Berkley titles by Betina Krahn

THE MARRIAGE TEST
THE WIFE TEST
THE HUSBAND TEST

THE
Marriage Test

BETINA KRAHN

BERKLEY BOOKS, NEW YORK

THE MARRIAGE TEST

A Berkley Book / published by arrangement with
the author

PRINTING HISTORY
Berkley edition

ISBN: 0-7394-4421-2

BERKLEY®
Berkley Books are published by The Berkley Publishing Group,
a division of Penguin Group (USA) Inc.,
375 Hudson Street, New York, New York 10014.
BERKLEY and the "B" design
are trademarks belonging to Penguin Group (USA) Inc.

PRINTED IN THE UNITED STATES OF AMERICA

For

Nicholas August Lord Krahn

May the road rise to meet you

Chapter 1

IT WAS A DEVILISH BAD NIGHT TO BE A traveler. A cold April rain had beat down steadily all day, and as night fell, the overflowing ruts in the roads merged to form ponds of sucking mud that would have given even the most seasoned of pilgrims pause. In view of those dismal conditions, the inhabitants of the Convent of the Brides of Virtue were surprised by a fierce pounding on the inner gate of the convent's courtyard just as they were preparing for the evening meal.

When the good sisters opened the door, two armor-clad figures were huddled under the eaves with water trickling down their faces. The two knights, one stout as an oaken barrel and the other lean as a Lincolnshire longbow, requested food.

"Axel of Grandaise, Reverend Mother. We've come from the Channel coast . . . headed to our home in the south," the shorter, rounder of the two declared, when they were allowed to step out of the weather.

The abbess slid her hands into the ends of her voluminous dark sleeves and looked at them in unblinking expectation.

"Greeve of Grandaise, Your Bountifulness." The taller, leaner one took up the explanation. "We have just escorted a shipment of wine to England. Wine produced by our lord's vineyards." The men seemed to hold their breaths as if awaiting a reaction. When there was none, Sir Greeve continued. "We stopped in the nearby village and inquired where we might find the best food in the area. The innkeeper said it was to be had at your most hospitable convent."

The abbess's eyes narrowed.

"We are famished, Reverend Mother," Sir Axel said balefully.

The abbess was a heartbeat away from ordering them back onto their horses when there came a subtle, metallic *clink, clink, clink* from between them. She knew the sound of coins eager to escape a purse when she heard it.

"We should have food enough to share. Come inside."

The abbess herself conducted the men to the audience chamber where a pair of old sisters appeared briefly to light lamps and lay a fire in the hearth. The knights accepted cups of heated wine and sighed in relief as they shed helms and gauntlets and lowered their hauberks to warm and dry themselves by the fire.

After a short time, the old nuns returned bearing a tray of food, and the knights seated themselves and produced eating knives from their belts. As the cover was lifted from the food and aromas began to curl above the table and around their heads, the knights inhaled deeply.

On the table between them sat a golden pie. Yellow golden. The color of sunflowers. In the vapors wafting through their heads came the unmistakable scents of saffron . . . and pork . . . and apples and plums . . . and cinnamon . . . and a peppery five-spice. Their mouths watered. They stared in amazement at each other for a moment, then dove into that beautiful, flaky, golden crust. With trembling hands, they scooped out slices and stuffed their mouths full.

For a moment nothing about the knights moved, not even a jaw muscle.

The abbess and the old sisters watched in growing concern as the men closed their eyes and turned their faces

Heavenward. From low in their throats came guttural, animal sounds that caused one of the aged sisters to cross herself. The nuns' uneasiness increased as the knights shivered, caught hard in the throes of gustatory shock. They looked to the abbess, who shoved her hands even farther up her sleeves and straightened her spine.

The second mouthful softened the groans and gave them a rising and falling vibrato that was almost melodious. The third bite turned the musical groans to sighs, and by the fourth, the sighs had become helpless whimpers.

"Ohhhh . . ." Sir Greeve swayed rhythmically.

"Yesss . . ." Sir Axel clasped his hand to his well-upholstered heart and looked as if he were about to swoon. "Ohhh, yes . . ."

By the time they scooped the last pieces from the pan, Sir Axel was humming and Sir Greeve was following along in close harmony. With those precious morsels in his hand, rotund Axel rose and turned from the table into an energetic step and twirl . . . staring at the pie as if it were his ladylove. Greeve burst into lilting "hey-nonny-nonnys" and began to keep time on the tabletop.

Oblivious to the stares of the abbess and nuns, Axel whirled giddily and bowed to his piece of pie before each new bite. Greeve soon joined him, warbling a sonnet in which womanly charms were replaced by tender golden crust and feminine mystery by the irresistible lure of sweetmeats and spices. As they popped the final bites into their mouths the knights locked arms and whirled first one direction and then the other, laughing, their eyes bright and faces ruddy.

They were still humming as they retrieved their helms and gauntlets, donned them, and bowed before the abbess with a flourish.

"We would thank the cook, Reverend Mother," Greeve said.

"That won't be necessary." The abbess stood taller.

"But a fine cook should be given his or her due," Sir Axel asserted.

"One cook is the same as another," the abbess declared

shortly. "They should all be grateful that God has given them hands with which to earn their bread and serve His glory. Now if you're quite finished—"

"Then, perhaps you would allow us to speak to your cook about this recipe." Sir Greeve produced a small leather pouch that clinked sweetly as he jiggled the contents with his fingers. The abbess's eyes widened as the knight dangled it before her. She tucked it into her sleeve before dashing their hopes.

"Out of the question," she proclaimed. "The sisters will show you out."

"But . . . but . . ." Sir Axel blinked and would have protested if Sir Greeve hadn't grabbed him by the arm.

"Our thanks for your hospitality, Reverend Mother."

As the knights exited the audience chamber, they paused by the table long enough to run their fingers round the empty tin one last time, look at each other, and sigh with unrequited curiosity.

As they exited into the stormy night, the abbess relaxed visibly and examined the pouch they had given her. Inside were six large gold coins—enough to pay for an entire year of such meals!

The sound of footsteps fast approaching caused the abbess to dump the coins back into the pouch and close her fingers protectively around it. When a young woman appeared in the doorway, the reverend mother cleared her throat and motioned to the old sisters to proceed with clearing the table.

"They're gone?" Julia of Childress brushed a few damp curls back from her forehead and the look of expectation drained from her heat-flushed face.

"They had to leave straightaway," the abbess declared, thrusting the pouch of coins up her sleeve.

"But I wanted to see how they—" Julia halted as the abbess's gaze tightened with disapproval. "What did they say about the pie?"

"I don't recall them *saying* much of anything," the abbess declared.

The sisters halted in the midst of clearing the table and

turned looks of dismay on the authority of their beloved order.

"They made no remark at all?"

"They ate, they drank, and they left a small donation. As usual." The abbess adamantly ignored the old sisters' accusing glowers. "Is supper ready?"

"Yes, Reverend Mother," she said, unable to hide her disappointment. "The same pie our visitors just ate. I was hoping to see if my new recipe—"

"No matter," the abbess declared with a dismissive wave. "I am certain it will be *sufficient.*"

JULIA OF CHILDRESS PAUSED ALONG THE colonnade surrounding the inner courtyard of the convent to watch the rain splash down into glossy puddles on the pavement. She felt just like one of those raindrops . . . being swallowed up . . . dissolved . . . dispersed into the larger life of the convent. She had seen plenty of raindrops plunge into puddles, in her time, but had yet to see a single one *climb back out.*

She glanced up at the dim gray outlines of the columns that ringed the courtyard at the heart of the cloister. Beloved as the Convent of the Brides of Virtue was to her and to the many other maids it had rescued from penury, abandonment, and a life of deprivation, it was not a place a young woman of spirit and capability would wish to spend the rest of her mortal days. And if Julia of Childress was anything, she was spirited.

It was precisely that "spirited nature"—as the more charitable of the good sisters termed it—that had gotten her into such trouble after her arrival at the convent. At the tender age of eight years old, she couldn't help that her luckless father had died and she had been tossed into a convent where suddenly she had to curtsy and cross herself, and to set to memory scriptures and housekeeping calendars and scores of domestic procedures and household remedies.

She spent many a day on her knees scrubbing and many

a supperless night standing in the darkened chapter room reciting imperfectly learned lessons aloud to a dozing old sister. The constant labor and discipline were all but intolerable for a motherless child who had been allowed to run unfettered over her father's meager and ill-tended holdings. And if she had to be miserable, she decided, she would share that misery with the good sisters who inflicted it on her.

Then when she reached ten years old, they had in exasperation assigned her to the most arduous and dreaded of all duties in the convent: *cooking.*

On the very first day of her duty there, she stood in the convent's big, bustling, overheated kitchens . . . smelling cooking food and burning wood . . . grain dust and pungent onions and sage and fresh dill and sharp aged cheese and tangy vinegar . . . and fell utterly, irrevocably in love.

From that day to this, she had spent her every spare moment in the kitchens, trying, testing, tasting, and mastering the culinary arts. She learned to read and write in four languages to uncover the secrets of recipes and ingredients from afar. She learned to cipher deftly to calculate amounts needed to enlarge and reduce recipes and make certain she was getting the most for the convent's coin.

The more she learned and developed her culinary skill, the more the convent and even the abbess herself came to see that her stubbornness was really "spirit," her bossiness stemmed from a God-given gift of "authority," and her penchant for flamming the local farmers out of produce and ingredients was merely a natural outgrowth of her Heaven-sent "resourcefulness."

Julia glanced over her shoulder at the door to the hall and the abbess's audience chamber beyond. Then she took a deep breath and headed back to the kitchens, thinking of the smiles and sighs of contentment her savory meat pies would elicit in the dining hall. Between the fasting-obsessed church calendar and the fact of feeding a strictly female population—females being widely known to fare best on fish, greens, and barley—she seldom got to cook red meats. She had been itching to try some new ideas

about roasting and spicing meat dishes, and a recent donation and a reprieve in the church's dictums of denial finally
gave her the chance.

She entered the busy kitchen and stood overlooking the
cooling tables on the open side of the kitchen. Twenty-two
perfect, golden crusts were laid out before her. Twenty-
one . . . the visitors had eaten one, she reminded herself.
She leaned closer and inhaled. Juicy pork . . . plums and
apples . . . saffron and cinnamon . . . and her very own special five-spice. She had mixed and seasoned the filling personally and rolled and shaped most of the crusts herself.
She'd put her very heart into them, and as she stood looking at them, she knew they would tickle the palates and
brighten the spirits of everyone who tried them. Even the
crotchety old abbess. See if they didn't.

God knew, the sisters of the Brides of Virtue loved her
cooking.

She expelled a heavy breath.

But did any of them love *her?*

Chapter 2

THE FEAST OF PENTECOST HAD COME
and gone, and the full spring sun had driven away
the rains and warmed the land into full, fertile glory.
Everywhere life was stirring: Sown fields were sprouting,
cows were freshening, town burghers were preparing for
hot fairs, and travelers were abroad on the roads and camp-
ing in the edges of woods . . . like the woods overlooking
the Convent of the Brides of Virtue. . . .

"We're in luck, Your Lordship!" Sir Axel came puffing
up the hill and charged into the undergrowth that hid his
liege lord, his friend Sir Greeve, and a dozen well-supplied
men at arms. Spotting his lord peering through the branches
at the stone-walled convent nestled in the valley below, he
braced against a bush to steady himself. "It's a feast day."

"Feast day?" Griffin, Count of Grandaise, turned to his
rotund, thickly cloaked spy with narrowed eyes. "Today
belongs to no saint."

"Not a saint's feast, seigneur. The Duke of Avalon visits
to thank the abbess and convent for something or other.
He's brought meat, and there's to be a special dinner for
the duke and *a distribution of alms.*"

Griffin of Grandaise turned that over in his mind.

"Alms? They're feeding the poor?"

"Yes, indeed. That's why those folk are clustered around the rear gate."

"How are we fortunate that those poor wretches get to eat alms bread?"

"Not just alms bread, milord." Axel parted the branches nearby and pointed to the knot of people milling around the rear gate. "They're waiting for the duke's leavings to be distributed. The sisters will give out all that's left."

"It's pure providence, milord," Sir Greeve declared, peering past Axel's shoulder toward the convent. "The duke will occupy the abbess . . . there will be men about the convent . . . and with the confusion of the poor milling about . . ."

"It would be the perfect opportunity to slip inside and have a look at this cook who's woven a spell on the pair of you," Griffin concluded, scowling.

Five weeks had passed since two of his knights stumbled fainting from hunger into this enclave of church-pledged females and came out intoxicated with gustatory pleasure. The pair rushed home to Grandaise to tell him about their find and had talked of little else since. Worse . . . every time they described that pie, the crust was a bit more golden and delectable and the meat a bit more tender and the spices a bit more subtle or bold or intriguing. . . .

And every time he heard them wax eloquent about the experience he wanted to put his fist through something.

Food, his men knew full well, was a sore subject with the Count of Grandaise. He never got enough. And what he did get never satisfied him. He could barely stomach half of what his beleaguered kitchens produced, and rather than force himself to consume common fare—which was as unpalatable to him as spoiled or soured food was to others—he often went hungry. And when he went hungry, his mood darkened and he earned the sobriquet that he had inherited along with his title from his grandfather: *the Beast of Grandaise*.

It was a curse of his lineage, passed down from his

grandfather, who raised him after his father died young in battle: a heightened sensitivity of smell that made ordinary food seem the equivalent of kitchen slops. He could distinguish a dash of pepper in a whole vat of stew . . . a single stalk of celery in an entire batch of stuffing . . . or a taint of vinegar in a barrel days before wine began to go "off." The scent of a dusting of mold, a hint of souring, or even the fermenting spoilage of a single apple in a barrel could ruin his appetite and linger sickeningly in his head for the better part of a day.

"Go, milord, and you'll have food fit for Heaven itself," Greeve urged.

"Divine," Axel added anxiously. "The abbess herself thinks so."

"That's why she guards the cook like a hawk." Greeve's head bobbed. "Wouldn't even let us set eyes on her. We had to spread a bit of coin about the village to learn she existed at all."

Neither of the devoted knights broached the question uppermost in their minds: What would happen if Lord Griffin decided the cook was all Axel and Greeve had said and insisted on having her? Trading anxious glances, they forced themselves to set such worries aside. It was enough that they'd managed to lighten his grim mood and turn his thoughts from the *impossible*—escaping the marriage the king had just commanded he make—to the merely *difficult*—wrenching a fine cook from a canny abbess's hands.

They and the dozen other men who had accompanied the Count of Grandaise to court and then farther north to this isolated enclave of females held their breaths as he turned and straightened to his full six-plus feet of height. They braced, expecting a blast, but he merely looked them over and demanded:

"Which of you has the worst-looking cloak?"

THE RAGGED FOLK GATHERED AT THE REAR gate of the convent jealously guarded their places in the line waiting for the distribution of alms. Nobody fed the poor like the Convent of the Brides of Virtue. There was no keeping back of the choicer morsels and reusing them for stew or pottage or broth and sops. The bread given out was not coarse "alms bread," but cuttings from the same soft, white flour loaves the sisters gave their guests. Sometimes the sisters set up tables in the rear yard and invited the poor and hungry to sit, and even mended their ragged garments for them as they ate. It was charity at its finest. And the poor and wretched, some of whom had been waiting since sunrise for a taste of a rare meat-day alms, were both hungry and contentious.

Thus, when a tall man in a ragged cloak appeared among them and strode straight toward the gate, they were incensed and demanded he wait at the back of the crowd. A few of the more intrepid souls grabbed his cloak as they insisted he wait his turn at the back. Some he shook off physically; others he pierced with a glare so fierce that they released him and skittered back to the safety of their fellows. By the time he reached the gate, opposition to his assumption had dwindled to shocked murmurs and shaken fists.

Griffin, Comte de Grandaise, walked boldly through the thick wooden gate, which, as it happened, stood ajar. But once inside he faded back against the stone wall and slid along it to a notch that offered at least partial concealment. From there he was able to survey the yard and orient himself.

Nearby, a gaggle of young girls and habit-clad sisters were struggling to settle planks across wooden braces to form makeshift tables. A pair of old men shuffled back and forth, carrying well-used benches out of what appeared to be a chapter dining hall. Periodically, some of the sisters would be called urgently back inside . . . leaving the young girls to chatter excitedly about their visitors and about the tasks they'd been assigned in the upcoming distribution.

The working parts of the convent were arrayed in a row along the outer wall, ringing the rear yard; the well, the cow byre, the stables, the shed, and the dovecote and chicken roost. Nearby was a stake-and-twine fence set atop a low wall of chiseled stone blocks. He edged closer and peered over it at well-tended rows of kitchen herbs. There was a surprising range of specimens: chervil, dill, lemongrass, mint, chives, onions, sage, leeks, rosemary, parsley, thyme, basil, summer savory . . . all grouped according to tastes . . . pungents, tarts, and savories. It was heartening. *Someone* here had a sense of culinary order.

He made his way around the herb garden wall. Pausing again behind a stack of old birch baskets and poultry ricks, he spotted the kitchens, identifiable by the plumes of smoke drifting out of sturdy-looking stone stacks that reached well past the roof. He watched the sisters and maids coming and going until an elderly sister came out to call everyone inside.

Seizing the opportunity, Griffin darted stealthily across the yard and inserted himself between the edge of the open kitchen wall and a dog cart that turned out to be filled with baskets of green tops, scrapings, and kitchen offal.

The Count of Grandaise reduced to hiding among the kitchen refuse to catch a glimpse of a cook. He groaned. *Grandfather must be turning over in his grave.*

Desperate for a better vantage point, he stuck his head around the corner of the kitchen opening and spotted a space between the wall and stacks of grain bags and barrels. Using the cover of the confusion of kitchen workers bustling thither and yon, he darted around the open wall to the safety of that new niche.

That was when he saw them.

Pies. A whole sea of them. Golden, perfect crusts mounded and laid out side by side . . . like undulating waves that stretched for yards atop cooling tables near the open wall. He recalled Axel's and Greeve's descriptions and against every disappointment-jaded impulse he possessed, his mouth began to water.

On the far side of the kitchen, in one of the four great hearths, fat pork shanks and legs of lamb were roasting over spits, flames flaring as grease dripped onto the coals. Nearby, pewter platters were laid out on tables, their handles tied with clean linen. Beside each was a boat and ladle ready to receive and dispense sauce. One of the old sisters was stropping long knives, preparing for the carving.

Fat tureens of pottage sat steaming on tables near the door, accompanied by baskets of beautiful golden bread. Farther still were platters piled with what looked like packets of fried dough—pasties of some sort.

His mouth was gushing water now. He had to have one of those pies . . . had to have a taste. Just as he slipped from his hiding place to the edge of the cooling table, a horde of chattering females came rushing back into the kitchen and swooped down on the pottage and bread. Orders and instructions flew from several quarters.

"You and you go before with the bread . . . you and you come behind with the bowls."

"Sister Archie brought a message and the abbess jumped up and rushed from the dining hall," he heard someone say with bewilderment.

"What do we do?" came another female voice.

"Begin serving the pottage," came a definitive response. "You . . . two by two . . . one holds while the other serves. And use your napkins!"

He was tempted to try to catch sight of whoever was issuing orders, but decided to focus instead on sampling one of the pies. Sticking his nose up over the edge of the cooling table, he seized the closest one, tucked it under his arm, and headed back to his hiding place.

Sitting on the floor amid barrels and grain bags, he drew out his eating knife and realized his hand was trembling as it poised above the pie. He cut a thick wedge, pried it out, and gave it a looking over . . . prolonging both the anticipation and the hope. Then he opened his mouth and . . .

Ahhhh.

The texture. The spicing. The delicate crust and tenderness of the meat.

By the blessed Saints, it was . . . he chewed, swallowed, and took a second bite before allowing himself to think it . . . *marvelous!*

Only long years of ruthlessly practiced self-restraint

prevented him from burying his face in that pie tin and wolfing down the contents.

It could be, he told himself desperately, that the cook simply had a way with crusts or got lucky with the combination of fillings. One dish was not enough on which to judge an entire kitchen. Or a cook. He licked his lips, savoring the lingering taste of spices, and stared ruefully at the pie. He needed more.

As soon as the tide of servers retreated back into the dining room and only a pair of elderly sisters and some kitchen boys remained to continue carving the meats and applying the sauces, he left his hiding place again and crept around the work tables. He watched from below and as the kitchen boys swung another spit from the fire and the old sisters turned away to supervise, he stuck his arm up and snatched a small leg of lamb . . . that burned his hands!

He fell back against the floor and dropped the meat on his chest to keep it from meeting the same fate. On the way back to his hiding place, he grabbed a napkin to save his hands, a loaf of bread, and one of the small pewter boats filled with what appeared to be a pink sauce. Emboldened by his success, he ventured still farther . . . determined to collect one of those pasties and to empty part of a tray of stuffed dates, almond tarts, sugared walnuts, small round cheeses, and what appeared to be spice-dusted crisps.

Then he spotted what appeared to be a pair of small animals—hedgehogs—sitting on a tray of greenery, apart from the others.

Hedgehogs? She cooked and presented *hedgehogs* to a duke? Opening the doublet he wore over his tunic, he tucked the sweetmeats inside and crept over to investigate. On closer inspection, the hedgehog quills were too thick and not nearly as sharp as they should be and the eyes seemed to be all crinkled and the nose bulged oddly. Edging still closer, he realized they weren't quills at all, but almonds—fried almonds! It was a hedgehog conceit, made out of edibles, intended for presentation to the duke!

Not an elegant peacock or swan or pheasant, but a

hedgehog. It could be seen as whimsy. Or disrespect. He scowled. This cook had either some skill or some nerve.

The sound of voices rumbling back toward the kitchen warned he was about to be inundated with cooks and servers once again. Frantic to taste this ambitious creation, he yanked out his knife and sliced off one of the hedge-hogs' hindquarters.

Crowded back into his hiding place, he spread out the napkin he'd snagged and deposited the lamb and sauce boat on it, then began to pull the rest of his booty from his doublet. Then with a half-uttered prayer, he sank his teeth into the lamb shank and closed his eyes. Grease dripped down his chin, but he scarcely felt it. He was too focused on the flavor sliding down his tongue and then rising up an aromatic back door into his brain.

For the first time in weeks—*months!*—he wanted to smell something. Fresh, tender lamb cooked to perfection . . . rubbed with garlic and stuffed with mint. He swallowed, ripped off another piece, and dipped it into the pink sauce. Pepper and garlic . . . in an almond milk base . . . with lamb juices and a hint of sweet grape for color and richness. Suddenly he was desperate to smell it, had to know the full effect of it, for good or for ill.

He reached greasy fingers up to the steel band he wore habitually across his nose and slid it off. Bracing himself, he held the lamb under his nose and inhaled. The scent of perfectly seasoned and roasted meat staggered him. He turned the hot lamb shank over and over, sniffing, absorbing, and luxuriating in every nuance of the combined meat, flame, and spice.

Biting off another huge chunk, he grinned and chewed enthusiastically, savoring every precious moment the meat was in his mouth. After several large bites, he turned to the pie again, smelling it this time before slicing and tasting. Cinnamon and saffron . . . oh, beautiful plums . . . tender, juicy pork . . . flaky crust with just the rapturously right amount of seasoning. Then he went to the purloined pasty that proved to be filled with chicken seasoned with sweet leeks and layered with spinach and what looked like a light-colored cheese. He sniffed—gratified to detect recently milled flour, new cheese, and fresh fat used in the frying—and dipped and sopped and devoured, growing steadily more enthralled.

It was nothing short of miraculous. Every dish, every sprig or dash of spice, every aroma blended uncannily with the others . . . not only in the same dish, but with all of the others in the whole meal. The pottage blended with the pasties, which blended superbly with the pies, then the lamb and the pork with the pink garlic sauce . . . which led to the rich entremets. . . .

And that hedgehog, whose rump turned out to be made of a dense, sweet yellow cake of sorts, studded with currants, soaked with almond milk and spices . . . cardamom, cloves, and nutmeg. The soft, melt-on-your-tongue interior presented a stunning contrast to the browned, crunchy almond spines.

He groaned with pleasure as he ripped more meat from the lamb bone, and stuffed his mouth full of the chicken-spinach pasty with the pungent light cheese. Quivering with pleasure, he finally abandoned all attempts at self-control. Bite after glorious bite, the juices ran and the aromas and scents filled his head as he closed his eyes and sampled and smelled and savored. . . .

Chapter 3

AT THAT VERY MOMENT, JULIA OF CHIL-
dress was meeting the abbess at the top of the steps
leading down to the kitchens. The head of the convent was
wringing her hands and nearly as pale as the white ruched
linen of her wimple.

"The bishop has just arrived." The abbess looked as if
the statement pained her physically. "Light-fingered old
trout. Says he heard the duke was visiting and hoped to pay
his respects to His Grace. *Humph.* Snooping about is more
like it. And he catches us serving meat. I suppose it's too
late for just bread and pottage." She gave the air a sniff and
winced. "The entire convent reeks of cooked flesh."

"Reeks?" Julia bit her lip to keep a bit of her "spirit"
from boiling over.

"You'll just have to carry on and serve what's been prepared. But no entremets or spiced wine at the end of the
meal." The abbess shook a finger. "I won't have the bishop
flogging me with canon law again for not fulfilling our
tithes. Heaven knows, he's already eyeing our prime crop-
lands along the river." She whirled and exited to the dining
hall in a fierce billow of black.

Julia watched her go with mounting anger. *Bread and pottage.* She ground her teeth. She understood the abbess's problem . . . distrust for the acquisitive, high-handed bishop she was forced to obey . . . but it was still *the abbess's problem.* It would take nothing less than a miracle to give one visitor the impression of wealth and another the impression of poverty with the same meal. And good as she was in the kitchen, miracles were still a bit beyond her.

As she stomped back down the steps to the kitchen, she carried with her the memory of the abbess's shaking finger.

No entremets. Her eyes narrowed. The devil she'd leave off the entire final course. She and her kitchen staff had labored for two long days to create this meal. She refused to wreck the menu just to make the abbess feel less conspicuous in front of the bishop. Truth be told, she wanted her food to be conspicuous. Memorable. Astounding. This was her first and perhaps her only chance to serve a nobleman of the duke's status. If she were ever to have a chance to marry and leave the convent, she would have to draw the attention and interest of someone as influential as the Duke of Avalon. This was her chance and she was not about to relinquish it because the abbess didn't want the bishop to realize the convent had substance enough to feed a duke like a king!

She made for the tables positioned near the hearth, stood watching, and nodded at the wafer-thin slices the old sisters were carving. Snatching a piece of meat, she rolled it and dunked it into the nearest sauceboat.

For a moment she stood with her eyes closed and her mouth busy, critiquing the spices, the roasting time, and the distance from the coals. After sufficient deliberation, she sighed, licked her lips, and produced a satisfied smile.

"Perfect." She wheeled on the young sisters and maidens collected to watch with widened eyes. "Don't just stand there. Let's go feed a duke!"

After a few moments of total chaos, Julia accompanied the train of servers to the bottom of the steps leading up to the dining hall, calling last-minute instructions as she sent

them two by two, carrying covered serving platters of meat
and roasted vegetables and boats of sauce between them.
Almost as quickly as it had risen, the confusion and tension in the kitchen subsided and she turned her attention to
the finale of the meal.

The trays of entremets—laden with stuffed fruits, can-
died nuts, almond tarts, and cinnamon-dusted pastry
crisps—seemed a bit sparse and she rearranged them to
make them look better. Thank Heaven she hadn't insisted
on producing something more exotic. When she learned
the duke's young son traveled with him, she decided something simpler, even playful would delight both father and
son. Perhaps the simplicity of the meal's finale would mit-
igate the penance the abbess would inflict on her for serving the sweetmeats anyway.

Then she came to what she intended to be the *pièce de ré-
sistance* of the meal and stopped dead, staring in horror at the
desecrated hindquarters of her precious hedgehog conceit.

"But—but . . . what . . . who . . ."

Strangling on her own juices, she turned to the trio of
old kitchen sisters who had just collapsed on stools away
from the heat of the hearths and ovens.

"Who cut into the—"

She halted at the sight of the veiled and wimpled trio
fanning themselves with their aprons, looking utterly exhausted. If they knew anything about it, they would have
said something. They had taken almost as much delight in
the creation of the hedgehogs as she had.

She turned back and with trembling hands tried to close
and tuck and repair the ruined creature. It was no good. The
little beast was beyond saving. Her heart sank. Who would
do such a thing? She clasped her hands together, grappling
with the hurt and sense of betrayal roiling inside her. Who
in the convent would be so callous or so greedy as to steal
a special dish intended for their most esteemed patron?

First the abbess demands she not serve the carefully
crafted finish of her feast and now this!

Seizing control once more, she forced herself to think

about how the situation could be salvaged. She hadn't made enough for all of the diners . . . perhaps if she presented the one remaining hedgehog whole, while quickly cutting and serving the other before they could see its missing rear . . .

Then she spotted a puddle of sauce on the planking beside the hedgehog tray. Dabbing a finger into it, she tasted it and recognized her pink garlic sauce. Someone had dribbled it on the table. She spotted another pool by her feet, and followed a string of dribbles leading across the floor to the far side of the kitchen. Whoever had stolen part of her hedgehog had stolen sauce. And what was sauce without something to dip into it?

She followed the trail to stacks of barrels, crates, and grain bags at the edge of the open wall, where she heard moaning and soft, unmistakable mouth-smacking sounds. Her eyes widened.

The wretch hadn't bothered to carry the food out of the kitchen before stopping to consume it!

She pulled a bag of grain from the top of the stack and realized that there was a opening between the stacks and the wall. Furious, she charged around the stacks and into that opening . . . to find herself facing a pair of tawny eyes set in a broad, muscular face smeared with grease, sauce, and pastry crumbs. It was a man, sitting behind the barrels and flour bags with a cache of purloined food, eating as if there were no tomorrow.

"Why, you miserable, thieving—" She leaned down to grab him by the top of his tunic to haul him out of his hiding place and spotted the food-stained napkin by his feet dotted with stray almonds . . . *slivered, fried almonds.* She braced and pulled with all her might. "Come out of there!"

Up he came, with a lamb bone in one hand and a pie tin in the other. By the time he reached his full height, she found herself staring up at a tall, dark figure with shaggy hair, broad shoulders, and a mouth covered with food.

She blinked, momentarily taken aback by his size. His features were angular, but he had none of the hollow, des-

perate malnourishment of the abjectly poor about him . . .
which stoked her ire even hotter.

GRIFFIN OF GRANDAISE LURCHED TO HIS
feet, emerging from his food-induced daze to find himself
caught between stacks of barrels and a kitchen wall holding a well-gnawed lamb shank and a mostly empty pie tin.
His awareness quickly broadened to include the food all
over his chin, the grease, crumbs, and flour on his padded
tunic, and the fury of a young woman pulling back a fist to
plow it into his midsection.

"Ooof!" He bent double, emptying his hands to grab his
stomach.

"How dare you sneak into our kitchens to steal food?"

He reacted instinctively to both the shock and discom-
fort, grabbing her by the shoulders and shoving her back
out the opening and around the corner of the open kitchen
wall, out of sight. He clamped a hand over her mouth to
muffle her cry of surprise as he shoved her back against the
stones and pinned her struggling form there with his body.

"Hush!" he commanded. She was choking furious and
croaking out something that sounded on the order of
"miserable . . . thieving. . . ."

Then it hit him . . . the smell of the dog cart filled with
kitchen parings and offal that he had fled for a niche in the
kitchen . . . the odor of sun-heated, fermenting waste and
burgeoning rot. It slammed through his head and his whole
body reacted, contracting in a wave of revulsion and nau-
sea. Groping frantically for his nose clip, he managed to
hold down both the feast he had just eaten and the girl he
had trapped against the wall while donning the smooth
metal clip that saved his senses and sanity.

After a moment, the onslaught of moldy onions, bloody
chicken feathers, and rotting carrot tops and cabbage
leaves subsided. He shook his head and forced himself to
take a few breaths. *Think*, he commanded himself.

She thought he was here just to steal food, he realized,

which meant his disguise was working. But a nobleman of his stature couldn't afford to be caught skulking about a nunnery, stealing food, and being assaulted by the kitchen help. He had to get away. *After* he learned more about the cook.

"I won't hurt you, wench," he ground out, staring into the girl's eyes. Big green eyes, that just now contained sparks enough to look like a grass fire in progress. "Nor will I release you until you tell me which is your head cook."

She glared mutinously at him and made it clear, as she tried to bare her teeth against his palm, that removing his hand to hear what she said would be unwise. Cursed female. He adjusted his grip to avoid those teeth.

"Is it one of the old sisters?"

She shook her head, but the fire in her gaze made it impossible to say whether that meant the cook wasn't one of the sisters or that she refused to tell him. He growled, fighting the scent of decay still rumbling in his head to think.

"Is your head cook one of the nuns? Tell me and I'll let you go."

This time his offer made an impact; she quit trying to bite him.

Again she shook her head.

"If I take my hand away, do you promise not to cry out?"

After a moment she nodded and he gentled his grip.

"What the devil do you think you're doing?" she snapped the instant his fingers departed her skin. "Sneaking into a convent and stealing food meant for the duke—"

"What is she like, this cook of yours?" he demanded, craning his neck toward the edge of the wall to look at the sisters collapsed in a far corner.

"Big enough and mean enough to make you wish you'd practiced your thieving ways somewhere else."

"Strapping, is she?" he deduced. Good cooks generally were. They had to be. There was always hauling, mixing, grinding, and pounding to be done. Wrestling massive iron kettles, griddles, and spits about the kitchen required a certain amount of brawn . . . not to mention the fact that skimmers, tongs, and ladles were the weight equivalent of lances, battle-axes, and maces, and demanded the same kind of stamina.

"She'll have your ears for candle wax," came the wench's reply.

"Strong, eh?" He narrowed his eyes, trying desperately to focus his thoughts through the mingling waves of exquisite and onerous sensation lingering on his senses. "But not overly smart . . . all she could come up with to present to the duke was *hedgehogs*."

The wench's mouth opened, then snapped shut.

"The duke brought his son. It was for *him* she made the hedgehogs, you big oaf. And if you don't get out of here"—she tried to push some space between them—"she'll stuff you headfirst into a vinegar barrel and leave you to pickle."

The mention of pickling unexpectedly reasserted the memory of the slurry of soured and rotting scents around him and conjured up the remembered scent of brine and vinegar and the half-rotten smell of pickling cabbage. . . . *Stop that!*

"Speaks both French and English, does she?" He forced his attention to his other senses . . . only now realizing that he was pressed hotly against the length of her body . . . that she was young and soft in the places a woman should be soft . . . and that he was having to work like the very devil to hold her there.

"And Latin. And Italian." She ceased shoving and twisting long enough to look up into his face and declare: "The abbess says she'd speak the devil's own tongue if it meant getting Old Scratch's recipes."

"A better cook than Christian, then."

She looked as if the comment outraged her, then abruptly nodded.

"She learned to cook from gypsies." She lowered her voice to a fierce whisper. "It was them that taught her to use all manner of secret herbs and eastern spices . . . like *devil's heat, curry,* and *paprika.* Makes food so hot, it flames a body's innards like a foretaste of eternal damnation." Her eyes narrowed. "You should try some. A few bites of her stew and you'd be on your knees praying for forgiveness."

She gave another furious push. He just managed to counter it and realized that he was now having to exert every bit of force he possessed to contain her. It registered in his mind that there was a reddish cast to her light hair. That made sense. Red hair always meant a pepper-hot disposition. He found himself wondering if she smelled like pepper, too. Or maybe tasted like it.

Good God. He quickly put some space between him and the wench.

"They also say," she continued in a taunting tone, apparently sensing the tide of power had somehow just turned, "the abbess uses her stew as a final test for the novices before she'll let them take vows."

"Which no doubt explains why *you* aren't wearing a habit yet," he snapped, feeling oddly defensive. "And her temper?"

"Like a badger in mating season."

She was lying, he realized. No one who made almond-and-spice hedgehogs for young boys could have that foul a temper. Only a woman of sensitivity and insight would think to please a father by delighting a son.

He'd learned what he came to find out: that he wanted— needed—the convent's cook for his own.

"You want to see her?" the girl asked with a purposeful edge to her tone. "She's in with the duke and the bishop and the abbess. I can go and call her for you." He allowed her to push him back and she bolted out of his reach, turning on him with eyes blazing. "So she can lay a fist to the side of your larcenous head!"

The instant she turned to run back inside, he wheeled and ran for the back gate.

Chapter 4

THE OLD SISTERS COLLAPSED ON STOOLS near the fire bolted upright on their seats as Julia came rushing back into the kitchen, calling out an alarm and heading straight for the dining hall. Midway up the steps, she was inundated by a tide of novices and maidens hurrying back down to the kitchen, their hands filled with empty platters and their heads with excitement.

They besieged her, all talking at once, recounting every comment and gesture of their guests' reaction to the meal. She tried in vain to part them and continue on up the stairs. As bits of their news pierced her turmoil, she had time to consider what she was about to report to the abbess and the duke.

Invaded? By whom? the abbess would surely demand. And what could she answer? A lone beggar who filched food from the kitchen? Scarcely a threat to the sanctity of the convent, the sovereignty of the duke, or the dignity of the bishop. In fact, the only one threatened in any way was herself. Why on earth would a man steal into the convent kitchen to stuff himself witless and—when caught—demand to know about their cook?

The chaos around her had subsided into expectant stares. She took a deep breath and grasped her bearings. She had a feast to finish and an angry abbess to placate afterward. Her gaze landed on the table below where one and a half hedgehogs waited to delight a duke's son. She clapped her hands for attention.

"Take the trays and linen to the scullery and tidy your sleeves and hands to serve the final course."

As she followed the servers back down the steps, she vowed to personally oversee the distribution of alms later. And if she spotted the wretch who had just assaulted her in her own kitchen, she would see that he rued ever setting eyes—much less hands—on her.

Half an hour later, under the abbess's scorching gaze, she presented the barrel-chested duke and his callow-faced son with a pair of charming, if somewhat abbreviated, creatures of the hedgerows. The young boy's eyes danced with merriment beneath his bowl-cut hair and the duke chuckled and bestowed an approving smile as she began to cut and serve. The bishop was moved to remark upon the choice of a creature of such humility, the confection's likeness to the real thing, and began waxing on about its suitability as a finale to a meal in a convent, when aged Sister Archibald hurried into the dining hall, curtsied to bishop and duke, then whispered urgently into the abbess's ear.

"What? Have they moved the road to Paris?" the reverend mother snapped, tossing her lap cloth on the table. "Now it runs right by our door?" She rose and apologized to the duke and then the bishop: "It seems we have more visitors. If you will excuse me, Your Grace, Your Worship."

The abbess hurried along the colonnade with Sister Archibald, who when asked, repeated the nobleman's name: the Comte de Grandaise. The abbess frowned, trying to recall why the name seemed familiar and where she might have heard it. He wasn't from the nearby region, to be sure.

She halted some distance from the inner gate, assessing the trio of armor-clad men standing just inside the entry with their helms in their hands. One spotted her and alerted the others, who turned to her while arraying themselves in formidable-looking phalanx . . . the two shorter men flanking the taller one . . . one telling step behind.

The abbess paused two yards away, face-to-face with a tall, broad-shouldered lord clad in mail armor, wearing what appeared to be a band of metal across the ridge of his nose, pinching it together. Aware that she was staring, she looked quickly down to the coat of arms emblazoned on a silk tabard over his mail. It was unlike any crest she had seen before: grapes, lumps of charcoal, and what appeared to be a wild boar rampant on a split field of pale blue and loden green. The lord's two companions, who bore the same coat of arms on their tunics, joined him in a light bow of respect.

"Please forgive the intrusion, Reverend Mother." The imposing lord's voice had a nasal quality that drew her attention to the metal band he wore. "I am Griffin, the Comte de Grandaise, of Bordeaux. I have ridden a long way to seek an audience with you."

"You arrive at an inconvenient time, sir."

"Your Lordship," the shorter, rounder knight prompted.

"Your Lordship." The abbess heeded the prompt a bit testily, backing up a step and inserted her hands into the ends of her sleeves. "We have guests. The Duke of Avalon and the Bishop of Rheims are with us and we must see to their comfort first. Perhaps I will have an opportunity to speak with you after dinner is finished."

"Dinner?" the tall, lanky knight whispered with an edge of longing. Suddenly both knights were staring at her with such naked hunger that she was startled for a moment.

"I suppose you haven't eaten."

"No, Reverend Mother," the shorter knight declared. "We are famished."

"Of course. You would be," she said flatly, thinking that something about that pair of knights seemed familiar. "You may as well join us in the dining hall for a bit of food."

When they reached the dining hall, the abbess gave three of the elder sisters at the head table a private signal to vacate their seats. Then she introduced the count and his knights to the duke and the bishop . . . which was when she realized why "Sir Axel" and "Sir Greeve" seemed so familiar.

"You appeared at our door some weeks ago, in a rainstorm," she said.

"And you were kind enough to provide us with food," round-faced Sir Axel responded, beaming with gratitude.

"What good fortune that we may now share with our seigneur the experience of your kitchen," Sir Greeve said while glancing wistfully at the sauce-stained trenchers on the tables.

"Yes. Fortunate indeed." The abbess watched the trio ogling the food and thought that perhaps she should have demanded to know the count's purpose straight off, then sent the trio on their way. But, they had left gold pieces to pay for a meat-day supper. . . . "Seat yourselves, good sirs."

The knights nearly tripped over themselves hurrying to the seats the abbess indicated, where they waited anxiously for their lord to return from holding the abbess's chair.

Julia stood before the head table with a long, sharp knife in her hand, having just served the last hedgehog's head to the duke's son. She gripped the bone handle tighter as a chill ran up her spine.

The man's size, coloring, and powerful bearing were the same. And that voice . . . pinched, as if he held his nose . . . just like the wretch who . . .

Then he looked up as he placed his helm on the table across from his place, and she gasped. He had the same dark hair—albeit somewhat tamed—the same angular face, and the same piercing golden eyes. The wretch who assaulted her as a beggar in the kitchen now appeared in the dining hall as a nobleman!

She could scarcely see the abbess nod to her, indicating she should retire to the kitchens to arrange food for these interlopers. Peeling her white-fingered hand from the knife grip, she glared at the thieving nobleman and exited to arrange the rogue's second dinner of the day.

Every eye in the dining hall was on the three men as they began to eat. The two knights dug into their bowls, trencher, and shared sauceboat with relish, groaning with pleasure as they experienced each new taste. The count, however, carved his food daintily and wiped his fingers frequently, seeming uncommonly restrained in the face of such exceptional fare. Only occasionally could he be seen closing his eyes as he savored an especially tasty morsel.

Where did the count come from? the abbess asked.

"The south."

Why was he so far from home?

"Summoned to court."

Where was he bound after that?

"Here."

"You have traveled all the way from Paris to come *here?* To our convent?" The abbess hesitated for a moment, torn between openly demanding his purpose in coming here, and allowing their hospitality to lay bare his motives in a less public manner. "And why have you sought us out, Your Lordship?"

Matrimony was the most common reason noblemen approached the gates of the Convent of the Brides of Virtue. The Order of the Brides of Virtue was known throughout the continent for taking in the nobility's destitute daughters and turning them into worthy brides for noblemen unable to acquire wives through more usual channels. Of late, however, the bride market had been a bit slow. The war between England and France had stripped many noble houses of dower lands and marriageable younger sons, and the number of wealthy merchants hoping to improve themselves with a wellborn bride had fallen off dramatically. She had to tread carefully here; she didn't want to insult a potential bridegroom and miss a chance to plump the convent's all-too-lean coffers.

"Have you come for a bride?"

"Not a bride," the count declared, pushing back from the table. "A cook."

"A what?" The abbess stared at the count as if he just sprouted a second head. "Surely you mean a bride who oversees a fine and worthy kitchen. The sisters of our order have answered the Almighty's call to train young women of noble birth to be *brides,* not common *cooks.*"

"Oh, there is nothing common about the cook I seek, Reverend Mother," the count declared, turning to face her. "Whoever stewed this pottage, roasted this succulent meat, and created this heavenly pink garlic sauce is far from common. And I've come to purchase her from you."

A communal gasp nearly sucked all the air from the dining hall.

"Purchase our cook?" The abbess lurched to her feet. "Out of the question." She looked rattled by the very notion. "Our cook is pledged to God Almighty and to the life of our convent."

"I have it on good authority that she has never taken vows." The count glanced about the dining hall and spotted Julia standing near the kitchen stairs glaring at him. His mouth quirked with recognition as his gaze moved on . . . searching the dining hall for a woman who looked capable of reducing a nobleman's ears to candle wax. "She is not a nun, I am told. Which means there should be no impediment to her leaving the convent."

"I care not what you have heard, *sir.*" The abbess's temper slipped the jess. "If you think you can invade these walls, take advantage of our hospitality, and then demand that we hand over our cook to you, you are sadly mistaken." She turned to find her trusted assistant standing nearby with an anxious expression. "Sister Archibald, please show these—"

"I am aware that what I ask is unusual." The count rose, drawing his wide-eyed men up with him, but showing not the smallest inclination toward the door. "My request is borne out of a great and pressing need." His words and tone became more entreating. "I have looked far and wide for a cook that meets my requirements, and yours is the first to even come close. I would have her for my cook, and I am willing to be generous with the convent in return."

"I will hear no more." The abbess raised both her chin and the imperative in her voice. "Take your men and leave these grounds immedi—"

"The Comte de Grandaise?" The bishop's imperious tones cut through the abbess's command like a knife, causing her to start. "Of course. Bordeaux. The Grandaise vineyards and wineries." He motioned to the grapes featured prominently on the count's coat of arms. "You are *that* Grandaise."

"The same, Your Worship." The count nodded to the churchman.

"You say you are willing to *compensate* the convent for the loss of this cook's services?" The bishop sought clarification, setting his wine cup aside.

"Most generously." The comte turned to Sir Axel to retrieve a sizeable leather bag that produced seductive clinking sounds as he jiggled it.

The sound of coins clinking produced a prim little smile on the bishop's face. "Well then, Reverend Mother, I believe you must listen more carefully to the good count. After all, the convent has certain fiscal responsibilities. . . ."

Which were desperately in arrears. The convent hadn't paid its tithe to the cathedral since before the English invasion, nearly two years ago. The coin in their coffers had been drastically reduced by the payment of dowries that accompanied five brides sent to England last year as a part of the Duke of Avalon's ransom. It was the duke's gratitude for that show of loyalty that had prompted this feast in the first place. He was their protector, their patron, and just now—the abbess saw—he was their only hope of holding on to the cook who had made the life of the convent contenting and harmonious in recent years.

She appealed to Avalon with a frantic look.

"The abbess is well aware of the convent's responsibilities, my lord bishop," the duke said in response to her prodding. "But she also knows the convent's needs and requirements. I would be inclined to defer to her judgment in such matters. If she says the cook must stay—"

"Is it true that this cook has not yet taken religious vows?" the bishop demanded of the abbess, clearly nettled by the duke's interference.

The abbess looked from the duke to the bishop to the kitchen stairs, where Julia stood with eyes as big as goose eggs.

"She has not, my lord." The abbess's gaze on Julia was hot enough to melt iron. Numerous times the abbess had urged her to take vows and don the order's official habit. Each time Julia had stalled and evaded and demurred, which was so unlike her that she might as well have shouted her refusal to the rooftops. After this, the abbess would cut her hair and stuff her into a habit before the sun set! "But she *will* take them as soon as it is humanly poss—"

"Then, I cannot see any impediment to granting the count's request," the bishop said, folding his hands at his waist so that his great ring, the visible symbol of his authority, was prominently displayed.

"Then look harder, Your Worship," the abbess said more sharply than was politic. "There is more at stake here than a bag of silver."

"Gold," the count corrected, drawing murmurs and exclamations from the collected residents of the convent, many of whom lurched to their feet.

The abbess shoved her hands even farther up her sleeves.

"It matters not whether it is silver or gold. Our order's resources—like those of the Holy Mother Church—are not for sale. We are merely caretakers. We have no right to barter away that which belongs to God."

"And yet, you manage to provide noblemen with brides from the 'resources' of your convent," the count said in an even tone, "for a price."

"*A donation.*" The abbess dragged clenched fists from inside her sleeves. "The men fortunate enough to find brides among our charges recognize their good fortune and make *a donation* to our work in gratitude."

"You sell brides." The count leaned forward with a glint of challenge in his eyes. "How is that different from selling a cook?"

"We most certainly do not *sell*—" The abbess turned to

the sisters of the order to support her statement and found
them and the girls and maidens in their care watching the
confrontation in deep dismay.

"It is time for Vespers," she announced abruptly, and
with an authoritative sweep of an arm, she ordered the assembly to exit through the far door. "Everyone into the
chapel and onto their knees!"

As the ashen sisters ushered their charges out, no one
had to ask the topic of the prayers they were being commanded to raise. There wasn't a soul in the convent who
wasn't horrified by the prospect of losing Julia of Childress's food.

"You, too, Julia," the abbess commanded. "Out!"

"But—"

"Silence!" The abbess cut off her protest. "Go."

Chapter 5

IT WAS AN OUTRAGE, JULIA MUTTERED furiously to herself, being excluded from a volatile confrontation where her fate was being decided. She exited behind the last of the sisters and maidens headed for the chapel, only to dart to the side of the door and inch back to the opening to see what was happening.

"Your petition is denied, Your Lordship." The abbess ignored the bishop's strangle of surprise. "I must ask you to take your men and leave our convent grounds straightaway."

The count's response was to spread his feet and set his hands on his waist.

"If I leave these walls without a cook, I will go no farther than the outside of your gate. There I will remain—camped with a score of men at arms—until you relent and give her to me."

"That will not be necessary, my lord count." The bishop rose with a face like a storm cloud. "There is no reason to deny you the services of a fine cook and the convent a chance to make good its obligation to the greater church. After all"—he speared the abbess with a furious look—"a cook, even a fine cook, can be replaced."

The abbess turned on her arrogant superior in a righteous fury.

"A cook may be replaced, you say . . . but what of a vocation? What of a commitment to God Himself? Would you deny our good cook the opportunity to pledge her love and service to God alone?"

Julia, listening at the edge of the door, nearly choked on the unuttered cry of protest that welled up in her. She had no desire to take vows! It was the abbess's desire that she forego all hope of her own home and hearth to bind herself forever to the convent's grates and griddles!

The hypocrisy of it. The abbess defended her right to choose her God-given vocation, while intending to deprive her of that same right the minute the duke and bishop were gone! It was all she could do to keep from stomping back into the hall and—

What? Agreeing to go off into utter servitude with this arrogant beast of a lord who wanted her enough to pay a goodly sum of gold for her, but clearly considered her no more than a commodity to be bought and sold?

"That is not a matter to be taken lightly, Your Worship," the duke rose to insert himself into the thickening fray. "If the cook has pledged herself to the religious life, then such a choice must be honored by the church."

The bishop shot a glare at the duke. They both knew, as did the abbess, that there was often a wide gap between the church's standards and actual practices. Vows and pledges to the church were considered inviolate . . . unless the church's interests were better served by negating or absolving them.

"Why is this cook so important to you, Your Lordship?" the duke asked.

"If I may, seigneur . . ." The tall, lanky Sir Greeve edged into his lord's sight, seeking permission to speak and was given a dark look, then a nod. "Our lord is afflicted with a rare condition that renders most ordinary food unpalatable to him. He has searched far and wide for a cook who can prepare food that allows him to eat normally."

"You cannot know the hunger and the anguish he must bear, Your Grace." Sir Axel lowered his voice to a confidential tone. "He hides his suffering from the world."

"So. Allowing him to take the cook would be an act of charity as well," the bishop declared, eyeing the bag of gold nestled in the comte's hands. "A sacrifice made for the good of this poor man and the glory of the Almighty."

"I will not allow it." The abbess faced the bishop in full defiance. "Infirmity or not, he's gotten this far without our cook . . ."

Julia was riveted to the sight of the formidable reverend mother defying both the wealthy count and their venerable bishop on her behalf. Her heart felt like it was beating in her throat. She would never have guessed that the abbess would risk bringing down the wrath of the Holy Church upon the convent in order to keep her. But, the warmth that thought cause to bloom in her chest quickly cooled. If only it were Julia herself the abbess feared losing, instead of Julia's food.

She peered around the dining hall, remembering the many expressions of praise—all aimed at the Almighty—her food had elicited from the abbess and sisters. She scowled. Not that she begrudged the Almighty His share of the credit, but it wasn't as if *He* had stood in the kitchens for hours on end, being roasted over sizzling griddles and spattered by hot skillet grease, and getting blisters from turning spits. . . .

The count took an abrupt step toward the abbess . . . the duke's men were on their feet in a wink . . . the bishop drew back in outrage . . . and the duke jolted between the contentious parties with his hands raised.

"Stop!" Avalon commanded, inserting both himself and a chord of reason into the escalating conflict. "There must be a way to settle the matter without resorting to threats and sieges." He swung a forbidding gaze from count to abbess to bishop, and after a moment shoulders eased and fists began to relax.

"Clearly, some compromise is called for. The count

needs a cook and is willing to compensate the convent handsomely for their cook's services. But the cook must be allowed to follow her cherished vocation within the church." He looked to the abbess, then the count, then the bishop. "Then, let the cook go with the count for a term of service . . . after which she will return to the convent and take up her vows."

"And how does that help me, Your Grace?" the count said irritably.

"It will give you time to set your kitchen in order." The duke scrambled to make it sound reasonable. "You will have the cook's food to eat while she trains another cook in her methods."

Julia's entire body was atremble with fear and expectation. Would they honestly consider sending her off with that duplicitous beast? A count who disguised himself in rags and stole food from a convent kitch—

Oh. She blinked. He hadn't been there to steal the food, she suddenly realized; he'd been there to *taste* the food and decide whether the cook was worth acquiring. So that was why the wretch had asked so many questions about her.

"Unacceptable," the abbess announced, eyeing the powerful count. "Once he has her at his home, in his kitchens, what guarantee do I have that he will ever return her to us?"

The count took visible umbrage. "*If* I agree, you will have my word."

"Which I have no reason to trust," she responded furiously.

"But you do trust the duke's word," the bishop put in with a taunting smile. "Our good duke would undoubtedly be willing to act as guarantor of the cook's safety. Wouldn't you, Your Grace?"

"And her virtue?" the abbess demanded. "If she is to return to take her vows, her gifts to God must not be sullied. What assurance do I have that she would be safe from vile interference?"

Alarmed, the duke looked to the count, who—to his credit—was keeping his temper mostly in check in the face

of assertions that he might be remiss in protecting the
cook's person . . . perhaps intentionally so . . . to prevent
her from taking vows.

"You would have the duke's personal guarantee," the
bishop put in, glaring with spiteful pleasure at Avalon. "He
has men at arms. If anything untoward should happen, he
would be obligated to avenge the wrong. Would you not,
Your Grace?"

The duke swallowed hard, assessing the count's presence
and strength and trying to think of what he'd heard about
Grandaise. His only recollections dealt with Grandaise involved in some sort of feud and going hot and hard into battle. The last thing he and his still-recovering estates needed
was the expense of mounting a small army to travel south
and go to war over a cook's virtue! The wretched bishop
was punishing him for interfering in a matter he considered
to be entirely under the church's authority.

"You would do that for us, Your Grace?" the abbess asked,
her expression pleading. He had once turned to her for help
as she now turned to him. It was impossible to refuse her.

"I would."

"Well then, it is settled," the bishop said with taunting
good spirits, eyeing the bag of gold. "Except for the
amount of payment and the term of service."

"Six months," the abbess proposed.

"Two years," the count countered.

"One year," the duke trumped the negotiation, staring
down both contending parties. "And half of the contents of
that bag."

Half a bag of gold, Julia thought. For one year of her
cooking. She clutched the edge of the door frame, staggered by the realization that an abbess, a bishop, a duke,
and a count had just engaged in heated bargaining over the
rights to her future. The doors and windows of her world
blew open and the wind of changing prospects took her
breath for a moment. She gasped and clutched her throat,
forcing herself to inhale and exhale sensibly.

Someone wanted her. For her cooking, true, but it was a
start. And once away from the convent, in a wealthy noble-

man's house, she would have a chance to see more of the world and look for a future of her own. After all, there would be knights and retainers and friends and neighbors. He would want richer food, so she would have to travel to spice markets in nearby towns and cities to procure supplies . . . which meant more opportunity to meet potential husbands.

Her excitement at the possibilities opening to her totally eclipsed, at first, the fact that all of this was being decided without consulting her.

Peering around the door frame again she saw the count nod and hold out the money bag, which the bishop quickly commandeered.

"Now if you will summon my new cook, we will be on our way," the count said to the abbess, watching the bishop sail out of the dining hall to divide the coin.

"I'm afraid you will have to wait until tomorrow to take our cook from us," the abbess said grimly, stiffening. "She will have preparations to make and must see that her duties are properly reassigned."

"Then I must at least speak with her," the count insisted.

"She is at prayer just now," the abbess declared, looking to Sister Archibald, who nodded and hurried across the dining hall and out the door toward the chapel. "As will we all be, shortly. We must pray that the beloved Queen of Heaven will watch over and protect our dear cook, and will keep us all from starving to death in her absence." She drew herself up to her full, intimidating height. "Sister Rosemary will show you out."

On the colonnade, just outside the door to the dining hall, Julia intercepted Sister Archibald, pulled her aside, and pressed fingers to her lips. When the old sister saw that it was her, she gave a huff indicating "I'm not surprised" and scowled at her. But Sister Archie could never stay irritated with her for long.

"Ye heard, I take it," the old nun said quietly, folding her arms.

"I did. I'm sold to this count and have to go with him and cook for him for a year."

"Then, ye must come back and take vows."

"And what if I don't want to go, or to come back and take vows? It seems to me everyone gets something out of this bargain except me."

Sister Archie pulled in her chin and studied Julia's face for a moment.

"Selfishness is a grave and slippery sin, child. Ye must think about the good ye can do in this world instead of the good ye can get out of it."

"Following Reverend Mother's example?"

Archie sighed. "The abbess has responsibilities and has to make hard decisions, betimes. But her first thought is always th' welfare of the convent."

"The abbess thinks of the convent, the bishop thinks of his new cathedral bell tower, the duke thinks of his obligations, and the count thinks of his stomach. But, does anyone think of me?" Julia straightened and, caught in a sudden crush of vulnerability, looked to her favorite sister with moisture springing into her eyes. "Has anyone ever thought of me?"

"Ah, Julia." Archie's eyes glistened, too, in the dim light. She put her arms around Julia and directed the girl's head to her broad, motherly shoulder. For a moment they stood in silence, one filled with need and the other with regret, both knowing the time for truth had come.

"*God* thinks of ye, my girl. And so do I." She drew back enough to cup Julia's cheeks in her gnarled hands. "That's why I must say, *go,* child. Use yer gifts to gladden hearts, and soothe bellies, and make a place for yerself in th' world. Find yerself a husband and make a family, if that's what yer heart desires." She smiled softly through prisms of tears. "I've always believed the Lord gives us desires just as he gives us the means to fulfill 'em. And He'll use the desires o' our hearts to lead us, if we'll let Him. Follow yer heart, Julia. And in whatever ye do, ask th' Lord to be yer guide."

Julia tightened her arms around Archie and received those words into her core as the heartfelt blessing they were meant to be. When she stepped back, they both had wet faces, and Archie reached into her sleeve for a hand-kerchief to dry their tears.

"Now, let's get to chapel before Reverend Mother does. I ate too much to have to listen to endless lecturin' on th' requirement of *obedience* tonight."

LATE THAT EVENING THE ABBESS SAT IN HER private solar with her assistant and dearest friend in the world, Sister Archibald. On the writing desk between them sat a flagon of spiced wine brewed specially for them by Julia . . . the last "evening treat" Julia would prepare for the abbess and the old sister.

"She didn't throw herself onto her knees and beg to stay . . . didn't rail about how high-handed and unfair it was . . . didn't tremble or burst into tears when I told her that she was leaving," the abbess said, still troubled by Julia of Childress's uncharacteristic display of equanimity.

Archie patted her friend's hand and poured her another cup of wine.

"She's a brave little thing, she is."

The abbess narrowed her eyes to search her friend's innocent smile.

"You are so full of horse manure, Mary Archibald. She's not brave, she's reckless. And hot tempered. And prideful, hardheaded, and disobedient. She served that blasted 'hedgehog' of hers when I specifically told her not to."

"Lovely almonds, those," Archie observed. "So crispy and brown on the outside, so pale and tender inside. That girl has a way with almonds."

"And with a saffron and plum-pork pie." Distracted, the abbess closed her eyes and allowed herself to be transported for a moment by the memory of it. "And with the crust for pasties stuffed with chicken and cheese. So flaky. So tender. So beautifully golden." She opened her eyes abruptly. "It's been years since we had a feast like that."

"*Humph,*" Archie said, shedding her slippers and propping her feet up on a stool. "We've *never* had a feast like that."

"We've never had a cook like Julia." The abbess focused her gaze past Archie, studying a vision only she could see. "She's God's gift to the convent. We've never had such harmony and contentment among the sisters. It was the best decision I've ever made, turning the kitchen over to her when Boniface died. She's my legacy to the order and I do not intend to see it brought to naught because some wealthy nobleman has an itch he can't scratch."

"A year passes quick enough."

"And what if she doesn't want to come back?" The abbess finally voiced the real cause of her anxiety. "What if she experiences the luxury and relishes the praise a silver-tongued nobleman can heap on a woman? She never took the slightest bit of interest in religious vows. What if we lose her to the world?"

"In the first place, her new master's tongue ain't exactly silver. He's arrogant and prideful and most likely has a temper. Ye heard how long he's looked for a cook. He'll not be an easy man to please." Archie frowned as she considered the pair together. "They'll probably get on like oil and water."

The abbess thought on her wise friend's observations and felt some of the burden lifting from her heart.

"You're right. It is *Julia,* after all. She'll be just as difficult and temperamental and disobedient there as she is here, and they'll have at each other fang and claw. And if the wretch even thinks about breaking his word, the prospect of answering to the duke will make him reconsider."

"An' thanks to the greedy old bishop, ye got the gold to pay the convent's tithe to the cathedral for four years," Archie reminded her. "Ye won't have to worry about his harangues for money for another two years. Almost makes you want to thank the old trout."

The abbess's smile soured.

"I wouldn't go that far."

Chapter 6

THE BEAST OF GRANDAISE WAS LIVING up to his name the next morning as he led his men on horseback through the convent gates. It had rained the entire night and every rock for miles around had somehow collected beneath his pallet as he slept. He had quit his bed of misery early, and two hours of predawn pacing in the cold and wet hadn't improved his mood. Now his head was pounding, his stomach was growling, and his rain-wetted garments felt cold and heavy and restrictive. But by far, the most annoying thing he had to bear just now was his own prickly conscience.

The moment he rode out of the convent's main gate last evening and heard it slammed and bolted behind him, he sensed he'd made a terrible mistake in allowing the abbess to dictate when he could have the cook for whom he had just bargained away half a year's wine profits. Given the abbess's attitude, how could he be certain the cook she handed him that morning would be the real one? *Dammit.* He should have insisted she produce the woman then and there and questioned her thoroughly before agreeing to such a costly scheme.

It was the food, he realized grimly. He'd been under the

spell of that magnificent lamb, those mouthwatering pasties, and that absurd but delicious hedgehog. All he could think about was getting the abbess to let him have the woman responsible for his first unblemished taste of pleasure in years.

Now as they entered the convent courtyard, he groaned at the sight of the throng of females gathered to bid farewell to the cook. The sisters and their maiden charges parted to allow him and his men to pass but then stood glaring at him as if he were the devil himself come to spirit off one of their blessed number. Thankfully, their attention was soon redirected to the inner gate, where several women in black habits and veils emerged and moved toward the cart.

He scowled and rose in his stirrups to see what was happening. There was emotion in the voices coming from that knot of nuns and he witnessed a great deal of spontaneous clumping going on here and there.

Hugging, he realized. Why was it females never went anywhere without endless rounds of hugging?

Seized by the need to reassure himself he wasn't being had, he urged his horse forward through the crowd until he spotted the top of a bare head crowned with a halo of reddish hair. It had to be her. She was the only one not wearing a habit and she was being hugged fervently by everyone else. He tensed for some reason as he watched her being passed from embrace to embrace and thought for a moment of his encounter with that kitchen wench . . . what she had said about the cook being strong. . . .

Then the woman with the reddish hair paused some distance away and held out her arms to several distraught little girls. Those arms, even viewed through heavy sleeves, didn't look sufficiently brawny. . . .

"Don't cry." He heard only snatches from where she knelt in the midst of them. Something about a "recipe for gingerbread with Sister Helena," "if you're good," and "tonight's supper."

Her condolences only elicited louder wails. She tried to move on; the girls attached themselves to sundry parts of her

anatomy and had to be peeled from her by equally unhappy
sisters. As she set the last child back into a pair of outstretched arms, she turned straight into his searching glare.

His heart stopped.

Her? The kitchen wench with the peppery tongue?

This couldn't be!

She met his gaze with a bold air of defiance, and then
continued on with her good-byes until she came full circle,
back to the cart.

"Sister Helena, I'm counting on you," she said to a
younger-looking nun dabbing at her eyes. "Don't forget the
older sisters' bedtime cups . . . to help them sleep." The
sister bit her lip and nodded.

He kneed his horse forward, sending sisters and girls
alike skittering out of his path.

"This?" He motioned to the red-haired vixen. "This is
my cook?"

"I am afraid so," the abbess said, making her way to the
fore and taking a stand with her hands lodged up her
sleeves. "We have decided to send one of our sisters with
her as a companion and chaperone. Sister Regine." She
nodded to the sister arranging herself on one of the planking seats that lined the sides. The sister lowered her eyes
and blushed as red as a berry.

"Chaperone?" Griffin scrutinized the abbess, seeing in
her aged face the sum of years of shrewd dealings. "Nothing was said about a chaperone."

"Nothing was asked. Julia of Childress is of noble birth
and as such is entitled to the same consideration we would
show to any of our charges forced to travel abroad in the
world."

"But . . . it can't be her," he said, gesturing irritably to her.

"And why can't it?" the wench "Julia" demanded
brazenly.

"You. You told me she could . . . you said she was big
enough to . . . you said . . ." He was halted by the taunting
spark in her eyes.

"I've said nothing to you, Your Lordship. How could I?
We have never met before this moment."

He looked from the kitchen wench to the adamant abbess and then to the hostile faces of the nuns and maidens gathered around them.

This was it. Whether she was the Angel of the Spit and Griddle he had purchased or not, this was the female they were handing over to him. He suffered a brief, alarming visitation of his body pressed hard against hers as he struggled to hold her against the kitchen wall, and prayed it wasn't a harbinger of force he'd have to use in dealing with her. His face reddened and he looked up to find Axel and Greeve staring with undisguised fascination between him and the fiery young maiden he had just paid a knight's ransom to procure.

"Into the cart," he ordered the wench irritably. "We're wasting daylight." Barking orders to his men, he swung his horse around and headed out the gate.

Behind them rose a wail of voices calling farewells. One would have thought he was stealing some holy relic from all the racket. Not that he was stealing anything. He'd paid dearly for the services of the tart-tongued female riding in the cart. Then it occurred to him that there had to be a reason they were so distraught at losing her. It was cold comfort to be sure, but better than none.

By the time they crested the first rise and started down the hill, he had decided to question the wench before they went any farther. If she were an imposter, he would turn straight around. He rode back to rein up beside the cart.

"Julia of what?" he demanded.

"Childress," she answered, without turning to look at him.

"That doesn't sound French."

"It isn't."

"And your father was?"

"The Baron Childress. Deceased."

"After which you were brought to the convent just like the rest of the 'maids awaiting.' Where did you learn to cook?"

"The convent."

When he was silent, she turned to glance at him. Green

eyes. Glinting in a way that made him wonder how much he would come to regret this bargain.

"Who taught you the kitchen?"

"Sister Boniface. She was the head cook before me."

"Head cook? You? You expect me to believe you were the convent's head cook?" He gave a snort of disbelief. "You're scarcely eighteen."

"Age is no indicator of experience," she said defiantly. "I've worked daily in the kitchens since I was ten years old, and have been head cook since I was seventeen. I am now twenty years."

"In charge of an entire kitchen at seventeen?"

"The abbess saw that I was capable and diligent, and handed over the spoon to me," she said defiantly. "She has had no cause to regret it."

"Of course not. How badly could you ruin a pot of porridge?"

She bristled at the implication that her repertoire of dishes extended no further than sops and gruel. "You ate my food. You know my worth."

"Do I?" He raked her with a look, taking in unblemished skin the color of fresh peaches, eyes the shade of new leaves in spring, and hair the colors of ginger and cinnamon. "How do I know you were the one responsible for the feast last night?"

"If you truly don't believe it was my work"—she folded her arms and tightened into an irascible knot—"why did you take me with you?"

Caught without a response to the very question he'd been asking himself, he glanced at the sister muttering and fingering a chaplet of prayer beads on the other side of the cart. *Pray for me, too, Sister.*

"The bishop left last night with my coin. When I saw you, it was too late to cancel the bargain. It appears I am forced to trust the abbess."

"Trust the reverend mother?" She gave a taunting laugh. "Oh, Your Lordship, you are in trouble."

Julia watched her new lord and master turn crimson,

spur his mount, and head not only for the front of the column but past it, motioning to Sir Axel and Sir Greeve to
stay with the cart. When she looked around, she found Sister Regine staring at her in horror.

"It's probably not my place to say," the round-faced
sister said, "but I think you might have handled that a bit
better."

"His Lordship is clearly used to having his way," she
declared. "I must make him respect me and my work or I'll
be finished before I've begun."

Sister Regine's wince expressed her opinion of Julia's
chance of success. Then she looked toward the count's di-
minishing figure and frowned.

"Why do you suppose he wears that bit of metal pinching his nose?"

"I was wondering about that, too." Julia frowned and
pursed one corner of her mouth. "Last night I heard them
say he was afflicted in some way."

She followed the sister's gaze, but ran straight into the
eager faces of the two knights who had accompanied the
count to the convent.

The pair, Sir Axel and Sir Greeve as they introduced
themselves, came rushing back to the cart, drew up alongside, and proved to be eager sources of information . . . including exactly where they were bound.

"Grandaise . . . east and a bit south of Bordeaux," Sir
Greeve said proudly. "Wine country. Cold ocean-borne
winds in winter, sizzling hot breezes in summer . . . a fine
mix for grapes."

"And what about His Lordship's home?" Julia asked.
"And his family? Who oversees his household? And what
are the kitchens like?"

"Good, sound walls . . . fine windows . . . real glass,"
Sir Greeve answered.

"Hearths in all the main chambers. His Lordship loves a
good warm fire," Sir Axel added, grinning in approval of
his lord's extravagance.

"And a cup of mulled wine after a hard day of riding
and training." Greeve added. "But you won't have to worry

about that. He has a cellar master to oversee the household wines and brew up his mulled drinks."

"He has?" Julia glanced at Regine with widened eyes, then back. "What other staff is there for the kitchens?"

"A larder, an oven man . . ." Sir Greeve's eyes flicked upward, as if a roster were written in the clouds. "A fire tender, a fueler, half a dozen turnspits . . ."

"What other *cooks?*" she persisted.

"Well, there used to be a woman who saw to the cold cellar and buttery," Axel said, looking uneasily at Greeve, who took it up.

"And there was that poulterer. Took care of all the seizing, chopping, singeing, and plucking. Haven't seen him for a while."

"But there's an army of scullions to do the washing up and sweeping. Oh, and a fine laundry, where they make sure the linen is smooth and free of spots."

"And the rest of the household?" she continued. "The housekeeper?"

"Well"—Axel glanced at Greeve—"there's not one appointed, just now. His Lordship's steward has been stepping in—"

"The kitchens, demoiselle, they are magnificent," Greeve intervened. "Half a dozen hearths, each with special metal ovens. Stone sinks . . . piped water . . . tall ceilings with louvers at the top. Good heavy oak tables and walnut chopping blocks . . . every size and shape of pot you could desire."

"His Lordship's father built the kitchen to Old Jean's specifications," Axel added. "Old Jean was the head cook some years back. In latter days, he was called Grand Jean to distinguish him from his assistant and pupil, Petit Jean. . . ."

Thus, the story of the count's former cook came tumbling out. For years, they said, the count's family had employed Jean de Champagne, the finest cook in the south of France. The old fellow was declining in health and had begun to train an apprentice to carry on his jealously guarded techniques when he suffered a massive stroke and died. On the very day Grand Jean was stricken, Petit Jean disappeared and was never heard from again. The kitchens reeled from the double loss of master and student and, from that day to this, had never recovered. It was a great mystery, they declared, bringing Julia's thoughts to a mystery closer at hand.

"Why does His Lordship wear that band of metal across his nose?"

Greeve and Axel exchanged glances and looked uncomfortably toward the horizon where the count had disappeared.

"His Lordship is afflicted with a wicked-keen sense of smell," Greeve answered in confidential tones. "Smells that to us are slightly unpleasant and fairly harmless make an unbearable assault upon his senses. He prefers to forego all smells in order to prevent the miasma that comes over him when he removes it." He leaned in and grew quieter still. "We've found it best not to speak of it."

"Mentioning it puts him in a temper," Axel added in a whisper.

"Hmmm. And is that temper responsible for the fact that he currently has no cook?" She knew she had struck a nerve when the pair drew back and looked as if answering would be tantamount to treason. "Just how many cooks has His Lordship had since Grand Jean died?"

Axel began recalling and tallying them on his thick, stubby fingers.

"Nine, demoiselle," he submitted.

"That is a quite a number—"

"In seven years." Greeve put it into perspective.

"Oh." She swallowed hard and looked to Regine, who blanched.

"But now all of that will change. You will transform His Lordship's kitchens and satisfy his hunger and sweeten his temper," Greeve said with something of a forced smile.

"Sweeten his temper." Julia straightened, thinking of the huge, irascible presence that had flattened her against the kitchen wall. "Of course I will."

Reassured, Sir Axel and Sir Greeve peeled away to ride

back to the front of the column, leaving Julia staring after them with a sense of impending disaster. How on earth was she to cook for a man who held his nose against the world? Half of the pleasure of food derived from the smelling of it!

What if he decided he hated her cooking? She grabbed the planking seat on each side of her and squeezed until her knuckles whitened. What if she couldn't please him and he packed her up and sent her back to the convent?

After a few moments, her reeling thoughts stumbled on the memory of him as she had first seen him: with gravy down his chin and crumbs all over his tunic. He had already tasted her food and found it so agreeable that he braved the abbess and bishop and Duke of Avalon to purchase her services. Her racing heart began to slow. The old cook they spoke of had managed to satisfy him. She would find a way to pacify his palate, and in pleasing him—

It suddenly occurred to her that while he was her main concern, there would undoubtedly be other people to please as well. His lady wife, for instance. Strange that Sir Axel and Sir Greeve had neglected to mention their lady. How could they forget so important a point in describing her new home?

She swallowed against the tightness that returned to her throat.

What kind of woman would be unlucky enough to be wedded to a powerful, hungry beast of a man who found the world just too smelly to bear?

Chapter 7

THE DAY WORE ON AND THE CART swayed, pitched, and bounced along the road south, past burgeoning fields of grain and fattening flocks of sheep, through orchards redolent with the fragrance of plum and apple blossoms, and between fields sown with turnips, cabbages, squash, and melons. The count was nowhere to be seen when they stopped, midday, to water the horses and stretch their legs. But as the sun began to lower, he appeared and directed them off the road to a site he had selected for the night's camp . . . within sight of a village.

There he ordered a sizeable fire built and metal rods tented above it to hold an iron pot. Nearby he had his squire unroll a leather pouch of knives, fire forks, and ladles and a chest of basic spices of the type carried by noblemen in hunting parties or on military campaign. Shortly, a rider arrived on a donkey fitted with panniers containing loaves of bread and a sack of provisions. Several of the men who had disappeared across nearby fields and into the woods near their camp returned with rabbits, which they laid in a pile beside the fire.

Julia had watched those preparations and the speculative looks aimed at her with mounting dread. When the count himself strode over, she knew what he would say before he opened his mouth.

"My men have provided the game and the fire. It's time for you to prove your worth and produce something edible for us."

"I beg your pardon, milord, but producing something truly edible under such crude circumstances would require nothing less than magic." She folded her arms and raised her chin. "And I am not a practitioner of the magical arts."

Her refusal clearly caught him off guard. He came alive, growing across her field of vision.

"Indeed?" His eyes narrowed. "I was given to understand that the convent's cook had learned a hot and spicy bit of magic from some gypsies."

"Really, Your Lordship." She looked positively scandalized. "How would I have encountered gypsies while living and working in a convent?"

His features tightened.

"You've been acquired at great cost to cook for me." He pointed to the preparations. "Pick up the knife and the game and do so."

"I am an artisan. A tempter of palates. A mistress of culinary secrets." She swept the makeshift campfire with a look of disdain. "Not a rabbit singer who works by the side of the road."

His fists were clenched at his sides as he leaned over her, adding the considerable persuasion of his physical power to his argument.

"You are my cook," he ground out. "I am ordering you to *cook.*"

She raised her gaze to his and thought she must have lost her wits. He was big and forceful and right now was overpowering her senses and rattling her teeth in their sockets. Then through her rising panic, inspiration struck.

"I will comply with your order, milord"—her gaze focused on that band of metal that clamped his nose together—"if you will agree to remove the band from your nose and smell what you are eating."

His shoulders swelled like rising bread.

"I'll do nothing of the sort. Who do you think you are, to lay down terms and conditions to me?"

"Your head cook, milord. You must be willing to trust me with your senses as well as your health and well-being. If you do not trust me to cook agreeably for you here—this humble fare—then I will not cook here."

For a moment, it looked to her as if he might try to enforce his order physically. Then he wheeled and stalked back through the camp, barking orders for his men to cook their own game. As he disappeared into the nearby woods, she felt every eye in the camp turn on her in confusion.

"If she's the new cook"—mutters reached her ears—"why don't she *cook?*"

Her cheeks burned, her fisted hands throbbed, and her legs might have given way if she hadn't been leaning against the cart. She climbed up onto the cart again and sat on the rear board watching the men's progress toward dinner and enduring Regine's baleful looks.

"I have to make him respect me and my work," she defended her course.

"And what about them?" Regine gestured to the men gathered glumly around the fire. "Don't they deserve a bit of help?"

"They've managed to feed themselves up to now."

"You know, hoarding talents is serious business with the Almighty," Regine mused, rubbing her own hollow middle. "Not to mention the fact that *we* will have to eat what they produce."

Regine had a point; they would have to eat his men's cooking for the week it would take to reach the count's home. That observation, along with the disappointment Sir Axel and Sir Greeve tried valiantly not to show, softened her determination. She left the cart to venture closer to the campfire and heard the arguments taking place among the men charged with cooking.

They had cleaned the rabbits and now debated whether they should stick them on a spit, as usual, or toss them into the great pot hung too close to the flame . . . where they would undoubtedly sizzle and scorch into a charred bit of rabbit leather. Heaven knew what they intended to do with the onions, cabbage, and parsnips piled nearby.

She paused by the basket piled high with bread and tested a loaf with her thumb. The crust gave nicely, surprising her, and the loaves smelled wheaty and fragrant. Next, she paused by a small barrel that stood nearby, wetted her fingers with the drips from the wooden spigot, and sniffed. Wine. Snagging the tin cup that hung on the barrel, she filled it and sipped. It was deep in color and redolent of raspberries and a hint of spice in a fine fume of oak.

Sir Greeve caught her standing there with the cup in her hand and a frown on her face. "If he doesn't mind buying bread and wine from locals, why doesn't he buy a decent joint of meat? Some pork or lamb for a proper meal?"

"He's . . . not partial to hung meats." Sir Greeve winced.

Julia blinked. That made as much sense as saying he didn't like water because it was wet. Aging meats by hanging them in a cool place and allowing them to tenderize was a cornerstone of good cooking. Half of the meat recipes Sister Boniface had imparted to her began: *"Take some well-hanged meat . . ."*

"He says if you hang pork it turns to worms. And lamb goes green and slimy." Axel appeared on the other side of her and sighed. "Won't even let us hang game birds . . . quail, wild geese, swans. Insists they be fresh killed."

"So, you have to find fresh meat when traveling with him."

"And we don't have time much for hunting. So if we can't find an agreeable cottager, we eat mostly small birds and rabbit," Greeve put in with a rueful look. "Very bad rabbit."

Julia looked at the stoic faces of the men crouched around the fire and felt compelled to do something. It wouldn't take much. Deciding, she drew a cup of wine from the barrel and strolled over to the cooks, missing the way Axel and Greeve grinned and elbowed each other behind her back.

"A pity you don't have a bit of bacon to season that pot before you chop up the meat and toss it in," she said, peering over them toward the pot.

"I think we might have a bit of bacon," one of the men declared, rising and pouring through the contents of a bag of provisions lying nearby. Producing a slab of bacon and a knife, he cut several thick strips from the slab and looked to her. She merely glanced at the pot, and he took the hint and tossed them in. They sizzled violently as they hit the hot metal and she suppressed a smile.

"Of course, if it were my kitchen, I'd say the pot was much too close to the flame. It will cook meat too fast and either burn it or make it tough."

Instantly, the men set about raising the pot and lowering the coals, looking to her until she nodded.

"And onions in the fat and a bit of garlic sweeten and impart flavor to whatever is added next. Lots of onions for wild rabbit stew."

A bullnecked fellow with a wild shock of salt-and-pepper hair, called "Heureaux" by the others, seized several onions and a few cloves of garlic from the spice chest, and sliced them into the hot grease. A pleasant aroma began to waft from the pot after a few moments, and as she gave the contents a look, she casually tipped the cup of wine she held into the pot.

"Oops." She shrugged with a scarcely apologetic little smile. "Well, it won't hurt those rabbits to have a bit of wine to simmer in."

Catching on, the men added four more cups of wine while looking to her, stirred the contents, and then looked to her again. In went the rabbit meat. Then the carrots. And some water. Then the lid went on. Parsnips were readied and added as the stew cooked. When a pleasant aroma issued from the pot, she stopped by the spice box and suggested a bit of salt, a few cracked peppercorns, a bit of cumin, and some lemon savory might improve the taste of the stew. When the spices had been added and given a chance to impart their flavor to the mix, she looked to the heat-reddened faces of the men collected around the fire.

"I think it needs to be tasted."

Sir Axel eagerly volunteered. When his eyes closed and he moaned softly the others laughed and headed for the loaves of bread in the nearby basket.

She appeared by the pot to help the first fellow slice his great round loaf in half, then she plunged her fingers in to pull out a great hunk of the soft middle and fill the opening with a cup of the stew. She repeated the process with the second half and carried it to Sister Regine, who fairly melted with longing as Julia thrust it into her hands.

"It smells wonderful."

"Not so bad," Julia said perching on the end of the cart with a mischievous grin, "considering what we had to work with."

Later, as dark was settling over the camp, the count reappeared and strode over to the fire, where the stew pot had been kept warm in the dying coals. He seized a hunk of bread and a cup of wine and headed for the sleeping canopy erected by his squire.

"Here, milord," Sir Axel said, calling after him, "we've saved you some of the stew." All eyes were on the count as he halted and glanced back at the fire.

"Bread is enough for me," he declared.

"Are you sure, milord?" The soldier Heureaux came up from a sitting position to his knees. Several others came alert with him.

Griffin of Grandaise glanced hotly across the camp to where his stubborn cook and her chaperone were settling into a pallet of blankets placed over a mat of dried grasses on the cart bed.

"I'm sure."

The words unleashed a scramble for the stew pot still warming in the coals. The men snatched up remnants and cuttings from the bread basket and scrambled to dunk them into the pot.

He watched in consternation as they gobbled the contents down like greedy children. As the rush slowed, he stalked back to the fire and peered into the emptied pot. There was one streak of sauce, one small morsel of meat left at the bottom. He tore a piece from his bread and sopped it up. Studying it for a moment, he cautiously took a bite.

It tasted of garlic and onions . . . bacon . . . salt and pepper . . . rabbit . . . and wine. His mouth defied him to water, anticipating more when there was none. When the hell did any of his men learn to cook like—

He wheeled to look at Axel and Greeve, who were suddenly busy rolling out their pallets for sleeping. Then he looked to his guardsmen. Heureaux intercepted his scrutiny and, with a smile, directed his glance across the campfire to the cart. It took a moment for the sense of it to register.

She was responsible. She might not have cooked exactly, but she'd done something to make their usual disaster edible. And he'd missed it.

He reddened and stalked for his cot with his stomach rumbling for more.

Dammit.

Chapter 8

GRIFFIN AWAKENED HUNGRY AND IRRI-
table the next morning and as they resumed their
journey, his mood darkened still further. Axel and Greeve
kept wending their way back to the cart, and each time his
own gaze went with them and lingered alarmingly on the
halo of reddish hair that belonged to his cook. Each time
he roared for them and sent them riding ahead on some er-
rand or other. But his attempt to discipline his own gaze
and thoughts was not so successful.

He kept recalling the defiant flash of his new cook's unusual eyes as he held her against the convent wall.

That was what bothered him most, he realized. Julia of
Childress might know something about kitchens, might
even be a cook of sorts. But to him, she would always be a
female first . . . a tart-tongued, pepper-haired wench who
was brazen and arrogant and entirely too full of herself.
And the last thing he needed was a temperamental female
meddling in what was left of his beleaguered kitchens and
bringing them to a grinding halt . . . especially as he was
preparing to take a bride he wanted about as much as he
wanted to have both of his legs broken on a rack.

Midday, they located a copse of trees near a stream and

stopped to be out of the hot sun for a while. The men watered the horses and tied them out in a grassy area, then removed their helms and sun-heated mail shirts to sprawl beneath the trees.

Griffin was in the process of joining his men when he saw his new cook and her chaperone slipping away along the leafy bank and followed, intending to order them back to the cart. But they continued, out of sight of the others, to a bend in the stream where the flow had gouged out a shallow pond. He stopped and watched for a moment, curious about what they would do.

Through the trees, he saw Julia of Childress raise and tuck her skirts into her belt and wade bare-legged into the cool water. She kicked up a spray and called to Sister Regine to join her. The good sister declined.

Rightly so, he grumbled mentally. What the devil was she doing out there in the water, exposing her legs. Smooth and muscular and neatly tapered. He watched her untie the top of her gown and open her chemise to splash water on her throat and chest. Smooth throat and creamy . . . a pang of frustration shot through him as she turned slightly and blocked his view of her bared breasts.

Look at her. No cook worth her salt splashed around bare-legged and bare-breasted in a stream. She was supposed to oversee the feeding and nourishment of his whole household, for God's sake, and here she was prancing around in a stream like some pagan water sprite. How could he possibly trust his health and well-being to a female who behaved like a deranged bacchanal—

A branch snapped somewhere and she snatched her chemise together and whirled to search the bank. His heart skipped at the sight of big green eyes set in a heart-shaped face and framed by a swirl of bright hair. All he could think was that in sunlight that hair seemed more like spun gold than dusky red pepper.

"What are you doing there, Your Lordship?" she called breathlessly.

He realized that the wood that had snapped was beneath his foot. He had inched forward into the sunlight without realizing it and now stood fully exposed on the bank above her. Appalled at being caught staring, he scrambled for an excuse.

"You're too far from the others," he managed to grind out. "The closer we get to Paris, the more travelers about. It's not safe for women to be abroad—"

"Paris?" She suddenly began wading toward the bank. "Did you say we're near Paris?"

"Yes." He blinked, dismayed to see her heading directly for him as she left the water. "We're . . . just over half a day's ride to . . . Paris." He stumbled back a step as she came toward him grappling with the ties of her chemise and pulling the top of her unlaced overgown together. When she reached him, the hem of her gown was still raised and tucked in her belt and her legs were bare and wet from the knees down. He backed another step and then another, reddening with embarrassment at his instinctive retreat.

"I have been meaning to speak to you about that, milord." She finally yanked her hem free and let it fall, then used her shift and gown to dry the water on her legs. He suffered equal impulses of fascination and horror as she pushed the fabric over those sleek contours that had just burned themselves into his brain. "Since we are so close to such wonderful markets, I thought it would be a good time to replenish your supplies of spices and—"

"Ohhhh, no." He rescued enough of his wits from the heat pooling in his loins to realize that this was no time and he was in no condition to engage in such negotiations. "We are not setting foot inside Paris. And that is *final.*"

He turned back to the camp, desperate to put distance between them.

"Not Paris proper, milord." She came after him, holding her hem up and picking her way through the dried grass and shrubby undergrowth. "The Hot Fair held to the north of Paris this time of year. I have never been there myself, but I've been told that the Paris merchants bring their wares out of the city to set up stalls in the open air. Merchantmen arriving from the East stop at the fair when sailing up the Seine on their way to the Hot Fair at Troyes. It's a grand market . . . everything imaginable . . . the freshest foods and spices . . . and good prices. . . ."

Her voice had begun to fade and, against his better judgment, he glanced over his shoulder. She was hopping up and down to keep her balance as she brushed her feet and shoved them into her slippers. Appalled by the way he had paused to watch, he wrenched his attention forward and struck off again, quickening and lengthening his stride. She soon caught up.

"How much do you spend in a year on spices and condiments, milord? Quite a bit, I should imagine."

He scowled and refused to honor her with a glance.

"My steward does the buying and keeps my household accounts. And he is under strict orders not to bother me with tallies of turnips and trenchers."

"In other words, you have no idea how much of your coin is spent each year to feed your household," she charged, breathless from the effort required to match his pace.

"*In other words,* how much I spend is none of your concern."

"I beg to differ." She darted past him and stopped directly in his path, causing him to arch and teeter to avoid touching her. "If I am to plan meals and bargain with local producers and purchase staples, spices, and equipment, I must know what I have to spend."

"Who says you will do the buying?" He tried to look through her instead of at her, but he could still see she had taken serious umbrage at that prospect.

"*All* cooks do their own buying, milord. How else can we be sure the ingredients we use are fresh and healthful? How else can we be held accountable for the safety and nourishment of the household we feed?" She yanked and tied the laces on the half-open front of her gown. "When was the last time your cook went to a spice market?"

"I haven't had a head cook for some time," he replied, refusing to watch what she was doing.

"Well then, your steward. How long ago did he attend a

fair or travel to a spice market to replenish your spice chest?" When he didn't answer, she finished the bow she was tying and tried another tact. "When was the last time your kitchen served you anything made with cinnamon or nutmeg or a good fine spice?" She drew a conclusion from his silence. "If you cannot say, then it has been too long a time, milord. If I am to revive your kitchens, then I must do some buying on the way to your home."

"So that's it. You want me to throw good money after bad." He bent closer to her, scowling. Wittingly or not, she had just provided the most convincing evidence to date that she was a true cook. He had never known a cook—young or old, seasoned or green—who didn't harangue his patron for more money or a chance to spend it at a market or fair. "You expect me to spend money at the behest of a cook who refuses to cook."

"A cook without the proper ingredients and tools cannot do much, milord. Surely you can see that," she said, straining to sound reasonable.

"Out of the question," he said, lowering his face still closer to hers.

He could see that she was trying to avoid meeting his gaze. Smart wench. Then in the silence that settled between them, she turned her head slightly and slid into his gaze like melted butter into bread. Perhaps too smart. Perhaps she sensed that some of the heat building in him had nothing to do with anger or outrage.

"What is your favorite spice, milord?" Her voice was suddenly full of texture and nuance that made his ears heat and sent a surge of anticipation prickling through his scalp. He felt a need to swallow, but found himself incapable of doing it. "What taste do you crave above all others?"

The growing tightness in his throat now prohibited speech as well. Was she leaning closer to him or was he swaying toward her?

"What makes your mouth water and your heart skip in anticipation? Cinnamon . . . a dusky red powder that tingles the tip of your tongue? Or could it be ginger . . . hot and bright along the back of your throat? Perhaps it is nutmeg . . . sweet and nutty . . . caressing your lips and bathing your cheeks with flavor. . . ."

Julia was mildly surprised by the words leaving her mouth. Tingles and caresses. Bathing in flavor. Someone else must be talking; she was too busy sinking in pools of hot Baltic amber to string together a coherent thought.

Every part of her body had come alive with awareness of him. She should move, blink, clear her throat . . . something . . . anything but stand here gazing into his eyes and succumbing to the mystery of a man who owned her time and talents and, despite the exorbitant price he had paid for them, seemed to value neither.

"Pepper," he said in a cracked whisper. "I love pepper."

"Red or black, milord?"

"Both."

"Short or long pepper?"

"Short."

"Is it the spiciness or the heat that you find most pleasing?"

"H-heat. Eye-watering, blood-searing, sweat-out-a-fever heat. Red hot. Like a glowing iron poker." His gaze flowed over her head and he curled his hands into fists at his sides.

She was warm from the sun, but felt her skin glowing hotter where his notice touched it. As she watched, feeling strangely sensitive in every womanly part of her, he parted and wetted his lips. Instantly, all of her awareness settled on his bold, generously curved mouth. Moist now. Glistening.

"I'm sure there will be wonderful peppers at the fair's spice market," she murmured, trying to rescue her senses from the puddle of melted resolve in the middle of her. "Pungent fresh pepper that will burn your nose and make your eyes water and your blood heat. I make a special three-pepper pottage with red pepper and horseradish and mustard and paprika. . . ."

"Say that again," he demanded, his voice deep and rough.

"Red pepper and horseradish and—"

"The name of the dish," he specified, his eyes darkening in the centers.

"Three-pepper pottage."

"Again."

"Three-pepper pottage." The words caused her mouth to draw into a bow and she felt his gaze on it like a physical touch. "Three-pepper pottage."

His head lowered.

She raised her chin one accommodating inch.

"*Ahem.*"

Sister Regine's voice from nearby startled them both and set them lurching apart with heat-burnished faces and luminous eyes.

"We . . . were just . . . I was just a-asking about . . ." she stammered.

"Spices." He cleared his throat with an authoritative rumble and glared at her. "Consider performing your rightful duties and I shall consider your request."

Sister Regine watched as he strode off and turned on Julia with a frown.

"What in Heaven's name was that all about?"

"I was asking for permission to attend a hot fair outside Paris," she responded, feeling damp inside her garments and oddly exposed.

"Oh, is *that* what you were asking for." Regine narrowed one eye. "All of that staring and breathing and blushing over a few grains of spice?" Her other eye narrowed. "Cooking must be more involving than I thought."

Julia's face flamed as she headed back to the cart.

"You have no idea."

THAT NIGHT, THEY CAMPED ON A HILL OUT-side of Paris, overlooking the city's hazy glow upriver and more distinct lights coming from the campfires in the market camps that littered the valley below. There was enough breeze from the west to keep the market smells at bay and provide a steady cooling. And when the men arrived in camp with fresh chickens bought from a nearby farmer and looked to her, she glanced at her brooding master and gave them a nod that set them scrambling for their knives and fire steel.

As she did the night before, she strolled the camp, peering, assessing, and giving advice that yielded some of the finest chicken sops the men had ever tasted. Her refusal to cook was compromised, but toward a higher good. And unlike the night before, the count also took a portion of bread, filled its soft center with the savory chicken, and ate hungrily.

When the meal was finished and the tools were cleaned and packed away, Julia retired to the cart to prepare for sleep. When she returned from visiting the bushes, she found the count sharing a silence with Regine.

"Milord." She paused warily at the side of the cart.

"A reasonable supper," he observed.

"Which would have been greatly improved by the addition of some sage and parsley, and rosemary." She looked pointedly at him, then away. "And perhaps some long pepper."

He scowled.

"You'll have your visit to the spice market tomorrow," he said, laying down the challenge. "And then we'll see what sort of a kitchen steward you truly are."

Julia contained her smile of triumph until after His Lordship had stalked away. She turned, eager to engulf Regine in a hug, and found the cherub-faced sister contracted into a defensive knot.

"I don't see what you're so happy about," the little nun declared with rising anxiety. "Fairs are noisy, smelly dens of mammon and iniquity."

Chapter 9

SISTER REGINE, AS IT HAPPENED, HAD it half right. The Hot Fair outside of Paris was a sprawling, noisy distillation of all that was worst and *best* about the great city. The gathering drew established merchants and itinerant peddlers, sly tavern keepers and gawking sheep herders, wool-clad burghers' wives and ladies in fine damask . . . as well as an army of wardens, notaries, and fee collectors, and their opposites: cutpurses, moneychangers, and short-weighting merchants. From the highest to the lowest, every aspect of Paris society was represented.

It was the haze they noticed first as they descended into the valley. Before the dew dried that morning, hearths, ovens, and braziers had begun spewing streams of smoke as bakers, wafer makers, confectioners, sauce makers, roasters, and food vendors prepared their wares for the day ahead. Shortly afterward the lanes of stalls, tents, and carts began to bustle with people and ring with the calls of merchants hawking wares. At the base of a growing din lay a hum of hammers, cart wheels, and grindstones, and over its top skimmed the laughter floating from taverns and jugglers' audiences and the squeals of racing children.

Sister Regine had chosen to stay behind and pray for her success, so Julia arrived at the fair with a cordon of escorts headed by Sir Axel and Sir Greeve. Her heart beat like a caged bird in her chest, both from the excitement of seeing something she'd heard stories about and from anxiety that in this foreign milieu, her judgment and ability would be put to the test.

Her first few impressions alone were worth whatever price she had to pay to gain them. She halted the party to watch two jugglers traversing a narrow plank while balancing balls on their noses, then went on to watch a banner maker at work, investigate a number of cooking tools at a tinsmith's stall, and laugh delightedly at a mummers' performance of a henpecked husband who finally evened the score. Sir Axel and Sir Greeve quietly pointed out the trick in a sleight-of-hand shell game and then closed ranks around her to usher her past a tavern fight turned ugly.

There was color, noise, and activity all around . . . things to attract the eye and extract coin from the purse. Not that she actually had a purse. His Lordship had decided to entrust his coin to the care of Sir Greeve and Sir Axel . . . who, she strongly suspected, had also been given the authority to override any purchases that seemed unwise. Annoying as such oversight was, it was not exactly fatal to her hopes for the day.

"Look, demoiselle," Axel whispered with awe, pointing to a series of carts draped with gaily colored trims and ribands, chaplets of flowers, and ladies' caps of all shapes, colors, and sizes. "It's like a rainbow."

"Lovely indeed. But not on my list." She turned away with a sigh.

"List? What list?" Greeve frowned as he thumped Axel's arm to wake him from his trance and hurried after her.

"I've made a roster of the things I use most commonly and are probably needed in His Lordship's kitchen. First on that list is bolting cloth."

"Cloth?" Axel lurched along after them.

"For wrapping, pressing, draining, straining, and sieving. Really, Sir Axel, I should think you would know how frequently cloth is used in a kitchen."

"Well, I . . ." Axel seemed a bit flustered. "But of course. *Bolting* cloth." The moment she moved on, he looked to Greeve and shrugged in bewilderment.

As they entered the cloth merchant's lane they slowed and perused the open tents filled with bolts of cloth. Sir Axel spotted some coarse bleached cotton and ducked inside a tent to hold a bit of the fabric up for her to see.

"You said you wanted a coarse, sturdy cloth." He tugged on the weave to demonstrate. "This seems sturdy enough."

Julia gave both merchant and merchandise an assessing glance.

"I'm afraid it won't do," she said distinctly, turning to leave.

The merchant rushed over to intercept her. "Oh, but look again, milady . . . it is excellent cloth . . . very sturdy . . . good for many uses."

"I'm sure it is fine cloth, monsieur, but le Comte de Grandaise must have only the finest in his kitchens." She smiled sweetly.

"Milady, this is the finest bolting cloth made." Seeing her under the escort of two knights, the merchant apparently assumed she was a lady, despite her simple garments. He was torn between expressing outrage at her conclusion and pleading with her to reconsider it. "I carried it all the way from Florence myself, a month back. The finest cotton Italy has to offer . . . woven with care by Florence's expert looms. Surely you have heard of Italian cotton."

"*I've* heard of it," Axel put in earnestly. Then he looked again at the cloth and frowned. "But doesn't it seem like it's been stretched in places?"

Julia looked up to find the portly knight staring at the cloth with widened eyes. So artless. So sincere as he pronounced an opinion guaranteed to curl a cloth merchant's beard. The first rule of good bargaining was to have more than one person in the negotiations, even if that other person was not a buyer himself. And so much the better if the third person didn't know he was part of the process.

"So it does," she agreed, rubbing the cloth between finger and thumb.

"That is the nature of the weave, milady," the merchant declared.

"Are you sure it hasn't been wet? Perhaps rained upon and dried?"

"Milady!" The merchant grew livid. "Never! My cloth is never wetted and stretched. A vile and deceitful practice employed by some of the ungodly heathens in my trade." He spit on the ground to condemn those unworthy wretches and glared at his competitors in nearby stalls. "I am an honest man . . . long a resident of Paris . . . respected in my hall."

"I did not mean to imply otherwise." She gave an apologetic smile. "But now that I look closer, I believe it may be an unfortunate gauge for kitchen work. Too gross a weave for finer straining and too fine a weave for thicker work."

"Can you not test it?" Axel proposed, drawing a gasp from the merchant.

"No need. I will just call on the other stalls," Julia said, backing toward the entrance. "Someone will have cloth perfect for my lord's kitchens."

"No, please, milady . . . save yourself the steps. You will only be disappointed by the inferior offerings of the others. Perhaps"—he looked unhappily at Axel—"we *could* arrange a test."

"I'll find a sauce vendor," Axel declared eagerly.

Half an hour of hard bargaining later, Julia exited the stall with seven bolts of excellent kitchen cloth and the knowledge that cloth merchants, at base, were no different than farmers with loads of cabbages, onions, and peas. Soon with the help of Sir Axel and Sir Greeve, who fell quite naturally into the role of the eternal skeptic and the overeager assistant, she added tinsmiths, waferers, basket weavers, dried fruit sellers, nut merchants, stone cutters, and oil merchants to the brotherhood of the susceptible.

Each bargain she struck added to her confidence and

carried her that much closer to the stalls of the spice sellers, merchants who knew the worth of their precious wares and were renowned to be shrewd and difficult traders. But each bargain she struck also added to the bolts, baskets, earthen jugs, and bundles her escorts had to bear. By the time they paused, midday, to purchase some meat pasties and apples roasted on sticks, the three guardsmen who accompanied them were groaning under the burden of those bolts of cloth, heavy bags of nuts, wooden flats of dried fruits, earthen jugs of spiced oils, bundles of dried herbs, a large stone mortar and pestle, and sundry small tools from the tinsmith. And Sir Greeve was counting the coin that was left with no small alarm.

"Only a few livres left and we have yet to buy a single grain of pepper," he said, paling.

Julia gave him a confident smile.

"I'm sure His Lordship has more."

GRIFFIN HAD REMOVED HIS SUN-HEATED TUnic of mail and sat in his leather jerkin, studying the parchment containing the royal decree that he must marry the daughter of the Count of Verdun by Michaelmas. He raked a hand through his hair and wished he could just toss the offensive document into the fire and pretend it didn't exist. But he couldn't, and he was trying to sort out what kind of dower lands he would be forced to settle on his unwanted bride. He searched the loathsome document for her name. Dammit—his fate was linked to the chit and he couldn't even remember what she was called!

A motion in the distance caught his eye and he looked up to find Greeve and three of his men struggling manfully up the path to their camp with arms full of all manner of bolts, boxes, bags, and bundles. Their burdens were so great that their legs fairly bowed from the weight they carried. He bounded up and directed them to the cart, where, to Sister Regine's chagrin, they dumped their cargo onto the cart bed and when that was full, piled it up on the seats. Groaning with relief, they stretched their cramped fingers and aching backs and stumbled over to the fire to collapse on the well-trampled grass around it.

"What the devil is this?" Griffin demanded of Greeve as the knight stared with dismay at the deep red marks Julia's purchases had left on his fingers. "Where is she . . . that cook of mine?"

"I came"—Greeve leaned against the cart, panting—"to bring these and get additional coin, milord. The demoiselle has begun to buy spices and I have only a few sous left. She bade me return and"—he swallowed hard—"get more."

"More?" Griffin lashed a glance at the fair in progress in the distance. "She's bought all of that and still wants *more?*"

"If you'd seen her, milord—she's a marvel. She can charm the chasuble off a bishop." Greeve smiled as if hoping to appease his lord. "I left her with Axel in the lane of the spice merchants. She said to tell you that her very next purchase would be *pepper.*"

Griffin felt as it he'd been punched. The nerve of the wench, taunting him with his own preferences. And the memory of how she had learned them.

"The hell it will." He shoved the parchment he'd been reading into his courier pouch and strode for the path down the hill toward the fair.

"Milord—wait! Ohhh, I was afraid of this." Greeve motioned irritably to the count's squire to take their lord his mail and sword. "Milord, wait for your arms! The fair is full of knights and squires—"

JULIA STOOD IN THE STALL OUTSIDE A RICH spice merchant's tent, listening to the yarn the merchant was spinning about the origin of the scrolls of cinnamon bark displayed in a long, narrow wooden box before her. With her were Sir Axel and a score of other folk who had heard her spirited bargaining and gravitated to the stall to witness her battle of wits with the canny spice seller.

". . . grown in a faraway land on a tree that is surrounded and tended by mighty winged beasts . . . with claws like scythes and beaks as sharp as swords," the merchant declared, each word more dramatic than the last. Murmurs went through the crowd. "They protect the trees so that they may use the bark and leaves to make their nests. The men who harvest the cinnamon must wait until the beasts are asleep before they can cut the branches. Very dangerous work. If the beasts should awaken . . ."

Julia stared pointedly at the voluble merchant.

"I don't care if the beasts' beaks are the size of long shields, monsieur. Two livres a pound is still too much to pay for cinnamon."

The merchant grasped his chest and groaned.

"You will not find cinnamon as fresh and potent as mine anywhere else." He could see his usual tactics failing and leaned closer to her. "But for you, lovely lady, I have something special."

"It will have to be nothing short of miraculous if you think it will blind me to the robbery you would practice on me," she said, rolling her eyes and drawing chuckles and calls of encouragement from the mixed crowd of men and women. While the merchant retreated to the interior of the tent to search his chests and spice boxes, she turned to Axel to whisper. "Not a denier more than a livre a pound. And we must have five pounds at least."

Her eye caught a trio of knights standing not far away, watching her intently. Realizing that they had caught her eye, one gave her an openly admiring smile that made her keenly aware of her exposed hair. Color bloomed in her cheeks. What would happen if she smiled back?

She dropped her gaze to the box of cinnamon the merchant's assistant was closing to protect it from the sun, and busied herself looking at the samples of other spices laid out for her consideration. She picked up a few of the peppercorns from the lot she had already agreed to purchase and tested them by rubbing them briskly between her palms and smelling them afterward. The friction produced a lovely true pepper scent, which she shared with Sir Axel. Then she picked up a sampling of cloves, smelled them, and put one clove in her mouth. The taste was pleasantly spicy and astringent.

From the corner of her eye she could see the knights
moving closer and felt her heart beat faster. They couldn't
know who she was, so it might be a chance to practice being a woman as much as a cook. She was, after all, looking
for a husband. . . .

"Here, milady. You must try these." The merchant returned with a box in which resided a bag of elongated
brown seeds that looked somewhat familiar.

"What are they?" she said, frowning, then catching the
scent of them in the warming sun. She lowered her head
and breathed deeply. "They're like cumin . . . only so much
stronger. And with more anise."

She popped a seed into her mouth and crushed it with
her teeth. Inhaling the scent as she savored the taste, she
found it strong, but clean and pleasant. "A variety of
cumin? What is it called?"

"Caraway, milady."

"And I suppose it comes from the Great Nile River,
where it is pulled out by natives with nets made of pure
gold," she said dryly, eliciting laughter all around. The
merchant reddened.

"It comes from the lowland regions to the north. And is
especially good in sour pottages, though I'm told it is
sometimes used in breads."

"I'll take half a pound," she said, not caring to hide her
pleasure. Then she realized she hadn't yet heard the price
and added: "*If* it's not too dear."

The merchant scowled. "It is rare in these parts. At nine
sous per half pound, you would be stealing it from me."

"Then call me a *clever* thief, because I'll have it for
seven," she declared, setting the onlookers laughing as she
retied the bag and handed it to Sir Axel. "And I'll have a
pound of galingale, a pound of mace, and a pound of grains
of paradise. Five pounds of loaf sugar. Half a pound of
powdered ginger. A pound of each of fennel seed, dill seed,
and coriander. Did I say cloves? Two full pounds of
cloves." She watched the merchant making tallies on his
wax tablet and setting his assistants scurrying with the indicated commodities to the nearby scales, and asked Sir

Axel if he would accompany them to see the weighing.

Watching the merchant adding up the cost, she arrived at the staggering amount well before he did. *Heaven grant that Sir Greeve return soon,* she prayed. *And with a healthy purse.*

"Now, about that cinnamon," she said.

"Before we settle on that price, let me show you one more confiture . . . something seldom seen in Paris, much less the rest of France."

"Give her her price, you skinflint."

She looked around to find that the three knights had worked their way forward in the crowd. The one who had spoken was standing not far away with his thick arms crossed and his eyes alight with an interest she sensed had nothing to do with her bargaining ability.

"The cinnamon." He clarified it. "Sell it to her for what she offered."

Her face flamed as a number of the crowd agreed noisily and began to harangue the merchant to do as the knight had said.

"But wait—how about this?" the merchant declared, pulling a handful of cloth from behind his back and opening it. She stood on her tiptoes to see what he held and caught a flash of orange. He held it out to her and everyone in the front of the crowd leaned forward to see it as well.

"Is that . . ."

"Orange. Sugared orange. Sweet and tart. And just look at the color. Have you ever seen such a—"

The bold knight broke through the front of the crowd to snatch a piece of the sugared orange, holding it up and turning it around in the bright afternoon sun. Startled by his action, Julia looked up and he caught her gaze in his.

"So this is what an 'orange' is like, eh?" He smiled. "I heard of them in Spain, when we fought there, but the Turks had stripped the trees as they retreated. Have you ever tried one, demoiselle?"

"I have not, sir," she answered, instinctively lowering her eyes.

"Nor have I. And there may be no better time than now." He broke the piece in half, took a bite, and thrust the second piece toward her. When her mouth opened in surprise, he slipped it between her lips. The merchant gasped at his outrageous behavior and ordered him to leave the stall, but the knight only looked to his friends and laughed.

"Here's for your wares, spice monger." He flipped a huge silver coin to the merchant, who caught it, glared at it, then looked up in surprise.

"But this is—"

"Too much, I know. I'll take the rest in your sugared oranges."

Julia's mouth watered wonderfully with the savor of the sweet-tart comfit. So this was the peel and meat of an orange, she thought, mildly astonished at the flavor and at how she had acquired this sample of it.

Across the table of wares, her benefactor watched her reaction with amusement. He was a tall, clean-limbed younger knight with a pleasantly muscular face, wearing a tabard of crimson and white over mail. When the flustered merchant handed him a small cloth bag containing several pieces of sugared orange, he offered them immediately to Julia.

"Thank you, kind sir, but I cannot." She shoved her hands to her sides.

"Oh, but you must," the knight said in a teasing tone. "For *I* will not take it and if *you* do not, our greedy merchant here will have both my coin and your oranges. Which will only encourage his penchant for overcharging and contribute to the endangerment of his immortal soul. Hardly a Christian outcome. Won't you agree, milady?" He continued to hold it out, until two voices from the crowd declared that if she didn't take it, they would. When she did reach for it, he held on to it for a moment longer to make her look at him.

"I must beg a favor, milady." His lowered voice sent a trill of excitement through her shoulders. "That you think of me each time you enjoy a taste."

"What the devil is going on here?" an all-too-familiar voice roared above the gathering.

Julia wheeled to find the count and Sir Greeve standing

to the side of the stall, watching in disbelief as she accepted costly treats from a strange knight. She had sent Greeve for His Lordship's money and he had brought His Lordship instead. If only the ground would open and swallow her whole.

"Your Lordship!" She gave a small dip of acknowledgment and thought better of trying to get through the crowd to where he stood glowering at her. A bit of distance between them just now seemed wise. "We were just trying a wonderful new sweetmeat. Sugared oranges. From Spain."

"Did I or did I not send you to buy spices this day?"

"Of course you did, milord."

"Then where the devil are they?" he demanded, invading the crowd and sending several onlookers scrambling out of his way.

"They are here, milord." She waved at the variety of samples spread upon the table while tucking the sugared oranges into the folds of her gown. "And the rest is with Sir Axel, who is watching the weighing. You will be pleased to learn that I have been quite careful with your coin." She nodded to the outraged spice merchant, hoping to induce him into a confirming nod.

"A veritable miser," he grumbled.

"And knowing how you love it"—she forced an excessively sprightly smile—"the first spice I purchased today was pepper."

At the mention of that spice, his face became as dark as a thundercloud. But that was only a pale forerunner of the fury that filled his countenance when he turned to face her orange-buying gallant. Julia was stunned by the drastic change in her already imposing employer; he seemed to grow a foot taller. The blood drained from her head so abruptly that she swayed.

"Who the hell are you? And why are you interfering with my cook?" Griffin ground out, addressing the knight who had been smiling at Julia of Childress. But in truth, he already knew. The knight wore the colors of the one house in all of France that roused in him true loathing . . . the

house and lineage that had brought his family nothing but
loss and grief.

"Martin de Gies, of the House of Verdun," the young
knight declared evenly, his gaze lowering with contempt to
the shield of blue and green on the tabard Griffin wore.
"And you can only be the Bea—the Comte de Grandaise."
He took a step back, watching Griffin carefully, his arms
tensed at his sides and the hilt of his sword suddenly visible as his leg nudged it forward. They were small movements that spoke of readiness to fight and of training that
would make that fight a pitched battle. Then he seemed to
realize what Griffin had said.

"What do you mean interfering with your 'cook'?" De
Gies glanced at Julia. "Do you mean to say this is your
cook?"

"She is."

"I had no way of knowing." He slid his gaze back to
Griffin, assessing him with the same eye for threat Griffin
employed. "I do not dally with turnspits or scullions."

Griffin saw Julia's eyes widen at the knight's words as if
she'd been struck, and he took an involuntary step closer to
the wretch. Suddenly Greeve was at his back and two
knights also bearing Verdun's colors were shoving their
way to the front of the crowd. Griffin's hand itched to close
around the hilt of his blade, but he glanced from de Gies to
Julia, to the merchant and shocked crowd.

It was a bad place for a fight. Property and innocents
would be at risk, and the odds were unknown. Greeve was
with him and Axel was nearby, but he had no idea how
many more of Verdun's men might be lurking about, full of
wine and spoiling for a fight. He could see de Gies making
the same calculations.

"She is neither turnspit nor scullion," he declared tautly.
"You would be well advised to hold your tongue in the
presence of your betters." Abruptly he turned and seized
Julia by the arm. "And you," he growled, pushing her into
Greeve's hands. "Go straight back to camp and remain
there until I return. Is that understood?" He slashed a glare
at Greeve. "See she gets there."

"Yea, milord," Greeve said with determination as he threaded Julia's arm through his and dragged her out into the lane.

"But my spices—" she protested.

"Go!" Griffin roared.

Both his fury and the danger of the situation finally registered with Julia. She ceased resisting Sir Greeve's grip and allowed herself to be hauled away.

It was some moments before she could sort out her tumultuous thoughts enough to demand an explanation. Sir Greeve said nothing at first, bustling her along the lanes and skirting the open areas, until they reached the edge of the fair. Only when they had left the last stalls and tents well behind did he slow his pace enough to respond.

"Why was His Lordship so furious?" she demanded, dragging her heels to slow him down. "Who was that knight?"

"A vassal of the Count of Verdun," Greeve said, spitting afterward as if the name fouled his mouth. Such a vehement action from the usually sanguine Sir Greeve shocked her.

"And who is this 'Count of Verdun'? Why does the very sight of his men cause His Lordship to go apoplectic?"

Greeve chewed on that question for a moment. Then, finding no one near them on the rutted road, he sighed and finally halted to face her.

"Verdun is His Lordship's closest neighbor. His sworn and bitter enemy. And soon to be . . . his father-in-law."

Chapter 10

WITH JULIA OUT OF THE WAY, GRIFFIN turned to his opponent with a soldier's acceptance of what would happen next. If it came to a fight, he was ready. If his opponent was not ready to engage, then he would gladly withdraw. He had to find out which it would be and took a calculated risk.

"What the hell are you doing in Paris?" he demanded of the knight. "Where is your lord?"

After a moment Martin de Gies allowed his shoulders to lower a degree.

"My seigneur is still in the city. He had to retrieve his daughter from the convent at St. Denis."

Griffin tried not to flinch at that reminder of his fate.

"Take your lord a word from me." He felt the charge of the air around him shift subtly as someone approached from behind and he prayed the eyes boring into his back did not belong to Bardot, Count of Verdun. "Tell him I will not expect to set eyes on him or his banner again"—his eyes dropped to de Gies's tabard—"until the event to which we both are commanded by the king."

He watched the knight's eyes drift to whomever was coming up behind him and held his breath until Verdun's vassal began to back away, turned with his comrades, and strode off in the direction of the city road.

A moment later Griffin nearly jumped out of his skin when Axel gave him a good-natured thump on the back.

"Ho, milord!"

"Where the hell have you been?" He wheeled, growling with relief that it was his own loyal knight.

Axel fell back a step and scanned the spice stall in confusion.

"I was just—where is the demoiselle?" He held up one of two meaty fists filled with bags and bundles. "She asked me to witness the weighing while she continued to—what's happened, seigneur?" He followed Griffin's stare to a glimpse of alarming red and white disappearing down the lane.

"Three of Verdun's knights." Griffin gestured toward that flash of dreaded colors. "I found your 'demoiselle' standing in the middle of a crowd making a spectacle of herself with one of them." Laughing. And glowing with the reflected interest that only a pretty woman could inspire in men.

His hands curled into fists as the memory replayed itself. His stubborn cook . . . smiling . . . opening her mouth. . . . He shook free of that vision.

"You were supposed to be overseeing her purchases and making certain that she bought spices and goods for cooking. What the devil were you doing playing servant and handmaiden?"

"Well, it seemed prudent to assist—"

"Pardon, milord." The spice merchant had recovered from his fright at the confrontation and now approached Griffin.

"What?" Griffin barked at him.

"The tally, milord." The merchant put forth his wax tablet for Griffin to see. "The lady—er—*demoiselle* had agreed to purchase a number of fine spices before she left."

Griffin was taken aback. He'd just caught his cook in a flirtation with his sworn enemy's henchmen and had damn near come to battle blows. Now it was all back to normal and hi-ho-milord-here-is-the-bill?

"And at very fine prices." Axel added the weight of his

own expectation to the harried merchant's. "She managed to get cinnamon for a livre a pound." He looked at the merchant, who realized that his entire sale hung in the balance, swallowed hard, and nodded. "Five whole pounds of cinnamon." He quivered with anticipation. "We shall have buckets of cameline sauce, and spiced pears, and spiced wafers . . . and imagine the tasty cups of hypocras of an evening. . . ."

"Eighteen livres, milord," the merchant announced with a hint of timidity. With good reason.

It was a bloody fortune in spices! Griffin came within a hairsbreadth of telling the merchant where to stuff his short-weighted and overpriced luxuries. But then he looked between Axel and the ashen-faced merchant and heard the whispers beginning to waft through the onlookers and spreading through the nearby stalls. There he was, they said, the Beast of Grandaise. In the flesh.

The slightest misstep on his part would be witnessed and repeated and retold, and would reach the heart of Paris before another day was out. The king would doubtless hear of it—Verdun would see to that—and his credibility with the king would reach another new low.

So, he did what any right-thinking lord would do when presented with a choice between a bill and a humiliation. He paid it.

Shortly, he was trudging down the lane with his back and arms straining to contain unwieldy boxes, bags, and bundles of spice. He had no choice but to act as a brute beast of burden; he didn't intend to spend one moment longer than necessary in these dangerous precincts and he certainly wasn't about to send his knights or men-at-arms back to retrieve her purchases. Axel trudged along beside him, equally burdened, but in perversely expansive spirits.

"Smell that?" The portly knight asked, shifting the bags and packages in his arms to thrust some part of a bag closer to Griffin's nose before remembering. "Oh. Sorry, milord." Little chastened, he rattled on: "It's cloves. Troth, I do love cloves. She bought two whole pounds . . . says she always uses more in the autumn. In pork, too, she said.

And—mercy—" He strained to get his nose to the side of a bag hanging at the edge of his burden and inhaled hungrily. "This must be the mace. You know, the smell of it always reminds me of those mace and anise wafers Old Jean used to make. Remember those, milord? Melted on your lips they did. Oh, and she got a new spice . . . something like cumin, only stronger Corraway. Carrenay. Anyway, it's a marvel. All pungent and musty and with a bit of a vinegary bite. They say it's great for cabbage and pottages of all sorts . . . and pork. I cannot wait to taste it on pork. Only imagine . . . tender, rosy meat dripping with juicy—"

"Axel!" Griffin roared at the top of his lungs, not caring any longer who might be watching. Another word and he was going to commit unholy murder.

"Yes, milord?" The knight's eyes were as big as goose eggs.

"Shut the hell up."

JULIA ARRIVED BACK AT THEIR CAMP DUSTY, exhausted, and thoroughly dispirited. Sister Regine rushed to meet her and pulled her back to the cart, where she pushed bags and packages aside to allow them to sit on the back.

"Ohhh, I knew I should have gone with you. What happened?" Regine patted and rubbed her white hands to restore warmth to them. "Sir Greeve came back with the men and His Lordship went storming down to the fair himself." When Julia didn't respond, she prompted: "You spent too much—was that it?" She groaned. "I warned you about that. Noblemen are notoriously close with their coin. If I learned anything from the reverend mother, I learned—"

"It's not that." Julia heaved a huge, shuddering sigh.

"What then?"

"I met a knight . . . at the fair . . . at the spice merchant's stall."

"You did? Well, that's no reason for . . . what do you mean 'met'?"

"I was buying spices and the knight came up and or-

dered the merchant to give me a good price and then
bought me some sugared oranges." She dragged the cloth
bag from her gown and handed it to Regine, who untied the
string and gasped.

"Oranges!" The sister stared at the morsels as if they
were holy relics. "I haven't seen these since I was a girl."
She exhaled pure awe. "Ohhh, Juuulia."

"A *handsome* knight . . . he gave them to me just as His
Lordship came charging up, bellowing like a baited bull. It
seems the knight is a vassal of the Count of Verdun, whom
His Lordship despises and apparently has fought in battle.
Sir Greeve said their lands adjoin in several places and
their families have been at it fang and claw for generations.
A feud of some sort. Of all of the awful happenstance . . .
the knight who was kind to me turns out to be His Lordship's sworn enemy."

"Terrible. Just terrible," Regine commiserated while
circling her finger above the oranges. "Would you mind if
I . . ."

Julia shrugged permission.

"What if . . ." She couldn't speak her fear aloud: What
if His Lordship bellowed like that whenever a man took
notice of her? He was always ordering Sir Axel and Sir
Greeve away from her. What if he kept her bound to his
hearths and pantry and she never got the chance to meet
any unmarried men?

"Then, as Sir Greeve was bringing me back"—her spirits
sagged even more—"he told me that His Lordship was just
betrothed to the count of Verdun's daughter, by order of the
king himself." Her shoulders rounded. "I thought it curious
that Sir Axel and Sir Greeve had failed to mention the lady
of Grandaise. I meant to ask specifically about it, but . . ."
Her voice trailed off and Regine's moaning was the only
thing audible. She looked over to find the round-faced sister's eyes closed and her face alight with joy transcendent.

"I had forgotten what they tasted like." Regine hugged
herself with happiness. "They're so sweet, so tart . . . a
work of heavenly splendor!"

Julia watched in dismay as Regine was transported to

some outpost of Heaven by the taste of a sugared orange, while totally ignoring her humiliating experience in the market, His Lordship's vile behavior toward the gallant knight who had flirted with her, *and* the tumultuous revelation that His Lordship had been forcibly betrothed to his enemy's daughter.

At least it was tumultuous to Julia.

It took her a few moments of grappling with that fact to realize that her reaction to the news of his betrothal was every bit as vehement as her distress over being denied the attention of a potential husband. Why should she care who her olfactorily afflicted master married? She was traveling to his household to revitalize his kitchen and train him a new staff of cooks. Nothing more.

In point of fact, his preoccupation with his marriage and unwelcome bride would probably make her task that much easier. He would be gone a great deal at the time of the wedding, and it would probably take some time for his bride to settle in and begin to take charge of the household . . . all of which would divert scrutiny from her kitchens and allow her more opportunity to search for a husband of her own.

A husband. Marriage. Being someone's wife. The notion seemed a bit depressing just now. Pledging her life to some moldering old knight with a thousand laurels and a yen to pour his hoary stories into little heads with ears like his . . . or a crafty merchant whose fortunes and girth had grown apace and who wanted a wellborn wife and a fine hearth tender, but could only afford one of them . . . was that what she had to look forward to?

Her maudlin thoughts were interrupted by His Lordship's arrival in camp and the sound of his voice booming with ire.

"Where the devil is she?" she heard him shout.

She was going to have to face him sooner or later. Girding herself with as much unwomanly arrogance as she could summon, she slid from the end of the cart and trudged toward the center of camp.

"There you are!" he thundered, standing over the pile of

parcels and bags dumped unceremoniously on the ground, his features bronzed with ire. "What in infernal blazes do you have to say for yourself?"

She drew her shoulders back and ignored the empty feeling in the pit of her stomach.

"Did we get the cinnamon for a livre a pound, or not?"

Astonished by her utter lack of contrition, he ranted and railed for some while. Sir Axel, Sir Greeve, Heureaux, and the others were wincing openly by the time he ran out of both wind and ire. But, insulated by a fog of distraction, she bore it all with remarkable equanimity and afterward nodded.

"Yes, yes. And did you remember to bring some meat for supper?"

He stared at her in outrage, threw up his arms, and stalked out of camp muttering things that were better left unheard.

She turned to Heureaux with a calm that owed more to numbness than serenity.

"I believe it's time to think about an evening fire."

THE NEXT MORNING, THEY ROSE EARLY, struck camp, packed the cart and horses . . . and quickly realized they had too much baggage to carry.

A night's rest and a bit of distance had greatly improved Julia's outlook and she adroitly inserted herself into the situation . . . to insist that the precious spices be protected along the way from weather and the predations of bugs and itchy fingers. They needed a proper spice chest . . . or two or three . . . she declared. And a second cart to carry them.

It took the count some time to come around to her way of thinking.

"Let me see if I have this straight," he declared, his voice constricted around an explosive core of emotion. "You badger me to let you buy spices, you squander my coin on things you don't need, you break our backs lugging mountains of God-knows-what up that hill . . . and now you expect me to buy another cart to haul this worthless nonsense all the way to Bordeaux?"

She paused a moment to gauge her distance from him and reconnoiter possible escape routes.

"I know it may seem excessive, milord, but I can promise you . . . you'll thank me when you're home in front of your hearth with a cup of mulled wine in one hand and a well-spiced joint of pork in the other."

"Don't . . . don't you dare . . ." Frustration choked off the rest and he raked his hands down his face.

Seizing the moment, she offered something of a defense.

"I did manage to strike some shrewd bargains." She adopted a confident stance. "Even if I do say so."

"Indeed." Sir Axel tried valiantly to come to her aid. "You could have easily spent four times as much for the same things, milord."

"No, I couldn't!" Griffin declared, his eyes a little wild and his dark hair standing out like a lion's mane. "I could never have spent even *two* times as much! I've never spent so much coin in all my life!"

The man wanted to eat like a king without spending any coin? She was seized by a defiant impulse that very nearly proved disastrous.

"Well, you can hardly hold me responsible for emptying your entire purse, milord. You negotiated the terms of your agreement with the abbess, yourself."

Now would be a good time to run, she thought, backing up.

"Damnation!" he roared. His eyes bulged. His fists clenched. His face turned an alarming shade of purple. For a moment she wondered if he might fly apart from the pressure building inside him. Out of pure desperation, he stalked over to the fire pit, seized the stones the men had set around it to contain the flames, and began to hurl them one by one down the hill and into the fields below. Each sizeable stone carried with it some of his anger and frustration, so that by the time they were gone, he was once again solidly in the realm of reason.

"Axel. Greeve," he called sharply, fishing inside his tunic for a small leather pouch. "Take this coin and find some wooden spice boxes down there." As those two hurried off to do his bidding, he called for Heureaux and two others to take another bit of coin to the local livery and purchase a second, slightly larger cart. "And have it here within the hour!"

THAT SAME MORNING, IN A RENTED HOUSE near the heart of Paris, Sir Martin de Gies and his two companions presented both themselves and the news of their encounter to their lord as he broke his fast. In the light coming through the open windows of the upper hall, Bardot, Comte de Verdun, sat in the great carved chair reserved for the master and honored guests of the rambling house, and gripped its carved wooden arms as he listened.

"I was told he left Paris a week ago." Verdun glared at his knights, reminding them that they were the very ones who had brought him that news.

"He did, seigneur," de Gies assured him. "My men followed him on the road north for nearly a day. He must have circled back."

Verdun's restless gaze caught the subtle imbalance of the knight's bearing and knew that such uneven weighting in a man's stance generally came from the pressure of something he carried inside. Something that should come out.

"And what was he doing at this 'fair'?" he asked.

"Buying spices. Lots of spices, seigneur."

"Spices? What for?"

"For a woman, seigneur." De Gies braced ever so subtly. "A young woman. Whom he called his 'cook.'"

Verdun broke into a wry laugh and sat forward in his chair. "You say that as if you have doubts, de Gies. Tell me, why would a man—even a man like the Beast of Grandaise—be buying spices for a woman who *isn't* his cook?"

"I cannot say, seigneur. But this woman—I have never seen a cook who looked like that." De Gies turned to his comrades, who murmured agreement. "Golden red hair. Fair skin. Clear eyes. A sweet, maiden form. When I spoke with her, he came charging up and took possession of her as if he owned her body and soul. She is most certainly his, seigneur. But I cannot believe she is his *cook*."

Verdun thought on the implications of that and came inescapably to the same conclusion de Gies had reached. A nobleman did not buy costly spices for comely young women unless she was his sister, his wife, or . . .

"He's taken a mistress." Verdun shot to his feet. The reason for his knights' reluctance to tell him was now all too clear. "With his marriage to my daughter a few months away, the bastard has taken a mistress!" He ground his fist angrily into his other palm. "Bound to my Sophie by royal decree, he drags home a harlot to lie in the bed he will soon share with her." His face hardened. "The pox-eaten cur . . . mocking my daughter's gentle goodness and purity with the indulgence of his beastly appetites! I cannot give my very own flesh and blood to that degenerate."

"But, milord"—de Gies lowered his voice and glanced anxiously at the thin walls of their rented accommodations—"the king himself has decreed—"

"The *king* does not have to hand his only daughter over to a slavering beast in three months!" Verdun roared, stalking back to his trusted First Knight. Treason or not, there were limits to what a man should be expected to yield to his sovereign. His eyes flickered over an as yet unfinished mental tableau.

"The king's precious 'peace' will not be bought with my innocent flesh and blood," he said in implacable tones. "I have to find a way to get Grandaise to violate the king's truce."

Chapter 11

 TRAVELING, JULIA QUICKLY LEARNED, consisted mostly of being rattled bone from joint in the rear of a cramped cart. The "cramped" part was her own doing, but the rest was simply the laborious process required in traversing broad distances. Except for occasional views of breathtaking scenery and the occasional stop near a nobleman's home to secure passage through his lands, it was the same hour after hour and day after day. It was deadly boring for a young woman used to constant and productive activity. Not even the nightly challenge of finding a way to make rabbit or the occasional bartered poultry more interesting was especially taxing, now that they had spices to vary the taste.

She began to think of the tasks that lay ahead and decided to make the fullest use of her time. When they stopped at the end of the second day out of Paris, she climbed up into the larger cart, located the sizeable mortar and pestle she had purchased and spices for grinding, and stowed them in her smaller cart.

The next day she made a seat for herself on the cart bed, positioned herself around the mortar and pestle, and began to season the stone by grinding some basic spices. Her first task was to replicate a "black spice" she used frequently in sauces and as a rub for roasting meat, which contained four broadly enjoyed ingredients: round pepper, long pepper, cloves, and nutmeg.

When they stopped in the hot midday sun for a stretch of their limbs and a bit of water, Axel wandered over to see what she had been doing all morning. When she told him, his eyes lighted and he asked if he might have a look. When she lifted the cloth covering her mortar, he inhaled the pungent smell, sighed, and ambled away rubbing his stomach.

That afternoon, he kept dropping back to ride near the women's cart. Periodically, he could be seen lifting his nose into the air and closing his eyes in concentration. Intrigued, Greeve dropped back to investigate and was soon riding beside him with his own nose hoisted Heavenward. Heureaux rode up to learn what was happening and stayed to sniff the air, too. Two more of his men abandoned their places to come and trail the cart with their noses quivering.

Griffin turned around, saw his men trailing the cart like hounds on a scent, and came charging back to find out what they were doing.

"She's grinding spices, milord," Axel told him with a dreamy look.

"Pepper and"—Greeve sniffed the air again—"cloves and something else."

"Grinding spices? Here?" Griffin filled his lungs with mercifully unsmelled air. "Get back to your posts."

When they rode off, he drew alongside the cart and peered over the parcels stacked along the sides. Julia of Childress sat on the bed of the cart with the mortar between her knees, wielding the pestle with forceful and rhythmic precision. The sight shocked him somehow. The sight of her legs wrapped around the bowl of the mortar . . . the intensity with which she wielded the pestle . . . the fact that he was probably going to consume those spices she was grinding between her . . .

"Dammit, woman," he growled, startling her. "What do you think you're doing?"

"I've decided not to waste the days I spend bouncing

around in this cart. I intend to use this time more productively." When she looked up with eyes wide and utterly innocent, he had to scramble for a plausible objection.

"The wind is carrying those spices for miles. Put them away until we reach Grandaise."

"Really, milord, I'm being quite careful. None of the savor is being lost, I promise you." She slid the stone bowl off her gown and scrambled up onto her knees on the bundles stacked along the side. "Here"—she held up the heavy mortar with a look of expectation—"smell for yourself."

Julia realized her mistake the instant the words were out of her mouth, and her gaze went inescapably to the dark band bridging his nose. She groaned silently. Now would be a perfect time for one of those great cinnamon-nesting beasts to make an appearance and swoop down and . . .

"Forgive me, milord." She lowered the mortar and cradled it in her arms. "I wasn't thinking."

"That is the last bit of grinding you will do on this journey." He jabbed a finger at the mortar, straining visibly to contain his anger. "The rest will wait until you reach Grandaise, where you can keep such unsightly tasks out of sight." He reined off and rode hard past the head of the column and out of view.

Julia set the mortar down on the cart floor and sank onto her bottom beside it, staring at the half-ground peppercorns, cloves, and nutmeg in dismay.

"You do have a knack for annoying His Lordship." Regine blew her nose for the tenth time. "But he'll come around once you start cooking for him."

"What makes you think he'll ever trust me to feed him?"

"Well, he didn't strangle you when you spent every coin in his purse. That's a start." She reached for Julia's hand. "Haven't you heard it said: 'The way to a man's heart is through his stomach'?"

"Why would I want to reach his heart?" she said in rising alarm.

Regine softened with a smile.

"Have your forgotten your lessons so quickly, Julia?

When our Lord was on earth He made it very clear: The most important part of a man is his heart. When a man gives his heart, the rest of him always follows." She patted Julia's hand. "If you cook, you'll reach his heart, and the respect you seek will follow."

It was meant to comfort her, Julia knew, but the guilty truth of it was, she wanted a good bit more than just the count's respect. She wanted his appreciation. No, his amazement. His adoration. His *awe*. She wanted to awaken his palate and astound his senses with her food and make him giddy with delight. She wanted him to take such pleasure in the taste and smell of her food that he would proclaim her skill from the rooftops. She wanted him to be so proud of his kitchens that he invited all of his neighbors—the whole countryside—to come and sample his wonderful food. More to the point, she wanted him to make him repent of every doubt and misgiving he had ever harbored toward her.

She picked up a grain of the spice she had chosen to begin grinding. Black spice. Comprised mostly of pepper. His favorite.

Perhaps she hadn't forgotten her lessons entirely.

For the rest of the day, the count's men took turns riding downwind of Julia's cart and breathing in the peppery aroma from the spice mixture she was making. That evening His Lordship returned after a long absence and directed them to camp in a spot he had selected near a stream. Sir Axel and Sir Greeve informed her that His Lordship had secured permission to pass the night there from an old friend of his family, a local baron who controlled the roads and provided both security and sustenance for travelers. The birds they secured from the baron's cottagers were rubbed generously with the combination of spices they had smelled all afternoon and were roasted to a turn over well-placed spits. The results were excellent, even by Julia's standards.

But the count sat off to the side by himself and added nothing to the heaps of praise and groans of satisfaction aimed her way. She refused to show her disappointment as she watched him from her seat on a stone by the fire. But after a while she decided to approach him directly on his opinion of the food.

Just as she started toward him, he rose and strode off into the gathering darkness. She stood on the edge of the camp, her arms folded, watching him escape into a small wood nestled alongside the stream where they camped. Sir Greeve joined her and followed her gaze to his lord's disappearing form.

"Where does he go at night?" she asked, only half aware she spoke aloud.

Greeve shook his head and cleared the campfire smoke from his throat.

"Away for a bit of solitude, perhaps. Who can say?"

Before her better sense could dissuade her, she headed after him.

"Where are you going?" Greeve asked, alarmed equally by her direction and determination. "Ohhh, no." He reached out, but quickly thought better of setting hands to her and jerked them back. "Not good. Not good at all."

Running helped her close some of the distance between them, but he still disappeared into the trees well ahead of her. The woods were pitch black, at first, and no air stirred under the dense canopy. The result was a stillness so profound that the trees around her seemed to be holding their breath. She closed her eyes, hoping to hasten their adjustment, and listened.

The telling shuffle of leaves and snap of twigs betrayed his position. He traveled carefully and steadily, with no attempt to disguise his movements. When she opened her eyes, she was able to detect fingers of silver-blue moonlight piercing the leaf cover and began to pick her way along.

The underbrush always seemed to thin in the direction she was drawn and she realized he was following a trail of some sort. Soon the sounds of his passage merged with the sounds of running water. The stream . . . they were some distance upstream from their camp. She halted, listening, but couldn't tell if he was still moving or not. Her heart seemed to beat in her throat as she decided to continue along the path. She had come this far. . . .

The silver-blue glow of moonlight bloomed ahead of her, through the trees. The air began to stir again; light branches swayed gently and leaves rustled with an almost human *shh-h-h.*

Then she spotted him on some rock ledge that jutted over the edge of the stream, standing perfectly still with his head back, staring up into the night sky. As she watched, he raked a hand down his face and turned into the breeze, letting it wash over his face and ruffle his hair. When his face turned toward her, she saw that he had taken the band from his nose.

Was this what he did each night when he left camp? He came to the forest to free his sense of smell and bathe it in nature's fresh and gentle scents?

Keeping to the shadows of the trees, she lifted her own face to the breeze and closed her eyes, hoping to catch whatever scents he might be experiencing. She was able to pick out the scents of moist wood and damp earth, the must of the leaves on the forest floor, and a tang of fragrant herbs growing between the woods and the stream . . . wild onion, tansy, butterwort. Was there still more?

Then his face lowered and it appeared that he focused intently on something just upstream, at the edge of the trees. She held her breath waiting. Something was there, watching him even as he watched it. Tension crept up her neck as she scoured the brush. Movement caught her eye.

A pair of dark, luminous eyes and pale ears became visible. A deer, little more than a fawn, stood with its nose up, trying to take his scent. He was downwind, just as she was downwind from both of them, and the animal remained wary.

The count continued motionless, patient, unthreatening, and the fawn finally took a step from the safety of the trees. Again its nose quivered for confirmation, and again the breeze carried away his scent. The animal approached cautiously, sniffing, and then halted a yard from him, looking him over. It froze as he slowly raised a hand.

He stood for what seemed an eternity with his arm outstretched, waiting for the animal to overcome its instinctive caution. Finally it came close enough to discern what was in his hand. But in so doing, it took his scent and darted back toward the safety of the trees. When he remained motionless, the fawn's hunger and curiosity provided grew greater than its fear of danger.

She watched in amazement as the deer came close enough to take something he offered and skittered back to eat it. For the next few moments, the man and the deer engaged in a dance of wariness and pleasure as the fawn satisfied its curiosity about him and took the treats he offered.

Wanting a closer look, Julia crept slowly closer, keeping to the cover of the trees. Soon she had a clearer view of his face as he stood in the moonlight. It was relaxed, almost peaceful. She was so absorbed in his expression that she hardly noticed the fawn withdrawing and springing for the trees. The count whirled and visually scoured the line of trees where she stood.

The wind had changed, she realized, shrinking partway behind a tree.

"Come out," he ordered angrily, *"Julia of Childress!"*

Chapter 12

JULIA STEPPED OUT INTO THE MOON-light, scrambling for an explanation of her presence and praying some fleet-footed minion of Heaven would bring her one.

"What the devil are you doing out here?" he demanded, striding to her.

"I-I was just . . . I wanted to . . . how did you know it was me?"

"Who else in these parts would smell as if they've bathed in pepper?" He seized her by her upper arms and her hands came up against his chest. "What are you doing out here in the dark?"

She sensed her only recourse was the truth.

"I wanted to see where you go each night."

"Where I go is none of your concern." He released one of her shoulders and with the other arm still captive, began hauling her back toward that trail through the woods. "You're my cook, dammit—not the keeper of my soul."

"What makes you think those are separate tasks?" she said, trying unsuccessfully to wrench her arm from his grip. "In order to feed you properly, I have to know what you need, what you like, even what you crave."

"What I *need* is a cook who knows his place and keeps to it."

"Well, you're out of luck there, milord. And how am I suppose to learn what pleases you? You eat each evening without showing the slightest bit of enjoyment in your food."

"You want compliments on your work, when all you do is stroll around the campfire and gossip with my men?"

"As you said yourself, I am not a turnspit or scullion. A head cook does not chop, roll, stir, turn, and baste every morsel in the kitchen herself." She planted her feet to resist and succeeded in pulling him to a halt. "I cannot carry out my duties properly if I know nothing about the one for whom I cook."

Griffin knew better, sensed it was sheer folly, but he turned in the midst of the moon-dappled path and grabbed her by both shoulders, holding her at arm's length. In the stillness of the woods, without the help of a breeze or even movement to dissipate it, her scent billowed up around him. And—God help him—he inhaled.

Pepper. He was positively greedy for it. *A strong hint of cloves and nutmeg* . . . the spices she had been grinding . . . the fine dust still clung to her garments. The combination made his mouth water. *And her own spicy, womanly scent.* Redolent of tangy-sweet oils and nutlike musk. That sensual essence made his very soul water.

Living without the stimulation of the strongest and most vital of his senses was like living in a continual haze or behind a veil. Without the input of his sense of smell, nothing was ever entirely clear and sharply focused. Nothing was ever entirely pleasurable or satisfying. Worse still, nothing brought him to a full and involving response; nothing touched him on all levels, roused his emotions, and reached deep into his soul. He lived at the very surface of his being, just beneath his skin, as if the depths of him didn't exist. On those rare occasions when he cast off those self-imposed restraints and filled his starved and ravenous senses, his responses sometimes leaped out of control.

Now, he could feel desires and hungers roiling up from his unplumbed depths. His nerves began to crackle and his blood began to heat. His skin came alive and tingled all over his body, hungry for sensation, aching for direct and potent contact. He pulled her closer, staring into her luminous, dark-centered eyes and then at her moist, fragrant lips. Every part of her was lush with possibilities for pleasure. And every sensually laden inhalation he took told him exactly where the trembling beginning in his body was leading. He was gripped by an overwhelming need to smell her . . . to taste her. . . .

With his responses spiraling out of his control, he released her as if she burned him and backed away, fumbling for his metal band and the sanity that lay in the cool restraint of polished steel. The familiar pinch, the cessation of smell, the fading of scent . . . it only took a moment for him to feel control returning.

"If you want to know something, you *ask*," he ordered roughly, striking off along the path by himself and leaving her to collect herself and follow.

"Fine. I am asking. What foods do you prefer?"

"I eat beef, lamb, most game . . . fish when the church requires it." He batted small overhanging branches out of the way. "Poultry. Eggs and cheeses. I like food I can carry with me. Pasties . . . be sure to make plenty of pasties."

He wasn't certain she was keeping up, but he wasn't about to turn around and find out that he was talking to himself. Truth be told, he could use some distance between himself and her. And if she somehow managed to get lost in the woods for a while, so much the—

"Pasties . . . sweet or savory?" From the thudding of her feet and her breathless question she was practically running to keep up with him.

"Both."

"Breakfast or not?"

"Breakfast."

"Raw fruit or cooked?"

He snorted. "Raw fruit's for livestock."

"Dinner or supper?"

His hesitation reached his feet. Which meal did he favor as the largest of the day? He thought of the sometimes erratic flow of life at Grandaise.

"Sometimes one, sometimes the other."

"Dining in company or separately?"

Would he take his meals in the hall with his men or separately in his own chambers, as was becoming the fashion in the cities?

"In company," he said stalking on. "Unless I say otherwise."

After a moment of silence came a question that stopped him in his tracks.

"And your upcoming marriage . . . what sort of celebration will I be required to mount?"

Marriage. A tremor of true horror rattled through him. He had fought battles all over France and faced blood thirsty opponents and desperate odds. And none of that had struck such fear and loathing in him as the prospect of wedding Verdun's nameless daughter.

"My marriage has nothing to do with you," he ground out, moving again, stepping over roots and batting back brush growing over the trail.

The oppressive urgency of his nuptial fate bore down on him. Whatever peace he had achieved in his household would surely be ripped asunder by her arrival. What kind of celebration was appropriate for a troth pledged in a blaze of antagonism that would leave both bride and groom charred and miserable?

"I will be in charge of your kitchens, and planning a wedding celebration will take time. The sooner I begin—"

"There will be no celebration," he declared without looking back.

"Oh? And how am I to serve your lady if I have not welcomed her and acknowledged her place and authority?"

"The wedding is still three months away," he said, realizing that against all odds, he harbored hopes for a reprieve. "And you won't serve her . . . you'll take direction from me and me alone." He wheeled to face her and jerked a thumb at his chest. "You're *my* cook. Is that understood?"

She stood her ground silently, her shoulders square and her chin up. He could see rebuttals vying for expression in her face and stalked back to stop just short of banging into her.

His head was still dangerously full of the lingering pepper-and-cloves scent of her and his blood was dangerously warm from the flint of her temper striking the steel of his determination. She was so hot and determined and breathless. Her flashes of defiance were so recklessly alluring. And she was so delectably unaware of just how close she was to being kissed. . . .

"You're *mine*," he repeated in a voice ragged with unaccustomed emotion. The saying of it created an imperative in his blood to make it a fact in the most basic and elemental way possible.

"For one year," she said quietly but adamantly.

"Or more," he corrected, speaking his unthinkable thought aloud.

"You cannot think of defying the abbess and the bishop and the Duke of Avalon, too. That would be madness."

He seized her and dragged her closer. If it was madness, it was damned compelling madness. Her eyes glistened in the dim light. Her lips were moist, parted, quivering with tension. He had to taste them . . . this very moment. . . .

She didn't pull away or try to avoid him as he lowered his head. His tensed muscles started to uncoil as he touched her soft, moist lips—

Wood snapped in the distance and suddenly branches in their path were jerking and thrashing. Out of pure instinct he lurched up, grabbed her by the wrist, and bolted back up the trail toward the stream. She stumbled and called to him to wait as she yanked up the hem of her gown.

Their pursuers approached on two sides and without much stealth, he realized. He'd have heard and evaded them easily if he hadn't been roaring at the top of his lungs and plowing through the woods like a stag in rut.

Outlaws, poachers, or Verdun? He could hear the wretches well enough now. Half a dozen at least. Most on foot, as far as he could tell.

On they plunged, until there was a brightening ahead that signaled the edge of the woods. He caught the glint of a blade off to the side and was spurred to even greater effort. If they could make it to the stream bank . . .

The trees ended abruptly; they were in the open, exposed by the moonlight. There was a desperate surge and crash all around as their pursuers closed in on them. Griffin wheeled and drew his knife, to put himself between Julia and the bandits, cursing himself for leaving his sword in camp. Then someone plowed into him from the side and knocked him into the undergrowth at the very edge of the trees. As he went down, he caught the flash of a moon-brightened blade and heard Julia scream.

Dazed but struggling fiercely against the weight of two men on top of him, Griffin looked up to see Julia in the clutches of armed men . . . wearing what appeared to be yellow and black. Not red and white, but *yellow and black.*

"It is a man and a woman, seigneur!" one of them addressed their leader.

Griffin heard a soft thudding and the swish of the brush nearby, and found himself staring up at a horse wearing familiar trappings . . . silks he had seen that very afternoon as he visited with the baron on whose land they camped.

"Crossan?" he managed to gasp out, past the beefy arm at his throat.

The man on the horse squinted down at him, and demanded, "Who calls me by name?" He dismounted for a closer look. "Grandaise?" Instantly, he was shoving his own men off their captive and offering Griffin a hand up. "Pardon, my lord count. We had no idea."

"What the devil are you doing out here in the dark, running people down?" Griffin demanded, jerking free and brushing leaves and grass from his tunic.

"Poachers. We've had a plague of unlawful taking. With the moon full, we set out to catch the wretches at their game. When we heard voices and saw you moving we thought—" The burly nobleman looked a bit uncomfortable and glanced away. His eyes fell on Julia and widened. "I am surprised to find you here, milord. I thought you were camped some ways downstream."

"My cook had gone off by herself and got lost," Griffin declared with an irritable gesture toward Julia, "and I had to come out and find her."

"Your cook?" Crossan barely covered his disbelief as he stared at Julia.

"My new cook," Griffin declared, setting off for the distant light of his camp. "Acquired on my sojourn to Paris."

"A cook from Paris." The Baron Crossan scratched his stubbled chin and produced a wicked chuckle. "Well, they do say that the best 'cooks' in the world come from Paris, milord. It's good to know you'll be feeding my son so well."

Griffin didn't care to correct whatever erroneous conclusion the baron had drawn. It would require more explanations than he intended to make.

"Care to join me in my camp for a bit of wine, Baron?" Griffin said, gesturing toward his downstream camp.

"*Your* wine? Damme, Grandaise. You needn't ask twice." The knightly fellow barked out a few orders to his men to escort "the cook" and struck off with Griffin to commiserate on poachers and discuss the news from the Paris court.

JULIA WATCHED HER EMPLOYER DISMISS BOTH her presence and her purpose as he strode off with his fellow nobleman. Moments ago he'd pulled her against him and weakened her knees with a look and stolen her breath with a lightning brief kiss. Now she was abandoned like a smelly old cheese rind.

She might be his personal cook, his expensive prize, and even his culinary salvation, but she was still just a cook. Whatever her birth, however she pleased him, whatever happened between them . . . a cook was all she would ever be. And a nobleman of his status did not dally with

mere cooks. She gasped as the full context of that interrupted kiss returned to her . . . unless, of course, he had
other motives . . . such as keeping her from returning to the
convent to take vows. If he kept her from being able to take
religious vows, she realized with widening horror, then she
would be ruined for taking marriage vows, too!

The wretch!

She came to her senses and found several men-at-arms
standing around her, glaring at her in both annoyance and
speculation. No one offered so much as a hint of an apology for their earlier bone-jarring handling of her. She
walked surrounded by a dozen armed men, feeling their
eyes on her and holding her head up to show she had nothing to hide.

It was only when they reached camp and the baron saw
Sister Regine run to embrace her and worry effusively over
her, that his lordship deigned to explain that his "cook"
had been acquired from the Convent of the Brides of
Virtue, and was sent under the chaperonage of one of the
good sisters.

"I have heard of that convent." The baron looked at her
with considerably more interest. "If they produce cooks to
equal their brides, then you can be sure I'll be paying you
and my son a visit soon, Grandaise."

Moments later, Julia looked up from Sister Regine's
comforting shoulder and saw Sir Axel and Sir Greeve
standing before her with a length of soft toweling and what
appeared to be a piece of soap.

"A thousand pardons, demoiselle," Axel said with a
pained nod. "His Lordship sent us with these for you and
orders to see that you . . . bathe."

"The sister is to go with you and assist." Greeve swallowed hard. "We are to stand guard near the stream and see
that no one disturbs you."

"Bathe?" Julia stared in disbelief at the items the
knights held. "I'm *ordered* to bathe?"

"His Lordship said"—Axel groaned softly—"you smell
like a pepper pot."

Julia flushed crimson with humiliation.

"She does not!" Regine said, glaring at His Lordship across the camp. "How dare he say such a thing?" Then she stiffened and transferred her widened gaze to Axel and Greeve. "How would he know what she smells like? He wears that metal thing on his nose to keep from smelling anything!"

It was a very good question.

Three noses gave covert sniffs. Three sets of eyes turned on Julia with dawning recognition. Whatever transpired between her and his lordship during their time together in the dark woods, he had at least managed to *smell* her.

"I have no idea what he—" Julia protested. "He didn't—I didn't—"

It was hopeless. The seeds of suspicion had already been planted.

Grabbing the toweling and soap from the knights' hands, she stalked out of the camp in the direction of the stream and was soon stripped to her chemise, standing waist high in the stream, scrubbing the scent of pepper from her.

The worst she could imagine was closer than she thought. She gave a terrible shiver. If Regine and Sir Axel and Sir Greeve could be made to think something improper had happened between them, then just think what the less charitably inclined would say.

Later, when she returned to the camp and warmed herself by the small, separate fire Sir Greeve had one of the men build for her, Sir Axel brought her a cup of wine and his own blanket to help her recover.

"Who is this baron?" she asked, shivering and glaring at the genial-looking nobleman drinking wine with her new master as if they were great friends.

Axel was delighted to be able to deliver that oft-told story to fresh ears.

"The barons of Crossan first won their spurs in the service of the counts of Grandaise. They went on the First Crusade with the Hospitaler knights and returned from the Holy Land wealthy men . . . able to purchase lands at the juncture of two well-traveled routes of commerce. They now make a tidy profit providing both safe passage and food to travelers. Ties between Grandaise and Crossan have remained strong. The current baron sent his second son to foster with milord's father. Sir Reynard de Crossan is milord's first knight and is watching over Grandaise in his absence."

Later as Sir Greeve assisted Julia and Sister Regine into their cart bed, he mentioned casually that the current baron boasted that he had inherited what he referred to as the "Crossan conjugal luck." At least half of the strapping, capable young men seated around the campfire with him were his own sons.

As Julia settled onto her pallet beside Sister Regine, she glanced back at the fire where the baron and his sons were passing around wineskins and trading stories with her employer and his garrulous knights. With a hollow feeling in her middle, she forced her gaze from His Lordship to the younger Crossans.

Blinking away a bit of moisture, she concentrated on those tall, manly frames. There would be eligible young men in His Lordship's circle of acquaintance; this was proof.

All she had to do was keep well away from His Lordship's devilish eyes and treacherous lips.

And *cook*.

Chapter 13

THE ENTIRE HOUSEHOLD OF GRANDAISE
turned out to greet the count and his men when they
returned home, four days later.

Lord Griffin had sent a rider ahead with word to prepare
his chambers and his bath, and to clean and freshen Old
Jean's chambers for the new cook. That offhand announce-
ment of a new cook's arrival raced through the household
like a flame in dry tinder. They had been braced for a dire
pronouncement from the Paris court regarding their lord's
fate and learned, instead, that he was returning home with
a new cook. From Sir Reynard de Crossan, who first received the message, to the steward, to the serving women,
footmen, sweepers, fire tenders, and even the boys who
carried coal and emptied chamber pots . . . everyone had
an opinion on this unexpected addition to the household
staff. After all, they had been through this before. Nine
times.

More work, the house women sighed. More standards to
meet, the footmen muttered. More expense with nothing to
show for it, the steward grumbled to the linen pantry ma-
tron, who grumbled back about the impending increase in
the use of linen. More wafers to pinch, the potboys in the

kitchen snickered . . . at least at first, while the cook was showing off his skill.

Nowhere was the impact anticipated more anxiously than in the kitchens.

"He better not make me change the grease every week."

"I'll put my pea broth up against any he's had!"

"If he don't like havin' a pig outside the door, he can just carry the cleanin's down to the pens himself."

"If he comes at me with that spoon of his—I'll not be held responsible."

By the time the count and his traveling party arrived, well after none, the hall had been swept, the bed furs aired and sheets changed, the torches and lamp wicks trimmed, and fresh herbs and flowers had been strewn over the permanent benches that lined the long sides of the hall. Knowing their lord's penchant for tidiness and his grim mood as he left, every household servant had washed face and hands, changed tunics or aprons, and brushed hair or donned a clean cap . . . even the reluctant kitchen staff.

As the news of their lord's approach came down from the watchtower, they hurried from all over the house to collect in the court outside the main hall to judge their lord's demeanor for themselves. To a person, they nodded, smiled, and waved to welcome their lord. But their attention moved quickly to the other men in the party, who all looked disappointingly familiar, and then to the carts.

They scratched their seldom groomed heads in confusion at the sight of a nun and a young woman in the smaller of the two carts. Who was the little wench with the red-gold hair? Why was His Lordship bringing home a nun? And where—they exchanged puzzled looks—was the new cook?

Julia held tightly onto Regine's hand as the cart rumbled through the gate of the stone wall and along a gravel path to the front doors of the castle.

Since they reached the borders of Grandaise, four hours ago, her heart had beaten faster and her stomach had contracted into a knot. They passed through stands of venerable old trees and two distinct ridges of hills planted with grapevines supported on wooden trellises. Everywhere she saw workers, patrolling the lanes that ran through the vineyards, grooming and tending the vines. They crossed two streams and entered an area of grain fields and crops that seemed to be lush and productive. Then, as they crested the final rise, she glimpsed the heart of the estate . . . a huge gray structure on a modest hill, surrounded by what looked like small village.

It wasn't at all what she expected. The keep looked more like one of the great houses they had passed outside Paris than a true fortification. There was no mote or inner curtain wall, though there were towerlike structures on all four of the main corners of the house. Surprisingly, there were several glazed windows in the upper part of the dressed-stone structure. On either side of what seemed to be the main doors were large stone columns that supported a triangular parament in which a carving of the Grandaise coat of arms nestled amid a voluptuous display of grapes and sinuous vines. Taken together the features presented a cohesive and well-planned welcome, which reminded her of the praise Sir Axel and Sir Greeve had heaped upon the present count's forward-thinking forebears.

The people who had turned out to greet their lord, however, were exactly what she had expected. Sir Axel and Sir Greeve had describe them with an uncanny eye for detail, and as His Lordship greeted them she was able to mutter several of their names to Regine.

The tall, well-dressed young knight who hurried down the steps to greet the count had to be Sir Reynard de Crossan. He was strong and well made and clearly resembled his brawny, amicable father. But his pleasant, blocky features wore a serious expression as he asked what had happened at court. When His Lordship said that things had gone as well as could be expected, he seemed relieved. Then his gaze darted over the familiar faces of the men in the count's party and finally came to their cart. Where, she heard him ask, was the new cook he had sent word to prepare for?

"In the cart," His Lordship said offhandedly, continuing

to greet his retainers. He accepted a half bow from a neat-looking little man wearing a chain of office around his neck, who had to be Arnaud the Steward. The thick-set older woman who curtsied briskly had to be Genevieve, the head of the house women and overseer of the linen pantry. Then came an aged, crookbacked fellow with one eye that wandered alarmingly: clearly old Brindle, a former assistant cook brought out of his pensionage to take charge of His Lord's kitchens.

"I've brought you some relief," His Lordship declared as if speaking to someone a few counties away. Clearly old Brindle was mostly deaf as well. "A new cook. I'll count on you to show her the kitchens."

"About time." Old Brindle shouted back, apparently unable to hear himself speaking. "M' spoon arm ain't what it used to be."

Julia was drawn from that absorbing interaction by Sir Reynard's visible confusion as he approached the cart and stared at her and Regine.

"I-Is one of you . . . ?"

"I am," Julia said, making her way to the back of the cart. "Julia of Childress. And this is my chaperone and companion, Sister Regine."

"Chaperone?" Sir Reynard reached up to help her down and then turned to assist the sister, looking as if he considered setting even helping hands to a nun appalling. He was so unsettled by the way Regine's veil brushed his face as he handed her down that he blurted out: "A cook with a chaperone?"

"The demoiselle is from the Convent of the Brides of Virtue," Sir Axel declared, rushing over to help. "The sisters and maidens never travel alone."

Sir Reynard looked rightly confused, but erred on the side of gallantry. "Demoiselle Julia"—he gave a light bow—"I am pleased to welcome you."

His uncertain chivalry became the template for others' responses to her. To a person, the other knights and major members of the household bobbed and nodded respect when introduced to her and the good sister. The knights eyed her with undisguised interest, but the householders' sidelong looks of dismay made it clear that they were not prepared for seeing a young woman made the head cook of Grandaise.

His Lordship had stood watching from the top step for a moment, then interrupted the introductions to assign the task of settling the new cook in her kitchen to Axel, Greeve, and old Brindle. Then he drew his knights and principal retainers inside with him, calling for wine and food and a full report of what transpired during his absence. Axel and Greeve traded uncomfortable glances and started toward a path leading away from the front entrance, no doubt to the rear and the kitchens.

Julia had watched His Lordship disappear into the hall and felt the sharp edge of reality whittling away the last of her illusions. He couldn't have expressed the difference in their status more emphatically if he had shouted it from the watch towers. He entered through the main doors; she was to be escorted around to the kitchen entrance.

In the last four days of the journey, she had suffered more than her share of his dismissal. After that night in the woods, whenever he was in camp he spoke and looked through her as if she didn't exist. Well, no more.

Squaring her shoulders, she headed for the main doors. The kitchen staff, seizing this excuse to enter their lord's great hall, hurried after her.

"But, demoiselle, the kitchens—" Greeve began as he reached her side.

"Will still be there in a few moments," Julia said determinedly.

The hall was every bit as surprising as the exterior of the house and was built on an awe-inspiring scale. The peaked roof and ceiling was supported by elegant carved wooden arches; clear glass windows were set high in the walls; and the smooth stone flooring was entirely bare of rushes. A great stone hearth and mantel, above which was carved a grapevine in full fruit, covered one entire end of the chamber. Before the hearth sat a wooden dais with a great rectangular table, and above the hall hung a series of three large iron rings bearing oil lamps, which Greeve informed her were lowered and lighted each evening in winter.

She stood looking up at the golden afternoon light filtering down from the high windows and drew a deep breath . . . which bore no scent of secret decay or must or mildew . . . no stale grease smell or smoky taint. . . .

Suddenly the crowd gathered around the great table parted and there stood His Lordship, glaring at her and Axel and Greeve.

"Well?" he demanded.

"*La demoiselle* . . . she needed to see the hall first, seigneur," Axel said.

"To see where the serving will be done," Greeve added uncomfortably.

"Fine. Now take her to the kitchens," he ordered.

Teetering on the edge of a disastrous retort, she spotted a large handwoven tapestry hanging on the wall and chose to investigate it instead. There were names and lines indicating boundaries and physical features, including the many vineyards. It was a map of the Grandaise holdings and bordering lands. She asked Sir Greeve to point out where they were and whose lands were nearby.

"Thank you, Sir Greeve," she said when he finished. "I believe I am ready to see the kitchens now."

"Demoiselle Julia!" His Lordship's voice rang out. There was a hint of defiance in her slow turn back. "I will expect you to begin your cooking duties tomorrow. Then we will see if you are worth the coin I paid for you."

If there was any doubt of her status in the household, he had just removed it. She might be a young unmarried female and under the church's protection, but she was still a cook . . . paid for and firmly under his authority.

Sir Axel ushered her to the kitchen passage and Greeve, Regine, and old Brindle followed in their wake. Traipsing behind them, gawking at the grandeur of the hall they served but seldom saw, were a score of under cooks, scullions, and potboys.

When she reached the covered walkway connecting the kitchens and the hall, the light breeze helped to draw away some of the heat from her face. She paused moments later at the arched doorway to the kitchens to prepare herself, and realized that there was almost no smell at all from the kitchens. No reek of stale smoke and burned grease, no air of charred meat or scorched beans, no stench of greens past their prime, no odor of soured milk. The lack of such common offenses was such a surprise that it yanked her from her irritable mood.

Within these walls and her own two hands were what she needed to make him regret every indignity of doubt he had heaped upon her in the last four days.

She entered the kitchen and paused at the top of the brick steps to look out over a cavernous octagonal chamber. Light and fresh air poured into the kitchen from louvers set just under the roof. In the center of five of the eight sides was a huge hearth fitted with different hooks, spits, trivets, griddles, and pot arms. Built into the side of each hearth was a brick and metal oven for specialized baking and warming.

In the middle of the great chamber were circles of heavy oak worktables, centered around a ring of poles studded with pegs, from which hung pots, bowls, and cooking crocks of every size and shape imaginable. On the sixth wall, by the stairs, were several stone sinks with pipes protruding above and spigots that allowed water to flow when they were turned. On the seventh and eighth were shelves laden with all manner of cooking utensils, boxes, linen, and pitchers.

Three of the four sizeable doorways leading from the kitchen provided access to the pantry, the larder, and the scullery. The fourth led to the yard and probably the kitchen gardens. Just below the stairs themselves, a small door opened into a cold well where buckets containing chilled items were lowered into a water bath from an underground spring.

Julia descended to the center of the chamber, looking around the amazing kitchen with its thoughtful organization, and realized that what Axel and Greeve had said about the family's history and love of food was only a small part of the story. For a lord to go to the expense of designing and constructing such a kitchen, food must have been of the utmost importance to him. She thought again of the count's unusual condition . . . said to have been inherited. . . .

Axel called her back to the present to introduce the rest of her new staff to her. It was then that she spotted the worm in this magnificent apple.

Nearly every member of the kitchen staff who was introduced individually had gray or white hair, few teeth, and a scowl that spoke of distrust or defiance. There was Fran, the plump and disagreeable larderer; Old Albee the Fryer, with hands as thick and scarred as battle iron; Old Mae the Saucer, who squinted continually; Pennet, the red-faced ovenman, who tended the small hearth ovens; Old Odile—who in truth should have been called *Ancient* Odile—who tended the buttery and cold well; and Cheval the Roaster, who had been sent to the kitchens to work because he was too often mistaken for the oxen he tended. There was a small army of fire tenders, turnspits, and fuelers . . . most of whom were older kitchen boys. And there were several young girls of general work, ranging in age from eight to sixteen, all of whom stared warily at the large wooden spoon tucked into Julia's belt.

"I have been instructed to begin my duties with you tomorrow," she said when the introductions were finished. "This evening, I will simply watch and learn how you are accustomed to working."

"WHAT A DISASTER," JULIA SAID LATER, kicking off her shoes and sinking onto the side of her bed in the spacious chamber reserved for the head cook. "They drop, they dribble, they slop and clump . . . they eat out of the pots, hack at meat like they are chopping firewood, and slap a boat of pureed peas and mustard seed on the table and call it a sauce."

"Well, at least you won't have to worry that they're set in their ways." Regine settled beside her. "They're so old they can't recall what their ways are."

Julia chuckled in spite of herself, relieved to be able to shed some of the evening's tension. "How will I ever get them to work for me? Every time I pulled out my tasting spoon, they flinched as if they expected a whack."

"They've had quite a few new masters over the last several years."

"Nine," Julia said, glimpsing the ramifications of that extraordinary number in human terms.

"And many cooks believe that 'if you spare the rod, you spoil the stew.'" Julia sagged under the enormity of the task ahead.

"I have to manage to please His Lordship, feed this entire household, and train a staff to do it without me after I'm gone." It was a daunting slate indeed.

They sat side by side in silence, watching the flicker of the tallow lamp on the nearby table.

"Well, you know what *my* advice would be," Regine said with a determined smile.

"I do?" Julia looked at her in confusion.

"If the way to a man's heart is through his stomach, just imagine where the path to a *cook's* heart must lie."

Inspiration dawned. "Oh, Regine—you're wonderful!"

The plump sister smiled with un-nunlike pleasure.

"The obvious. It's my gift."

Chapter 14

WHEN THE MAIN KITCHEN STAFF AR-
rived in the kitchens the next morning— tottering
stiffly, stretching arthritic limbs, and rubbing bleary
eyes—they were stunned to find their new cook present,
freshly scrubbed, and wearing a pristine apron . . . already
hard at work.

The lamps were all lighted and she had already taken
stock of the larder and pantry, organized a number of spice
boxes she had brought with her, and selected and set out
bowls and tools for the day's work. She had roused the fuelers and fire tenders early and had substantial fires going
in two hearths. She had claimed the first new loaves of the
day from the bakers, pulled up butter and cider from the
cold well, and found some fruit preserves in the larder. Before their disbelieving eyes she arrayed the warm bread,
butter, and jam on the table on trays, and returned from one
of the hearths with a pot of freshly boiled eggs.

"Be seated," she ordered the lot of them, pointing to
benches she had instructed the fuelers to carry to the work
tables from the sides of the kitchen. When they were a bit
slow to comply, she added in no uncertain terms: *"Now!"*

"Once a week we will break fast together and I will give

you your assignments," she declared when the scramble for seats at the two long tables had finished. "You will carry out those duties until our next breakfast." They muttered about which duties they would and would not accept. She drew her tasting spoon from her belt and folded her arms so that it stood upright . . . the symbol of her authority.

"Anyone who disagrees is free to leave." She met eye after eye. "Those who agree may break open those loaves, peel those eggs, and make a good start on the morning."

There was a pregnant moment as they looked at each other, then at the warm, fragrant loaves, sweet, creamy butter, and still steaming eggs. Then Old Albee the Fryer grabbed one of the loaves and tore it in two. The potboys, who were used to having to wait until everyone else was fed before receiving the scraps, dove eagerly into the pile of loaves and grabbed at the butter and jam with their fingers. Their horrified betters began to smack their hands and box their ears.

"Everyone eats their fill today. Everyone," Julia said, striding into the fray. Then she looked down at the boys. "And everyone uses manners. If you don't know what manners are, watch your elders and copy them. Now *sit!*"

Clutching their warm, fragrant prizes, the boys sank onto the benches, tore open their loaves, and filled their mouths as if they hadn't been fed in years. Soon, the rest of the kitchen staff was doing the same . . . pouring cider, spreading butter, and piling on precious jam they served regularly in the hall but never got to enjoy themselves.

As they peeled their eggs, Julia strolled around the tables, pausing and holding her hand over each naked white oval. A twitch of her fingers released a pinch of salt mixed with ground pepper. They stared in amazement at the flecks of spice on their eggs, inhaled the familiar scent, and melted with pleasure.

By the time she handed out assignments for the week and roused the servers to carry huge baskets of bread and eggs and sliced bacon to the hall, for the rest of Grandaise's hall to break fast, the kitchen staff were disposed to give her direction and methods a try.

Thus, when she had them heat water in sizeable cauldrons and drag out bags of hulled wheat berries from the pantry, they were puzzled, but complied. She measured out grains, sent runners to the dairy for fresh milk and to the chicken roost for more eggs. The kitchen workers knew now that she planned to make frumenty. But they were confused by the apparent quantity, considering that in the hall, frumenty was usually for breaking fast or eaten as a side dish. Where was the meat for His Lordship's meal?

When Cheval the Roaster, who was assigned to continue "roasting" for now, asked about the rest of the menu, she gave him a piercing look and told him to warm his hearth for a few birds. A few birds? The workers shook their heads. They had at least a hundred mouths to feed, morning and night.

GRIFFIN HEARD HIS STOMACH GROWLING AS he sat in his great chair in the hall, sipping watered wine and waiting for his dinner. He hadn't eaten since that infuriating display of culinary ineptitude last night, and it was well past none. He had already sent his steward twice to check on when the food would arrive. Twice Arnaud had come back saying that they would be served soon. Each time the suspicion that something was amiss gnawed deeper into his empty stomach.

Then the first course arrived. He sat forward eagerly. A simple round loaf of bread was put before him . . . not trimmed of crusts as was usual in bread presented to a lord. They just plopped a crusty loaf down in front of him for him to cut himself.

Probably on her orders. Brazen chit.

Shifting irritably in his chair and feeling the stares of a dozen knights and four times as many men-at-arms . . . not to mention his steward, bailiff, head vintner, head taster, head vintager, and estate wardens. He thought of the shock and dismay on the faces of his kitchen staff the previous afternoon. He should have stopped by the kitchens earlier to see that she was taking things in hand.

But, in truth, he hadn't wanted to see her taking things

in hand . . . hadn't wanted to see her at all. It was a damned relief to be back in his own bed and at his own table, not having to look across a campfire each night and see her sitting with her chin up and eyes adamantly averted. Or to look back at his men and find them clumped around her cart, basking in her smiles. Or to have to fight the urge to look every time she stepped from the cart and bared a leg. . . .

He wanted her to keep to the damned kitchens and be totally invisible as she worked her culinary miracles. If he could stuff her in a damned barrel for the next year, he would!

He ripped off a piece of that fragrant loaf, dipped it in his wine, and stuffed it into his mouth. Up and down the main table and the lesser boards, his men followed his example.

Shortly, a number of pairs of servers came rushing up from the kitchens bearing massive crocks of something steaming and headed straight for him. The tightness in his middle eased . . . until they began to ladle out a lumpy, thin golden pudding with dark bits floating in it.

"Frumenty? That's what I get for a first course?" He nearly choked.

But in the interest of order and dignity, he seized a spoon and made himself try it. It was faintly sweet, seasoned with cinnamon and nutmeg . . . and the floating lumps of color were raisins, apricots, and dried cherries. It was like a fruit and rice pudding, made with shelled wheat. Suddenly he was looking at the bottom of the bowl and licking his lips. He signaled the servers and they quickly brought him more.

Pacified, if not entirely satisfied, he sat back and waited for the next course to arrive. When some time passed, he beckoned to the closest server.

"Where is the main course?"

"Pardon, Yer Lordship. Ye just ate it."

"What?"

"That's it. Frumenty. Ye want some more?"

He tore his napkin from his lap, shot to his feet, and strode for the service passage. The kitchen door at the end of the covered walkway was barred and after rattling it for a moment, he set the side of his fist to it, demanding entrance.

Moments later, as his temper hit a rolling boil, he heard the bar being drawn back and Julia of Childress slipped outside and closed the door securely behind her.

"What the devil do you think you're doing—barring me from my own kitchens?" he demanded.

"A regrettable but necessary measure, milord. I am having to assert proper discipline and teach some of these old heads the very basics of cooking."

"Frumenty? I pay a king's ransom for you, haul you all the way from the brink of Normandy, allow you to spend a bloody fortune in Paris—"

"A very *fine* frumenty," she inserted defiantly.

"—and all I get is *porridge* for dinner?" he finished in a bellow.

"Simple though it may be, frumenty is the most nourishing dish known to humankind." She folded her arms with her tasting spoon sticking up like a royal scepter. "And a perfect dish to test the working of a kitchen."

"What kind of *test* could you possibly—" Deciding to see for himself, he stepped around her to reach for the door handle, but she stepped into his path.

"Dammit." His face flamed. "I would have a word with my cooks."

"*I'm* your cook, remember? For you to charge into the kitchens now would undo everything I've worked to accomplish this day." She stubbornly raised her chin, despite the fact that it brought her face closer to his. "I must be allowed to run my kitchen free of interference, even from you."

There was a moment, as she raised her face to him, that he felt a delicious trill of panic at being so close to her. It was all he could do to keep from wheeling and running back down the passage to escape.

"Your kitchen?" He almost strangled on the words. *"Your kitchen?"* He teetered on the edge of an explosion for a moment. For the first time in his life he had no idea what was sensible or reasonable or even sane! The chit pulled every usual standard of judgment he'd relied upon from under his feet. Giving her free rein in the kitchens might be the wisest thing to do or the most foolish. And he had no idea which. What the devil was happening to him?

Then he looked into those green eyes. Warm. Open. Beguilingly clear.

"Dammit, woman—"

Charging back down the passage, he ran into Reynard, Axel, and Greeve holding back a tide of others who had streamed out of the hall to witness the confrontation. Servants, men-at-arms, and retainers flattened themselves against the passage walls to allow him to pass, then followed him back to the table.

Reynard again took his place at Griffin's right hand; he frowned at the bowl of tepid wheat berry pudding in front of him.

"A whole dinner of just frumenty?" he said with a wince.

Griffin gave him a look that could have seared a side of bacon.

"It's good for you. Shut up and eat it."

THE KITCHEN STAFF HAD STOPPED STOCK-still to listen to their head cook's confrontation with their lord and looked at each other in wonder. Any cook who had the nerve to serve the Count of Grandaise *frumenty* for dinner had to be either very brave or quite mad and they had yet to decide which applied to their mercurial new cook. Their confusion deepened as the afternoon wore on and she continued to have them carry, clean, and rearrange the kitchen to suit her . . . and perform the most basic of kitchen duties.

She had the kitchen staff, from the most experienced to the greenest beginner, demonstrate how they measured, blanched, ground, peeled, seeded, chopped, grated, strained, larded, sliced, pounded, and fileted . . . while she watched and assessed their abilities. There was considerable mumbling . . . until Sister Regine cheerfully tried her hand at each . . . with such ineptitude that she had many of them laughing at and with her.

While the younger staff practiced such mundane skills, she had the position cooks create some of the mixtures and substances basic to the cuisine of noble houses: almond milk, pea puree, soured cream, mustard sauce, strong dough, soft dough, aspic from a marrow bone, rose water, fruit sauce, and sundry colorings. They, too, grumbled and chafed at being required to demonstrate their competence at tasks they had been doing for years.

But all was forgiven when the demanding new cook sailed around the kitchen seizing various chopped, ground, diced, blanched, roasted, and mixed ingredients they had just produced and carried them to a cleared center table. There, with winning deftness of hand and eye, she rolled dough and assembled luscious-looking chicken and vegetable pasties dusted with a savory fine spice. The cooks' and workers' mouths watered as she slid the packets of dough into the hot grease of Old Albee's frying pans and tended them until they were golden brown. As each batch came out, she dusted them with herbs and salt and piled them up on her work table beside crocks of yellow mustard in wine and soured cream into which she had stirred garlic and spices.

They could hardly tear their eyes from the pasties long enough to hand the crocks of reheated frumenty out the doors to the waiting hall servants. Quickly, they closed and barred the doors, as she ordered, and huddled around the center table of the kitchen, staring at her flushed face.

"The tasks you carried out today were boring, each unto itself. But taken together, the results of your separate labors"—she picked up one of the cooling pasties and held it aloft for all to admire—"the diced chicken, chopped spinach, grated carrots, strong dough, ground spices, and snipped herbs have created a beautiful and delicious dish. Fit for a fine lord."

She could see the wistful hunger in their eyes, and the disappointment dawning. She smiled.

"But as our Lord Jesus said, when He was here on earth: The first shall be last and the last shall be first," she declared resoundingly. "I think it only fair that you taste first-hand the delight you will be providing for His Lordship and those who dine with him in the hall. Dig in!"

Without a moment's hesitation, they seized the pasties and dipped them in the sauces. The kitchen filled with groans and titters of pleasure and excitement. Their lord was having frumenty in the hall while they were eating like kings in the kitchen! By the time the last pasty was consumed, most of the staff were pinching themselves to make certain it wasn't a dream. One or two, however, were scowling in disapproval at what they saw as a scandalous use of food that rightly belonged on their lord's trencher. She saw those scowls and the sly, speculative looks of the wily potboys.

"Do not mistake the meaning or the uniqueness of this lesson," she declared, stalking to two of the more fractious boys and grabbing them hard by the ears. As they howled, she yanked sharply upward. "I expect hard work, obedience, and loyalty. Otherwise, I can be a hard and difficult mistress." She looked down at her captives. "Isn't that right, boys?" She pinched a bit harder and they yelped agreement. "If anyone asks, you'll be sure to tell them." More agreement. "Let me hear you say I'm a terrible hard and ruthless mistress."

"You're a terrible hard and roofless mister!" the boys called out, scrambling up onto their knees to relieve the tension on their ears.

She released them with a satisfied smile.

"You bet I am."

LATE THAT NIGHT, AT THE HEAVILY FORTI-fied keep of Verdun a cloaked rider arrived at the gates insisting he had a message for the count. The guards ferried him by lantern light up the winding stone stairs to the count's quarters.

All was dark in the count's bedchamber except for the

flicker of a trio of costly beeswax candles. The lines of the count's stately bed were barely visible at the outer reaches of the candles' glow, but closer to the source, color bloomed. Parti-colored silk pillows were strewn on the chairs and stools, and a tufted wool panel from the Orient lay on the floor beneath the count's slippered feet.

"Milord." The messenger went down onto one knee before taking the chair the count offered.

"You could have chosen a better time to make your report." Verdun glowered at his informant and waved a ringed hand. A cup of wine appeared.

"Supper was late, seigneur. Lord Griffin has brought home a new cook."

"So I have heard." Verdun sat forward. "Have you seen her?"

"*Non*. But I hear she is young and"—he made a face—"I know she is not much of a cook. We had frumenty for dinner. And for supper."

"So?" The count sat back and sipped his wine again.

"That is all, milord. Just frumenty."

The count choked mid-sip and lowered his cup. "Grandaise was served pap for dinner *and* supper?" He chuckled. "He tries to pass his tart off as a cook and actually puts her in his kitchen. The man's an idiot. What did he do?"

"He stormed out to the kitchens. Then he came back and ate it. Along with the rest of us. The entire garrison was up in arms—some talked of marching on the kitchen to demand a fighting man's ration."

The count was on the edge of his seat.

"And did they?"

"*Non*. Sir Reynard caught wind of it and set the grumblers back on their heels." The count's hopes deflated visibly as his informant continued. "He said the new cook merely finds her seat in the saddle, that the food will improve."

The count smiled vengefully.

"Don't hold your breath waiting for that. She's a whore, not a cook. I'll wager she doesn't know the first thing about running a kitchen."

The informant considered both assertions and nodded.

"This is good. This 'cook' business has possibilities." Verdun sat back with his intense ferret eyes darting back and forth as ideas materialized in his mind. He glanced at his spy. "Watch her, Bertrand de Roland, and report back. I want to know how she spends her days . . . and where she spends her nights."

Chapter 15

BEFORE SUNRISE THE NEXT MORNING, Julia rousted the fuelers and fire tenders and lighted several lamps to begin the day's work. As she headed into the larder to begin selecting ingredients, she caught a whiff of aged onions and rotting greens and stopped dead. It was a testament to the uncommon cleanliness of the kitchen that she hadn't smelled such things until now.

Investigating, she pulled a forgotten pail of waste from behind a stack of large willow baskets. One of the potboys had thought to save himself steps and tucked it there instead of carrying it out to the offal cart. Averting her nose, she carried it out the side door to the dawn-lit yard and—

—screamed, dropped the pail, and lurched back . . . banging into the kitchen wall beside the door. A huge rounded snout, glossy eyes, and a fleshy, pinkish face closed in on her and her cry shriveled to a gurgle.

"Come, come, *ma chère*. Let *la demoiselle* be," came a voice from the edge of her vision. "You see? She has more for you to eat."

Julia swallowed her heart back into place and kicked the bucket away from her feet. The huge pig—she finally rec-

ognized the shape of the beast—abandoned her to follow
the rolling repast and stick its snout into the middle of
those stinky greens.

"Who are you? What are you doing here with that—that
creature?"

"I am Jacques." The smell of pigsty and the sight of
ragged clothes on a lanky frame struck her in the same moment. He gestured to the walking barn that accompanied
him. "This is my Fleur. We come each morning to take
away the scraps and tops and peels." He motioned to a
small heap of waste on the ground where the offal cart
should have stood. Julia sucked a breath. That pungent
smell seemed to be coming from the man, not the pig.

"Well, take your pig back to the sty and keep it there,"
she commanded.

"And ask the old cooks to bring their tossings to us?"
He shook his head in dismay. "It is a long trip to the pens,
demoiselle. Besides, my Fleur likes stretching her legs and
greeting her friends here at the kitchens. Don't you,
chère?" He reached over to scratch the pig's ears and she
stopped munching long enough to lift her head and tilt it at
him in what could only have been agreement.

"Her *friends*?" Julia stared at the amicable Jacques—
who was clearly a few inches short of an ell—and at Fleur—
who seemed to have found the very inches Jacques had lost.

A pair of potboys burst from the kitchen door carrying a
second belated pail of kitchen offal. "Fleur!" they cried
and launched themselves at the pig, before one spotted
their mistress and grabbed the other back. They reddened
as they followed Julia's glower to the bucket they held.

"We . . . um . . . forgot a pail last night," one said,
shrinking back a step.

"Two," she corrected, pointing at the one Fleur was
emptying.

They blanched, looking at the stout spoon tucked into
her belt.

"Fleur!" Two older kitchen girls came running up and
sobered to a walk under her critical gaze. "How are you this

morning, Demoiselle Fleur?" They greeted the pig with a respectful bob before they greeted Julia the same way.

Then a deep voice came from the corner of the kitchen, followed closely by a pair of tall boots and a pleasant, manly face.

"Demoiselle!" Sir Reynard waved as he approached. "Good morning."

Julia wondered if the greeting was for her or the pig.

"I see you've met Fleur," the courtly knight reached down and gave the pig's ear a friendly scratch that it acknowledged with a grunt.

"I hardly know what to make of her," she said, grateful to be able to summon that much diplomacy at this hour of the morning.

"Fleur, you see, is no ordinary pig," Reynard said with a hint of the ironic to his genial face. "She is a finder of lost objects." He looked to Jacques, who nodded with obvious pride.

"She is better than most dogs at tracking," Jacques said. "When Solange's little daughter wandered off—"

"Fleur followed the girl's scent and led us to her," Reynard finished for him, nodding. Then he chuckled at Julia's dubious look. "We are not flamming you, Demoiselle Julia. She is truly an extraordinary pig."

"Well, then," Julia said, trying to reorient her thinking to accommodate one *extraordinary pig*. "I believe I can find something to feed a helpful knight." She looked from Sir Reynard to Jacques with a bemused smile. "And the keeper of an extraordinary pig."

Jacques accepted the food but declined to enter the kitchen, saying that he wasn't much for being inside any building. But Sir Reynard sank onto a stool and drank some of the sweet, frothy ale she set out for him as she accepted the day's deliveries: baskets of hot, crusty loaves from the bakers, meat from the butcher, and a number of fine, plump capons that were already plucked from the poulterer. She negotiated with the butcher for lamb to be served the next day, and then had to check the baskets of freshly picked onions, greens, turnips, and small carrots the gardeners hauled to the kitchen in a cart.

At Julia's direction, Fran the Larderer began collecting and portioning out ingredients for the day's dishes, and the recently arrived cooks and girls began to drain and rinse beans that had soaked overnight, clean and slice vegetables and greens, and prepare a dozen capons and several joints of beef for the spit.

Then she finally was able to turn to Sir Reynard with an apology for keeping him waiting, and set forth a warm, crusty loaf, sliced, salted butter, fruit preserves, and hard-boiled eggs.

"I came by to compliment you on your fine frumenty of yesterday," Sir Reynard said between mouthfuls of food.

"Thank you, sir." She flashed a smile, doubting that and wondering what he was really doing in the kitchens. "It is a simple dish, but nourishing and versatile. It can be spiced many ways and eaten any time of the day."

"You're not thinking of offering it to Lord Griffin again this morning, are you?" he asked, looking at her over the edge of his tankard of ale.

"And if I were?" she said raising her chin.

"Let's just say that"—he measured his words carefully—"Lord Griffin is expecting something more *substantial*. And we're all hoping you give it to him."

"Who is 'we'?" she demanded, propping her fists on her hips.

"His knights and his eighty-man garrison. His entire household. His tenants and villagers. Essentially, everyone who meets him in the course of a day or has dealings with him. We need him to be at his best. And he needs good food to be at his best." He leaned forward across the table, staring into her eyes, and said quietly, "He faces several difficult challenges."

His pleasant voice and disarming gaze tweaked her sense of the personal.

"Challenges. Such as . . . his upcoming marriage?"

Reynard froze for a moment, assessing the question and the questioner, then nodded. "There will no doubt be some 'provocations' before Verdun finally hands his daughter over to Lord Griffin. Verdun is a treacherous man."

"This feud, Sir Reynard, how did it begin?" she asked earnestly.

"No one seems to know for certain. But the killing started when an early Comte de Grandaise tried to bar the lords of Verdun from hunting or taking from the forest. Verdun then laid claim to what had always been acknowledged as Grandaise land. Blood was shed, and has continued to be shed until this present generation. Lord Griffin's grandfather was killed in a fierce battle when Lord Griffin was still a stripling. Then Lord Griffin's younger brother was killed in the woods four years ago."

"Sweet Heaven." There had been killings. Of his closest kin. Small wonder His Lordship had no desire to celebrate his upcoming marriage.

"By Verdun's son and heir, who was gravely wounded and also died. Other houses were recruited by alliances into the fray, and the king—fearing all-out war if the side-taking didn't stop—vowed to end it."

"By ordering His Lordship to wed the count of Verdun's daughter."

Sir Reynard nodded. "He believes their children will unite both houses. And well they may." He shook his head and added under his breath, "If His Lordship lives long enough to produce any."

"What is she like, his intended bride?"

"I have no earthly idea. She was sent to a convent for safekeeping, and was brought home recently. She's fairly young." He shrugged. She noticed that his shoulders were wide and that he had a pleasant masculine scent. Her eyes began to sparkle with interest in more than just his story. "That's all we know. There isn't any traffic between Grandaise and Verdun, and Lord Griffin doesn't usually have neighboring lords in to dine."

"He doesn't practice hospitality?" She thought of his visit with Sir Reynard's father, the Baron Crossan, where wine and good humor had flowed freely. "Why?"

"Could it be that my cooks are too busy gossiping to see to my food?" came an irritable voice from the kitchen door. She looked up to find His Lordship leaning with his arms crossed against the door frame.

Galvanized by the sight of him and suddenly aware that her face was only inches away from Sir Reynard's—and her thoughts had been closer than that—she lurched back and blushed. All activity ceased as everyone from cook to potboy watched their lord stroll inside with his gaze fixed on their head cook.

"Sir Reynard came by to comment on yesterday's menu . . . and I . . . invited him to break his fast here with us." She looked around the silent kitchen and, with a glare borrowed from her employer, ordered her people back to work.

"Your choice of menus is one of the reasons I am here." His prowl-like gait and cool smile were ominous enough to send Sir Reynard sliding off his stool. "The other reason is that I was looking for you, Reynard. I want a report on the forest patrols sent out last night."

"Yes, milord. On my way." He nodded to Julia and withdrew.

"I was just about to send some food up to the hall, milord," she said.

"I'll take mine here." His Lordship settled onto the stool the knight had occupied and looked deliberately around the kitchen. "I want to see firsthand how you fare in my kitchens."

"Well enough, milord. There really is no need for you to—"

"What are you preparing for dinner?" It was not a casual question.

"A bean pottage, Roast Capon with Jance Sauce, Roast Beef with Lamprey Sauce, Pasties Florentine, and Baked Apple Rissoles." She folded her arms. "Does that meet with your approval?"

"It may. I'll decide when I taste the final results."

With a quiet huff of exasperation, she set out the same breakfast for him, then prepared baskets of food for the servers to carry up to the hall. Just before they departed, Axel and Greeve strode through the open kitchen door, fresh from their morning ablutions and hungry as wolves.

"Milord! What a surprise to see you here." Greeve yanked Axel to a halt at the sight of their seigneur.

"I'm so hungry I could eat a horse," Axel said, staring at the food spread on the table and ignoring the way Greeve tried to hold him back from it.

"Fortunately, you won't have to." Julia said with a smile.

In short order, they were drinking ale she had dipped from the barrel and were groaning with gratitude as she paused to pepper the eggs they peeled. They were so intent on their food that they didn't notice the count's face darkening.

"Don't you two have men to train this morning?"

No sooner had they stuffed their eggs into their bread and exited than another strapping young knight appeared.

"Milord! I didn't expect to see you here."

"Obviously."

"But where else would one go to see the prettiest face in all of Grandaise?" the young knight declared, eyeing Julia with an admiration that brought more color to her already pink cheeks. "Bertrand de Roland. Head of His Lordship's archers." He made a courtly bow and was quickly invited to break his fast. As he watched her cut his bread, he complimented the previous day's dinner and the wonderful smells coming from the hearths.

"Bertrand," His Lordship said without looking up from the egg he was peeling, "do you have a score of men yet who can reliably hit a bull's-eye?"

"Not yet. But we have at least thirty who can reliably hit the second ring." He smiled as he accepted the partial loaf Julia had buttered for him.

"Then you have work to do," His Lordship declared in tones that were clearly dismissive. The knight stilled and his face sobered.

"So I do." He nodded briskly to Julia, and exited.

Julia was furious. The nerve of His Lordship . . . sitting there barking at every man who came through the door . . . a blessed dog in the manger!

She slammed down her bread knife and went back to work, assigning two of the more rambunctious kitchen boys to grind spices and several of the younger girls to mince vegetables and grate hard cheese. Then she busied herself measuring flour for dough and inspecting the hearths.

Albee the Fryer grumbled about having to change the grease in his skillets, and Old Mae the Saucer muttered that she'd been making Jance sauce since Moses was adrift in a basket and nobody had complained. But under their lord's watchful eye, both did as they were bade and prepared for the next phase of the morning's work.

When she spotted the hulking Cheval standing near his hearths just watching the heat-flushed turnspits working, Julia dragged the big fellow to the dough trough, thrust a wooden paddle into his powerful hands, and bade him stir as she added the combined water and ale to the flour. Periodically, she halted him to add a bit of salt and check the consistency. When the dough met her standards, she sent four of the younger girls to wash their hands, then put them to work cutting and rolling circles of pastry.

A trio of young knights came bursting through the door; two laughing at the third's dripping wet head, which had obviously been pushed completely under in the trough. They were so busy enjoying their jests at their unfortunate comrade's expense that they didn't recognize at first that it was their lord's back they saw seated at the table.

"There she is," one declared broadly. "All that was said and more."

"Sugar and spice made flesh," the second declared with a gallant bow.

"A sight to make the heart beat fas—" The third didn't get his compliment fully out of his mouth before he stopped dead, skewered by his lord's glare.

"Milord." The first gallant straightened and nodded to his lord. "We came to welcome our lovely new cook to Grandaise."

"*Whose* cook?" Griffin said, turning slowly to face them.

"Why, *y-your* cook, milord." The second fellow said uneasily, sensing they had trespassed, and reading in their lord's face that he was right.

"Some bread and eggs for my loyal knights to take with them to the practice field," he ordered Julia, making the dual point that she was his to command . . . and so were they. When there was no movement from where she stood, he turned to her with a scowl. She met his gaze with a stubborn look, squared her shoulders, and wiped the flour from her hands.

"Have a seat, good sirs, while I fetch you some ale."

"They can get ale in the hall," he said sharply.

"They can get it here as well, and save themselves steps." She nodded to the stools and the three looked uneasily between their lord and his cook.

"They take morning ale in the hall with their fellows. There is no reason to change that."

"Except to offer hospitality," she declared, striding to the table where he sat. "It appears to me that you would benefit from a greater spirit of hospitality, milord . . . even within your own household. Hospitality makes for alliances and alliances make for strength." She sliced a loaf of bread three ways and slathered each piece with butter. As she handed it to them, she nodded again to the stools.

Griffin reddened. Tossing the last of his food aside, he shoved to his feet and glowered at his men.

"Take your food and go. *Now.*"

They didn't have to be told twice; they had seen that look in his eyes too many times not to know what it meant. The instant they quitted the door, he turned on her with his anger blazing.

"Don't *ever* take it upon yourself to interfere between me and my men again. When I give an order I must have complete and immediate obedience—lives may depend on it. Fighting men cannot look with respect on a lord who is countermanded and ordered about by a *cook!*"

Some of the high color drained from her face.

"I am sorry, milord." She seemed genuinely stunned by

the intensity of his reproach. "I did not meant to intrude between you and your men. I had no thought of doing any such thing."

Griffin felt his nerves vibrating inside his limbs as he stared down into her huge green eyes, and felt a bit ashamed of the magnitude of his reaction. If only she wasn't so arrogant and outlandishly brazen, he wouldn't have to—

"But truly, milord, a kitchen is nothing like a battle-field." Her voice grew measured and insufferably reasonable. "Your men surely know the difference."

"They were not where they were supposed to be," he said irritably, feeling his ire rising again. "And they were intruding on my kitchens."

"But they weren't in the way, milord. And they have to eat somewhere. Why does it matter if they break fast here instead of in the hall?"

"If it were only a matter of food," he said tautly, knowing now that she would not let it lie until her suspicions and his motives were both aired, "they would never have come to the kitchen."

"Of course it was a matter of food." That defiant edge was creeping back into her voice. "What else would they seek in a kitchen?"

He looked up to see every hand in the kitchen still and every eye turn on them with eager fascination. He seized her by the arm and pulled her out the door with him into the dubious privacy of the open kitchen yard.

"You may have spent most of your life in a convent, demoiselle, but you cannot be that blind."

"Blind?"

"You cannot think they came here for food."

"Sir Axel said he was famished, as did Sir Greeve. My food is worthy of seeking out. You yourself—"

"Look." He seized her other shoulder and drew her up to face him, intent on making an impression on her. "I know these men. I've trained them and taken them into bat-tle and into relief after battle. I know their intents and their desires. And I know they do not pour out honeyed words and flattery in a woman's ear unless they seek something in return."

"Of course they seek something: *breakfast!*"

He gave her a shake that only made her more resistant to his meaning.

"Don't feign innocence with me, Julia of Childress. You know they came to see you as a woman, to flatter and court you. And I tell you now, I will not allow that . . . not now, not ever." The vehemence of those words reverberated in his very core. "I have sworn to preserve you and return you to your convent in a year so that you may take vows and offer yourself to God. I intend to do exactly that. If I have to lock you up in the kitchen in order to do it—so help me God—I will!" He knew beyond all doubt that it was more than just keeping his word in an ill-begotten bargain that created such vehemence in him . . . there was beneath his determination a thwarted and unsettling urge for possession.

She wrenched her arms free. As she stood glaring at him with all the heat and passion she possessed, her eyes filled with moisture and her body began to tremble. Her voice came low and full of emotions that found resonance in the hollow that had opened in him the moment she set eyes on his knights and opened like a morning glory.

"And what if I don't want to go back?"

She whirled and charged into the kitchen, slamming the door behind her. He stood staring at the door for a moment with her words rumbling about in that alarming emptiness inside him.

Dear God.

What if she wouldn't return to the convent?

Chapter 16

AN EDICT WENT OUT THAT DAY, SPREAD quietly through the house, grounds, and garrison: The kitchens were off limits to all but the assigned kitchen staff. There was more grumbling among the men of the garrison, some of whom who were accustomed to stopping by the kitchens on their way to and from the stables and practice fields to get a sample of dinner and flirt with the kitchen wenches. But Reynard, Axel, and Greeve quelled the dissent by reminding them that the improved food that resulted would more than make up for the inconvenience.

As if to prove that assertion, dinner arrived just after midday in the hall, heralded by clean cloths on the tables, salt cellars aplenty, and cups ready for the cellar master to fill. Julia herself escorted the first round of servers into the hall, bearing baskets of wooden bowls and bread trenchers. As they were being distributed, the huskier servers arrived carrying heavy kettles of beans cooked with generous chunks of rendered bacon and baked in a pepper, onion, mustard, and honey sauce. The aroma wafted up from the kettles to set mouths watering and tongues wagging.

She stopped first by Griffin's chair to watch them ladle out his portion.

"What are you doing here?" he demanded.

"Overseeing the serving, milord. As a good cook should."

"That won't be necessary. Return to the kitchens."

He could see that she was annoyed by the dismissal. She stood for a moment, studying him as if deciding whether or not to obey.

"Where is your taster, milord?" She glanced up and down the long table.

He glowered. "Are you saying I have need of one?"

"I would think it a necessity for a nobleman in your situation, milord," she answered. "Having enemies close at hand and a cook who clearly has not yet earned your trust."

"Fine." He shoved the bowl across the linen toward her. "You taste it."

"Very well. To assure you that your cook and kitchens have nothing but your best interest at heart . . ." She pulled her tasting spoon from her belt, lifted his bowl, and took a bite of the bean pottage.

"Mmmm." She licked her lips and made a show of waving some of the vapors toward her nose, inhaling, and closing her eyes briefly. "I love this dish. It combines the heat of mustard and the sweet of honey with the meaty richness of beans. The flavors create an unexpected harmony. That is what fine cooking does, you know . . . it brings about unexpected harmonies."

He realized his mouth was drooping and clamped it shut.

"I believe it's safe to eat this one, milord." She nodded to order the servers to continue around the tables.

Stifling the urge to strangle her, he dragged the bowl back in front of him and dug in with his spoon. In two bites he confirmed all she had just said. It *was* good. Dammit. As pottages went, it was neat and tasty and rather novel. None of his other cooks had presented such a combination to him. He looked around as he munched. His men were wolfing it down and calling for seconds.

"How is it, milord?" she asked, a smile teasing one corner of her lips.

He didn't bother to look up.

"Different."

Soon the kettles were removed and replaced by platters bearing a second course: pasties fried to golden perfection and dusted with herbs and spices. Chicken, spinach, onion, and a dry and tangy cheese were wrapped in a tender, delectable crust. All over the hall there were groans of anticipation.

Griffin took several from the tray and would have begun eating straightaway if she hadn't appeared at his side with her arms crossed.

"I would not keep my men from eating," he said defensively, referring to the custom that the lord of the hall must open each course. She took the pasty from him and broke it open. Steam rose from the meat and cheese packed inside, and she inhaled ostentatiously.

"A very nice balance of humors and flavors, if I do say so." She took a bite. "Next time, I think I'll try minced lamb, mild cheese, and add a bit of nutmeg." Finishing the morsel, she licked her lips. "It is quite safe, milord."

No, it wasn't, Griffin thought as he dragged his eyes from her glistening lips and bit into what was left of the first pasty. It wasn't safe at all. This tingling in his fingertips was like an alarm bell. She was up to something.

But his attention was quickly stolen by the pasties . . . the firm, golden crust, the flavors of the filling—savory to piquant—which were blended into a tasty and satisfying mouthful. They were even better than he'd hoped. First the pottage and now the pasties managed to tantalize him entirely without the help of scent. Only genuinely fine food could accomplish that. As he looked around the hall at the jovial faces of his knights and men and retainers, he envied them the pleasure their ordinary noses added to their eating.

"You said you liked pasties, milord. How do you find these?"

He could tell she was smiling by her voice and refused to look at her.

"I'll eat them," he declared flatly.

By the time the third course arrived, Reynard, Axel,

Greeve, Bertrand, and the rest of his knights were licking their fingers and scooping out the soppy centers from their bread trenchers. When they saw the capon and beef, both roasted to brown-tinged perfection, and smelled the sauces meant for the meats, they began to joke about fighting all comers for the rights to an entire platter.

When Griffin was served meat and bowls of sauce, he tensed with anticipation and felt his heart beat more vigorously . . . even without the heavenly aromas. When she didn't appear at his side straightaway, he looked around and found her down the main table, speaking with his younger knights. Her eyes were sparkling, her cheeks were glowing like ripe peaches, and the idiots were staring at her as if she were sugared and set on a tray.

Suddenly he knew: She was here in the hall for more than just seeing that her food was served properly . . . for more than tormenting him with the limits of his unique affliction. . . .

"And what if I don't want to go back?"

The image of her that morning in the kitchen yard returned to him with a vengeance. At the time, part of him had felt a guilty twinge of satisfaction at the thought that she might rather stay here and cook for *him.*

Now, with deepening alarm, he watched her working her way down the table past Reynard to Axel and Greeve and Bertrand and beyond. The gracious smiles she aimed at his knights raked his pride like cat's claws. It occurred to him that if she didn't want to go back to the convent, it might not be because she wanted to stay here and cook for him. She might have other ambitions, other plans . . . which would of necessity involve finding someone to beguile into helping her . . . a man . . . of his garrison, his hall.

Dammit. He'd have to find a way to keep her at his fingertips and then keep those fingertips at a full arm's length from the rest of him.

"Demoiselle Julia!" he called irritably. The sound of his raised voice reduced the noise in the hall by half. When she abandoned her new friends to approach his chair, her face alight, he felt a disconcerting heat ignite in the pit of his stomach.

"Yes, milord?"

"Since you have appointed yourself my taster, I suggest you see to your duty." He gestured sharply to the untouched beef on his trencher. The smile left her face as she bit back whatever it was that she was tempted to say.

She rolled a slice of the beef on his trencher and dunked it into the sauce.

Against his better judgment, he watched her lips close around that meat and felt every muscle in his body tense with expectation. When she chewed, clearly savoring the tastes, he felt his mouth begin to water. Her swallowing conjured the same action in his tightened throat.

She borrowed his napkin to wipe her fingers and dab her lips.

"As you can see, milord, I am still hale and well," she said crisply.

He took a bite and the meat all but melted in his mouth, leaving a lingering sensation of sweet and sour on his tongue. Damned, if this wasn't excellent beef! He ate several more pieces, reveling privately in the beefy flavor, juiciness, and tender texture. Then he tried the capon in Jance sauce and quelled an involuntary groan. Ginger tingled his tongue at the top of other piquant sensations, and he briefly closed his eyes. For all the trouble she caused, the woman certainly knew how to—

Musical, feminine laughter reached him, floating above the coarser male rumbles in the hall, jolting him back from the realm of satisfaction. Alarm filled him as he spotted Axel and Greeve trundling one of the hearth stools over to the table to seat Julia in the midst of his knights.

"Axel! Greeve!" he called out. The pair snapped upright. "Bring that over here." The two complied with such visible disappointment that he felt compelled to add: "If the demoiselle insists on being my taster, she must stay close at hand." Then he thumped the seat of the stool they had placed between his chair and Sir Reynard's. "Sit, demoiselle. By your own word, you have made this your place in the hall."

She sat, sensing she was being reined in, and gripped her knees.

"How is the beef, milord?"

"It melts to nothing in my mouth." He didn't make it sound like a compliment. She supplied the proper term.

"So it is *tender,* then. And how about the sauce, milord?"

He chewed for a moment, apparently thinking.

"Not very . . . peppery."

Julia settled onto the stool, watching him plod through the trencher of meat and poultry as if he were an ox munching hay, and longed desperately for a club. A *big* one.

How dare he behave as if her food were unworthy of compliment?

She glanced down the table to Axel and Greeve, who were consuming the same meat and sauces with an almost worshipful demeanor. Admittedly, the pair were more appreciative of good food and more effusive of expression than most men. But up and down the head table, knights and retainers were moaning with pleasure and exclaiming with surprise and delight at the quality of the fare. Of the over four score people in the hall, only His Lordship acted as if the food were unremarkable. Why?

It wasn't the food. She knew that was pleasurable; she had tasted and corrected and brought it along herself, and knew it to be at a peak of flavor and desirability. Why wouldn't he just admit it was good? She stared at the flexing muscles in his jaw as he chewed, and felt a curious trickle of arousal that might have been rising anger or rising interest. Scowling, she sat straighter to banish it. Was his taste so linked to his sense of smell that he couldn't appreciate food without it? If so, why had he bothered to bring her here?

As he turned from speaking to one of his vintagers, he caught her staring at him and she flushed and turned quickly away. When she could refocus her gaze, it ran into

Sir Reynard's and he gave her a somewhat apologetic smile that spoke volumes. She turned to him on her stool.

"It has been some time since we've seen you in the kitchen, Sir Reynard."

"I've been busy overseeing patrols and training with the men."

"All of this wretched training you do . . . surely you could make a little time for yourself." She gave him a wistful smile. "And us."

"The men and I"—he glanced up, past her shoulder, and the look that registered in his face made her realize His Lordship was watching them—"have important duties, demoiselle."

"Important, perhaps. But none half so pleasant as tasting cherry and cinnamon rissoles, fresh out of the fryer."

"I cannot argue that." He smiled ruefully, his face almost boyish. "Alas, duty must come before pleasure, demoiselle." He turned adamantly back to his food, cutting off further conversation.

Frustrated, she looked around and ran headlong into His Lordship's gaze. This time, he leaned toward her and lowered his voice.

"Don't waste your time there, demoiselle." When she frowned as if she hadn't taken his meaning, he nodded to the noble Reynard. "He's sworn to God and to me, until he swears to a wife. And he takes his vows most seriously."

"Really, milord—" She was taken by surprise and couldn't mount a proper protest.

"*Really,* demoiselle," he responded. "You would do well to consider your own future vows." Then he dismissed the topic as he waved to the fritters. "I may as well save Fleur the trouble of eating a few more of those things."

Her vows.

Stinging privately, she served him more fritters and folded her arms with a huff. So, he knew she had ulterior motives; that was the real reason he isolated her on a stool beside his chair. It should be no surprise; she had all but admitted she had mutinous intentions that morning in the kitchen yard. And she could scarcely blame him for wanting to interfere with her plans. He had, after all, given his word.

Her face reddened as she kicked a few absurdly personal conjectures about his motives back into a dark corner of her mind.

But if he thought he was going to hand her back to the abbess at the end of the year, he was sadly mistaken. She would find someone to marry her, even if she had to court an entire garrison with her food. She looked at the eager faces of the men up and down the tables. One of them was going to be hers. It was just a matter of finding one who loved her food enough to defy a duke, a bishop, and an abbess to have it.

DETERMINED TO CONQUER HER EMPLOYER'S stubborn palate, Julia spent part of each day visiting another area of the house and grounds, getting to know those who supplied the kitchens with consumables and letting it be known that there would be a healthy reward from her kitchens for high-quality berries, herbs, verjuice, game, and honey. Everywhere she went people seemed eager to offer her the best from their stores and private larders. And everywhere she went, she bumped into the porcine Demoiselle Fleur. At least she thought it was Fleur.

"*Non, non,* demoiselle." The young man accompanying the large pink and gray pig on her rambles shook his head. "This is Margarite, not Fleur. Fleur is Margarite's mama."

Then at the gardens, she ran into another, somewhat smaller and pinker beast accompanied by a lad who smelled suspiciously like Jacques the Pigman.

"I don't suppose this is Fleur, either," she said as the beast snuffled around at her feet as if trying to decide if she were edible.

"This is our Isobel," he declared, grinning proudly and scratching the pig's back. The pig shivered with pleasure. "Fleur is Isobel's *grandmère.*"

Fleur, it happened, was the matriarch of a clan of pigs who wandered the estate with human companions, munching castoffs and leavings, and keeping the place surprisingly tidy. Everyone seemed to greet them and feed them . . . and to accept as normal the fact that animals who were disdained as low and filthy elsewhere, at Grandaise were being accorded an extraordinary amount of respect.

It was only as she watched Isobel lumber toward a woman tossing a basket of peelings from her door that Julia realized that His Lordship had omitted pork from his list of desirable foods. Curiously, now that she thought about it, few pork products other than bacon and fat were kept in the larder.

Other than the roving "pigs of renown," the estate seemed to be an exemplary demesne: well organized and capably kept. The people were proud of their vineyards and wines, but were no less pleased to speak of the cheeses they made and aged in the cavelike cellars used to hold the casks of wine.

Within days she was garnering the best of the estate's wild produce and private gardens, poultry, dairy, cellars, ovens, and butcher's stock . . . turning it into savory Chicken with Fennel and Lasagne with Herbs and Cheese. . . .

"Filling," was His Lordship's assessment.

Roast Goose with Black Grape Sauce and Gravé of Quail . . .

"More blessed bird and gravy."

Haricot of Lamb with Mint Sauce.

"Never really cared for mint."

Knowing she must improve the kitchens if she were to charm and win His Lordship's stubborn palate, she selected and assigned some of the older kitchen girls to serve as apprentice cooks. To her surprise Sister Regine declared she felt guilty just watching the bustle in the kitchen and asked to join them. Both Regine and the girls threw themselves into their new duties and began to ease some of the burden on Old Albee the Fryer, Pennet the Ovenman, and Old Mae the Saucer. The kitchen staff began to catch her determination and take more interest and pride in their work. The courses and accompaniments became increasingly delectable and elaborate.

She was able to produce a lovely Cream Flan and a Blancmange Lyonese.

"Pale." His Lordship pronounced them.

Poached Eggs in Custard Sauce and Herbed Chard and Cheese Pie . . .

"More eggs? What—is it Easter again already?" he muttered.

Whole Pear Tart and Layered Dried Fruit Pudding . . .

"I'll spend the day dragging my men out of the damned privy."

Leek and Mushroom Torte, Meats in Aspic, and Porée of Greens . . .

"Why is there never any vinegar on my table anymore?"

Cherry Almond Pudding and Spiced Plum Mousse with Honey . . .

"Fruit and sugar. Sugar and fruit. Do I look like I'm sick?"

The astonishing variety and quality of the food sent exclamations of pleasure and delight throughout the hall. Folk who did not regularly find a place at their lord's table contrived to present reports and petitions to their lord just before serving began, and eagerly wedged themselves onto the benches and dug into the plentiful platters and aromatic stews. Tensions and rivalries between knights, men-at-arms, and retainers were momentarily lost in pottage bowls, savory filled crusts, and sauce-sodden trenchers. And that improved humor carried forth from the hall into all aspects of the estate and nearby village . . . easing mistrust and conflict between merchant and patron, tavern keeper and soldier, and vineyard worker and vintager.

But His Lordship's reaction to the ever improving cuisine was a maddening mix of silent indulgence and vocal criticism that grated ever more harshly on her nerves. For every bite that made him close his eyes to trap and savor a taste or texture, he was sure to toss a dark look or sharply barbed comment her way.

When she served a Parsley-studded Lamb with Pink Garlic Sauce . . .

"Garlic is too common an herb to deserve such prominence on my table."

A tender Poached Tuna with Yellow Sauce for a day of abstinence . . .

"It lacks the proper strong 'fish' taste that reminds a body of repentance."

And sweet and savory King's Fritters for supper one evening . . .

"All this sugar they're rolled in sets a body's teeth on edge."

She was proving herself—she thought furiously as she perched on her tasting stool by his chair and watched him wolfing down those woefully "imperfect" fritters—and he was dead set against admitting she was the best cook he'd ever had. Why? Would it kill him to say he liked her food?

She turned to glare at him and found him leaning toward one of his knights seated on the far side, listening. Something in the angle of his jaw and the corded smoothness of his neck trapped her gaze and held it.

Then he smiled. A slow, spreading grin that bore an unexpected hint of mischief. Her stomach collapsed and slid to somewhere in the vicinity of her knees. As he turned, his eyes glinted with irresistible golden lights and his lips glistened with the residue of the wine he'd just sipped.

That was what pleasure looked like on his face.

A sharp and unexpected ache of longing pierced her. Her eyes began to dry as she stared, unblinking, and her breathing grew shallow.

She wanted to make him smile like that. No. She wanted to make him smile *at her* like that.

She transferred her attention to the band on his nose and

the longer she stared at it the more important it seemed. It was that wretched band, she told herself irritably. What did she have to do to get him to remove it and succumb to the pleasures she set before him?

Chapter 17

THAT SAME NIGHT, ACROSS THE ROLL-ing hills to the west, the Comte de Verdun and his allies were sprawled over chairs and benches in his rush-strewn hall, gorged and wined to insensibility. Around them lay dirty platters, puddles of soured wine, and the contents of overburdened stomachs . . . the debris of a long and determined rout. The torches burned low and the stench-laden air shook with penetrating snores. A pack of stringy hounds roamed the ruined bowls and platters on the tabletops, picking bones clean and licking up spilled sauces, while their fatter, more successful cousins lay sprawled in the rushes under the table, satisfied and snor-ing as vigorously as their masters.

Two days of hunting and celebrating had taken their toll on the comte's fellow nobles and their knights. And when the results of their successful "hunt" were discovered, they could be counted on to take a toll on the count's prime en-emy—Grandaise—as well. Verdun, as was his custom, had celebrated with moderation and now merely dozed in his chair. Thus, when a servant hurried in from the side court, he roused and demanded to know what was happening.

"Pardon, milord." The servant lowered his gaze. "But that rider ye said to watch for . . . he's come."

"In the middle of the damned night?" Verdun rubbed his eyes.

Bertrand de Roland halted at the door for a moment and took in the devastation and the pack of dogs feeding on the remains. Then he spotted the compte and strode for the dark figure blearing at him from the head of the table.

"About time you showed your face," the comte snapped, struggling to focus both his vision and his ire.

"He keeps us busy, seigneur. I could not get away."

"And?" He made a winding gesture, demanding Bertrand get to the point.

"And . . . the Beast trains his men as if he expects to have to fight."

"As I suspected. And what of the garrison?" When Bertrand looked around them at the bodies caught somewhere between Verdun and oblivion, the compte dismissed his concern. "In their condition, they're deaf as posts."

"He drives the men hard of late, but they don't mind. They are too busy looking forward to their next meal." When the comte frowned, he continued. "It's his new cook, seigneur. It seems she really does cook."

"A tart who cooks?" The compte was not pleased. "Are you certain?"

"I've seen her working with my own eyes, seigneur. She is indeed in charge of the kitchens . . . and feeds Grandaise and his garrison well. Of late, the Beast has lost some of his lean and hungry look."

"Has he indeed?" Wheels began to turn in Verdun's mind.

"And Grandaise is fiercely protective of her. He has barred the men of the garrison from the kitchens and gets furious if one of his knights so much as speaks with her." He pause for a moment, frowning, recalling. "I tossed a girl who cleans in the main house and learned that the cook shares her chamber with a nun who accompanied her from a convent. The house women say that this 'cook' is bound to take religious vows someday."

"A tart posing as a cook who intends to become a nun."
Verdun gave an incredulous laugh and sat forward, fully
alert. "This just gets better and better." His eyes darted
back and forth as he looked for elements in Bertrand's
story to assemble into something useful.

"A cook, eh?" He rubbed his chin. "So much the better.
Losing a bit of bed sport is one thing, but losing his
food . . . a man cannot wage war or even defend his own
lands if he has nothing to eat."

"What would you have me do, seigneur?" Bertrand de
Roland asked, watching carefully the cunning unfolding
before his eyes.

"She is a cook, yes? And is this not the season for mushrooms in the forest?"

ON SUNDAY, SINCE MOST OF THE FOOD WAS
prepared in advance for the day of rest and cooking duties
were light, Julia dragged Regine with her up and down the
stairs and through every accessible passage and portal in
the great house. Corralling Genevieve, His Lordship's recently appointed housekeeper, they enlisted her help and
had her try her keys in every lock they encountered.

They finally discovered in one of the watch towers a
small chamber made to serve as quarters for the men who
stood sentry duty in times of peril. When Regine and
Genevieve helped Julia open a set of weathered wooden
shutters that stretched from floor to ceiling, they discovered a semicircular balcony beyond, complete with stone
benches built into the thick stone walls. From the
crenelated edge, they could see fully half of the estate's
buildings and housing, and the vineyards to the north and
south and the fields and forest to the west.

Julia stood for a few moments in the lowering afternoon
sun, lifting her face to the gentle breeze and closing her
eyes. She had found just the right place. Air, a beautiful
sunset, seclusion . . .

"This is it." She turned with a glow of excitement.
"We'll need brooms, buckets, and scrub brushes . . . plenty

of water . . . and we'll have to find a table and some pillows for the bench." She grabbed Genevieve's hands and squeezed, trying to force some of her enthusiasm through them into the stoic housekeeper. "This is where His Lordship is going to dine tomorrow."

GRIFFIN STRODE INTO THE HALL THE NEXT evening, fingering a small bunch of green grapes and listening to his head vintager's ideas on how to protect the estate's far-flung vineyards in the event of a war with Verdun. In the history of their family conflicts, both sides had made a point of avoiding damage to the long-lived vines that were so much a part of each estate's economy.

But this Comte de Verdun, Griffin knew, made his greedy father and grandfather seem reasonable by comparison. He cared nothing for the traditions of the land and the natural wealth that lay around and between their holdings. If it couldn't be dug, drained, chopped, hunted, or eaten, he had no use for it. Though the venerable vines on their lands produced some of the finest grapes and wines in all of France, to Bardot of Verdun they were merely crops. And crops could be replanted. Never mind that some of the best bearing vines were more than two score years old and would take at least that long to replace. . . .

The hall lamps were lighted above, tables were set in place, and only the head table was draped with linen, as was usual for the lighter evening meal. He didn't notice, as he washed his hands and splashed his face with water from the basin that a boy brought him, that his silver wine cup and trencher were missing.

"Milord." Sir Reynard met Griffin by his chair and cleared his throat nervously as he blocked the way. "I have been told you are needed in the old west lookout."

"Can't it wait?" he asked glancing toward his chair. "I'm ravenous."

"It's Demoiselle Julia, milord. She insists it is of the utmost importance." Reynard winced at the annoyance that bloomed in his lord's face.

"She does, does she?" Griffin glanced once more at his chair, deciding. "With her it's always something urgent . . . or desperate . . . or *expensive*."

"This way, milord." Reynard started for the arched opening that led to the stairs, but Griffin grabbed him back.

"I know the way," he growled, striding for the stairs.

What the hell kind of emergency a cook could be having in a little-used lookout tower? If this were a ruse of some sort, he was going to strangle her. He was already perilously close to it—just on general principles.

He'd spent the entire day out in the fields and vineyards and had purposefully missed dinner, intending to avoid the sight and sound of her. He had awakened that morning with a dream that recalled in stunning detail their brief encounter in Crossan's forest. And he rose with her scent lingering alarmingly, in his head: pepper . . . cinnamon . . . cloves . . . a hint of smoke . . . bacon . . . yeasty bread . . . She was a whole damned dinner menu on the move. A portable feast. For the rest of the day he had been unable to get the unsettling impact of that potent blend out of his head.

When he reached the top landing, he paused a moment, looking down the narrow passage that led to the lookout. This had better be important.

Turning his wide shoulders so that they didn't brush the sides of the passage, he headed for that aged door and used the rope handle to pull it open. Light flooded the darkened passage around him and he blinked rapidly, trying to adjust to the brightness before he stepped into the sun-filled chamber.

As his vision cleared, there she was, standing on the balcony with the lowering sun behind her turning her hair to spun gold and the sky around her to a thousand shades of red. He tried to turn and stalk right back out the door, but his limbs were totally unimpressed by the panic rising in him and refused to obey.

"What the devil am I doing here?" he demanded. "Better yet, what are *you* doing here?"

But even as he spoke, his gaze slid to a linen-draped table on the balcony, laden with plate service and covered dishes. Behind her he could see pillows strewn on a stone bench. Silk pillows—his eyes widened in recognition—from his own chambers.

"You're having dinner, Your Lordship," she said, moving out of the light.

"I'm what?" His balking limbs managed to propel him forward enough for him to glimpse his own silver wine cup and trencher. "This is ridiculous—"

"It is not meant to be an assumption or imposition, milord," she declared. The way her hands were clasped tightly together at her waist betrayed a disarming bit of anxiety. "It is meant to be a pleasure." She waved to the mostly empty chamber. "Here you will have privacy and plenty of air to bear away any unwanted scents. You will be able to enjoy your food completely—aromas and all—for once. And I will serve you myself with as little intrusion as possible."

He should have banished her from the hall entirely, that first day. He should have locked her in the damned pantry that entire first week, and let her out only to cook. He should have sent her straight back to the convent and resigned himself to a diet of frumenty for the rest of his benighted days.

But he hadn't.

Now he should turn around and walk back down the stairs and demand to be fed in his hall, in his chair, as usual.

But he wouldn't.

She was moving closer, swaying, her supple body moving.

God help him.

That glow was back in her eyes and that tingling was back in his fingers.

"Please, milord, come and sit." When she reached for his hand he jerked back involuntarily. He could see she had to force herself to try again and, this time, let her succeed. "I believe you'll enjoy the food we have prepared for—"

"My men—"

"Have been told you'll be dining alone this evening." She poured some of the rich, red wine into his cup and pressed it into his hand. "Sit, milord. You won't be disappointed."

Most likely.

If he survived.

Chapter 18

GRIFFIN LOOKED AROUND THE MOSTLY empty chamber. The floor had been scrubbed scrupulously clean; there wasn't a trace of bird droppings or a spider web. Stacked against a near wall were several willow hampers, kettles, and crocks, and a set of poles for transporting them. Nearby was another small table laden with cloth-covered trays and bowls. He turned back to the table laid for him . . . trying to keep his wits about him . . . making himself think about what motives might lie behind this exceptional display.

The linen was as white as new. His own silver trencher and wine cup nestled in rings of pristine napkins. He needed a drink but when he started to sip, his cup was empty. The heat igniting in his stomach told him where the wine had gone. That alarmed him; he didn't remember drinking it.

Knowing he would probably regret it, he allowed himself to be pushed toward the bench and sat down onto the cushions. She nudged the table closer to him and lifted a lid on a thick earthen crock sitting on it. He could almost see the vapors curling around her head as she inhaled the aroma of the pottage.

"Ahhh." She smiled and began to ladle out what she called "Oxtail Brewet." It was a rich broth thick with beef and marrow, in which steeped barley, onion, pepper, and small, sweet red carrots. His mouth began to water.

"All I ask is . . ."

Here it comes, he thought, bracing his hands against the edge of the table. The change that came over his face made her hesitate.

". . . that you take the band from your nose and smell the food."

"Don't be absurd." Something akin to relief flooded through him.

"If you'd like, I'll leave. I'll wait outside and you can call for me when you're ready for the next course."

Was she serious? Gripping the table, he looked around and weighed her words. A light breeze ruffled his hair. She'd chosen a place high above the miasma of smells that came from the stables and pens, the smithy and storage barns, the dairy and slaughterhouse, the privies and middens. A place with a light breeze to dilute the intensity of the sensations. A place where he and his reactions couldn't be seen or heard or judged.

He stared at her without speaking. How had she known the exact conditions he needed in order to free his sense of smell? Then he realized: She had seen him without the band on his nose in the forest. She was certainly clever enough to deduce why he was drawn to it.

She had thought about him.

The pulse of warmth that idea generated in him said he was in trouble. He couldn't summon a grain of resistance to this calculated appeal to his senses.

He looked down at the rich brewet, picked up the spoon, and took a bite.

He closed his eyes. Beef and marrow and onion and pepper . . . with a touch of rich red wine. It rolled over his tongue and down his throat, sending a wave of response through his body. Ahhhh. He opened his eyes, chagrined to find he had closed them. What were those herbs that blended with the wine enough to speak their presence, but not enough to say their names?

By the third bite, he couldn't keep from groaning. By the fourth the curiosity and the impatience to experience the food fully were gaining the upper hand. By the fifth, he braced himself and ripped the steel band from his nose.

The assault of sensation he always feared and frequently encountered on his first breath . . . didn't happen. It was the breeze that saved him. His entire body relaxed as mild, clean air filled his head along with his lungs. Among the scents of hay and ripening oats and grinding wheat from the mill, he caught just enough of the remaining scents of horse and stable to feel at home. Then he lowered his head toward the bowl and inhaled.

The succulence of the beef broth and marrow seeped through his head, blending with and enhancing the tastes. Bay leaf and basil . . . wine from his own cellars . . . pepper freshly ground . . . beef . . . a trace of applewood smoke . . . it was ambrosial. He ate spoon after spoonful, holding each to his nose and relishing the complex blend of flavors and essences. And he felt the tight grip he held on his apparatus of sensual appreciation begin to slip.

He looked up, surprised to find her standing not far away, and shoved the bowl toward her with one ragged word.

"More."

As she refilled the bowl, he realized she was keeping downwind. Smart girl. He kept forgetting just how clever she was. As he consumed a second portion, she began to pull things from hampers to assemble the second course.

"Pie, milord. A golden pie of cheeses, mushrooms, crisped bacon, and onions." She cut a generous slice, set it on his trencher, and withdrew several paces. "I saw how you enjoyed the Herbed Chard and Cheese Pie and thought you might enjoy this one even more."

She was right.

He groaned fully now, no longer willing or able to hide his pleasure.

"Spices," he declared with his mouth full, pointing at the pie. "What herbs and spices are in there?"

"Thyme, milord. And pepper, of course. And lesser amounts of marjoram and rosemary." Her eyes widened as she watched him begin to sway on his seat, as if to some unheard melody.

"Do you have any idea how long it's been since I ate food like this?"

"Yesterday," she answered. "And the day before and the day before that. You've been eating food like this for two weeks, milord."

"Dear God."

He stuffed the rest of the piece in his mouth while she drew a bread trencher from a basket and slipped it onto his platter. Then she produced a crock and a covered pewter dish from another basket, and served him medallions of vinegar-marinated venison covered with a thick, aromatic civet made of raisins and almonds, bacon and onions, wine, and a blend of ginger and cinnamon. He gasped and grabbed a slice with his fingers.

"This is heavenly. Nectar. Fit for the angels themselves." He filled his mouth with it and moaned, concentrating on how the sweet and sour flavors blended flawlessly and filled his head.

Somewhere in the middle of that Sweet and Sour Civet of Venison, his appetite slid beyond his control. His mouth watered profusely, his stomach contracted as if it were still ravenously empty, and his belly and loins both ached with physical longing. He wanted more . . . wanted to smell it, inhale it, absorb it . . . revel in it. It was suddenly all he could do to sit still.

"Demoiselle Julia . . ." His voice scraped the bottom of its register as she came forward again with the flagon of wine to refill his cup.

"Yes, milord?"

"Sit."

"But, milord—"

"Sit!" He flung a finger at the end of the bench.

Julia sat. Clutching the flagon of wine to her breast. As far from him on the stone bench as she could get.

"I don't wish to taint the food with my own scents, milord," she said, her heart beating like the wings of a trapped butterfly.

"It doesn't matter where you stand, demoiselle. As long as you are in this chamber, I will smell you."

"Surely not, milord." She flushed, fighting the urge to stare at him. "I . . . I bathe regularly."

"Every two days. With a soap that has lavender in it."

"How do you—" Her brow knitted in dismay at the thought that occurred to her. "You can tell that?" He nodded.

"Just like I can tell that you spent the day with your hands in dough."

She glanced down at her hands, looking for evidence that lingered on them. They seemed spotless . . . even her fingernails. Then she realized there was probably flour dust still clinging to the apron she had worn all afternoon.

"I should really—" She started to rise, but he seized her hand and held it. When she sank back onto the bench, he brought her fingertips to his nose.

"The cherries with cinnamon . . . almonds . . . and raisins . . . can wait."

"How could you—did you really smell that? Or did you glimpse it when you came in?" She forced her gaze from his pleasure-bronzed features to the preparation table, across the chamber.

"You still don't understand," he said, leveling a penetrating look on her and reeling her closer. "Then I'll have to show you." He put her hand to his face and inhaled along each of her fingers. "Pastry . . . made with lard . . . and flour. You rolled them out yourself . . . and filled them with the fruit and nuts and spices . . . cinnamon and nutmeg." He closed his eyes as he smelled the back of her hand before turning back to her palm. "You draped the table yourself . . . the scent of new linen is on your hands." He worked his way across her palm and paused at her wrist. "Here, you used soap from the kitchen earlier . . . a harsh soap, heavy with lye."

"How"—she swallowed hard, mesmerized by the sight of his chiseled face pressed against her naked skin and the deep, intimate sound of his voice—"could you know that?"

"I know the scent of the soap Old Damon makes for my household." He pushed up her sleeve as he ran his nose along the pale, sleek skin of her inner arm. "And here is your lavender . . . and a hint of salt . . . the heat of the hearths in the kitchens made you sweat."

"Please, milord . . ." She could feel heat flooding her skin as if she were standing before Cheval's blazing hearths. "There are some things a woman prefers to keep to herself."

"Unfair, demoiselle." He reeled her still closer. "If I must give up my secrets to satisfy your wretched curiosity . . . then you must give up your secrets to assuage mine." He inhaled his way up her upper arm and then clamped a hand around her waist to draw her against him.

"But I have no secrets, milord," she said on a forced and nervous whisper. This unusual and determined seduction was *not* what she had in mind.

"You won't when I'm through with you," he murmured, pulling her onto his lap and burying his nose in the hollow of her throat. "Ummm . . . a touch of vinegar and a hint of honey . . . that damned lavender again . . ."

"Really, milord, I don't think—"

"Good. *Don't* think."

She could feel his breath at her ear and realized he was tracing her ear with his nose and lips. Every bit of marrow in her body began to turn liquid and seep out of her bones. She suddenly wished that his tantalizing stream of breath would slide inside her garments and flow over her entire body . . . bit by bit . . . shiver by shiver . . . thrill by entrancing thrill. Frissons of excitement raced along her shoulders and down her spine to coil in her lower body.

As he turned her to face him, she met the molten amber of his eyes and told herself that this was a very bad development. She shouldn't be here, on his lap, looking into his dark-centered eyes, and drinking in his scents even as he did hers . . . a vinegary tang of male sweat, sandalwood, sun-warmed hair, a hint of oil and metal from his hands and garments . . . the must of aged and well-worn leather . . . mint from the water he'd used to wash his hands in the hall . . . the sweet and sour spiciness of the venison on his breath. . . .

"Cherries," she said weakly, saving the rest of her strength for pushing away. Her movement must have surprised him; he allowed her to lurch up and scramble along the bench to find her feet. Once she was solidly on her own legs, she hurried to the table and began to stack sugar-dusted rissoles on a small wooden platter. The way her hands trembled and the unsteadiness of her knees alarmed her. Another moment or two on his lap and . . .

She turned and gasped, nearly dropping the platter. He was standing close behind her, simmering in a stew of sensory provocation and raw male hunger. And when he leaned toward her with his eyes glinting and his lips parted, she panicked and stuffed a cherry rissole in his mouth. He choked in surprise and grabbed the pastry from his mouth—not, however, whole. Fully half of the succulent pastry was still in his mouth and he had to either spit it out or chew and swallow.

She could have sworn she saw him shiver as the juice of the cherries filled his mouth and sent a burst of tart sweetness through his senses. As he chewed, he looked at the half-eaten pastry in his hand and bit into it again with a groan. Then he reached for another, then another. And then he reached for her.

He was so quick and she was so startled that she had no time to react. He pulled her hard against him, upending and trapping the whole tray full of pastries between them. She sputtered and tried to push away . . . but his muscular arms clamped around her like a band on a barrel and tightened. Then his lips closed over hers and all resistance, all thought . . . even time itself . . . stopped.

Her only surviving impulse was to melt and give herself over to the exploration of a kiss that had been interrupted on the road from Paris and had haunted her every night since.

His mouth was sweet with cherry juice and redolent with cinnamon and sugar and sweet almond cream. It was mildly shocking to her that he would share the taste that lingered in his mouth with her so intimately, and that she would find it so enjoyable. Her arms came up to clasp him as she responded with the urgency of an exploration a long time in the making. Heaven help her, she couldn't separate the taste of the pastry from the taste of him.

He slanted his mouth over hers, massaging, kneading her lips . . . teasing her tongue with his . . . and she opened to him, making small, helpless sounds of discovery with each new sensation and every new delight. His hands ran up and down her back and sank into the base of her thick braid. She arched upward to press harder against him, running her fingers up his corded neck and into his hair.

"Ummm . . . platter . . . ," she muttered against his lips.

"No problem," he muttered back, ripping the platter from between them and sending it clattering onto the floor. "Better?"

"Much."

She forced his mouth harder against hers and felt his groan of response vibrate all through her. Suddenly she was moving backward—it felt as if she were falling, weightless, floating, until she smacked into the wall and felt his body cover and press her back against it. Every part of her body came alive, demanding attention and craving fulfillment of the promise of pleasure washing through her. She molded herself against him, opening to his kisses, returning them without restraint . . . no longer capable of resisting the pleasures being spread before her. . . .

Banging came at the door and the sound seemed to explode around them.

She froze, her lips still captive, her heart still beating like a drum.

He froze, his body curled over and around her, taut and focused with desire and expectation.

Reality was being pounded back into the chamber with every fall of a fist on those weathered planks. "Milord!" It was Sir Reynard's voice. Something about "news."

Suddenly His Lordship was peeling himself from her body and staggering back, staring at the rattling door with something akin to fury. Then something of the urgency of his first knight's tone apparently penetrated the blood roaring in his head, and he called out: "Come in!"

The door flew open and Reynard ducked his head to step inside. Behind him were Axel and Greeve, their noses in the air, sniffing.

"Sorry to interrupt, milord," Reynard said with genuine regret. "But I knew you would want to hear straightaway— there's been hunting in the south forest." His expression became even more grave. "With *dogs*."

"Dammit." The count's big hands curled into fists. "You're certain it was hunting?"

"Packs. Ten to twenty animals each. And men on horseback . . . heavy mounts . . . riders most likely wearing armor."

"Verdun." His jaw clenched visibly. "What damage?"

"Deer. Fox. Wild boar. All savagely torn, half eaten, and left to rot."

The words seemed to carry some taint of the carnage they implied. Blinking, His Lordship staggered back and fumbled in his leather jerkin for the band to clamp across his nose.

"A thousand pardons, milord." Reynard glanced at her and his eyes widened. "I would not have disturbed you for anything less."

When the band for his nose was in place, His Lordship straightened, took a pair of breaths, and was once more in full control of his faculties.

"You did right, Reynard." Then he glanced at her and was jolted by the sight that held Reynard, Axel, and Greeve transfixed.

His look of horror caused Julia to realize that her lips felt hot and swollen and conspicuous. She look down at herself and found her apron and gown, from breast to knee, covered with squashed cherry rissoles. Her face flamed as she looked up and glimpsed a similar mess on the front of His Lordship's jerkin and tunic. The knights looked with astonishment from cook to count and back. As she tried frantically to think of a plausible explanation, one of the moist cherry pastries peeled from her gown and fell to the floor with a gooey *plop.*

"Dammit!" His Lordship roared, his face nearly as crimson as her own. Then he stalked across the chamber, struggling visibly to clamp a tighter control over his impulses. A moment later he turned back, his thoughts already shifted and fury etching its way across his face.

"Verdun and his damnable dogs—it's no less than we expected. He's trying to provoke me into an armed exchange."

Without a word to her, he stormed out of the chamber and down the stairs with Reynard at his heels. Axel and Greeve stared at her with broadening grins, then turned to follow their lord, muttering:

"Those must be some rissoles."

Outside, as they strode for the stables, Reynard scooped a finger full of cherry filling from Griffin's jerkin and popped it in his mouth.

"Ummm—"

"Not a damned word, Reynard, or I'll run you through. I swear it."

Chapter 19

THE HALL WAS ABUZZ BY THE TIME JU-
lia collected herself, cleaned her gown, and wobbled
her way downstairs. Fortunately, the topic of feverish interest in the hall had nothing to do with her or squashed
cherry pastries. With knee-weakening relief, she heard the
men talking about dogs—packs of dogs in the forest—and
finally it registered that it was something about dogs in the
forest that had sent His Lordship storming from the sentry
chamber.

"Damnable dogs," growled Lucien, the head of His
Lordship's sword and pike men. "They rip game to shreds
just for the pleasure of it."

"A dozen deer . . . a half dozen foxes . . . a whole score
of wild boar, I heard," a nearby fellow supplied a group of
eager ears. "The forest's knee-deep in blood."

"That's nothin' new," came a harrumph from another
soldier. "That bit o' forest's cursed. Time and again, it's run
red with gore."

"It's them devil dogs," one of the serving women declared, glancing around the hall. "Thanks be . . . His Lordship don't allow them filthy beasts to roam Grandaise, or to
skulk about in the hall chewin' on folks' ankles."

Dogs, it seemed, suffered grave disrepute on Grandaise . . . which accounted for the absence of hounds in the hall and on the estate grounds in general. On her way back to the kitchens, to oversee the evening cleaning, she paused long enough to glance about the hall and recall her surprise that there were no rushes on the floor and no dogs running about to pick up the scraps and bones that fell from the tables.

"Well?" Regine and the rest of the kitchen folk gathered around to hear the results of their most valiant culinary effort to date. "His Lordship . . . what did he think of our Oxtail Brewet?" The little nun's eyes sparkled with anticipation. "Did he swoon with pleasure?"

Julia tried heroically to ignore the way her face caught fire.

"He was more than pleased. He removed the band from his nose and smelled it all and proclaimed it fit for the angels." The others murmured excitedly and grinned at one another. "He wanted to know every ingredient in the Lorraine Pie. And the venison—that was when he spoke of feeding the angels."

"And the rissoles?" Old Albee looked at her with hope in his age-faded eyes. "What did he say about our cherry treats?"

"He"—she flushed crimson—"couldn't say enough about them. It wouldn't surprise me if he requested them again, soon."

Smiles and congratulations broke out all around.

"So, tell me. What really happened?" Regine demanded later, as the door of their chamber closed behind them and they settled, exhausted, onto their beds.

Julia removed her slippers and began to rub her feet.

"It was as I said. He thought the food was wonderful."

"And?"

"And . . . it took a while for him to remove the band from his nose. When he finally did, I glimpsed the intensity he lives with day by day. You know . . . he smelled the rissoles and told me what was in them before I even took them out of the hamper." She grew thoughtful and spoke her thoughts aloud. "What must it be like to be besieged by such powerful sensations? To perceive so many things, so strongly that they all mix into a great, oppressive slurry? To feel such a potent invasion on every breath that it is tempting at times not to breathe at all?" She shook her head. "It's no wonder that he refuses to smell anything."

"Goodness." Regine was clearly disturbed by Julia's description. "I had no idea." Then her gaze came back to the cherry stains that had seeped through and around the edges of Julia's apron. "But, he liked the food."

"He loved it."

"He didn't throw anything at you or knock anything over?"

"Of course not." Julia frowned and sat straighter.

"Then how did you get rissole filling all over you?"

Julia's face flamed and glanced down at her gown. "Oh. Well. I-I was holding the tray of pastries when Sir Reynard and the others burst through the door with news about dogs in the forest. They startled me and I stumbled and fell right into that tray of sweets." Abruptly, she tilted her head and launched into an altogether different subject. "You know, I wondered why I seldom saw hounds about the demesne. It always struck me as odd, considering how noblemen usually love to hunt. Some of the men tonight said that His Lordship does hunt, but with falcons rather than dogs."

Regine blinked at Julia's abrupt change of topic.

"I thought that was strange, too," she finally said with a shrug. "And look at Fleur and her clan. People hand-feed them and talk to them and even pet them. Pigs seem to have replaced dogs here. How could such a thing have happened? I mean, hounds have fur and pigs have . . ."

As she prepared for bed Julia listened with one ear to Regine's dissertation on the unprecedented reverence of pigs on Grandaise. But her thoughts kept returning to His Lordship . . . the way the breeze tugged at his dark hair . . . the way his jaw muscles flexed as he ate . . . the trill of expectation that swept her as their eyes met . . . the pleasure that suffused her when he claimed her lips.

Her time with him had been intensely personal and pleasurable. She had intended it to be. She had wanted to see his eyes light, his features soften, and his broad shoulders lose their defensiveness and rigidity. She wanted to see passion and pleasure in his face and to know that she'd had some part in the making of it.

Now, as she slipped into her narrow bed, she felt a lingering glow within her own heart and realized that she had never felt such warmth and such a sense of belonging as when he wrapped his arms around her and caressed her lips with—

She froze mid-thought, mid-breath.

His pleasure . . . his embrace . . . his kisses . . .

Heaven help her . . . she had searched for a path from his stomach to his well-guarded heart, but what she had found was a path to her own stubborn desires! It struck her with a horrifying clarity of vision that the giving of pleasure brought a unique and beguiling pleasure of its own. And such pleasure, once experienced, begat a growing need for more of the same. Already she had been thinking of more dinners, more embraces, more kisses. . . .

She sat up in the dark, her heart beating frantically.

Madness.

What about her sane and sensible plan to provide herself with a future? What about courting and wooing the men of his hall and the visitors to his table until one of them agreed to marry her? Desperately, she tried to banish the memory of the heat and possession of his kisses. But the more she tried to sweep it aside, the more vivid and emphatic it became in her mind.

She wanted him with every particle of her being, even knowing he was destined to live his life with another. And the worst of it was that she couldn't imagine wanting another man—any other man—the way she wanted him. How was she supposed to look for a husband—someone to share her bed and board and the balance of her days— knowing that His Lordship already occupied the choicest parts of her heart?

* * *

AT DAYBREAK, THE NEXT MORNING, HIS
Lordship rode out with Sir Reynard and a party of men to
inspect the damage firsthand and take steps to make sure
the wholesale slaughter of game in his forest did not happen again. The hall was unusually quiet as Julia led her
servers up the steps with bread and eggs and crisp fried bacon to break the fast of the remainder of the garrison.

As she strolled along the undraped tables, greeting the
men of the garrison and chatting with the men and women
of the household, Bertrand de Roland entered, spotted her,
and headed straight for her.

"The very face I had hoped to see." He gave her a
courtly nod. "I have something for you, demoiselle."

"Oh?" She watched with interest as he reached into a
small leather pouch that dangled from the side of his belt.

"Here they are." He produced three perfect white mushrooms, displaying them on his open hand. "What do you
think?"

"They're lovely, Sir Bertrand." Her eyes widened.
"Where on earth did you find them?"

"In the woods—not far away." His smile broadened. "I
saw them and thought of rice and mushroom stuffing . . . a
cheese and mushroom tart . . . sausage-filled mushrooms. . . ." He placed a hand over his heart as if to slow it.
"There are hundreds, thousands of them, and this is the
perfect week for harvesting. They are just beginning to
open." He slid the mushrooms into her hand. "I am due out
on patrol shortly, but I had to come and tell you about
them."

She closed her eyes and smelled their earthy, woodlike
fragrance, already thinking of a dozen dishes that would
tempt the palate and try the will. Opening her eyes, she
grabbed him by the sleeve.

"Please, Sir Bertrand. You have to show me where they
grow before you leave on patrol. I simply must have these
for His Lordship's dinner."

That was how she, Regine, and a trio of the kitchen
girls—cooks in training—came to be traipsing into the
woods west of the vineyards that morning. They carried

willow baskets, linen napkins for protecting the precious cargo, and small knives for harvesting. The student cooks listened eagerly on the way to Julia's explanation of the humors and culinary properties of mushrooms and of how to tell an edible from a poison one. Sir Bertrand, who escorted them on foot while leading his horse, added bits of lore regarding the woods they had entered.

"The southern part of this wood was where the count's brother was killed." He waved down the gasps and jitters of anxiety. "But the mushrooms are at the northern edge, and the Count of Verdun's holdings are well to the west. You're in no danger." He gave Julia a roguish smile. "Not with me along."

Julia smiled back, thinking that his eyes shone with a peculiar glint just then. But that fleeting thought escaped as they came to the first patches of mushrooms growing in the dark, woody soil at the foot of a stand of venerable trees. She instructed the girls how to pick so as not to damage future production, and left a pair of them to collect those mushrooms while she and Regine and a third girl headed farther into the forest with Sir Bertrand.

Soon they came to a stretch of forest floor that seemed to be paved with small white cobblestones. It was a veritable sea of mushrooms! Laughing with surprise and delight, she set Regine and the other kitchen girl to harvesting, and hurried forward to see how far the growing bed extended. It went on and on through the huge old trees whose leaves provided the rich compost that nourished the edible buttons. She followed, fascinated by the way it sometimes trailed off and then reappeared around the next bend of the narrow path.

For a time she heard Sir Bertrand behind her, but he was scarcely able to keep up with her eager pace. With her thoughts occupied with ways of drying and storing the mushrooms for use during the rest of the year, she paid no attention to the rustle of leaves behind her or the snap of a small branch nearby. After a time, she stooped to pick several additional specimens and examine them for evidence of the red pigment that would mark them as poisonous.

Happily, there was none. She began to imagine great strings of mushrooms drying in the sun outside the kitchen, and didn't notice a trio of stealthy figures moving up behind her.

Hands clamped tightly over her mouth and she flailed as she was yanked and fell backward onto her rear. Men—two, young and powerful—pinned her to the ground, one stifling her screams and grappling furiously with her arms while the other knelt on her legs to keep them from thrashing.

"She's stronger than she looks," one of them muttered breathlessly as they worked to contain and bind her.

"She works as a cook," came a familiar voice that caused her to cease struggling and look up. Towering above her was Sir Bertrand, holding several loops of rope. "Yes," he declared to her unspoken charge, "I'm afraid I've led you into something of a trap. But you won't be harmed, demoiselle. And you will see . . . it will all work out for the best."

She condemned him to the farthest reached of perdition, though not a word of it reached his ears. She thrashed her head trying to free her mouth to scream, but they snatched a bit of linen from her gathering basket and stuffed it into her mouth. The thirsty cloth wicked up the moisture in her mouth and throat, rendering her incapable of anything more than a parched croak.

They used Sir Bertrand's ropes to bind her hands and feet, then hoisted her across the saddle of a horse, face down. She kicked and thrashed, trying to relieve the pressure on her ribs, struggling to draw breath. Then someone mounted the horse behind her and it took off as if it were launched from a bow. The constant bouncing and jostling pounded the breath from her and—robbed of air—she felt everything going slowly darker until she lost consciousness.

It was some time before Sister Regine topped her basket of mushrooms and stood up to arch backward over her hands and relieve the strain on her muscles. She asked the others if they had seen Julia and, hearing that they hadn't, went to look for her. Some distance farther down the path, she found Julia's basket, empty and discarded, beside a badly trampled patch of mushrooms. She called repeatedly for her friend and charge, but there was no response. Alarm filled her and she rushed back to the others.

"I can't find Julia. She seems to have dropped her basket and . . ." She held it up and discovered that it had been crushed on one side. The ominous implication of that damage caused her face to drain of color. "Something has happened to her." She whirled around, peering through the trees in every direction in an attempt to locate their knightly escort. "Quickly—where is Sir Bertrand?"

THAT SAME EVENING, GRIFFIN, REYNARD, and their men rode back through the stone and iron gates of Grandaise with grim expressions. They had spent most of the daylight riding the borders of the estate, questioning cottagers and tenants, and inspecting the sites in the forest where game had been slain and left to rot.

"It looked like a damned slaughterhouse," Reynard said.

"Worse." Griffin turned to the guardsman Heureaux, who rode on his left. "I want you to choose some men and take them out to the sites of the kills tomorrow morning. Whatever is left . . . bury it."

The burly guardsman nodded and rode straight to the garrison barracks to draft several men.

Griffin watched him go, then instead of riding to the stables and handing off his mount, he headed for the front doors of his hall. As onerous as the day's duty had been, it at least had kept him from dwelling on that debacle with Julia last night. He'd made a fool of himself . . . sniffing and pawing her like some damned animal. Then he'd done exactly what he'd vowed never to do; he'd kissed her and set hands to her as if she were his for the taking.

The memory of her standing there with her lips kiss swollen and her apron and gown covered with squashed cherry rissoles sent a shudder of humiliation through him whenever he thought of it . . . which he had done roughly once each hour since it happened. He deserved every sly and suspicious look his men had tossed his way. He was sworn to protect and defend her, after all, from the very predations he'd subjected her to last night.

It was no good arguing that she didn't mind or that she'd participated willingly, even eagerly, in that lapse of sanity and judgment. He was a nobleman who'd won knightly spurs and was bound by a strict code of honor. He was responsible for her virtue . . . had promised to safeguard, not seduce, her.

"Milord!" Arnaud the Steward came rushing down the steps to meet him, his silver chain of office bobbing on his chest. The little nun, Sister Regine, was at his heels. One look at her reddened eyes and strained countenance and Griffin knew there was trouble.

"She's gone, milord," Arnaud declared, wringing his age-thinned hands.

"Taken. She's been *taken*," Sister Regine corrected, then addressed Griffin directly. "Abducted, milord. Stolen. You're sworn to protect her—you have to find her and get her back!"

"Abducted?" He slid from his saddle and bounded up the steps to seize Sister Regine's wringing hands. "When? How?"

"We went out to collect mushrooms," Regine declared in a tearful voice. "Sir Bertrand said he'd found some in the forest and she insisted on going to see them and pick some for your dinner."

"The *forest?* Which direction?"

"That way." She pointed to the west and tension wrenched tighter in a band around his chest. "Sir Bertrand took several of us. We were all together at first, but she wanted to see how large a crop it was and wandered off with him."

"Where is Bertrand now?"

"Gone, too, milord." Axel came hurrying out of the hall in time to answer that question. "We've looked everywhere."

"We thought he had just ridden off on patrol like he said he was supposed to do," Sister Regine said, looking a bit sick at the admission. "But when we got back to the house,

Sir Greeve said he hadn't appeared for duty. Perhaps he was taken, too."

"Bertrand?" Griffin straightened. "He would never have allowed her to be taken. Or himself, for that matter. Not without blood being shed."

"I did see him give her mushrooms in the hall this morning, seigneur," Axel said reluctantly, producing the damaged basket from behind him. "And there were hoof-prints around the place where they found this."

She was gone. Then it struck him: "gone" did not necessarily mean "abducted." She had ambitions of her own. And Bertrand had shown interest. . . .

"Sister, has Sir Bertrand been visiting the kitchens?" he demanded. She looked a bit surprised, then quickly denied that possibility.

"You've forbidden the men to visit, milord, and they've obeyed," she said. "Sir Bertrand included. Only kitchen folk venture into the kitchens now."

Assuming that was true—Lord, he was doubting the word of nuns now!—it only meant that Bertrand was not likely to have run off with her. Thin comfort. There were probably at least sixty others in his garrison who were equally besotted . . . with either her or her food . . . it was hard to tell which.

He scowled, thought for a moment, then took Sister Regine by the elbow and ushered her to the path that led to the western gate. "Show me where he took you." He called over his shoulder to Reynard: "Follow us with fresh horses, and roust a score of men to help with the search."

As they hurried along the path—him striding along with his mail clinking dully and her trotting alongside trying to hold her hem up and her veil down—he glanced at her anxious face and felt the damnedest urge to reassure them both.

"I'll find her, Sister," he declared from between clenched jaws. "And if she's been abducted, I'll do whatever it takes to get her back."

Griffin studied the hoofprints and the destroyed mush-rooms at the side of the path, reading in those signs confirmation of his fears. There had been a struggle. He sent Sister Regine back up the path, out of sight, telling her to keep the others back until he called for them.

When he was alone, he took a deep breath. It had been a long time since he had tried to harness and control his sense of smell. He had once, with the help of Grand Jean, learned to concentrate enough to select out the things he wanted to smell from the waves of sensation that bombarded him. But it had been seven years. . . . He removed the band from his nose, braced himself, and took a long, slow breath.

Mushrooms and dark, damp, faintly fetid soil . . . old decay . . . rotted wood now mostly dust. Through that brownness came a pungent tang of green leaves and undergrowth and wild herbs. As he knelt on one knee and braced on his arms over the place where the mushrooms had been trampled, he caught a hint of something familiar.

Closing his eyes, he focused desperately and began to pare away the clutter of sensation that kept him from pursuing the scents he needed to find.

Suddenly there it was. Her scent. Faint, but distinctive. A heart-stopping blend of pepper, wheat flour, cinnamon, woman musk, and lavender. His heart began to pound with both longing and anger, and he lost the scent amid a storm of rising emotions that splintered his concentration.

Once again he was assailed by the scents of broken mushrooms and churned earth and horse smells. It took a few moments for him to regain enough control to realized that he hadn't just lost her scent . . . it had been overtaken . . . transported . . . on horseback.

Shoving to his feet, he followed that horse scent along the path and stood for a moment facing the direction it seemed to have taken her. West.

It was Verdun. He would stake his life on it. But did he trust his volatile perceptions enough to risk Julia's life and the lives of his people on the things that they told him?

Chapter 20

JULIA FELT HERSELF BEING HOISTED and then draped over something—someone— and realized she was being carried into a house or a building of some sort. Her thick braid dangled and jiggled freely from the back of her head, attracting the attention of several parti-colored hounds, who made a game of nipping at it while dodging the feet and fists of the men who carried her.

Before her tortured gaze, a badly worn tunic and a pair of oft-patched woolen tights strained to contain a monumental pair of buttocks. Given her proximity to that part of her abductor's anatomy and the fact that she had to drag each inhalation through her nose, she was almost overcome by the fumes he emitted every time he strained and rose a step. By the time they reached the top of a set of spiraling stone stairs, she was woozy and nauseated and had wicked ringing in her ears.

"So"—came a strident-sounding male voice—"this is Grandaise's *tart*."

She was dumped unceremoniously onto a bench and had to twist to the side and hook her legs beneath the seat to keep from tumbling off. A man leaned close and grabbed her chin to look at her. Apparently he couldn't see her much better than she could see him, for he ordered her captors to remove her gag to better appraise her.

"You're sure this is the one?" he demanded, clearly expecting something other than a tousled young female with unfocused green eyes and a burnished gold braid tainted with dog slobber. She worked harder to make her eyes both focus on the same thing, and soon found herself face-to-face with a tall, slender man in a wine-colored velvet tunic with matching hose and sleeves. He scowled at her and she would have answered in kind, but she was too busy trying to get her aching jaws to close and her parched mouth and throat to moisten.

"She's little more than a green twig." Her captor made a face. "Grandaise has appallingly common taste in females."

He drew back out of range before she could make her jaws work well enough to bite his nose. Then he strolled back and forth, fondling a small, elegant eating knife. With a wave of his hand he ordered her feet released, and her abductors went one better and pulled her upright on the bench.

"Do you know who I am?"

With her vocal apparatus not sufficiently primed, she was forced to answer with a shake of her head. But, the motion must have shaken her wits back into place, for in the next instant she realized he could only be—

"Bardot, the Comte de Verdun. Your lover's bitter enemy. Although"—he rolled his eyes—"*bitter* may be understating it a bit. I'd like to cut off his head, scoop out his brains, and use his skull for a drinking cup." His sardonic tone undercut none of the seriousness of that desire. "But until I have that pleasure . . . until he gets off his dead arse and comes out to fight me like a man . . . I shall have to make do with capturing and holding his scrawny little mistress." He gave a smirk and pointed to her with the knife. "That's you."

"Not . . . mistress," she rasped out. "Cook." The effort of speaking produced painful tearing and stinging sensations in her throat.

"Whichever." He brushed the distinction aside. "The

important thing is, he wants you. By now Bertrand will have scurried back to Grandaise to tell him you were carried off by my men. What do you think . . . will the Beast be enraged enough at losing you to break the truce our sovereign has imposed on us?"

Before she could respond, door hinges creaked nearby and he swung his razor-sharp glare to whomever had just entered the chamber.

"Well, well. Here is someone you might remember. I believe you encountered our Martin de Gies in Paris."

She had to turn her whole body in order to move her throbbing head. By the door stood the knight who had bought her sugared oranges at the spice merchant's stall. He wore the same red-and-white tabard and a carefully contained expression.

"Martin, look who has just arrived . . . your little friend from the fair." His smile was the kind that gave pleasure a bad name. "I'm putting you in charge of securing her under lock and key, and making sure she is suitably uncomfortable."

Soon she was being trundled back down the winding stairs, bustled along a passage that gave her a glimpse of an impressive hall, and up another set of steps to another tower room. This one was far smaller and more spare than the count's silk-draped quarters. There was one shuttered window set deep into rounded stone walls that at one time had been whitewashed. The stone floor was strewn with rushes that were disintegrating from sheer age, and the place had a chilled and musty air of disuse. Sir Martin strode to the window and threw open the shutters to admit some fresh air. With a snap of his fingers, he ordered his men to untie her.

"This will be your home for the foreseeable future," he said, looking around the chamber . . . everywhere but at her.

"Please . . . you cannot do this," she declared in a whisper, rubbing her wrists.

Sir Martin ignored her as he lifted and dropped the straw-stuffed ticking on the bed, watching the *poof* of dust it emitted with a glare. "That will have to go."

"As soon as His Lordship learns where I am, he'll—"

She halted, realizing that she wasn't certain what he would do . . . besides have frumenty for dinner. But she needed a threat of some kind. "He'll come after me. There may be bloodshed."

"That, I believe, is exactly what milord Verdun is counting on," he responded grimly. Then he waved his men out the door and strode to the portal himself. "I'll send up a fresh ticking, some linen, and some heated water." He turned back for a moment and looked directly at her. There was a trace of true regret in his sober brown eyes. "There will be men outside your door at all times with orders to bring me word if you should need anything."

The moment the door closed behind him, she launched herself at the window and stretched across the deep window well to reach the modest opening. It was as she feared; the chamber was high up in a corner tower. Below were buildings and walls, beyond them stretched a swath of what seemed to be fields and vineyards, and beneath her lay a sheer stone wall. No possibility of escape here. She dragged a stool from the corner and brushed away the dust before sinking onto it.

Misery poured over her in waves as the full impact of her situation settled on her. She was captive in the stronghold of Griffin of Grandaise's hated enemy, sitting in a tower with her entire body aching and her throat cracked and burning with dryness. When His Lordship learned where she was, he would face the choice of either battering down thick stone walls to get her back or simply cutting his losses and looking for another—

She held her breath.

What if he just left her there? Her heart began to beat frantically, which, perversely, helped to restore feeling to her stiff, swollen hands. Surely he wouldn't do that. He had to answer for her whereabouts and condition to the abbess and the duke of Avalon in a year or so. She looked around the musty, little used chamber and felt her spirits sink.

A year.

Tears formed in her eyes and she refused to let them fall.

Surely His Lordship would get sick of frumenty before that.

FROM THE DEEPENING SHADOWS OF A STAND of ancient trees, a cloaked figure watched an armored horseman arrive in the glen and dismount. The rider searched the trees and after a moment, the cloaked figure stepped out and lowered his hood to reveal a shock of wispy white hair on an age-shrunken frame.

"It took you long enough," the old man said. "Is it done?"

"It is." Bertrand de Roland removed his helm and stood towering above the gnarled figure. "The girl is at Verdun's. Grandaise is no doubt in a fury."

The old man studied both the knight and his response.

"If you went back to Grandaise, as I told you, then why do you speak of doubts?" His dark eyes bored into the knight, who shifted silently and uncomfortably from foot to foot. "You didn't go, I take it."

"Grandaise returned early. By the time I delivered the girl to Verdun, his men were already scouring the northern woods," Bertrand said tautly. "If they'd found me, alive and unharmed, I would have had to explain how I managed to escape while I allowed her to be captured. I decided it was better that I not return to Grandaise."

"Damn your eyes!" The old man brandished knotty fists in Bertrand's face. "You were to take the girl to Verdun and then go back to Grandaise—to learn Lord Griffin's plans." The old man fairly vibrated with rising anger. "Now we have no way of knowing how close we are to a fight between Grandaise and Verdun."

"It will happen soon enough, milord. Grandaise is fiercely possessive of the cook. When he learns Verdun has her—"

"And just how will he learn this, Bertrand, eh? If you are not there to tell him it was Verdun's men, how will he know where to look for her?"

"Before I headed south, I saw him and his men searching

the woods. I'm sure they came upon the tracks Verdun's henchmen made and followed them toward his castle."

"You're sure, are you?" The old man glared furiously at him. "Coward." He struck Bertrand across the face. "You were afraid to face him—afraid he would see the mewling, sniveling coward in you!"

Bertrand staggered back, holding his cheek, shame and fury erupting in him.

"You have no idea how it has been for me, old man," he shouted, stepping forward, then back, then to the side in agitation. "Living and training under his hand . . . eating at his table . . . sharing quarters with his men . . . pretending to be his loyal vassal . . . and all the while—"

"All the while forgetting your purpose," the old man spat through shrunken lips. "I can see you need reminding." He studied Bertrand for a long moment, then gave a short, sharp whistle.

Out of the shadows four men materialized. Big men who moved with stealth and purpose. And their purpose was to carry out the orders of the grasping hand that now gestured to Bertrand's braced form.

"Make him look as if Verdun's men caught him, and he actually put up a fight."

"MILORD!" AXEL CAME BARRELING INTO THE hall of Grandaise the next morning, out of breath and stumbling, frantic with haste. "It's Bertrand . . . come . . ."

Griffin jumped up from the head table where he was meeting with Reynard and rushed out of the doors. He stopped dead at the sight of Greeve and one of the younger knights riding hell-bent for the front doors with a body draped across a horse between them. He bolted to intercept them and helped Axel and Reynard lift the injured Bertrand from the horse and ferry him into the hall, where they laid him on one of the tables.

"We found him in a field north of the forest," Greeve said. "He was trying to make his way back, milord, and his strength gave out."

Griffin assessed the damage and sucked a breath at the blood on Bertrand's battered face and bare hands. The loyal knight was battered and bleeding in more than one place. Who knew what injuries he carried inside him.

"The bastards," Griffin ground out, cradling the battered knight in his arms and peeled the knight's hauberk back. "Bertrand, you're home . . . you're safe." He winced at the sight of the blood matted in his hair. "Who did this? Who took Julia and beat you like this?"

Bertrand managed to crack open his blackened eyes and move his swollen lips. His voice was weak but audible enough to tell Griffin what he needed to know.

"Ver-dun."

They carried Bertrand to one of the upper chambers and sent for the physician that served Grandaise. While they waited for word of Bertrand's condition, Griffin paced and sorted his options, and then called for parchment, ink, and his quills. By the time it was announced that Bertrand's wounds were not as severe as they first appeared—he would recover, Griffin had charted his course of action.

He called a council of his elder knights in the hall to announce his decision.

"Reynard"—he laid a hand on his first knight's shoulder—"I intended to send you to your father, the baron, to ask for a force of men to bolster my garrison. Now I must ask you to do that and something more . . . something that I would entrust to no one else." He looked around the circle of solemn faces and back to Reynard. "I am sending you to the king with news of Verdun's treachery."

A murmur of response went through the others. A difficult task indeed.

"I have written a letter telling of my obligation to the convent and the Duke of Avalon regarding Julia of Childress. I ask the king to command that Verdun return her to me, unharmed, as soon as possible. If the king will not do so, or if he does and Verdun fails to comply, I am under an obligation of honor to retrieve her from Verdun by force of arms." He stared into the earnest face of his most trusted vassal. "You, Reynard, must convey that which my letter cannot . . . my desire to obey his commands . . . my hope to avoid bloodshed . . . and my determination to fight if she is not returned. You must make him see that it is a matter of honor, not vengeance. That I am the one trespassed upon."

"You may count on me, milord," Reynard said soberly.

Griffin took a deep breath and handed Reynard the sealed leather pouch containing the letter. "Give your father my best. And Godspeed."

The knights clasped his arm, thumped him on the back, and escorted him out to his mount. Three guardsmen on fast horses waited to accompany him. As they watched the foursome race down the road and out of the gate, Griffin was already planning his next step.

"We have to be prepared to fight," he told his men, "with or without Crossan's men and the king's permission. I must send a message to Verdun, demanding that he return Julia." He gave them a rueful smile. "Which of you feels like pulling an ogre's beard?"

THE TWO LONGEST DAYS OF JULIA'S LIFE passed as she waited, isolated in her prison chamber. Conditions slowly improved; they brought her a new mattress and blankets and at her request, a scrub brush and a pail of water and some vinegar. She gathered the old rushes and tossed them out the window, scrubbed the stone floor, and then swept the cobwebs from the room with the cloths they provided. Having done all she could to improve her surroundings, she was reduced to pacing and thinking about Sir Bertrand's betrayal and her capture, and then to reciting prayers and recipes and Proverbs and whatever else came to mind. She asked for a priest to hear her confession, hoping to be able to persuade the priest to intercede for her in the human plane as well as the heavenly one. But she was told she would have to wait until he returned from blessing the grapevines, which might take several days.

The nights were the worst. Lying there in the dark, feeling the strangeness of the place and the animosity that seemed to emanate from the very walls, she sought comfort in the memories of Grandaise and of its enigmatic master. One thought led to another and before she knew it, she was reliving his kisses, the feel of his strong arms around her, and the pleasure of watching him consume her food and revel in the scents and tastes she had prepared specially for him.

But the pleasures of those dreams always gave way to destructive images of Grandaise in flames and the men of the garrison lying sprawled on a battlefield, and she awakened with guilt settling on her chest like a hundredweight of iron.

She rose that third morning to another empty day, feeling tired and dispirited and worrying about what was happening at Grandaise. Was Sir Bertrand back in the hall, back at His Lordship's table, plying his duplicitous comradery? As she splashed water on her face, she heard voices outside the door and suddenly the planking panel burst open to reveal the guards tussling with a flurry of hair and silk.

"Let me go, you brutes! How dare you lay hands on me? I could have you drawn and quartered!"

It was a young woman at the center of what could only be called a storm of hair, bashing the startled and anxious guards with her fists.

"Let me go! I have a right to go wherever I please!" Clearly, the guards disagreed. Desperate now, she stiffened and summoned her most potent threat. "I'll tell my father you touched me—that you fondled me—that you tried to force me—"

They jerked their hands from her as if she scalded them and she scuttled back into the chamber, glaring furiously at them.

"Fine." She wrenched her disarranged gown back into place and brushed her wildly tangled hair back out of her face with exaggerated dignity. "Now close the door. Unless you want your prisoner to escape."

The door slammed shut and the maid smoothed her rumpled blue silk as she turned; her cheeks were rosy from the exertion of trying to break *into* Julia's prison.

"Can you believe that? The wretches wouldn't let me in!"

"Why on earth would you want to get in?" Julia asked.

The girl halted in the midst of taming her hair and looked her up and down.

"I figured I should have a look at you. Seeing as how we're fellow prisoners." She folded her arms. "And you're bedding my future husband."

Chapter 21

JULIA'S JAW WENT SLACK AS SHE STARED at the lovely young woman who had invaded her prison. After a moment she recovered enough to say: "You're the count's daughter?"

"I have a name," the girl declared defiantly. "Sophie Marie. Everybody seems to forget that." She stalked a bit closer to Julia. "Here, I'm just the count's daughter, the count's 'issue,' or the count's spawn . . . depending on who is talking." She stalked still closer. "But I'm *Sophie*. Sophie of Verdun."

"Well, Sophie of Verdun, I'm Julia of Childress." She squared her shoulders. "And I've never bedded anybody, much less your future husband."

Sophie studied her skeptically.

"That's not what my father says. He says you fornicate with the Beast regularly. Constantly. Incessantly."

"There is no 'fornicating' at Grandaise. Believe me. Least of all with your future—what do you mean: *the Beast?*"

"The Beast of Grandaise. The count. He's a raging, ravenous beast."

"He is not."

"Of course he is. That's why they call him the Beast of Grandaise."

"He is *not* a beast." Julia planted her fists at her waist. "He's a good man. An honorable and noble man. He's handsome and strong and capable and generous and considerate and honest—"

"How handsome?"

Julia blinked at the interruption.

"Very handsome."

"Of course, you'd say that," Sophie said with a huff. "You're bedding him."

"I am *not*." Julia folded her arms irritably. "He's tall—quite tall—and has broad shoulders and a noble carriage. His dark hair is silky and his eyes are an unusual golden color. He has a strong jaw and chin, but his features are nobly cut."

"Well, if he's so handsome, why do they call him 'the Beast'?"

"I have no idea," Julia said. "I didn't know he was called 'the Beast.' "

"Well, I won't marry him," Sophie insisted. "I'd rather go back to the convent."

"You had a calling to the religious life?" Julia recalled Reynard saying that Verdun's daughter had recently come home from a convent.

"Me? A nun?" Sophie fairly choked on an involuntary laugh. "I hated the convent. All of that prayer and penitence . . . always 'forgive us' this and 'cleanse our sins' that. When did we ever have a chance to get besmirched with sin in the first place?" She headed for the narrow bed and sat down forcefully on one end. "Not that things are much better here.

"When I found out what my father planned for me, I hoped that I could get somebody to bed and corrupt me so he couldn't marry me off." She gave a defiant huff. "I've tried Sir Martin and then every knight in the garrison . . . not one of the cowards will lay so much as a finger on me. They're all scared witless of my father. And *he* behaves as if I'm a bother to have around . . . he's constantly sending me to my chambers." She looked around Julia's chamber and gave a sigh of disappointment. "It seems I've just traded one prison for another. And I have yet another prison waiting at Grandaise."

Silence descended as Julia studied the young woman and felt a kinship with her desire to be granted a person-hood, an identity, a life of her own.

"You know, don't you, that your marriage was decreed by the king himself?"

"Yes, I know." Sophie clasped her hands between her knees, looking dejected. "This stupid feud . . . no one even remembers how it started. All of that fighting and hurting and even killing . . . I don't see how disposing of one reluc-tant virgin will somehow make everything right."

There were probably all kinds of arguments to be made in favor of the peace-through-marriage approach to diplo-macy, but just now, sacrificing Sophie's virtue and freedom and forcing His Lordship to make babies on someone who was terrified of him made no sense to Julia. She settled across from Sophie on a stool.

"You know, I came from a convent, too."

"You did?" Sophie looked up. "How did you fall into the Beast's clutches?"

Julia gave her a censuring look.

"Contrary to what your father believes, I am *not* the count's mistress. I was brought from the Convent of the Brides of Virtue to cook for His Lordship." When Sophie looked askance at her, she raised her right hand. "It's true—I swear it. His Lordship has a condition that renders most ordi-nary food unpalatable to him. His men stumbled upon our convent, ate some of my food, and carried word of it to him. When he was in Paris not long ago, he traveled to our con-vent and hired me from the abbess for a term of one year. She sent one of the sisters along—Sister Regine—to chaperone me, so that I can take vows when I return to the convent."

"You want to take religious vows?" Sophie was clearly horrified.

"No, no . . . I don't. That was why I agreed to come in the first place. I hoped to get out of going back to the con-vent by finding someone willing to marry me."

"And how have you done?" Sophie studied her. "Found any possibilities?"

Julia thought of the dismal prospect of trying to win a husband under His Lordship's nose. Assuming, of course, that she ever made it back to Grandaise.

"No. His Lordship has taken a vow to 'preserve' me and answers to the duke of Avalon for both my safety and my purity. So, he has ordered the knights and men of the garrison to stay away from the kitchen and keeps a hawk's eye on me . . . to make certain my 'gifts to God' aren't sullied under his roof."

Sophie digested that for a moment, then shook her head in disbelief.

"If a woman can't get ravished under the Beast's roof, where *can* she get ravished?"

Julia couldn't help laughing and liking Verdun's salty little daughter.

"You're a handful, Sophie Marie," she said. "It's a pity you're not in charge of things at Verdun."

Sophie laughed . . . a sweet, throaty sound that made Julia feel sorry for Verdun's abstemious knights.

"Well, give me a little time." The girl's eyes twinkled. "After all, I've been here less than a month."

WITH GRIM THOROUGHNESS GRIFFIN SET THE forges blazing and the smiths and arrow makers to working around the clock. Then he threw himself into completing a newly devised complex of defenses for the vineyards. While his men worked to erect the temporary fortifications and dig the covered trenches intended to protect the vines from horsemen bearing torches, he had his herdsmen secure the flocks and herds in defensible locations and he worked on gathering as many of his people as possible inside the walls of Grandaise.

As preparations proceeded, he sent a message to his neighbor to the south, the Baron Thibault de Roland, informing him of his grandson's injuries and vowing to see Bertrand well cared for during his recovery. Old Thibault responded via an aged-looking messenger, thanking Griffin for his concern and pledging the services of Roland's fighting men if or when it came to blows with Verdun.

Griffin tried to remember how many men Old Thibault was said to keep. From what he and Axel and Greeve could recall, it wasn't many; the old baron didn't have funds to maintain a proper garrison. Griffin would have to rely solely on Crossan for aid in that regard. He sent his thanks to the old baron all the same.

There was no response to the message Griffin had sent to Verdun, demanding Julia's return and declaring her to be under the protection of the bishop of Rheims and the duke of Avalon. With each day that passed, the sense of urgency and tension rose in the hall, and Julia's wonderful food was not there to assuage them.

Fortunately, the lessons Julia had imparted in the short time she had been there had not fallen entirely on fallow minds. Most of the new practices she brought to the kitchen continued, with a little help from Sister Regine. The nun's stubborn hopefulness regarding the return of their head cook set an example for the kitchen staff. By the fourth day, they were looking to her for direction as well as encouragement. She, in turn, looked to Griffin for guidance.

"What shall we do, Your Lordship?"

"The best you can, Sister," was his terse response.

That night they had frumenty for supper.

Griffin hardly noticed. The last thing he needed to think about right now was food. Especially Julia's food.

Every idle moment allowed her to rise into his thoughts dragging a whole feast of both worries and remembered pleasures with her, so he strove to not allow a single one. He planned and discussed and ordered and rode and oversaw . . . wielding a hammer as they erected wooden extensions in place atop the walls and personally deciding on the quarters for the families relocated inside the modest fortifications. He dragged his steward around to check on supplies in the barns, granaries, wood bins, and coal piles. He had his men go to the river to fill barrels with water for the kitchen cistern, and found himself remembering the way Julia had waded in the stream north of Paris. He dismounted straightaway and began dipping buckets of water himself.

But at night when he fell exhausted across his empty and silent bed, there was nothing to distract him, and the last thing he saw before the darkness claimed him was her face, flushed with pleasure, warm and inviting. Painful thoughts of what must be happening to her at Verdun's hands rose and he focused his dimming awareness on the sensations of food and woman and warmth she had brought to him each time he had smelled her. And kissed her. And caressed her.

He would get her back, he vowed as he lost consciousness.

Whatever it took.

"BUT I THINK SHE MAY REALLY *BE* A COOK," Sophie said to Sir Martin as she trotted to keep up with him across the bustling side yard of Verdun's great redoubt. "She talks about food constantly and can recite recipes until she puts you to sleep. I doubt 'mistresses' bother to set such things to memory."

"How would you know what mistresses do or don't do? Stay away from her, Sophie." Sir Martin halted to glare at her and punch a finger against the tip of her nose. "Keep this meddlesome member of yours out of her chamber. I catch you in there again and I'll have to report it to your father."

"And what do you think he would do about it?" Sophie jammed her fists at her waist. "Marry me off to some hideous beast?" Her eyes widened in mock surprise. "Oh, wait—he's already doing that."

"Don't try his patience, Sophie. Or mine. Heaven help me, I've tried to keep news of your activities among the knights from him. He thinks you're as pure as the driven snow."

"Well, thanks to you, I am." When he gave her a dark look, she amended it. "All right . . . maybe slightly sooty, top-of-the-roof snow . . . but I'm still *snow.*" She strode after him. She hated the way he assessed her with those warm brown eyes of his and then glanced coolly away and spoke to her as if she were a child.

"If you're so diligent about keeping him informed, don't you think it would behoove you to learn whether it's true, what she says about being under the Beast's protection . . . and about how he is answerable to that duke of something?"

"It's not your business, Sophie."

"Well, you should at least help me find out if she's really the Beast's cook."

He halted again and scowled at her.

"What are you up to?"

"I just want to know if she's telling the truth . . . about the cooking. If she is, then she's probably truthful about other things."

"What other things?" He scowled, trying to imagine what might have passed between the two before he discovered Sophie in their hostage's chamber yesterday.

"Woman things. You wouldn't understand." She raised her chin. "So are you going to take her down to the kitchens to see if she can cook, or not?"

"Absolutely not. She's to stay as far away from the kitchens as possible." He shook a finger in her face. "And *you*—you're to stay away from *her!*"

LATE THAT NIGHT, A PAIR OF WARY GUARDS-men under the direction of a nervous young knight escorted Julia of Childress from her chamber, through the darkened hall and corridors, to the kitchens of Verdun. Sophie, who had both seduced and coerced Sir Gerard into helping her, hurried along before them, scouting the way to be certain it was clear. When they finally entered the kitchen Julia paused on the steps, staring in amazement at the massive chamber.

It looked exactly like the kitchen at Grandaise. There were eight sides, five of which were anchored by huge hearths, a high ceiling, and windows with louvers for ventilation overhead. In the center was a now familiar arrangement of poles studded with pegs to hold hanging pots and utensils. The poles were surrounded by a score of sturdy oak and maple work tables. How on earth could there be such identical kitchens in such adamantly opposed houses?

Julia allowed Sophie to pull her down the few steps toward the banked and slumbering hearths. In the center of the kitchen, at one of the work tables, sat a white-clad figure perusing a wax tally tablet and making marks in columns. He looked up with a frown, which he quickly transferred from Sophie to Julia.

"This is the cook I told you about," Sophie declared. "Julia of Childress."

The head cook leaned back from his work and jammed his fists at his ample waist, looking over her trim figure. "She must not taste much of her own cooking," he said testily. "You can't trust a cook who doesn't eat."

"Or one who overindulges in pleasures wrought by his own hand," Julia responded tartly, gazing at his girth.

"Now, now, Francois." Sophie wagged a finger. "You agreed to let Julia come and see your kitchens."

"Because you said she was a cook. A *fine* cook."

"So I am," Julia declared, tucking her arms and raising her chin to a combative angle. "And a truly good cook never foregoes a chance to gain methods and recipes from another cook . . . even if he is arrogant and inhospitable."

"Arrogant, am I?" Francois was on his feet in a flash. "Inhospitable?" It was the worst thing one could say about a cook. "We'll see who's a proper cook and who isn't."

He bustled around the kitchen, nudging the fire tenders awake and pulling a linen apron from a stack on shelves along one of the walls. He slapped a new apron and a freshly carved wooden spoon down onto the table before her with a burning challenge in his broad face.

"Let's see what you can do."

As Julia took stock of the huge larder and selected items necessary for the pastry she had in mind, Francois came along behind her . . . watching her and selecting ingredients himself, clearly intending to do some cooking, too. Sophie stationed herself at the table where Julia worked and Francois rousted one of his undercooks from a cot in the pantry to assist him. Lamps were lighted and soon the kitchen was humming with activity.

Four hours later the guards' mouths were long past watering as they sat with their heads propped up on the tables, waiting for the verdict in this culinary match. The smells were heavenly . . . spiced crust, sweet custard filling, wined cherries and plums, sliced almonds, spices and sugar . . . beef roasted with garlic and pepper and served with a rich claret wine and mushroom sauce.

When the two dishes were placed on the table, side by side, each cook eyed the other's creation with grudging respect. Julia sliced into her elegant cherry custard tart to a chorus of *ahhhs* and presented a dish of it to Francois. He produced a porcelain dish and served several slices of peppered beef with the sauce and mushrooms and handed it to Julia. Eyeing each other so as not to seem overeager, they sat down opposite each other at the same time and watched each other carefully as they simultaneously took a first bite.

Two sets of shoulders lowered, two pairs of eyes closed, and two sighs issued forth. Julia and the portly Francois opened their eyes and looked at each other with dawning respect.

"Magnificent beef, Monsieur Francois." Being the guest, Julia went first. "It melts on the tongue. And the wine sauce . . . with both the tang of new wine and the depth of a fine rich claret. But the mushrooms . . . they are pure heaven . . . the very soul of the soil is in them. I've never tasted anything like them! The way they draw the other tastes together . . . make each flavor seem more intense and unique. You are a master of both spit and sauce, monsieur." She rose and curtsied deeply.

He smiled with a satisfied curl to one side of his mouth, then he turned back to her offering.

"Those wretched ovens have never been so kind to *my* crusts. And this custard is light and creamy—perfectly set." A high compliment indeed, for a fine and delicate custard was the universally accepted credential of a fine cook. "The balance of tartness and sweetness in the cherries is perfect . . . a whole bouquet blooms in the mouth upon first bite . . . and the heart soars upon the second."

Sophie looked from Verdun's opinionated cook to her new friend, grinning.

"I knew it. I just *knew* you were a real cook!"

Sir Gerard and Julia's guards were offered generous helpings of both in compensation for the risk they took in escorting Julia to the kitchens. Francois, surprised and delighted to find another knowledgeable cook with brains enough to pick, broke out a cask of exceptional claret and insisted they sit down and share a bit of fine food and wine.

"I have to ask, Monsieur Francois," Julia said as she pushed back from the table later, sighing with unexpected satisfaction. "What kind of mushrooms are those? I have never tasted the likes of them."

"Not mere mushrooms, demoiselle. *Truffles*. A rare and exceptional sort of mushroom that grows in this region. A true delicacy." He chuckled. "I confess . . . I knew if you were a true epicure, they would give me a secret advantage."

"For such an enthralling sauce, I would gladly yield you that advantage any time you wish." She wiggled her eyebrows and the cagey Francois laughed.

"But I have another question, monsieur," she said after a few moments. "How on earth can there be two such remarkable and identical kitchens as the one here and the one at Grandaise? How did they come to be so alike in such bitterly opposed households?"

"What?" Francois choked in the middle of a drink of wine and lowered his cup to reveal ruby liquid dribbling down both sides of his mouth. "I can't imagine what you mean, demoiselle. There is but one kitchen as grand as this"—he thrust his arms out to praise the culinary splendor of his kitchen—"in all of France."

"Has no one ever told you? Have you never seen the—"

One of the potboys came running down the passage and burst into the kitchen, shouting, "'Is Lordship—'e's comin'!"

Chapter 22

FOR AN INSTANT EVERYONE FROZE, then Francois, Sophie, and Julia jumped to their feet all at once, and Sir Gerard and the guards weren't far behind.

"There's no time to run—they'll hear us—we have to hide!" Sophie cried, looking wildly about for a safe haven.

"The larder!" Francois shouted in a whisper, shoving the women and frantic guards all toward the door to the main storerooms. Beyond was a stone chamber hung with strings of dried herbs, dried beans and condiments, and garlic; shelves loaded with boxes, jars, and bundles; and stacks of barrels, bags, and willow hampers. Julia and the others scattered, ducked, and crawled into whatever accessible niche they could find.

Julia slithered into an opening behind the main door, flattening herself against a set of shelves in the corner, just beyond the hinges. Through a crack around the heavy planks, she could see part of the kitchen and the main door leading from the hall. Shortly, the Count of Verdun burst through the doorway, clearly in a temper, and paused to scour the grand chamber with a glance. Sir Martin entered next and as they descended the stairs, the count demanded to know if his daughter had been in the kitchen that night.

"She's not in her chambers nor the hall, nor the upper solar," he declared. "Martin said she often visits the kitchen of an evening."

"It's true that Lady Sophie visits often, milord," Francois's voice was believably anxious. "But as to whether she was here this evening . . . I confess, I cannot say. I have been so concerned with the tallies and orders for food for the extra mouths I am now charged with feeding." He moved toward the count and into Julia's line of sight, wringing his hands. "Milord . . . I must have more help. I have the bakers running their ovens nearly day and night as it is. All of these extra mouths to feed . . . I must have more meat and beans and cheese of all kinds . . . more rice and pears and pepper and cinnamon and ale—and oil—I must surely have more olive oil—"

Julia bit her lip. Clever man, Francois. There was no faster way to get a nobleman out of a kitchen than to beg him for goods or money.

"Yes, yes . . ." The count put up both hands to ward him off. "You'll have what you need. If my daughter appears, you are to report it to me immediately."

"Of course, milord."

Julia watched the count turn toward the stairs and then back. "What is that?" he demanded. She gasped and drew back from the edge of the door.

"What is what, milord?" Francois asked in tones a bit higher than usual.

"There, in those dishes." The count turned toward the table where sat the remains of their cooking bout, and Julia edged back to the crack in the door. "Is that your beef with wine and mushrooms?" He leaned closer and sniffed. "And a tart?"

"Y-yes, milord."

"What—were you having your own private feast?"

"No, milord. I was just . . . trying a new recipe or two . . . hoping to serve it to you when the Comte de Lombard arrives."

The count looked alarmingly interested. He stuck a finger into the custard of the tart and then into his mouth. Impressed, he sat down on the very stool Julia had occupied moments earlier and demanded a spoon. He made quick, noisy work of both the remainder of the beef with "mushrooms" and of the cherry-custard tart.

Julia shifted for a better look and something fell onto the floor at her feet. Francois cast a look of alarm at the larder door. When the count looked up and demanded to know what was wrong, he cleared his throat and demonstrated once again the agility that had served him well at the helm of Verdun's kitchens.

"I—I just realized . . . we may not have enough cherries to make that dish for the count's entourage. Perhaps I should begin to scour the countryside for more, milord. It will be expensive . . . this being the end of the cherry season."

"Money, money, money. It's always 'money' with you, Francois." The count shoved to his feet and was halfway up the steps before he made his decision. "I can't afford to look miserly when I'm asking him to send men into battle on my behalf. Yes, dammit, scour the countryside for your cursed berries."

And he stormed out.

Julia waited—they all waited—to be certain he wouldn't return.

When the door swung open and light from Francois's lamp brightened the inside of the larder, she looked down to see what had fallen by her feet. It was a book, a large, leather-bound volume covered with dust. It had been tucked away on the bottom shelf in the corner and her movements had dislodged it.

She picked it up as Francois moved farther into the larder, saying the count was gone, and she brushed away some of the dust. What sort of book would canny Francois have hidden away in his kitchen? Books were precious and fragile . . . more suited to a lord's private chamber or solar.

She opened it. There she made out neat lettering on the parchment leaves: lists of ingredients followed by instructions. Recipes! As she turned page after page and neared the front of the book she stopped dead, staring at the elegantly illuminated word *Grandaise.* She turned her back to the rest of the larder and opened the front cover. There in elegant colored ink and gilt was a coat of arms bearing a tripartite shield decorated with grapes, a boar pig, and several strange little lumps that looked like coal. It was the coat of arms of Grandaise.

"Demoiselle Julia—"

She had a decision to make. Instinctively, she slipped the book up inside her apron and held it there with her folded arms as she turned.

"Here I am." She waved as she slipped around the door and back out into the kitchen. When the others joined her, she pulled Sophie in front of her and headed straight for the steps, declaring that they both needed to get back to their chambers straightaway. With a quick wave to Francois in the kitchen, and a hurried hug for Sophie at the bottom of the stairs, she raced ahead of her guards up to her chamber. It was empty. She sagged with relief and asked her guards, who arrived shortly, to light her lamp from theirs.

After the door closed behind her and the bolt was thrown, she raised the wick on the lamp, drew the stool to the small table, and sat down before that curious volume. She ran her fingers over it, wiping away the dust of years, and then opened the heavy cover.

Grandaise. In the frontispiece of the binding was a chart depicting the lineages of the ancient estate, all the way down to the present count, Griffin de Grandaise. She studied the names and the dates, wondering how such a vital record came to be in Verdun's larder. Then she opened the first pages and began to read a short history of Grandaise . . . as handed down by the estate's noteworthy cooks and written down by the last and most beloved of those kitchen masters . . . Jean de Champagne . . . otherwise known as *Grand Jean.*

*   *   *

SOPHIE REACHED HER CHAMBER UNDETECTED and took a deep breath of relief as she opened the door . . . then froze. There, in the middle of her chamber sat her father, with his arms crossed and his eyes as cold as January. A hand pulled her inside and closed the door behind her. She looked up to find herself in Sir Martin's I-told-you-so grip.

"Where the devil have you been?" her father snapped like the tip of a lash.

"I was just . . . I went to the kitchens . . . and then out for some air. . . ."

"The hell you did. We've been all over Verdun looking for you. From the ramparts to the kitchens to the gardens to the cellars. Where were you?"

She was in deep trouble. But she was also every bit as resourceful as her irascible father. She swallowed her trepidation and raised her chin.

"I was doing what I have repeatedly asked Sir Martin to do. I was investigating the truthfulness of your hostage's identity and claims." She folded her arms, mirroring her father's judgmental pose. "And you know what I found? She *is* a cook. The Beast's cook. He acquired her from the Convent of the Brides of Virtue to come and cook for him for one year. Before she could come, he had to swear to return her at the end of one year so that she may take religious vows. Thus . . . she is not only under the Beast's protection . . . she is also under the protection of the Duke of Avalon."

She unfolded her arms and stood tall, looking quite confident and self-contained.

"I already know all of that," he said irritably. "Grandaise sent a demand for her release laying out those very claims. The idiot. As if I can't figure out that *he* is the one who is really in trouble if she isn't returned intact."

"And what happens when he goes to the king . . . tells the king that you have abducted his cook and violated the truce?" Sophie demanded. "Unless you can point to a worse violation, the king may choose to believe him and punish you."

"He can't even prove the chit is here."

"There is Bertrand, seigneur," Sir Martin reminded him diplomatically. "He did not return with the girl as expected. Grandaise must have learned he was our spy and detained him."

"There is one way to be sure he violates the truce," Sophie said, dragging them back to her point. "A way to bring him to his knees before the king that will save you a dangerous and destructive battle."

"Why would I want to avoid a battle?" her father snapped, flinging a hand at Martin. "That's what I'm keeping him and his lot for . . . fighting."

"Oh, I don't know." Sophie narrowed her eyes. "Because it's *costly* and *stupid* to fight when there are better, *less expensive* ways of handling things?"

"And what ways are those, *daughter?*" Her father reddened and gripped the arms of the chair, his patience ominously thin.

This was her moment, Sophie thought. She had to do this right.

"Tell the Beast he may have his cook back only if he marries her."

Verdun's face fell. "He's supposed to wed *you*. What makes you think he would stoop to wed a—especially when she's protected by—" A rush of anger erupted through him. "You're doing this to get out of marrying him yourself!"

"Of course," she said brazenly. "I don't want to wed him any more than you want me to wed him. This is a perfect opportunity to keep me from having to marry him *and* to bring down the wrath and fury of both the king and a duke on his head. When he comes to get her . . . tell him he can have her . . . only if he marries her."

"What makes you think he would do that—marry a mere cook?"

"She is from a convent and he has sworn to protect her. And from the way she talks, she has beguiled him as much as he has her. He cares for her." Sophie watched the calculation in her father's face and gauging how much more was needed to convince him. "Give him reason to believe she is in danger and he'll marry her."

A devious grin spread slowly over the count's lean, aristocratic face.

"You've done well, my girl." He rose and rubbed the velvet covering his chest with a self-congratulatory air. "The apple hasn't fallen far from the tree."

He strode to the door and turned back to find Martin only a step behind him.

"Stay here," he ordered the knight. "Don't let her out of this door or out of your sight. She's a devious chit." He gave a wicked chuckle. "She may be more valuable than I thought."

The door closed and Martin stared at it in dismay. Then he heard a soft throat clearing behind him and wheeled to face her.

"Well, well, Sir Martin," Sophie said, swaying toward him, loosening her hair. "By my father's own command, it looks like you'll be *watching* me tonight."

Martin took a step backward and banged hard into the door.

"Now, Sophie . . ."

THAT SAME NIGHT, SEVERAL MILES AWAY, Old Thibault de Roland sat in his shadow-shrouded hall glowering at the men who had crowded around his tables, gorged themselves on his wine and food, and then fallen into a drunken stupor. They reeked of soured sweat and oiled metal. Their garments were rough and dirty and some had rags wrapped around the disintegrating leather of their boots. But the swords at their sides glinted, blades bright from care and use. They were a filthy, hungry, dangerous barbarian horde, just waiting to be unleashed.

But tomorrow—he let his head drop back against the threadbare cushions of his chair—they would don his colors over their pathetic rags. His precious green and white. And for a few splendid hours they would rise above their pathetic lot to become the instrument of his revenge on the two houses that had risen to wealth and prominence over the bones of his ancestors.

He looked around the dimly lighted hall, recalling the days when the tapestries had been bright and the stone walls free of soot and years of neglect. He recalled the sound of music in the hall and the flirtatious looks of pretty women . . . of one particular woman. . . .

Movement in the open doorway drew his attention and he sat straighter and called out, demanding to know who was there.

"A message, milord." A meagerly garbed old man scurried forward, clutching a tattered cap, and casting anxious glances at the burly figures snoring over the tabletops. He stopped some feet from the baron. "From Sir Bertrand. He bids me say . . . they will move on the morrow."

Old Thibault sagged back against his cushions, drawing a rattling breath into his wasted frame.

"Good." He nodded, thinking that the boy was finally coming around . . . proving his worth . . . remembering his true and rightful allegiance. "Take him back this word from me," he ordered the servant. " 'It is time to come home.' "

Chapter 23

FOUR DAYS AFTER JULIA'S ABDUCTION, the Baron Crossan arrived midmorning at Grandaise with half a dozen knights and three score men-at-arms.

"Any word from Reynard?" Griffin rushed to greet him at the front doors.

"None. I decided to wait no longer in bringing my men to you." The blocky, amicable baron clasped his shoulder and gestured to the force filling the courtyard and stretching down the path and through the gate, arms and armor glinting in the morning sun. "We are well rested and ready to move." He turned back to Griffin. "You, on the other hand, look as if you haven't slept in days."

"Who sleeps well with a wolf at his door?" Griffin ran a hand down his face, feeling his eyes burning dryly. Then he looked from the baron's knights, standing by their mounts in the courtyard, to his own knights behind him in the hall.

"We're ready, milord," Axel said, his round face uncharacteristically somber. "Greeve and I have taken over Bertrand's archers . . . he has done well with them. And Heureaux has the scaling ladders and battering rams ready."

"Let's hope it doesn't come to that," Griffin said. "Verdun has thick walls and who knows how much aid he has recruited."

"I am your right arm, Grandaise, you know that." The baron stepped closer and lowered his voice. "But, all of this over a *cook*?"

"She is not just a cook, Crossan. She is . . ." He reddened as he struggled to keep his head above the memories inundating him. Julia splashing around barelegged in a stream, following him into a darkened forest, demanding to be let into his tightly controlled world; Julia cooking for him, tasting his food, tantalizing his palate, provoking him, tempting him; Julia prying into his inner workings, trying to understand him and then to please him. She might have begun as a cook, but she was much more than that now. She was the reason he lay hot and wakeful in his bed each night. She was the reason he rushed down the steps to break fast each morning. She was the one person in his entire life who had cared enough to try to reach the man inside the protective barrier he had erected around himself. She cared for him.

And, God help him, he cared for her . . . above duty, above honor, above his own safety and the safety of his men. He was desperate to have her back.

"She is well-born. A maid of great worth." His throat constricted. "And I am honor bound, pledged to a bishop and a duke of the realm to guard and defend her." He saw a hint of recognition and sympathy in the baron's perceptive gaze and straightened. "*And* . . . she makes the best cherry rissoles in all of Christendom."

The baron's laugh boomed like a kettle drum.

"Then by all means, Grandaise," he slapped Griffin's shoulder, "we must get her back!"

THEY MOVED IN DOUBLE COLUMNS ACROSS pastures filled with sheep, along the edges of lush fields of grain, and through the broad, grassy paths crossing the vineyards that usually carried harvest wagons laden with grapes to the wine presses on Grandaise. Knights and

mounted men led the way and food soldiers came behind
with carts bearing extra arrows and weaponry.

As they reached the edge of the forest-rimmed valley of
Verdun's seat, Griffin pointed out the agreed location for a
battle line and sent his younger knights to form a double
line stretching out across the fields. When they reached the
midpoint of the valley, Griffin raised his arm to halt them
and, leaving Crossan to command the lines, proceeded on
toward the gates under a white parley banner.

"Verdun!" he roared, looking up at the ramparts above
the iron portcullis in Verdun's main gate. "I've come for
Julia of Childress. I know you have her. I'll give you a
quarter hour to send her out unharmed through those gates.
If you don't, then I'll come for her. And I'll take your head
in the bargain."

A long, deep silence followed, where the only sounds
heard were the creak of saddle leather and the snort of anxious horses. The sun bore down as they waited. Heat built
inside Griffin's gauntlets, hauberk, and helm, and making
him feel all the more keenly the pressure of his responsi-
bility for Julia's safety.

What if Verdun wouldn't bring her out? What if she
were injured or ravished and unable to walk? What if—

The massive portcullis at the center of the stone gate began to lift. Beyond, he could see Verdun and some of his
red-and-white-clad knights. His knees must have tightened
along with the rest of him; his mount snorted and shied.

"So you've finally come!" It was Verdun himself who
came forth, flanked by knights, carrying a white banner
like the one that whipped in the air above Griffin.

"Bring her out, Verdun," Griffin demanded.

"In time, Grandaise." Verdun walked down the slope
that led to the open field where Griffin stood, and stopped
twenty yards away. "First, we talk."

"Your actions speak louder than your words, Verdun."

Verdun scanned the lines of men in the field behind
Griffin and focused on Crossan. "You've done some re-
cruiting, I see. Both men and alliances."

"Bring her out," Griffin repeated his demand. "Or we will come in."

"As if you could." Verdun strode forward a few steps, his dark eyes blazing inside his polished helm. "There is only one way you will get your tart back." Verdun turned partway and pointed to the gate, where several other figures had appeared while Griffin focused on Verdun's movements.

There stood Julia, dressed in a white gown, her hands bound before her, and her hair loose and flowing around her shoulders. Her face was pale but she appeared to be unharmed. Beside her stood a tonsured man in a dark cassock.

"She is alive and well. A state that can change with a simple movement of my hand." He gave a flick of his hand and his men seized her by the arms.

A bolt of fury shot through Griffin.

"You wouldn't dare." He raised his hand halfway up his side and several archers in the front rank of his men drew back their bows and took aim on Verdun.

"Listen well, Grandaise," Verdun said in a tightened voice, then shifted slightly as if subduing his temper in the service of something even more dangerous. "Beside your wench is my priest. He is here to administer rites. Either the rites of marriage or the last rites. The choice is yours. You will wed the wench, here and now, or she will begin her journey to Heaven here and now. My priest will preside over whichever you choose."

"Damn you, Verdun—if you harm so much as a hair on her head—"

"That is no longer up to me, Grandaise. You are the one who decides whether she lives or dies. To have her . . . to take her home with you . . . all you have to do is speak vows of marriage with her."

The anger surging in Griffin's blood was hindering his reason. This had become a game of strategy, and now of all times, he needed clear thinking. Taking a deep breath, he struggled to cut himself off from all interfering emotion . . . even his concern for Julia.

"Speaking those words of binding would keep me from

fulfilling the king's command that I marry your daughter," Griffin declared. "You are forcing me to go against the king's command."

"No, I am giving you a choice," Verdun said, not bothering to conceal his pleasure at having Griffin's fate in his hands. "You must choose which means more to you: your king's approval or your cook's life."

"And if I refuse to choose? If I decide instead to take her by force of arms?" Griffin stalled for precious moments in which to consider his course.

"There will be much bloodshed," Verdun said with icy determination, all trace of humor gone. "And I promise you, she will be the first casualty." He turned to the men holding Julia in the gate and raised a hand. One of the knights drew his sword and the blade glinted in the sunlight.

The distance made her face indistinct, but Griffin's memory filled in the green of her eyes, the curve of her cheeks, and the velvet texture of her lips to bring a haunting image to his mind's eye. He could see in the proud carriage of her shoulders outrage at the way she was being handled. She must glimpse him and freedom and wonder why—did she know what he was being asked to do? Was the intensity of her gaze a plea for rescue or an expression of anger at being used as a pawn in a game of power?

Part of him wanted nothing more than to draw his sword and dispatch Verdun on the spot, but another part of him recoiled from adding yet another chapter of death and destruction to the chronicle of hatred that lay between their houses.

"Time is up, Grandaise. What will it be? Your king or your cook?"

Griffin straightened his spine, fixed his gaze on her, and spoke those fateful words: "Bring on your priest, Verdun. I will speak vows with her."

As he dismounted and ordered his men to do the same, Julia was ushered out alongside the priest. As soon as she came within reach, Griffin grabbed her by the shoulders and stared at her for a long moment.

"Are you all right?" He fought a massive urge to pull her against him.

"I am whole and well, Your Lordship." She met his gaze with warm eyes.

A frightening surge of emotion crashed over him at the sight of the relief and trust and longing in those clear green eyes. Impulses for possession and protection seized him with such force that he trembled and had to squeeze her arms to keep it from becoming visible.

"The price of your freedom is a marriage vow. You will give consent when the priest asks," he ordered. Her eyes widened with confusion, but she nodded, speechless for once. Having her so near caused an easing in his inner turmoil. He turned her by the shoulders so that she faced the priest with him, but she turned back and held out her bound hands.

"Please, milord. I would not be wed in bonds."

For one brief, heart-stopping moment their gazes met and the air around them crackled with the tension of words unspoken and feelings unacknowledged. Then he cut the ropes binding her wrists and once again turned her to the priest.

He would not remember, later, much of what the priest said or what she had said. But he would recall until his dying day the words he spoke. He pledged to love and cherish and keep her, to live with her through all the conditions and trials of life, and to be faithful to her only. And in that brief and terrifying moment, he wondered if the spell those words cast on his future would be the making or the destruction of him.

As soon as the priest pronounced them husband and wife, Griffin scooped her up in his arms and carried her back to his horse. His men folded in behind them to protect his back.

Shortly, he was riding across the fields with her on his lap, holding her against him with desperate intensity. The battle lines folded in behind them as they rode through, and soon the entire contingent was headed for the forest path they had just traversed.

*   *   *

"WHAT THE HELL IS GOING ON?" THIBAULT
de Roland snarled, squinting toward the blurs of color on
the far western side of the field. He reached over to smack
the arm of his grandson, who was mounted on a horse beside his. "What are they doing down there?"

"Parley flags." Bertrand himself was having to squint to
make out what was happening. "They're talking."

"What the devil could they have to talk about?" The old
man shook a fist toward the reluctant combatants. "Get on
with the fighting, damn you!"

Suddenly there was movement from the clump of men
at the edge of the field.

"Aha! It begins!" Thibault turned to look around at the
men shrouded by the trees and brush at the south end of the
valley. Clad in his green and white colors, they were waiting
sullenly for orders that took too long to come. "Get ready!"

There was a rustle of interest and attention among the
men and Thibault turned to his grandson.

"Remember, both sides will see our colors and think
we've come to their aid. Once you're into the fray you must
reach Grandaise and Verdun before they realize you're not
engaging the enemy. The lords must go down first and stay
down for you to seize the field and—"

"Wait—look there—" Bertrand scowled past his grandfather and pointed.

The old man wrenched himself around in his saddle and
glared toward the center of the field, where the Comte de
Grandaise was riding right through his own lines. His
ally—Crossan—was turning and joining him in his retreat
to the forest. It didn't look like they were running for their
lives and Verdun's forces weren't pursuing them.

"He's got the cook!" Bertrand said, pointing to
Grandaise.

The old man squinted harder and just made out the pale
figure on the horse in front of the imminently recognizable
count. He let rip a string of oaths that brought his hired
henchmen to fierce attention.

"Verdun—spineless cur—he gave her up. Handed her over without a drop of bloodshed!" He thumped a withered thigh with a bony fist. "Damn him!"

The old man turned his mount and headed back through his mercenaries to the road leading to Roland. Even though the old man was approaching seventy, Bertrand had to ride hard to catch up with him.

"What now, Grandfather?" he said tersely. "All of your planning . . . all of our work . . ."

Some of the choler left Old Thibault's face as he set aside the failure. There had been so cursed many near misses in his lifetime that he was accustomed to recovering quickly and planning anew.

"We've been content to stay in the background, working silently, sight unseen," the old man said, rubbing his shrunken and bristled chin. "The time has come for more direct action. If they won't provoke each other to bloodshed, then we'll just have to do it for them."

JULIA RODE ACROSS THE FIELDS AND through the forest in Griffin's arms, relishing the feel of the wind in her face and the thundering rhythm of the great war horse beneath her. It was dazzling, confusing, and for the moment exhilarating. All she could think was that he'd come for her and he'd rescued—*married*—her! It all happened so fast she couldn't catch her breath.

The previous day she had spent in anxious solitude, pouring over Old Jean's book, in desperate need of someone to talk to about the things she was reading. She had expected that Sophie would slip in to see her that morning, but she didn't come. As the sun began to lower she wheedled and cajoled her guards into carrying messages to Sophie and Sir Martin. They returned shortly saying that neither Lady Sophie or Sir Martin had been out and about the castle all day, and that there was some talk that the count had confined his impetuous daughter to her chambers the night before.

Then the next morning, Sophie's waiting maid appeared

at her door with word that Sophie was well and a lovely ivory silk gown that seemed to be rather large for Sophie's diminutive figure. Julia tried it on, as she was asked to do, and it fit surprisingly well. Then the maid helped to brush her hair and then whisked away her old woolen gown, saying Lady Sophie insisted it be cleaned and freshened.

Midday, she heard voices and commotion below her window and looked out to find the castle's workers scurrying toward the center of the enclosure, while men-at-arms were rushing the opposite direction . . . for the walls. Then, when the sun was almost overhead, Sir Martin and his men came for her, bound her hands, and led her down the tower steps and through the great hall.

Sophie, looking rosy and confident and pleased to see her, fussed and tugged at Julia's dress and then gave her a warm hug that allowed her to whisper "don't worry" into Julia's ear. After that, Sir Martin ushered her out the main doors.

She heard Griffin's voice thundering at the Count of Verdun before she saw him. Everything within half a mile, even the wind itself, seemed to have stopped to listen. When she reached the gate, she understood why. He was huge and terrifying and magnificent . . . astride a huge black horse draped with blue and green trappings and a silver clad saddle and bridle fittings. His armor enhanced his already sizeable shoulders and arms and he looked ready to ride down the very walls of Verdun.

Then he saw her. She could tell the moment he set eyes on her; his mount stopped its pawing and he froze in the saddle. She could feel him reaching for her across the distance, touching her, examining her . . . reassuring her. Her fears eased at Sophie's cryptic "don't worry" and his powerful presence, combined with arrival of a priest at her side.

Then the guards seized her, and one drew his blade. Something was happening between His Lordship and the count. Lord Griffin looked at her again and she felt his anxiety and anger like physical vibrations on the air around her.

By the time His Lordship dismounted and the priest dragged her forward, she realized something had been decided. She couldn't have imagined that it was the price of her freedom, or that it would prove to be that he speak marriage vows with her. When he told her what was required of her, she asked him to repeat it, thinking that she couldn't have heard properly.

Was that what this was about? All of these men, these preparations for battle, this anger and fear . . . it all came down to speaking marriage vows?

Suddenly Sophie's advice made sense. She had known what her father was about to demand of Lord Griffin. She looked down at her new silk gown. She had even provided clothes for the occasion.

Now it was done and she was on the way home. She relaxed back into His Lordship's arms and felt surrounded, secure, safe. He had married her in order to rescue her. It was proof he *cared* for her. And it also meant that her heart and her future were at last set on the same tumultuous path.

She turned her face up to the sun, closed her eyes, and felt like the luckiest maid in the entire world. She refused to think any further than the circle of his strong arms.

They picked up the pace as they neared the walls of Grandaise and soon they were galloping past the waving sentries and thundering through the eagerly opened main gate. The courtyard quickly filled with cheering folk. House servants, retainers, villagers, and knights just dismounted, all crowded around to welcome Julia back and to hear and tell the remarkable story of her rescue. It was Sir Axel who shouted the news of the nuptials to them.

Married? The folk stared at their little cook in amazement, which quickly melted into acceptance. They'd known all along that she was wellborn and different from the usual kitchen master. Truth be told, it was a modest step in their eyes from presiding over the kitchens to presiding over the rest of the household as well . . . the kitchens being the acknowledged heart and lifeblood of the estate.

Julia was lifted down by the Baron Crossan, who was the first to kiss her hand and call her "milady." Axel and

Greeve presented themselves to her with exaggerated courtesy, squeezing her extended hands and volunteering their assistance to her as she launched into her new role. Arnaud the Steward bowed and Genevieve the Housekeeper curtsied awkwardly. With everyone talking excitedly and all at once, she scarcely noticed Sister Regine pushing her way through the crowd with a shocked expression.

"It's really you!" Regine looked at her as if she were a ghost, then threw eager arms around her. "We were beside ourselves. We lit candles in the chapel every day. You just disappeared and then we learned—you're all right?"

"I'm fine," she said beaming. "Never better."

Regine looked her over and then turned to His Lordship with a teary smile. "You did it, milord. You brought her home safe, as you said you would."

Everyone looked to Griffin, who had not yet dismounted. He sat above them watching her reception with a taut expression, and he cleared his throat.

"Yes. And now things can return to normal." He swept the crowd with a look. "Everyone can go back to his or her duty. And perhaps we can get some wine and ale in the hall for the baron and his knights."

After a few more hurried greetings, the householders hurried back to their duties, leaving the courtyard to the soldiers, squires, and grooms. His Lordship dismounted and, setting a hand to the small of her back, propelled her through the throng of men toward the hall.

When Sister Regine lifted her hem and bustled along after them, he halted the sister to suggest that she check on the progress of supper in the kitchens.

"I've been helping in the kitchen since you've been away," she said to Julia, as she backed away, grinning. "I get to give orders and people actually *obey*."

Julia watched her depart, smiled, and continued into the hall.

"Thank you, milord, for coming to my rescue," she said, slowing as she approached the door and then stopping just outside to have a moment with him. "I never imagined that you would go to such lengths to retrieve a cook."

"I wouldn't have gone to such extremes to rescue just any cook," he said thickly, his gaze sliding to hers and his body leaning closer. She saw his gaze drop to her lips and for a moment wondered if he meant to kiss her. But he suddenly snapped upright and looked at the men filing past them into the hall. "I have a great deal invested in you. I could hardly let Verdun and his band of cutthroats deprive me of the best food south of Paris."

He escorted her briskly into the hall, where the Baron Crossan and several of Grandaise's knights crowded close to ask questions. As she began to recall for them how it all began, she suddenly remembered the one responsible for her abduction.

"Oh—Sir Bertrand—" She turned to His Lordship and grasped his sleeve. "It was he who betrayed me and put me into the count of Verdun's hands."

"Bertrand? Betrayed you?" His Lordship froze, staring at her with disbelief. All around the hall, Grandaise's men halted in their tracks and turned to look at her. "But that can't be. He fought—was beaten and wounded trying to—"

"It's true, milord. On my honor." She looked from him to Sir Axel and Sir Greeve and the others. "He followed me as I searched out the mushrooms, and when the two men came out of nowhere and seized me . . . it was Sir Bertrand who supplied them the ropes to bind me."

His face blanched as he turned to Axel and Greeve.

"Bring Bertrand to me. *Now.*"

Chapter 24

THINGS WERE EXCEPTIONALLY QUIET IN the hall as His Lordship ushered her to a seat on the dais to wait for the knight to be brought from the barracks. The baron joined them and His Lordship removed his helm and gauntlets—handing them off to a squire—then called for Grandaise's best wine to be served straightaway.

She watched him pace the dais and was unable to understand why her charge was met with such skepticism from him and the rest of the knights. He had mounted an armed force to retrieve her from Verdun, but he refused to believe her story about who had betrayed her into captivity?

"I'm telling the truth, milord," she said, looking from him to the baron and back. "I have no reason to lie about who abducted me."

"Nor, we thought, did Bertrand," His Lordship said grimly. "He was brought back to Grandaise beaten and bloody." He looked to the main doors of the hall, where Axel and Greeve had disappeared. "If he wasn't beaten by Verdun's men, then who beat him?"

She shook her head, having no explanation and feeling suddenly like she was the one against whom evidence was being gathered. She had a number of other things to tell him, but if he wouldn't believe her on this, he surely wouldn't believe the rest of what she had to say.

It seemed an age before Greeve reappeared in the doorway and strode quickly through the hall with Axel panting along behind. Greeve glanced with a misery-laden smile at Julia before announcing to his lord:

"He's gone, milord. His bed, his garments, his armor—everything."

"Absconded," Axel added. "His horse is gone from the stable."

"Dear God." His Lordship broadened his stance, bracing, looking shaken by the news and its implication. "Bertrand. Verdun's foil. He never gave a single indication . . . and he was brought back injured. . . ." He stood for a moment, letting the news sink in before lifting his head and forcing himself to shake off the vile feeling of betrayal.

"Let it be known," he announced to all in the hall, "that if Bertrand de Roland is found on Grandaise, he is to be seized and brought immediately to me." A muscle flexed in his jaw as he took Julia's hand and pulled her to her feet.

"Come. You look tired, demoiselle."

"I feel fine, milord."

"Believe me, demoiselle, you are more fatigued from your ordeal than you realize," he declared, pulling her toward the arches leading to the steps. She was surprised that he whisked her away so forcefully. But she was even more surprised when he took her straight to the chamber she had shared with Regine instead of his own quarters.

For a moment, he stood looking around the sparsely furnished quarters, as if collecting and assembling his thoughts from the chamber's unused corners.

"Why did you bring me here, milord?" Some of the tension visible in his face migrated into her.

"I wanted to tell you out of others' hearing. . . ." he said, looking at the bed, the table, the stools, the floor. She braced privately. "There will be no change between us or in my household as a result of what we were forced to do today."

"I don't think I understand, milord. What are you saying?"

"Verdun contrived this wedding to ruin me with the king. No doubt his messenger is on the way to court even now with word of our vows." He dragged his hands up and down his face. "I don't yet know how the king has responded to the word I sent him of your abduction. But I am sure Verdun will try to make it appear that I have violated the truce and the king's command in wedding you.

"To make matters worse, it will also appear that I have just violated my agreement with your abbess and the duke of Avalon. If my lands and title are not stripped from me by the king, I may lose them to the duke and the convent in reparation for dishonoring our agreement."

Dishonor? Reparation? He was speaking of their vows in such terms? She fell back a step, found herself at the edge of the bed, and sat down with a thud. She hadn't expected him to be pleased about wedding her—not at first—but she could scarcely believe that he thought being bound to her in wedlock was nothing more than his enemy's damaging contrivance.

"I wedded you to keep you safe, but a wedding does not a marriage make. As long as the vows are unconsummated, you may still be allowed to return to the convent. I will seek an annulment, but if that fails . . . I believe you may still take vows with my permission."

"I don't want your 'permission.'" She felt as if everything in her chest was melting, creating a hollow where her heart had been. "I don't want to go back to the convent. I've never wanted to take vows."

"What you want has nothing to do with it." He stalked closer to her, his arms pressed tightly to his sides. "I am bound by honor to fulfill my agreement with your abbess and the duke."

"You speak of honor—what about honoring the vows we spoke this day before a priest?" she said, anger rising into the stunned void inside her.

"We spoke *words*—that is all."

"Words that were powerful enough to make Verdun release me," she declared hotly, shooting to her feet. "Words powerful enough to make you fear the king could strip you of your lands and title."

"What I am saying is . . . words don't make a real marriage."

"Tell me, milord, what do you think *does* make a real marriage?"

Something in the tone and timbre of her voice made him look at her, and the moment he did it he knew it was a mistake. Her cheeks were flushed, her burnished hair was sweetly tossed, and her eyes flashed like faceted emeralds . . . dark-centered wells of feeling and response he had experienced and been unable to forgive himself for wanting again and again.

"I-I don't know." He felt an alarming surge of heat that had nothing to do with anger. "But I do know that *this*"— he gestured between them—"is not it!"

He backed with jerky motions to the door and exited. After he cleared the landing, it felt like he was falling down that incline of steps . . . catching himself with first one leg and then the other . . . always just one lurching motion away from being flat on his face.

His talk with her had been every bit as bad as he feared it would be. She thought their vows had somehow affirmed and ennobled the desire between them, and made it into something acceptable. But with duty, diplomacy, and destiny all against it, how could it be anything but a disaster?

He was a lord; she was a cook. He was ordered to marry another; she was promised to God. He had to think of an irate king and duke and bishop and abbess, while defending his lands from a dangerous, grasping neighbor; she didn't want to think of anything but their mutual desires. She had no idea of the dire ramifications of what had just happened to them. All she cared about was—

What? Being held in his arms . . . melting against him . . . the way she had as they rode back from Verdun? If he had anything to do with it, that would be the last time he suffered the sweet torture of holding her in his—

He stopped in the hall as wave after wave of memory

fanned through his senses . . . the softness of her against him, the prisms of tears in her eyes, the way she curled against his chest and made him feel as if she were melting into him. It suddenly felt like the very foundation of his determination was dissolving and leaching from him like chalk from old bones.

She cared for him. He swallowed against the emotion filling his throat. And he cared for her more than would be wise to admit, even to himself.

The intensity of his longing suddenly jarred him back to reality.

But a noble marriage wasn't about harbored passions and feelings run amuck. Marriage was about advantages of property and power and alliance, about duty and heirs and obligation. Marriage was an organizing, civilizing influence to be entered into with deliberation. *Not* at the tip of an enemy's sword.

He scowled and proceeded into the hall.

Why the hell couldn't he have thought of such things when he was talking to her just now?

JULIA STUMBLED TO THE BED AND SAT down, feeling drained and hollow and strangely more bereft and alone than she had as a prisoner at Verdun. She had said marriage vows, but according to her groom, wasn't truly married. She was to go back to the kitchens and cook and pretend nothing had happened.

She looked down at the ivory lutestring silk of her gown. It was a lady's gown. A fitting bridal garment. For a wellborn lady.

The hollow feeling in her center grew.

She closed the door, untied her side lacings, and drew off the lovely gown to pack it away in the small chest she had brought with her from the convent. Sophie had kept her other, better gown, so the only thing she had to wear was an older brown woolen one she had cleaned with fuller until it looked the color of rusty ashes. Thinking that it would have to do, she donned it over her chemise and tied the laces at the sides. She looked down at the patch on the skirt that covered a hole burned by a popping ember, and reached into her chest for one of the two aprons she had stitched long ago when learning to sew. As she pulled the drawstring over her head and wrapped the fabric around her, she fingered the girlish, uneven stitches and recalled the hope and anticipation with which they had been made.

She had a sudden and powerful yearning for old Sister Archibald, with her sage advice and warm, sensible wisdom. Her throat tightened and her eyes began to burn. A moment later she was running down the steps and out a side door, headed for the one place on Grandaise where she could come close to the comfort she missed . . . the chapel.

Father Dominic, the priest who served the lord and people of Grandaise, was busy tending a small plot of earth at the side of the chapel when she arrived. When he saw Julia running for the chapel doors, with tears streaming down her face, he rose and dusted the soil from his hands and cassock. He entered the chapel and found her kneeling by the altar railing, pouring out her heart in a stream of sobs and half-audible prayers.

"Here, here, my child. It can't be all that bad," he said, patting her on the shoulder. She gave a start and looked up. Seeing it was the priest, she swallowed back a sob and turned to sit on the step in front of the railing.

"The sun still treads its appointed course, the seasons come and go, and the Creator still looks upon it all with a smile. Everything else is subject to change, my child." He smiled. "Including human hearts."

"Not all hearts, Father. Some are made of stone." She sniffed and wiped her eyes with her palm. "Or they wish they were."

"Hardened and stony hearts are God's own personal grief," he said with a sigh, sitting down on the kneeling step beside her. "They're the very reason for all of this, you know." He waved to the chapel and altar and their trappings. "The Almighty wants to crack open our crusty and difficult hearts . . . to fill them with such peace and joy and goodness that they overflow into the world around us and make it a better place." He gave a rueful shrug and looked around them. "Unfortunately, we have quite a way to go."

She nodded and he gave her hand a squeeze.

"It may help you to know that many fervent prayers were answered by your return to Grandaise." Father Dominic chuckled. "I saw faces at mass in these last few days that I usually only see at Christmas and Easter. We are all grateful for your safe return, demoiselle. Or should I say 'my lady'?"

She winced.

"I'm not anyone's 'lady,' Father. Least of all His Lordship's." She halted and struggled with how best to say what was on her mind. "What makes a marriage, Father? A real and true marriage?"

"Ah." The little priest nodded, understanding now what was troubling her. "I've heard of these vows of yours. The village, the barracks, and the barns are abuzz with talk of them." He searched her troubled face. "Unfortunately, the church law is not as clear as we would wish it to be on such matters. There is the matter of spoken vows—which, I take it, were said." She nodded. "Then there is the matter of volition. The vows must be said of one's own will. Which, I take it, may be where the problem lies."

"The vows were forced," she said dejectedly.

"And then, there is the matter of consummation. I take it you have not . . ."

"How could we have?" She looked so horrified that he smiled.

"I thought not. I do hear all of the confessions, hereabouts, you know."

"Are there laws prohibiting nobles from marrying . . . non-nobility?"

"No. In fact, there have been some famous instances of French noblemen wedding common-born women. But, didn't I hear that you are wellborn?"

"My father was a baron. But a poor one. And not well-known."

"A status shared by half of the nobility of France." He chuckled and clapped his hands on his knees. "It appears to

me, my dear, that your problem is mostly a matter of volition—willingness. If you want to be married, you are."

"But what if only one of us wants to be married?"

He scratched his tonsured head and sighed again. "Then
I believe one of you will simply have to convince the
other . . . one way or another."

TRUDGING BACK UP TO THE HOUSE, HER
thoughts were on her conversation with Father Dominic
and on convincing His Lordship they *were* truly married
before he could convince her they *weren't*. That was no
small task, considering that he would have to accept her as
his lady wife while knowing as he did that it meant he
would have to stand up for her to the duke and the abbess
and even the king.

She bumped into something and jerked back with a
gasp. Her feet had, out of habit, carried her to the kitchen
door, where a moveable pink wall named Fleur stood
munching stolidly under the watchful gaze of her keeper.

"Welcome back, milady," Jacques said, dragging his hat
from his head and giving Fleur a nudge with the staff he
carried. "Go on, Fleur—give 'er a nod."

The pig looked up, and Julia could swear she bobbed
her head before going back to her bucket of peels and
slops. Jacques grinned, revealing a new gap in his teeth.
Feeling an odd trickle of warmth, Julia smiled back and
ventured a scratch of the pig's bristly ears.

Just then, one of the potboys ambled out the kitchen
door, saw her, and darted back inside to shout to the others:
"She's here! Laydee Jul-ya's here!"

Heartbeats later she was being dragged inside the
kitchen, where the folk bowed and curtsied awkwardly and
some grabbed her hands to squeeze. The heat-polished
faces and the familiar smells of flour and cabbage and
onions and roasting fowl unleashed a torrent of emotions in
her; it was all she could do to keep from dissolving into
tears.

"Sister Reggie, she was a great help," Old Mae declared, putting an arm around Regine, who blushed becomingly. "Kept us all hard at it."

"Helped us remember what was in th' dishes," Old Albee added. "I'll 'ave ye know, I been changin' my grease regular."

"I'm sure you all did very well." Julia blinked away moisture as she patted his huge, scarred hand.

She looked around the substantial stone walls, glowing hearths, and soaring ceiling. This was her kitchen, her home, the source of her strength and her hope. Whatever she did to win his heart and her future, it would have to begin here.

"I'm proud of you for working so hard while I was gone." She reached for an apron and began to roll up her sleeves. "Now, let's get to work and make this a fine supper for His Lordship and his guests."

They stared at her with mouths agape, until one of the older girls spoke up.

"But surely ye ain't gonna still work in th' kitchens . . . are ye, milady?"

"Of course I am. I'm still head cook. It's what the Almighty and His Lordship have put me here to do, and it's what I intend to do until they tell me otherwise." She looked around with a growing sense of determination and her gaze fell on the wooden trough used for mixing dough.

"Look at those lumps. Oh, Cheval"—she looked to the brawny roaster with a stubborn smile—"we have work to do."

Chapter 25

ALL EVENING AS JULIA OVERSAW THE cooking and planned the week's menus and acquisitions, the kitchen folk watched her with mounting dismay. Even they knew a lord's wedding day was supposed to be a time for feasting and merriment. But their lord hadn't mentioned a keg, pudding, or wafer, much less a whole feast of celebration. Even stranger, their new lady spent the balance of her wedding day working like a common cook. Then she closed down the kitchen and sent the other cooks off to their rest before she went to hers.

It wasn't right. They wagged their heads as they shuffled off to their beds.

Sister Regine agreed with them.

"So, you're sleeping in *our* room tonight," she said as Julia trudged along beside her, up the steps toward their shared chamber.

"And every night," Julia responded. "For the foreseeable future."

"I thought husbands and wives were supposed to share bed and board. If you're married, why are you not sharing either one?"

"The problem seems to be that we were wedded at

sword point. Since we didn't have the proper 'volition,' His Lordship is of the opinion that ours isn't a real marriage. And he's determined that our 'almost-marriage' won't change anything in his life or his household."

Regine folded her arms in indignation.

"Well, if you ask me—*and I'm very well aware that you didn't*—that man could use a few changes. In fact, he could use a wife."

"How is that?" Julia opened the door of their chamber. "What could a wife give him that he doesn't already have?"

"You honestly don't know?" Regine looked surprised, then her eyes narrowed. "You didn't pay attention in Sister Rosemary's lectures on marriage."

"I was always getting called out to the kitchens," she said crossly. "Unlike some of the girls, *I* had a full slate of duties to attend."

"Then listen carefully and I'll try to summarize. Sister Rosemary's 'principle of necessity' is that a wife is indispensable in three areas: a man's heart, a man's home, and a man's future. Her 'principle of pride' is that there are three areas in which men believe they need no help or interference: their passions, their possessions, and their futures. It doesn't take but half a wit to see that the 'principles of necessity' and the 'principles of pride' are bound to clash."

"My respect for Sister Rosemary's wisdom grows," Julia said. "Go on."

"Men have to be shown how much women can improve their hearts, their homes, and their futures. Women have to show them by becoming lovers of their hearts, partners in their homes and possessions, and gentle guides toward good and worthy actions."

"And that's it?" Julia sat on the bed, slipped off her shoes, and curled her legs beneath her. "That's the test of a good and proper wife?"

"According to Sister Rosemary."

"Then what is the test of a marriage?"

"Well"—Regine scowled and her voice trailed off—"following Rosemary's logic, I suppose that would be if people take vows and become lovers and partners who help each other through life."

"It's all about that wretched 'volition.' He has to want it, too. He has to want—" She stopped short of saying *me,* but that was the long and the short of it.

She sat for a few moments in silence, thinking about that evening in the tower room . . . of how he had kissed and caressed her and held her as if he wanted to pull her inside him and make her a part of his very heart. The combination of her food and his powerful sense of smell had cracked open his tightly guarded composure and allowed her to touch his passions and emotions, however briefly.

He had wanted her then. He could want her again.

She had to get him alone, feed him, and remove that wretched band from his nose long enough for her food to free his passions and emotions.

Then, of course, she'd have to keep him from putting it back on.

As she finished her evening ablutions and prayers, doused the candles, and climbed into bed, she felt a spark of stubborn determination relighting in her.

"Regine?"

"Uh-huh?" Regine's voice came through the darkness, clogged with sleep.

"What did Sister Rosemary say that women need men for?"

"I don't believe she ever got around to that," came the drowsy reply. "She's a nun, you know."

THE KITCHEN FOLK WERE NOT ESPECIALLY surprised to find the hearths already alight the next morning when they arrived, and the tables piled high with fresh produce and berries and cheeses and herbs brought by folk who had heard of Julia's return and had come to wish her well in her marriage to His Lordship. Julia stared at the piles of edible gifts through a mist of rising tears and declared that with such a bounty they would do some fine cooking indeed.

The kitchen folk seemed to understand that she was throwing herself into her work for a reason and, with plenty of opinions but no prying, they forged ahead with her. The older girls were set to cleaning and seasoning baskets of trout for dinner, it being a fast day, and Cheval was set to stirring a heavy dough that would encase them. Mae was set to making a walnut and garlic sauce while Old Albee worked on sugaring nuts of various kinds. Fran the Larderer grumbled as she searched for storage for the many gifts and Pennett the Ovenman was assigned to assemble and tend large pots of rice.

The younger girls were put to cutting and grating winter squash from the cold cellar and Ancient Odile set about measuring butter and cheese of various kinds. Julia measured spices and set the potboys to grinding, and Regine and the younger girls cut dried plums, dates, and apricots and stuffed them with blanched almonds and sugared pieces of walnut.

When all was ready, Julia donned a fresh apron and accompanied the first course into the hall. The great chamber was almost as crowded as the kitchen. The baron and his knights were crowded around the head table with His Lordship and Grandaise's knights. The lower boards were lined with Grandaise's men-at-arms and a few of Crossan's luckier warriors, sitting shoulder to shoulder . . . their eyes gleaming with anticipation, and their interactions oddly both tense and polite.

The first course, intended to "open the stomach," was a lovely Green Porée, made of chard, tart verjuice, garlic and pepper, into which a scoop of Tredura, or hashed leeks, was dropped. His Lordship and the baron looked at each other in puzzlement; those two fast-day staples had never been combined, to their knowledge. His Lordship was about to take his first bite when she appeared at his side with her tasting spoon and her stool.

"*Tsk, tsk,* milord. You didn't wait for me." She pulled out her spoon and dipped it into the fragrant pottage. She sighed as she tested the dish, then nodded. "By all means, eat. It's quite safe." She gestured to the baron's bowl. "Truly, Baron. I believe you'll find it a lovely combination."

Crossan pursed one corner of his mouth and leaned around her to look at His Lordship.

"Your bride is your taster?" he asked, not bothering to hide his dismay.

"I—um—she has been my head cook until n-now and volunteered to—" He was speechless with embarrassment. Julia hadn't imagined him like that.

Crossan took a bite, and his eyes closed just as His Lordship's did. Their joint sigh ignited a murmur of anticipation all around the hall. As the serving proceeded and the knights began to eat, sighs and groans and exclamations began to rise from every part of the hall.

His Lordship was soon staring at the empty bottom of his bowl. When he looked up, she was staring at him and could have sworn he blushed.

"Good, milord?" she asked with a musical lilt that made his hands curl around the arms of his chair. "Wait until you see what else I have planned."

Winter Squash Tart, as it happened, was the next course. Litters filled with rows of deep golden pies arrived from the kitchen. She cut one into fourths and served a quarter each to His Lordship and the baron.

"Winter squash and almond milk . . . spices like nutmeg and cinnamon and ginger and a bit of cheese and sugar," she detailed the contents of the tart as she tasted. Again she sighed and pushed the silver trencher over to His Lordship. "I confess, it would be better with cow's milk. But since it is a fast day . . ." She leaned close to him, making certain that her breath moved his hair and bathed his ear. "Promise you won't tell Father Dominic . . . but I put a few eggs in them."

He froze until she moved away. Then he took a bite . . . and then a larger bite . . . and then a still larger bite. Then he called for a whole tart.

"Troth—you'd better save me a piece of that!" the baron demanded, licking his fingers as he eyed the tart being cut.

The next course—it being a fast day—was fish in cases of dough. Each packet of dough was cut in the shape of a fish and pinched together around a trout such that a fin stuck out of the top. When she broke open the first of the hard pastry shells, there was a tender succulent trout on a bed of savory rice . . . to which she added Old Mae's Walnut Garlic Sauce. She inhaled the vapors with a flair, then took a taste and smiled.

"I had forgotten just how indulgent 'fast' days can be with the right fish and sauce." When His Lordship made to retrieve his trencher from her, she pulled it back. "Oh, no, milord. I really should have a second taste. One cannot be too careful these days." When she took a second bite, she chewed with exaggeration, though, in fact, the fish nearly melted in her mouth. She laughed with a teasing rasp of half-exposed desire. "As you can see, milord"—she looked straight into his eyes and unveiled for one breathtaking instant the heat simmering inside her—"it's perfectly safe."

Yanking his gaze from hers, he pulled his trencher back in front of him with hands that trembled visibly. She watched him dig into the fish and rice and savory sauce like a driven man. He focused so intently on the flavors and pleasure of the food that he hardly noticed when that demolished pastry fish was replaced by a fresh one and a hand intruded to drizzle sauce over it for him.

"Damme, Grandaise," Crossan said with his mouth stuffed full, "do you always eat like this?"

"Since *she* arrived," His Lordship said, pointing at her with his knife.

She folded her arms and gave the baron a confident smile.

"Saints! She's worth her weight in gold." He gazed at her with undiluted awe. "Now I see why you were dead set on having her back, Grandaise! Hell, if *my* cook could produce food like this, I'd marry him, too—beard and all!"

Laughter rolled around the hall. By the time the final course of entremets was served—sugared nuts and stuffed dried fruits intended to "close the stomach"—the atmosphere in the hall was downright jovial.

As the platters and bowls and trenchers were cleared away, Griffin watched Julia wander up and down the head table, collecting admiration as she chatted with Grandaise's knights and Crossan's sons. The young men were unfailingly polite and even charming as they extolled the virtues of her golden tarts and clever "fish in crust." But every good word they spoke and adoring glance they aimed at her took a bite out of his food-mellowed mood.

What the devil was she doing, playing the coy maiden with his and Crossan's men? She had spoken vows with him only the day before, and until he was granted a proper annulment, her status lay somewhere in the murky region of *more than a cook but less than a wife.*

He began to search for a proper description of her status, and quickly eliminated all possibilities until he came to the word *bride.* He shrank from that designation at first, but soon realized it was the most accurate and useful description of her role. "Bride" indicated the legal status of spoken vows, but implied newness of relation . . . a not-yet-completed exchange of intimacy and transfer of domestic power. In the end he decided it fit his situation and requirements exactly: Perhaps it could be used to rein in her behavior while keeping her at something of a distance.

He turned to call her to his side and saw her bump into a servant carrying a pot of her Green Porée . . . which went all over the front of her apron. There was a flurry as Axel, Greeve, and several others jumped up to assist, but in the end, she removed her apron, which had prevented the spillage from reaching her gown, and all was well.

"Julia!" He called and motioned her to his side. She came with a smile and a sway that he tried unsuccessfully not to watch.

"Yes, milord?"

"Sit down and tell the baron how and where you learned to cook," he said, pointing to the stool between his and the baron's chairs.

She sat as she was bade and began to tell Crossan her story, including details Griffin had never heard. A baron for a father. A lady for a mother. An abbess that assigned her to the kitchen when she was only ten years old . . . for punishment. He found himself leaning closer to hear her vivid and sometimes humorous descriptions of the sisters, the maidens, and the abbess's clever management of the convent's affairs.

"Oh, and I've some interesting news for you, Your Lordship." She turned to him with a new light in her eyes. "Did you know that Grandaise and Verdun have identical kitchens? Right down to the eight sides, five hearths, and the cold well under the steps."

"How would you know that?" he demanded, pausing in the midst of reaching for more sugared nuts and stuffed dried fruits from a nearby tray.

"I visited it. Lady Sophie—the count's daughter—went on and on about the wonderful kitchen and I asked to see it. She secreted me there, late one night."

He almost choked on an almond-stuffed apricot and had to look at her.

"The count's daughter?"

"The very one." Her eyes were full of mesmerizing lights. "She visited me in my prison chamber. She is quite a young woman. It seems I was abducted because the count believed I was actually *more* to you than a cook." She glanced at Crossan with outraged innocence. "Can you imagine?"

"Julia—" he said in a warning tone, feeling pricked and irritable.

"If you will excuse me, milord," she said with a pointed little smile at his reaction. "I am no doubt needed in the kitchen."

As they watched her go, the baron leaned toward Griffin.

"She may have been your cook and even your taster, once upon a time. But she is your bride now, Grandaise. What the devil is she doing still in your kitchen, tending a blazing hearth and wearing patched garments?"

Griffin's ears caught fire. He had seen the patch on her gown, too, and for some reason it infuriated him. He thrust to his feet and headed for the passage to the kitchens. Catching up with Julia in the covered walkway, he pulled

her by the wrist out of the covered stone arches and down
the slope that swept around toward the kitchen yard and
outbuildings.

"Milord—"

"Just what the devil do you think you're doing?" he demanded, pulling her around to face him and backing her
against the nearby wall. "Wearing patched garments . . .
flirting and playing fair and free with my men . . ."

"You told me yesterday that nothing would change as a
result of the words we spoke. That I am still your cook.
And as your cook, it is my duty to—"

"Well, you're no longer my cook." He startled himself
with what he'd said. "That is . . . you are to cook . . .
still . . . but you are no longer *just* my cook. You are also
my bride. And until this marriage nonsense is sorted out,
you must be more circumspect in your behavior and appearance." His gaze dropped to her worn gown with its of-
fending patch. "They reflect on me."

"I cannot possibly be both 'cook' and 'bride,' milord,"
she said looking up at him with those huge green eyes and
a stubborn angle to her chin. "I have neither the patience
nor the garments for it. Anyway . . . I believe you need a
cook far more than you need a bride."

"What?" He paused a moment, feeling that he'd been
flanked and not quite certain how it had happened. "What
do you mean, I need a cook?"

"Well, when you consider what cooks are good for . . .
securing, storing, and preparing nutritious foods . . . building your strength . . . guarding your health and safety . . .
concocting savory dishes . . . tempting and pleasing your
palate . . . entertaining your allies. . . ."

"Julia," he growled.

"And then you consider what brides are good for . . . demanding fine clothes . . . decorating your hall with their
presence . . . spending your manly strength in bed . . . wasting your precious hours with lustful pleasure . . . distracting
you from duty with fleshy thoughts and temptations. . . ."

"Dammit, Julia—"

"Which would you rather have, milord?" She edged

close enough to brush up against him. "Me clothed and industrious in your kitchen or me naked and demanding in your bed?"

His tongue was so thick that he could hardly swallow. Visions of naked curves and tangled hair and sweaty sheets erupted and took over his mind. A reaction flashed through his skin. It was instantly hot and sensitive, screaming for a more direct and pleasurable contact everywhere his garments touched it.

"Cook," he choked out. Then he lurched back, wheeled, and strode away.

Her breath came hard and quick and her eyes glistened as she watched him flee. She folded her arms, nodded, and gave a little laugh.

"That's what I thought."

Chapter 26

SIR REYNARD DE CROSSAN ARRIVED IN the banner-lined antechamber of the king's audience hall, and sat down, propping his helmet on his knee, his elbow on the top of his helmet, and his head in his hand. Nearly a week ago the king's chamberlain had listened to his report and ushered Lord Griffin's letter and then Reynard himself through that massive set of doors to the king.

"I thought I had this damned thing settled!" King Philip had roared.

After his councillors talked him into a less ferocious royal mood, he quizzed Reynard on the alleged abduction. His first reaction was skepticism that Verdun would be so reckless as to defy a royal order. His second was disbelief that the loss of a mere cook would rouse such outrage in a nobleman of Grandaise's status. His third was to demanded proof that the maid in question was under the protection of not only the Count of Grandaise, but of the Convent of the Brides of Virtue and the Duke of Avalon as well.

"Good God," he snapped, "if it's true, a cook in my realm has more defenders than I have!"

He sent immediately for the Duke of Avalon and for

three days Reynard had sat in the king's outer chamber waiting for the duke to appear.

Now the chamberlain called his name and ushered him into the king's presence. Finally, Reynard thought, there would be some resolution to—

But when he stepped inside, his heart all but stopped. King Philip was seated at his writing table with his councillors gathered around him and a clerk seated nearby, taking down whatever the king indicated must be recorded. Standing before the king was a mud-spattered knight in mail and spurs . . . wearing a red-and-white tabard. Verdun's colors.

"Sir Thomas de Albans has brought disturbing news." The king's comment and glare were both aimed at Reynard. "It seems your lord has married his mistress, and in so doing has dealt a terrible insult to the house of Verdun and to our own royal authority."

"B-but, Majesty," Reynard stammered, momentarily unmanned. "Lord Griffin could not possibly have wedded his m-mistress. He doesn't have one."

"He brought this female with him from Paris a few weeks ago, Majesty," Sir Thomas protested with a fierce look at Reynard. "She has masqueraded as his cook. And now he has wedded her."

Reynard's eyes flew wide. "Majesty, this 'cook' he is supposed to have wedded is the young woman who was abducted a week ago."

"One and the same?" Philip thought on that for a moment, sitting forward. "So is this female a cook or a mistress?

"*Cook.*"

"*Mistress.*"

The knights answered at once, then looked daggers at each other.

"What have you to say for your lord, Sir Reynard?" the king demanded.

"I have been gone from Grandaise for a week now, Majesty." Reynard braced. "There may have been developments, but I am certain Lord Griffin would not wed anyone in defiance of your command."

"He did, Majesty," Sir Thomas insisted. "I saw it with

my own eyes. Grandaise came to get the wench and when milord Verdun brought her out . . . the Beast wedded the wench on the spot . . . right on milord's doorstep. An insult to my lord's honor and a shocking defiance of Your Majesty's expressed will."

"Damned if I'm not sick of dealing with the lot of you." Philip shoved to his feet and leaned toward the opposing pair with a face like granite. "Calais is under siege . . . the northern provinces are a shambles . . . and the Flemish merchants are near revolt. I'll not hear another word until Avalon—"

"Here, Majesty!" came a breathless voice entering from the antechamber. All turned to the barrel-chested figure in ducal robes, hurrying to join them. He paused some feet away for a graceful bow. "I came as soon as I got your letter."

"And not a moment too soon." Philip sank back wearily into the cushions of his great carved chair. "This girl—this cooking wench of Grandaise's—are you or are you not pledged to protect her?" Philip demanded.

"Cooking wench?"

"The chit from the Brides of Virtue!" the king snapped.

"Oh. The *cook*." The duke nodded with a wince. "She was sent from the convent to revitalize the comte de Grandaise's kitchens."

Philip searched out the name in Grandaise's letter. "Julia of Childress?"

"That sounds like the name. The abbess of the convent did not want to let the girl go, but the bishop liked the color of Grandaise's gold and ordered the abbess to send the girl with him."

"Grandaise had *gold?*" the king said, his eyes widening.

"A deal was struck: The maid would go to Grandaise and work for him for a year, establishing his kitchens, and then would return to the convent to take vows. I was to act as guarantor." The amicable duke looked alarmed. "Are you saying, Majesty, that something has happened to the maid?"

"Grandaise may have wedded her . . . in defiance of a

royal command that he marry Verdun's daughter to end their long-standing feud." Philip looked to his councillors, who nodded affirmation. Then he picked up a letter in each hand and frowned, weighing them against each other.

"So. This Julia of Childress is a cook . . . who may or may not have been Grandaise's mistress . . . before he may or may not have made her his wife," he mused irritably. "Verdun is seeking compensation for the violated betrothal." He tossed both letters onto the desk in disgust. "Troth—the man has ballocks . . . demanding compensation, when a month ago he stood in this very chamber and said he'd rather put his daughter to the sword than hand her over to Grandaise!"

"Majesty, this is a grave insult to my seigneur, but also to the crown of France." Sir Thomas tried to steer the king back to considering his lord's plea.

"But it was Verdun who provoked it, by abducting the maid in the first place," Reynard countered. "How else would she have come to be there?"

"I-I . . . believe she was lost in the woods . . . and . . . found and taken back to Verdun." Sir Thomas was thinking on his feet, but too slowly.

The king gave a snort of disbelief.

"What the hell kind of female has a convent, a duke, and two counts up in arms over her?" Philip asked no one in particular. "What? Is she Helen of Troy?"

"A fetching wench, as I recall, but not a face to launch a thousand ships," the duke said, rubbing his eyes and trying to recall that night at the convent. "I believe her attractions lay more in the culinary realm. She is a remarkable cook, Majesty. She made a hedgehog conceit for my young son that he still speaks of. I believe the abbess would have gladly killed the bishop in order to keep her."

"Which bishop?" the king asked.

"Rheims," Avalon answered.

"Well, that's understandable."

At that time a figure who had gone unnoticed rose from a silk-upholstered bench beneath the large window at the side of the chamber. The king looked up as the dignified woman in a silk brocade gown, wimple, and veiled head-dress glided across the floor and through his advisors to his side.

"Milord husband," Queen Jeanne said as she placed a hand on his velvet-clad shoulder, "too often you are France's indulgent 'father.' You let these squabbling children divert you from more important matters of state. Why not send a representative to learn the truth and deal with it for you?" She glanced at Avalon, who sensed what she intended and groaned audibly. "The duke, who already has an obligation in the case, could carry the royal interest south and investigate for you."

"Please, Majesty," Avalon said with a wince, but sensed it had been decided the instant the words left the queen's lips. Jeanne of Burgundy was a formidable woman, and some said the power behind the throne. Clearly, the king took her council to heart . . . evidenced by the fact that his councillors stepped back to allow her access as she approached. "I already must see to the interests of the abbess and convent."

"Surely, Avalon, you would not consider putting the interests of a gaggle of nuns above that of your divinely anointed sovereign." Philip engaged the duke's gaze and forced a surrender.

"Never, Majesty."

"You already know more about this mess than anyone at court. Go. Figure out what's happened and bring these two rabid hounds to heel. I may have need of their garrisons soon, and I'll not have their strength and substance squandered in senseless battles." He motioned to his secretary to begin drawing up the official document embodying his decree. "Do whatever you have to do, Avalon. Make them see reason."

FOR THE NEXT TWO DAYS, JULIA COOKED her heart out. And Grandaise—both the man and the people of the great hall—ate very well indeed.

Chaudumé of Pike . . . Turnips with Chestnuts and Sage . . . Fennel and Leek Torte . . . Cold Pork with Sage and

Caraway dressing . . . roasted carrots in ginger glaze . . .
Summer Squash Torte with Cheese . . . poached pears in
spiced syrup . . . apple mousse with almond milk . . . sugared
almond torte . . . and wafers. Lots of wafers. The potboys
were ecstatic. And the Baron Crossan declared that when
these present "troubles" were over, he might just forget
which road led home.

Despite His Lordship's insistence that she needn't
"taste" his food any longer, she appeared at his side at each
meal to receive firsthand his reaction to what was served.
The way he struggled to contain his pleasure in the food,
the way his eyes lingered ever longer on her, and the in-
creasing frequency of incidental brushes of his hands
against her hinted that his resolve to keep their vows from
changing anything in his life was wavering.

With each dish she produced and each meal her kitchen
served, Julia refined the plan that had been developing in
her mind and set another part of it in motion. Critical to her
success, however, were two things available only at Verdun: Grand Jean's book and a quantity of truffles. To that
end, she sent a message to Sophie of Verdun by one of the
older and shiftier potboys.

"That's a cinch," Raoul said with a mischievous glint in
his eye. "I'm good at gettin' in an' out, wi'out bein' seen."

"You must place this letter"—she wrapped his fingers
around the rolled parchment—"directly into Lady Sophie's
hands. Only hers. She is shorter than me and pretty, with
dark hair and eyes. She shouldn't be hard to spot."

"I'll find 'er, milady. She'll have it a'fore nightfall."

It was risky, sending a message to Sophie. If the boy
was caught it might be seen as disloyalty—Bertrand's betrayal had pierced Griffin of Grandaise to the core. Even a
suspicion of betrayal would ruin her with him. But she had
to try.

It was late and the lamps were burning low that night
when a bedraggled and breathless potboy burst through the
kitchen door. Julia rushed to help her messenger to a stool
at the table.

"Are you all right?" she asked anxiously and sagged with relief when he nodded. "And did you deliver it? Into her very hand?"

The lad nodded, grinning. "She's pretty, milady. But not as pretty as you."

Julia laughed and set a whole plate of wafers before him.

THE NEXT MIDDAY, JUST BEFORE DINNER, ONE of the potboys came rushing into the kitchen calling for Julia. "Come, milady—there's someone askin' for ye."

Julia wiped her damp hands on her apron and hurried outside, thinking it might be a messenger with the truffles from Verdun. She stopped stock-still at the sight of Lady Sophie standing in the kitchen yard, wearing a hooded cloak and a determined expression. In her arms were a large black book and a cloth-covered basket, and behind her, a groom holding her baggage-laden horse.

"Sophie!" Julia was so surprised she could scarcely say the name. "What are you doing here?"

"You asked for these"—she held out the book and basket—"and I decided to bring them myself."

"Oh, Sophie!" She opened her arms and hurried to engulf the lady of Verdun in a huge, boisterous hug. "I can't tell you what this means to me! How can I ever thank you?"

"I had a devil of a time getting into your old chamber to search for that book. And Francois—ever since that night you cooked with him, he's been snarly and secretive. I had to wait till he was out of the kitchen and steal into the larder to filch these 'truffle' things." Sophie drew back enough to unload the things into her arms. "This better be important." At closer range, Julia noted an uncharacteristic trace of strain and uncertainty in her expression.

"It is. Very important," Julia said, touching Sophie's cheek. "Goodness, Sophie, you've taken a terrible risk coming here. If your father finds out—"

"He'll have a royal fit. He'll stomp and swear like a devil and probably behead somebody." She tossed her head strongly enough to send her hood sliding down to her shoulders. "But it won't be me."

"Don't be so sure—" Julia recalled her encounter with Bardot of Verdun.

"Oh, I'm sure," Sophie said tautly. "Because I'm not going back there."

"What?" Julia blinked, thinking surely she had misheard. "You mean—"

"I'm not going back to Verdun. Ever." She squared her shoulders and raised her chin. "I need shelter and protection. Do you think your 'beast' would be willing to take me in?"

Julia took her in to the kitchen and sat her down at one of the empty work tables. Sophie looked around in astonishment.

"This is exactly like Francois's kitchen at Verdun," she said.

"Exactly. Remember, I said to Francois that our kitchens were identical. He didn't seem pleased to hear it."

"Why would he be?" Sophie said. "He brags about how he planned it and how unique it is in all of France." She frowned. "But that's not true."

"No, it's not." Julia smiled, wondering what she would say when she met *the Beast*. "There may be quite a few surprises in store for you at Grandaise."

She introduced Sophie to Regine and enlisted the sister's aid in keeping her presence there a secret until the appropriate time to reveal it. Together they got her some wine to steady her nerves and, between sending the two evening courses up to the hall, listened to her story.

"I thought when you married the Bea—*the count* that I would be free . . . that perhaps my father would consider making me a match with someone I know . . . someone who . . ." Sophie lowered her gaze to her cup, cleared her throat and composed herself. "But as soon as you rode off with your count"—she looked up at Julia—"he was already scheming to barter me off to some German prince."

Tears came to Sophie's eyes, but she glared so hotly that they dried before falling.

"I heard my father laughing and saying the prince is

monstrously fat . . . that his first wife died when he rolled
over on her in bed."

Julia made a choked sound that was halfway between a
laugh and a gasp. She and Regine looked at each other and
reached for Sophie's hands.

"Well, you're safe here," Julia declared. "I'm sure His
Lordship will give you sanctuary." She chewed the corner
of her lip, thinking. "I just have to find the right time to tell
him that you're here."

FROM THE COVER OF OUTBUILDINGS AT THE
edge of the village around Grandaise, Martin de Gies
watched the front gate for sign of a gray horse and rider.

"Dammit, Sophie," he swore quietly, glancing up to
judge the late hour by the red streaks in the sky overhead.
"What do you think you're doing?"

He thought of his men and the column of smoke they
had been riding to investigate that morning when he spotted a familiar gray horse and cloaked rider headed along
the edge of the trees across the fields from Verdun's main
gates. By now, Gerard and the men would have assessed
the situation, rendered what aid they could, and reported
back to the garrison. All without him. And he would have
to explain, when he returned, what had made him send the
patrol on without him.

Sophie. If he went back now he would have to reveal
that he'd spotted her on horseback, unescorted, riding east,
and that by the time he tracked her through the woods, he
had found her riding furiously for the gates of Grandaise.

He couldn't imagine what had possessed her to head
straight for the seat of her father's sworn enemy, but he had
a good idea of what had set her to flight in the first place.
For the past three days she had teased and enchanted and
out-and-out seduced him . . . had melted his reason, resolve, and resistance . . . and all but succeeded in reducing
his defenses to cinders. He'd been on the brink of throwing
her down on her bed and giving her exactly what she was
asking for when she whispered into his overheated ear that

both she and Verdun were his for the taking . . . words that seemed like a betrayal of his oath to his lord and his sense of honor . . . words that rattled his very bones with their potent allure.

After following her to Grandaise, he stopped long enough to remove his armor, hide his colors, and swipe a ragged cloak from a clothing line to cover his leather jerkin and sword. By keeping to the edge of the outlying barns and sheds he had managed to escape detection. But if Grandaise's men found him here, just outside their walls, his life was probably forfeit.

And if he returned home without Sophie, he could face a similar fate. Her father had trusted him with her safe-keeping. If anything happened to her . . .

A stab of loss struck him, sending an ache of longing fanning through his chest. If anything happened to her—to those big brown eyes, sweetly petulant lips, and saucy tongue—he would never be able to forgive himself.

He couldn't imagine what she was doing in the hall of her father's dreaded rival, or how he was going to convince his seigneur that she had gone there of her own free will. His only hope was to get her out of there and home again before her father found them *both* missing.

"Go home, Sophie. Don't make me come in there after you."

Chapter 27

IT HAD BEEN A LONG, ARDUOUS DAY and showed every sign of getting longer. As Griffin entered his hall, he removed his sooty gauntlets and brushed at the combination of dust and ash that had collected between the links of his mail. He had ridden out early to investigate a column of smoke spotted by one of the tower sentries. On the way, he encountered a family of displaced shepherds and discovered that their cottage, situated on his pasture lands, had been set on fire by ill-dressed but well-armed men who wore no colors.

They might as well have worn their red and white, Griffin thought. He knew exactly where they had come from.

It was a cruel and cowardly attack, coming just at dawn and aimed at simple people who had nothing to steal and no weapons to defend themselves. The worst of it was, they had returned to their cottage just yesterday, after having spent several days in the safety of their lord's walls. He and his men spent the rest of the morning and early afternoon riding to other outlying cottages and bringing the vulnerable folk back into the safety of Grandaise.

He and his patrol had missed dinner and as they returned, all the men could talk about was what they hoped Lady Julia would have for them at supper. They each had favorite dishes and described them in such loving detail that he felt his stomach rumbling and his patience dissolving in the water his mouth was making. Now he felt fatigued and gritty and ravenous . . . in no condition to have to encounter Julia's delectable food and even more delectable presence.

Night after night he sat there in his hall, in his chair, watching and wanting her . . . being stewed in his own damned juices. He knew what she was doing. Being cooperative and reasonable and diligent. Letting his own passions do her work for her. And they were. Dammit.

He wanted nothing more than to scoop her off her feet, bear her straight up to his chambers, and love her until he worked out the ache in his body and the fever in his blood. But his desire for her had already wreaked havoc on his standing with the king and brought him to the brink of war. Imagine what catastrophes awaited should he ever truly tried to make her his wife!

"Supper is a bit delayed, milord," Arnaud the Steward said to him as he strode onto the dais and handed off his gauntlets and helm to his squire. He looked at Griffin's streaked face and dusty mail and smiled apologetically. "If you would like, milord, I can have water sent to your chambers so that you may bathe and change your clothes as you wait."

Grumbling at the delay in supper but grateful for a few moments of solitude, he trudged up the steps to his chambers, where a crew of house women had begun filling his great copper-lined tub with heated water. At that moment, the sight of the steam rising from the water and the prospect of soaking his aching body in warmth were every bit as welcome as a platter of well-peppered beef.

His squire helped to remove his armor and boots. When the women left, he stepped naked into that beckoning tub, sank into the water, and groaned as his squire brought him a tankard of mulled wine. He drank and soaked and let his

head drop back and his eyes close . . . gradually letting go
of the day's strains and worries. Around him footsteps and
scrapes indicating movement told him his squire was dusting and putting away his garments and laying out fresh
ones. . . .

"Wake up, milord. Your supper awaits." A voice cut
through the pleasant darkness . . . a familiar voice . . . a
woman's voice. He sat up with a jerk and fumbled to keep
from emptying the dregs of his tankard into his bathwater.
Sitting on a chair across from the end of his tub was the
subject of the tantalizing dream he had just been forced to
abandon. There she was. In the flesh. Looking warm and
fresh and delectable enough to eat.

"What the devil—" He reddened, checking to see how
much of him was exposed. Thankfully, not much; the water
was gray from the soap. "What are you doing here?"

"I came to give you a taste of something," she said,
leaving the chair to kneel beside the tub. That was when he
realized she had a covered dish in her hands.

"You invaded my bath to—to—"

"Bring you something to eat. You are hungry, aren't
you?" she said calmly, discarding the lid and drawing out a
wedge of what appeared to be custard pie or tart. "I think
you may remember this." She held it up toward him, urging
him to take a bite.

"This is absurd. You shouldn't be here." He looked
around frantically, feeling a prickle of anxiety running
over his scalp. "Where is my squire?"

"Not here. Try this, milord. I made it specially for you."
She smiled and he hoped it wasn't because she could see
his growing panic.

"Cooks do not invade their lords' chambers and force-
feed them tarts," he declared irritably, staring at that
morsel and feeling his mouth begin to water. "I am about to
leave my bath, and if you don't remove yourself, you'll
have only yourself to blame when you're subjected to the
sight of a man's nakedness." When she didn't move, he
glowered and leaned forward with an air of threat.

"Don't expect me to pick you up when you faint," he announced, clapping hands on the side of the tub as if preparing to rise. "If you swoon, you'll lie where you fall until my squire comes and scrapes you up."

"I'm a cook, not a bride, remember? Nothing on your person could possibly unhinge me." She narrowed her eyes defiantly. "I've seen oxen and capons and even *sausages* being made."

She shoved the pie an inch closer, with a stubborn look. She was calling him on his threat, and he wasn't certain which was more alarming . . . his desperation to have her go or his desire to have her stay.

"All right, dammit. If it will get you to leave," he said, his voice suddenly thick. He bit off a piece and as he chewed, his heart all but stopped.

He knew that taste. An egg-based custard flavored by chunks of rich pink-fleshed fish and a musky, garlicky, mushroom-like flavor that coated his mouth like culinary velvet. It was a heaven-inspired pairing of the very best produce of land and sea . . . *salmon and truffles*. He chewed slowly, luxuriating in the tastes, feeling the flavors seeping up the back of his throat into his head, rattling the closed and padlocked gates of his sense of smell.

"Where did you get—" He looked at her with his mouth drooping and she stuffed another bite of the torte into it. He chewed, feeling a shiver course through him. He seized the remainder of the piece and took the third bite on his own. "How did you ever find—where did you get this recipe?"

"We cooks have our sources, milord. You do recognize the taste?"

He caught the knowing glint in her eyes and felt a quake of anticipation run through his body. She knew something she couldn't possibly know. But just now the larger part of his consciousness was focused on that well-remembered and often-longed-for taste.

"Truffles," he said thickly, his mouth already watering for more.

"Salmon Truffle Torte," she said, then braced on the side of the tub and pushed to her feet. "There is more, milord. Lots more." Her voice was low and earthy and as thick with the potential for pleasure as the torte she had just fed him. "But you have to get out of the tub and come with me to get it."

At that moment he would have followed her to the end of the earth. Stark naked.

He rose out of the water like Neptune himself, and stalked out of the tub and across the stone floor to the toweling draped over a stool. His legs were a little weak and he could feel memories and emotions stirring in him . . . palpable and volatile and not a little alarming. He turned his back to her so she wouldn't see how his hands were trembling. He pulled on a pair of tights and then a long shirt and simple tunic. The moment his belt was on, she took him by the hand and led him out the door and up the winding stairs.

The sentry lookout was much as it had been a fortnight ago. The large wooden shutters were thrown back to the open air and there were hampers stacked around, and a linen-draped table was set before the bench on the balcony. His mouth began to water and the hollow feeling in his middle intensified as he sank onto the edge of the cushion-strewn seat and watched her light several candles and place them just out of the breeze. In the sky overhead, the dusky rose of evening had given place to encroaching purple hues. He gripped his knees and watched her swaying toward him with something in her hands.

She slid onto the cushion-littered seat beside him and held out a spoon of something. After a moment, he opened his mouth and was rewarded by another taste he hadn't experienced in more than seven years: Oyster and Truffle Soup.

Upon his first bite, his eyes closed. On his second, he gave a ragged sigh. His third he rolled around in his mouth, savoring the meatiness of the oysters, the richness of the broth, and the pungent flavor of the mushrooms.

"It's been a long time since I had oysters," he said, his voice resonant with pleasure he couldn't suppress. "Especially with truffles."

"The oysters came from Bordeaux," she said, edging closer.

"And the truffles?" he asked, taking another bite.

"We cooks have our—"

"Sources," he finished for her, staring into her softened smile and shimmering eyes. He lost track of everything else for a moment . . . until she guided his hand to fill the spoon and raise it to his mouth. And while he was occupied with imbibing that liquid paradise, she slipped the band from his nose.

"Hey!" He tried to grab it back but she refused to release it, looking steadily into his gaze, making him think about what she was doing.

"You won't need this tonight," she said softly, exerting just enough force to take it from him and lay in on the table by his trencher.

He stared at the curled band of metal on the white linen and realized what she was doing. For the last seven years that band of steel had been his sole defense against both the sensory assaults of the world and his own charged and overpowering emotions. Tonight, she was stripping him of that defense and demanding that he let his emotions run wherever his potent senses led. The alarming thing was that she had no idea where those complex and volatile emotions could lead. And for once, he didn't, either.

"This isn't fair, you know," he declared.

"Fair? You expect 'fair' from a maid who was sold by an abbess to a nobleman who all but imprisoned her in his kitchen and made her cook for hours on end without a single word of praise or simple gratitude?"

He stared at her heart-shaped face with its stubborn chin; at the clear, bright mind visible inside those haunting eyes; and at the strong, sleek little body honed by exertion to withstand hours of intense labor. She was right. She was no shrinking violet or easily bruised lily. She was a strong, capable, intelligent young woman. And she was demanding to be let into the heart she had already laid siege to and won.

He closed his eyes and prayed he wasn't making a huge

mistake. Because, if she were willing to weather the storms that were coming their way . . .

Then it was done.

His decision made, he lifted the bowl of soup to his nose and took a long, slow breath. His eyes closed as the vapors—mingled scents of earth and sea, perfectly blended—curled through his deprived and ravenous sense, reaching for the very core of him.

"He made them for you, didn't he?" she said quietly, near his ear. "Grand Jean." He opened his eyes and nodded.

"How did you know?"

She smiled and left the bench. He continued to eat and by the time he reached the bottom of the bowl, she was back with an uncovered platter.

Rich scents billowed up from an artful fan of slices of golden, sautéed capon . . . basking in a sauce made of truffles and mushrooms in wine and almond cream. For a moment he couldn't speak, couldn't move, couldn't even blink.

Then she draped a slice onto a finger of bread and offered it to him.

Flavors and smells that seemed to come from both the depths of earth and the heights of Heaven filled his head. He ate that piece, then another, and another. . . .

Memories and old lessons mingled with new desires and awareness to burst through the last of his carefully wrought restraints. He looked up into her eyes, his head filled with potent scents from his past and his body filled with warmth from her nearness, and saw his past and future merging.

He reached for her, drew her close to him on the bench, and startled her by putting a piece of the capon into her mouth. She groaned softly and melted against his shoulder. Her eyes glistened and her lips reddened as she licked sauce from them. When she looked up at him . . . open and heart naked . . . he glimpsed what this dinner, this special bid to his senses and passion was meant to accomplish. She wanted to be fully that which fortune, guile, desire, and perhaps even the Almighty Himself had conspired to make her.

The next instant his lips covered hers. Her scents curled through him . . . the dark soil and garlic fragrance of truffles on her hands and near her mouth . . . she tasted while cooking. The hint of long pepper remaining on her fingers . . . the musk of warm cream and newly ground flour . . . the tart, winey sweetness of early pears . . . cinnamon and nutmeg . . . the dust of ground almonds . . . the more subtle layering of lavender and fresh soap . . .

She was not only the cook, he realized, she was the feast.

His feast.

In that moment he knew. Abbess, count, duke, king . . . none of them, not even all of them together were going to keep him from having this woman. Pulling her onto his lap, he kissed her and accepted unequivocally—for better or for worse, for richer or poorer, in sickness and in health—everything she had just offered him.

With a triumphant laugh, she hugged him and covered his face with kisses before turning back to feed him more of that magnificent bird and truffles. Sauce dripped down his chin and she laughed and caught it with her tongue . . . following it up to his lips and offering him the taste of it on her.

Long, sensuous, truffle-flavored kisses gave way to wine-sweetened sighs and groans of mounting pleasure that were carried away on the gentle evening breeze. She fed him truffles shaved over a creamy rice and almond pudding . . . then wined-spiced pear and almond custard tart. . . .

Between bites they kissed and explored the pleasures of touch as well as smell and taste. He sought out her shape beneath her simple woolen gown and she traced the mounded muscle of his chest and the broad plane of his back. She nuzzled his neck and ruffled his hair and ran her nails against the grainy texture of his beard stubble . . . satisfying her curiosity, setting to memory every texture and line of him. He caressed her curves and teased the tips of her breasts through her garments and relished her response to the delicious new pleasures he showed her.

Drunk with wine and truffles and Julia, he finally slid her from his lap, rose, and pulled her to the door and along the passage to the steps. There, he scooped her up into his arms and carried her down to his chamber.

Kicking the door closed behind them, he bore her to the great draped bed and sank onto it with her beneath him. The exertion and change of location cleared his head more than he would have liked. For a moment he lay looking down at her, savoring every tantalizing detail of the view.

"Want to change your mind?" he asked. "Last chance."

"Let me think," she said with a hint of breathlessness. "A lifetime of abstinence, scratchy woolens, and making the same frumenty every morning . . . *or* . . . a lifetime of loving a handsome, strong, honorable man who knows me and wants me and has chosen *me* over safety, sanity, and the king's favor? No . . . no change of heart here, milord."

"But if you had to choose again?" he said. "If you could start over, what would you want to do?"

"Exactly what I have done, milord. *And*"—she reached for his hand and slid it onto her breast, her eyes twinkling—"I do believe I would choose this, too."

With a growl, he sank his arms around her and prepared to kiss her within an inch of her life.

She slid her arms around his neck and gave him a searing hot kiss that melted him all the way to his loins.

With a groan, he pushed up onto his knees and stripped off his shirt.

Julia watched him towering above her, drank in the movements of his big, powerful body, and felt like her every muscle had turned to mush. When he reached for the lacings of her gown, she tried to help, but she seemed to be all thumbs and limp fingers. By the time they were both naked, she was breathless with laughter and gloriously embarrassed.

"As your husband," he said, eyes glowing, "it's comforting to know that the one thing you're *not* good at is getting out of your clothes."

She laughed and held her arms out to him, but he remained on his knees, astride her, for one more eternity-bound moment.

"You are beautiful," he murmured as he sank over her, running his nose along the hollow of her throat and up to her ear, inhaling her. "So very beautiful."

"Fresh rose water," he said against her hair. "And new linen."

"I remembered that you liked the smell," she said.

"Ummm. You were right." His kisses trailed down the side of her neck to her shoulder. "The lavender and cream of your soap . . . you bathed last night."

"I'll never have secrets from you, milord," she said, inhaling as he reached the tip of her breast. There he stopped and tensed . . . smelling, tasting her nipple. "Honey," he said in desire-tattered tones. "Your breasts smell like honey." She gave a soft, knowing laugh as he licked and suckled and tantalized her the way she had just tantalized him. After a few sizzling moments, he raised his head to look into her passion-darkened eyes.

"You put it there for me?" he whispered.

"I have a few more surprises for you, milord." Her smile was temptation incarnate. "If you can find them."

"Oh, God," he groaned, realizing it was indeed half a prayer.

Hungry for all of her secrets, he covered her naked skin inch by inch. At her elbows he found a hint of sweet, tart pear and in the cleft between her breasts was a stunning blend of fine spice . . . cinnamon and ginger and cloves and pepper. Behind each ear was a hint of heliotrope, and at her knees he found the must of grapes.

But beneath it all, blending those exquisite scents into a harmony, was the deeply moving scent of Julia herself. A hint of salt and tang of vinegar . . . a musk that spoke of arousal and invitation . . . a salty, roe-like fragrance that mingled with the fruitlike sweetness of her skin.

And he could smell it all . . . in layers . . . opening levels of sensitivity when he wanted them . . . focusing all of his awareness on her . . . just her.

He raised his head from the curve of her hip and found her looking at him with her heart visible in her eyes. She was the key, he realized. It had come full circle. His salvation had begun with a cook, and now was completed by one.

Who else but a woman of her sensitivity to flavors and scents could understand the strange workings of his internal world? Who but a brave and profoundly compassionate woman would be willing to open her heart to a man who had closed off his own emotions to the world? Who but his Julia would risk everything to follow her heart and in doing so, help him to find his?

He kissed and caressed her with care, plumbing the depths of his own feelings and capacity for tenderness, drawing the power of restraint from the lush and enervating pleasures she offered him.

She gave herself wholly . . . nothing held back . . . never guessing that the subtle scents with which she had marked her body had become a path to freedom as well as a path to love for him. Needs she had never experienced before began to uncoil in her body and carry her into a deepening response. He showered attention on her throat and breasts and waist and limbs and she felt the pleasure of it all the way into her bones. By the time he slipped between her thighs and began to tantalize her with slow, rhythmic motions, there wasn't a part of her body that wasn't marked permanently by the possession of the pleasure he gave her.

The deeper, richer contact she craved came at maddening slow pace. Her impatience to have more of him bore testimony to the care with which he introduced her to each new pleasure. As a hot and urgent haze of need built in her, she began to understand that some of the delight of joining came from the anticipation of still greater pleasure. She began to meet his movements and then to encourage them with her sighs and responses. Gradually, the tension and longing reached unbearable levels in her body and she tensed and arched against him, seeking whatever would shatter that tantalizing bright bubble of tension in her body.

Then, as that delicious strain and expectation reached some divinely ordained limit, it felt as if she burst and shattered into a thousand little pieces . . . flung in all directions, disappearing into pure light.

It was some time before her senses cleared and she felt him withdraw and pull her close against him. She was floating slowly back to the here and now, when she felt the rumble of his chest against her ear and realized he was speaking.

"I love you, Julia of Grandaise. There's no going back now."

SEVERAL HOURS LATER, WELL INTO THE night, Julia awakened to find Griffin propped on his arm beside her, watching her. Somewhere in the night, he had pulled a quilted coverlet over them. She roused, responded to a gentle kiss, and snuggled closer to him. The silence was sweet, but the sound of his voice speaking her name was sweeter.

"Julia, how did you know?" he asked, looking down at her in his arms.

"About the truffles?" When he nodded, she smiled. "Grand Jean's book."

He sat up as she pulled away and slipped from his bed. "What book?"

Chapter 28

JULIA WRAPPED HERSELF IN THE QUILT and padded across the moonlit chamber to Griffin's writing desk. She came back with the large, leather-bound book and held it out to him. While he sat up and piled pillows and bolsters behind him, she lighted several tapers on the candle stand closest to the bed.

"I brought this with me to your chamber last night, intending to show it to you. But then . . . you were very hungry and supper awaited."

By the time she climbed in beside him, he was staring in shock at the frontispiece of the great book, which contained a listing of the names, dates, and relations of several generations of his forebears. He turned to the first real page and discovered a rendering of Grandaise's coat of arms. On the second page was a sample of the distinctive script found throughout the book. She could see from Griffin's face that he recognized it.

"Where"—his words came out a hoarse whisper—"did you get this?"

"Remember that I told you I visited Verdun's kitchen? Well, while I was there I met the head cook, Francois. He told me he arrived at Verdun exactly *seven* years ago. Then

I asked and learned that his first name is 'Jean.'" She leaned forward, eyes bright with pride of discovery. "Milord, I am certain that he is the same 'Petit Jean' who was once your second cook and Grand Jean's eager pupil. I know this because he had this very book—written by Jean de Champagne, 'Grand Jean'—in his possession."

"You're saying that my former under cook is at Verdun?"

"Exactly that."

He was astounded.

"Jean occasionally spoke of wanting to write down his recipes to pass down to the next generation," he said as he ran his fingers over the elegantly written pages. "But I had no idea he had actually done so."

"Your Jean was a keen observer . . . devoted to Grandaise and you." She paused here and met his gaze. "You know, he includes in these writings what he believed caused the feud to start almost a hundred years ago."

"He did? What was it?"

"Treasure."

"What?"

"In the forest."

"Treasure. In the forest," he said dryly. "If he believed that, don't you think he would have mentioned this to someone—*like me*—when he was alive?"

She pulled the book onto her lap, turned pages, then slid it back to him.

He read the words where her finger tapped the page. "Treasure." His jaw went slack. "He calls it the 'Treasure of Grandaise.' Why didn't Jean ever talk to me about it? Have you read it all? Did he reveal what this treasure is?"

"I haven't read every entry completely, but he says that the lords of Grandaise and Verdun disagreed over how to claim it. Hard feelings developed and came to blows."

"Exactly where is this 'treasure' located?"

"He just referred to it as 'the riches in the south forest.'"

"That's the disputed part of the forest—the part both sides are forced to avoid. Our grandfathers fought each other and died there."

"And then Jean went on to record his finest and most

beloved recipes, many of which contained truffles. I thought that rather odd at first, but then began to understand from some of his comments on the recipes. He mentions you numerous times." She turned several pages and pointed to his name and the comments Jean had written about him. "That's how I knew which recipes would be your favorites."

He stared at the script until it began to blur.

"He saved me. Jean. From my earliest days, I was deviled by a great sensitivity to the smells around me. I remember feeling like I was breathing poison sometimes and scratching and clawing to get free of it. My head throbbed at times and at other times I felt like I was suffocating. Frightened by what happened to me, I would lash out in pain and anger. I hated being out of control like that—sometimes I tried not to breathe at all.

"I finally found a remedy a bit better than refusing to breathe. I abandoned all smells and began to wear a band on my nose. I was still quite young when my father died. Jean set out to help me learn to control my reactions. He thought that if I could learn to focus on one smell at a time and ignore all else, I might be able to live more normally. To begin my training, he chose a smell that was rare and pungent and—oddly—didn't make me ill in large doses."

"Truffles," she supplied. He nodded.

"Gradually I learned to control how much scent I perceived and with it, the emotions that seized me when smells became too much. For a time I lived almost normally. Then Jean died and his wretched assistant disappeared and my kitchen went to ruin. Then I was called to take my garrison to Spain to fight. The battlefield smells overcame me and I lost control again." He gave her a pained smile. "There is a reason they call me 'the Beast.' "

She smiled through the haze of moisture in her eyes.

"You know, I can actually smell your tears," he said, running his thumb across her cheek. "I hope you're not regretting what we've just done."

"Never," she said.

"There may be drastic consequences."

"There would have been drastic consequences if we hadn't." She gave a teary laugh. "And we would have totally missed this. . . ."

And she kissed him until his toes curled.

THE SUN WAS HIGH OVERHEAD BEFORE THE Lord and Lady of Grandaise exited their chamber together, heading for the hall to face whatever the fleet chain of estate gossip and their conspicuous absence from duty that morning had wrought. They stopped halfway down to the first landing where Sister Regine stood with a pretty, young, dark-haired maiden wearing fine garments and a worried look.

"Well?" the girl said looking at Julia.

"Oh, well . . . I'm afraid we didn't get around to it yet," Julia said with a wince, then she looked up at Griffin. "How much do you love me again?"

He gave her a startled look.

"We have a visitor, milord," she said as if every word had a cost. "And she has a most urgent request. May I present Lady Sophie Marie . . . of Verdun."

Griffin must have felt as if he had been poleaxed. He certainly looked like it. "Lady Sophie of Verdun?" He looked from Julia to the girl with a shock-delayed reaction rising. "The one you said you met when you were captive?"

"The very one," Sophie answered for her, giving him a deep curtsy. "And I've come to beg your aid, milord. I am in desperate need of sanctuary."

It took a moment for that to register. Verdun's daughter . . . the one he was once commanded to wed, now asking him for . . . He clapped his hands over his face.

"Dear God!"

A cup of wine, some shouting, and a fair number of heartfelt apologies later, Griffin had redonned his nose band and sat in his empty hall—cleared of everyone but the

Baron Crossan and Axel and Greeve—glowering at Julia and her cohort in diplomatic disaster.

"When I sent to her, I never expected she would bring the truffles and book herself," Julia said. "But, milord, you must see that she is desperate. To have to wed a man who squished his first wife like a bug in their marital bed."

"My father is a monster," Sophie declared, producing another wave of perfect tears. "He's scheming and cruel and has no natural affection for his own child. To him, I am no different than a turnip field . . . to be plowed and planted . . . so he can reap a rich crop. I have no say in my future at all."

"Well, who does?" Griffin roared, lurching forward in his great chair. "Noblewomen have obligations and duty to perform—even duty to wretched scheming fathers." He shook a finger at her. "It's your role, your fate, your cross to bear. Your earthly burden is to take that fate and do the best you can with it—not go gallivanting around the country begging people to protect you from it."

Julia could hardly believe those words were coming from him. It could only be the dry bones of some long-decayed ancestor speaking through him.

"And yet only a few hours ago, milord," she spoke up, aiming a warm yet challenging look on him, "we were taking our future into *our* own hands."

He looked at her with fire in his eyes and for a moment she wondered if she had just made the biggest mistake of her life. Whatever possessed her to test their vows, their determination, and the fragile new bond they had forged in private, so openly?

Still, the words had been uttered. She straightened her back and held her head high, showing him that she was unafraid to face the ramifications of what they had done together and praying he would not shrink from them, either. His gaze sought hers and she saw the moment he affirmed that life-giving connection between them and decided to conform his life to the new state of his heart.

"So we did." He sat back and after a few moments, looked to the baron for comment. Crossan shrugged and wagged his head.

"A bad business, Grandaise. She gets the freedom. You get the blame."

The baron's succinct assessment struck a chord in Griffin, he looked back to Sophie and cocked his head, studying her. "You ask for sanctuary, milady. But in any alliance, benefit must accrue to both sides. If I offer you protection and support, what can you offer me by way of compensation or advantage?"

Just as Sophie turned a frantic look on Julia, she was visibly struck by an idea. She straightened and her lively dark eyes darted back and forth.

"Only the satisfaction that comes from knowing that you're depriving my father of a most lucrative alliance," she said. "And that he'll be furious about it."

There was a heartbeat of stunned silence before Crossan's mouth fell open and Griffin choked on a laugh.

"Heaven deliver us from such daughters!" Crossan crossed himself.

"Oh, I don't know," Griffin said to the baron while looking at his new wife with unabashed adoration. "It may be that Heaven is the very agency responsible for them. My guess is that they're sent here to test us, and—if we pass—to give us a little taste of paradise."

THEY MOVED POSSESSIONS AND REVISED sleeping arrangements that afternoon. Julia's things were moved into the lord's quarters, Sophie was given a chamber of her own just down the way from the master's chambers, and Regine was given the head cook's quarters and for the first time in her life, had a chamber all to herself.

The house and outbuildings and the village beyond began to buzz with talk about the lady guest that had appeared in Grandaise's hall. There was some speculation that she might be from the convent that supplied the new Lady of Grandaise. But she didn't wear a nun's habit and was reportedly quite a beauty. Folk were so preoccupied by the news that they didn't notice a ragged fellow with incongruously fine boots lurking about the walls and various gates.

Over the day, Martin de Gies had made a thorough study of Grandaise's walls and gates and found them solid and well-guarded. So much for hopes of an easy entry and a quick retrieval of his wayward lady.

Evening was coming on again, and by now both her absence and his own had been marked and cast in the worst possible light. It wouldn't take long for the count to extract from some of the younger knights the fact that Sophie had courted ruination among them. And it wouldn't take him long to deduce that if she had tried to seduce the others, she had tried it with his First Knight as well.

That meant that even if he got Sophie safely back to Verdun, he would be walking into a maelstrom of fatherly fury and retribution, and Sophie would be imprisoned and sent away to wed a gluttonous German pork pie. He would never see her again. Salty little Sophie with her delicious brown eyes and throaty, musical laugh . . . her curvy little body and pouting mouth. His chest ached as if he had just been emptied of everything that made living possible.

Duty. Honor. Loyalty. They made hard masters.

He spotted a caravan of carts carrying wood and hay into the narrower rear gate and quickly fell in beside the last cart, bending his head and rounding his shoulders, imitating the trudging walk of the men accompanying the goods. He tucked the hilt of his blade under his arm, pinned his scabbard to his side, and held his breath as he passed by the sentries. A coughing fit from the man leading his cart diverted the guards' attention enough for him to pass through undetected.

Once inside the walls and away from the gate, he darted to the cover of a wooden shed near the stables and surveyed the place. His heart sank. He was between the stables and the garrison . . . a location that placed him square in the path of the frequent traffic between the two. He backed away from the corner and crept in a broad arc back toward the wall and then past sheds and animal pens and smithy and barns.

Ordinarily he would have been alert to everything, assessing the buildings, the locations of forge and armory and wells, and the supplies of livestock in the pens as military assets or liabilities. But just now, he was so busy planning what he would say to Sophie to persuade her to return home with him, in fact, that he didn't see the pig. . . .

The huge pink creature staggered only slightly as he banged into it, and he narrowly avoided pitching over its back into the pile of peelings and kitchen offal it was devouring. The disaccommodated beast looked up at him with a snort of indignation and a ragged, unwashed fellow grabbed him by the shoulder. "Watch where you are going! You have disturbed Fleur's—"

"Keep your cursed pig out of the way," Martin snapped, trying to thrust the smelly wretch aside. The man grabbed Martin's cloak in both fists.

"How dare you speak of Demoiselle Fleur so?"

"Take your hands off me."

"Not until you give my Fleur an apology."

Martin shoved against the outraged pig keeper's grip, but the fellow was not as insubstantial as he seemed. A tussle ensued and in the scuffle, the sword Martin was taking pains to conceal hit the ground.

A trio of soldiers had paused on the way back to their barracks to watch the confrontation, mildly amused by the pig man's indignation . . . until that sword fell. Peasants and workers didn't carry swords, much less ones wrapped in finely wrought scabbards. And no man carried such a sword and wore such boots beneath such a cloak unless . . .

Martin saw them emptying their hands and rushing him, and he tried to bolt. They were on him in a heartbeat, ripping off his cloak, discovering his padded leather jerkin with its clear imprint of mail . . .

"MILORD!" ONE OF THE SQUIRES CAME RUNning into the hall just after supper. "Milord, come quick! We've caught a spy!"

Griffin was on his feet in a flash, striding for the door. Crossan, Axel, Greeve, and several of the other knights grabbed their swords and rushed out after him. In front of the barracks they found a crowd of men gathered around a pair of guardsmen holding a battered but struggling figure. Griffin paused to look him over before approaching. The man had a bruised jaw and a cut above one eye; he had obviously put up a fight.

"I am no spy," the prisoner declared.

"Who are you and what are you doing here, within my walls?" he demanded, striding closer, taking in the man's battle-worthy frame and examining the sword one of his men handed him. Something about the man seemed familiar. "You're a knight, by the looks of you and your weapon. Who is your lord?" He stalked close enough to stare directly into the man's eyes and roar: "Answer me!"

The knight ceased struggling and stood straight in his captors' grip.

"I am Martin de Gies, First Knight of Bardot of Verdun and protector of Lady Sophie of Verdun." He glanced up at the hall and braced himself to announce. "And I've come to take her home."

Chapter 29

"YOU'VE COME TO TAKE HER HOME?" Griffin choked back an involuntary laugh at his claiming of the thankless role of "protector" for a pig-headed young lady who clearly had her own ideas about how she should be protected and by whom. "I expected that sooner or later Verdun would find out where she was and would move to get her back"—by now, a messenger was probably on the way to Paris with news of Sophie's "abduction," and from court, it was sure to look like a bla-tant case of an-eye-for-an-eye—"but he sends one lone knight? Sneaking into my walls disguised as a beggar?"

He scowled, studying the tension in the knight's face and recalling the name. "Martin de Gies. You're the one . . . from Paris . . . the fair."

"I know you have Lady Sophie within your walls . . . I followed her here. I ask that you turn her over to me imme-diately so that I may escort her home."

"Do you hear that, Crossan," Griffin said, turning to glance at the baron. "He *asks* that she be returned."

"There's a story here," the baron observed. "No knight would undertake such a mission singlehanded . . . not when he has an entire garrison at his disposal."

"You've come here—alone—to demand Lady Sophie return with you to Verdun?" Griffin turned back to his captive. "You must be mad."

"Far from it, Lord Griffin." Martin of Gies stood his ground and raised his chin. "I may be your best hope for getting out of this without violence and bloodshed."

"How so?" Griffin demanded, scrutinizing the handsome knight with grudging admiration. He had not an arrow in his quiver, but he still tried to negotiate.

"If you are indeed the man Julia of Childress said you are . . . you will first seek to settle a dispute without fighting and bloodshed. And that is what I offer you. You see, I know that you did not abduct Lady Sophie, that she came here on her own. And I know that it may be a misguided bit of friendship on Julia's—"

"Lady Julia!" Griffin corrected.

"*Lady* Julia's part that she has taken Lady Sophie in. But surely you must see, Lord Griffin, that if she is not returned—and soon—that a peaceable solution will no longer be possible."

Julia, Sophie, and Regine rushed down the slope to the garrison's quarters shortly after one of the potboys brought word that a spy from Verdun had been caught near the barracks. But as they arrived, they were barred from making their way through the crowd by Axel and Greeve, who had spotted them and moved to intercept them. When they demanded to know who it was and what was happening, Axel said that Martin-of-Something had been caught inside the walls and was demanding Lady Sophie be returned to her home.

"Sir Martin?" Sophie grabbed Julia's arm and squeezed. "Martin is here? He came for me!" She would have rushed to his side, but Axel and Greeve—along with Julia—held her back.

"Sophie, he hasn't just come for you, he's come to take you back to your father," Julia said anxiously. Even though it was the truth, she regretted saying it when Sophie's spirits plummeted. Then Griffin's voice rumbled forth again and she looked to Axel's sympathetic face. "We have to get closer to hear what they say."

"So Verdun did not send you," Griffin was saying.

"No. I followed Lady Sophie here and waited . . . hoping she would think better of her rashness and return home. When it became clear she would not, I hoped to meet with her secretly and persuade her to return before blood is shed."

Griffin studied that for a moment. De Gies was as decent as he was bold. How did a cur like Bardot of Verdun ever manage to claim a knight of such foresight and principle?

"I am willing to escort her back to her father and to attempt to make him see that the entire venture was simply the result of Lady Sophie's thoughtless whims leading her astray."

Within the gate Sophie heard those words and gasped.

"Thoughtless?" She grabbed Julia's hands in horror. "How can he say such things about me, when he knows the reason I fled was—"

"Was what?" Julia forced the girl's chin up, feeling a little sick at the realization that there was more to the situation than Sophie had revealed. "Why did you flee? Don't tell me there is no fat German prince. . . ."

"Oh, there's a prince all right, and he's fat as a watered sow." Sophie's eyes rimmed with tears. "But I fled because I'm in love with Sir Martin and it's impossible. He's my father's First Knight and champion . . . the prime defender of Verdun's honor. But he won't speak for me because he knows my father is greedy and because he has no prospect of a title or fortune."

"But, Sophie—"

"He loves me, too, Julia." Sophie's tears were all too real this time. "He said so. And I can't let my father send me off to wed some slavering beast. One of us has to fight for our— Help me, Julia." Her lip quivered. "I helped you."

Julia saw the events surrounding her vows in an entirely new light . . . Sophie's questions about Griffin and his treatment of her . . . the dress Sophie sent for her to wear . . . Sophie's assurance as she went out to the gate. . . .

"It was you," Julia said, more to herself than to her friend. "You told your father to make Lord Griffin marry me as the price of my—"

Caught in the grip of a sudden idea, Julia grabbed Sir Greeve and told him to carry an urgent message to Griffin.

As it happened, her message came at a good time. Griffin stated that he had promised Lady Sophie sanctuary and needed to confer with her before making any decision on her future. He turned aside to look at Julia, thinking that it was her infernal knack for making friends out of enemies that had gotten him into this disaster. A moment later as he emerged from the crowd he found himself facing the pair.

"Sophie is desperate to avoid marriage to the monster her father has in mind for her," Julia said to him in private tones. "And the only way to both get her to go home and honor your agreement to protect her is . . . tell Sir Martin that if he wants to take her home, *he'll have to wed her first.*"

It was such an appalling idea that he tried to distance himself from both it and her. "Dear God—you've lost your—do you know what that would—you're saying I should force some other poor wretch to marry the daughter of the man who forced me to marry you."

"Exactly."

"That's monstrous!" He looked at her in horror.

"It is not. It's justice . . . of a sort. And to make it even better, it's Sophie's idea." She edged closer to him and lowered her voice. "Just as it was Sophie's idea to make you wed me. Apparently *she* suggested it to her father."

He looked at her in astonishment, then at Sophie, who was standing a few yards away, looking both innocent and cunning in the same moment. After what Sophie had said that morning about taking revenge on her own father, he wouldn't put anything past her.

"And if I force him to do this . . . how does that benefit Grandaise?"

"Well, Sophie and Martin will go home and we will

have allies in Verdun." She brightened. "This could be the beginning of the end of the feud!"

He wavered, thinking of what the pair—if wedded—might face at the hands of his ruthless enemy. Julia added the *coup de grace* of persuasion.

"Milord, they're in love. That's why Sir Martin risked coming alone to retrieve her. That's why he'll marry her. He loves her. And she loves him. Perhaps a 'forced marriage' is the only way they can be together."

She had him. Dammit. And she knew it. Why was it when women failed with rational and sensible arguments, they brought it all back to the personal and wiggled their way in through your emotions?

Because it worked, that's why.

He looked into her warm, liquid emerald eyes and surrendered.

"Take Sophie back to the hall and keep her there," he ordered.

Making his way back to the prisoner, he astonished Sir Martin, the Baron Crossan, and his gawking garrison by declaring his terms for returning her.

"I'll allow you to take her back to Verdun with you on the condition that you speak marriage vows with her first." He folded his arms with determination. "She will leave my protection a married woman, or she will not leave it at all."

Sir Martin looked thunderstruck. He stammered and then got angry and then roared that Griffin had gone mad with a thirst for vengeance. But it was clear from Griffin's calm, determined demeanor that he was anything but irrational or seething with hatred. Soon enough, Sir Martin realized that no amount of protest or posturing would alter that shocking requirement.

"Perhaps you would like to speak with Lady Sophie yourself," Griffin suggested, motioning to the guards to release their captive.

As Sir Martin climbed the rise to the great hall, he spotted Sophie on the steps, silhouetted by the light coming through the doors. Griffin, striding along beside him, glimpsed the way the knight's heart rose into his eyes at the sight of her. He ordered everyone out of the hall except the bride and groom, then exited to the front steps himself . . . where Crossan found him.

"You're either blinding brilliant or screaming mad, Grandaise. And I haven't a clue which," the baron said, shaking his head.

Voices were raised between the couple in the hall. As everyone outside strained to not listen to what was going on, they managed to hear every word that was said.

"This whole thing is your doing!" Martin charged, seizing her by the shoulders. "You stubborn little—have you any idea how much trouble you've caused? Your father will be out for blood, Sophie, unless you come back to his house with me right now!"

"I will not." She raised her chin. "I've decided to heed the advice of my host and protector . . . to return to Verdun only if you marry me."

"Don't be absurd—"

"Is it so absurd to try to find a way to marry and live with the man you love? Is it beyond thinking that our marriage may actually *help* to end the hatred and resentment that has bled these noble houses for three generations?" She seized the open edges of his jerkin in desperate fists. "Don't you see, Martin . . . if I go home and my father sends me off to his German coin-purse . . . he will use the money he gains for more weapons and men, more fighting. But if you and I wed, and we can get him to accept our marriage—"

"He won't, Sophie. Dear God, don't you think I've gone over this a thousand times already? I'm just a knight—"

"His First Knight," she protested, fiercely. "A man of honor and valor and of no little standing at Verdun. The men of the garrison respect you . . . support you . . . they'd *die* for you. If worse comes to worse, we can remind him of that."

"Sophie," he groaned, his misery evident, "don't do this to me."

"To *you*?" She straightened and shook his jerkin to make him look her in the eye. "You think I haven't—" She released his garment and took a step back, still in his grasp. "Fine. I'll go home. I'll marry that barrel of pork fat. *If* you can honestly tell me that you don't want me." She crossed her arms and tried to blink back the tears beginning to form. "Go on—let me hear you say that you have no love or desire for me . . . that you have never lain awake at night imagining us sharing a bed and a life."

Martin stared at both the prisms of tears growing in her eyes and the undimmed defiance of her chin. It wasn't foolhardiness that brought her to such drastic action, he realized, it was the stubbornness of her loving heart.

"Tell me, Martin. Say that you don't love me." Her voice was a whisper and her eyes were brimming with love she was willing to risk everything for.

"I-I can't do that, Sophie." He could barely force the words past the lump in his throat, not knowing whether they would prove to be salvation or doom. "Because I do love you. You make me furious and you make me crazy and you make me defy both duty and common sense. But I do love you. And if you still want me tomorrow morning . . . I'll marry you."

"Oh, Martin!" She threw her arms around him and covered his face with kisses.

There was a long and potent silence before the couple came to the door, arm in arm, and Sir Martin announced that he would comply with Griffin's requirement.

There was a flurry of congratulations as everyone poured back into the hall and Griffin called for his best wine and offered toasts to the bride and groom. Griffin sent word to Father Dominic to prepare to read marriage vows in the chapel the next morning, and Julia and Regine whisked Sophie off to her chamber to begin preparations for her wedding.

It was strange, Julia and Griffin thought separately the next morning, how the air of Grandaise warmed and brightened at the prospect of a wedding. The kitchens were bustling with preparation for a fine dinner . . . to which they now added a few special entremets . . . and the house women began freshening and decorating Sophie's chamber for the bridal night . . . and there was much joking and teasing among the men about who should wed next and why. It was almost as if one of their own were being married.

When Sophie came downstairs to the hall, midmorning, there was a collective *ahhh* from men and women alike. Sophie had brought a fine sky-blue gown with her and the potboys managed to find enough flowers in the kitchen gardens to make a garland for her head. With her hair flowing around her shoulders and her eyes bright and cheeks glowing with pleasure, she was the very picture of the joyful bride. Sir Martin's knightly reserve melted at the sight of her. It was plain to all present that part of him was eager to make her his own.

Julia and Regine escorted her to the chapel, even as Griffin and Crossan escorted Sir Martin. Father Dominic met them at the chapel door, where marriage vows were always said. On the broad stone step Sir Martin took Sophie's hands in his and looked at her with all of the turmoil and love in his heart. She gazed up at him with more joy and adoration than any one person should be able to hold.

Julia wanted to tell them it would be all right, that things would work out for them as they had for her and Griffin. But she knew there was no guarantee that the couple could convince her father to accept them. If he didn't, where would that leave them? And what revenge would Verdun exact upon Grandaise for taking his daughter in and helping her to wed someone against his wishes?

It might be madness, Griffin and Julia both thought as they stood together, her arm in his. But if it was, it was a very fine madness.

HALFWAY THROUGH THE VOWS A LOW RUM-bling sound began that seeped in around and underneath the edges of Griffin's awareness to make him glance toward the main gates, the upper parts of which were visible from the front of the chapel. As the promises and assurances of the vows were stated and repeated—"honor and obey . . . love and cherish . . . for richer or poorer, in sickness and in health, till death do us part"—the sound became audible and through the gathering there were numerous glances toward the gates.

"Faster, Father, if you please," Griffin declared, looking around at his men's faces and realizing that each one was having the same thought. *Verdun.*

The priest did speak a bit more quickly, but was still barely through with the giving of the rings when the sound of many horses burst through the gates and the horses and riders themselves followed close behind. A galvanic shock flashed through Griffin and his men at the realization that the sentries hadn't moved to close the gates and the invaders were inside, filling the front court and probing the estate's weaknesses from the *inside.* The men began to run for weapons and shout "to the walls." Those who had blades drew them fast; metal sang as it raked scabbards.

Griffin had drawn his blade and now thrust Julia behind him as he realized that the main force had turned and was headed straight for the chapel. Then he realized why the sentries had been confused and why the gates hadn't been closed; at the front of that invading force rode none other than Sir Reynard de Crossan, wearing Grandaise's own blue and green colors.

Sir Reynard spotted the blades bristling among his comrades and reined up, staring in dismay at them and at the people assembled at the front of the chapel.

"Milord!" Sir Reynard called, and when Griffin raised a hand of greeting and called out his name, he dismounted into a crowd of greatly relieved knights and men-at-arms. The first to reach him and give him a burly hug of welcome was his own father, the Baron Crossan. Axel and Greeve were next and shortly after them, a number of others sheathed their weapons to clasp his arm and demand to know if he survived the pleasures of Paris. Reynard worked his way toward Griffin, who stood near the chapel doors with Julia now at his side.

"Ho, milord!" Reynard called as he approached and clasped Griffin's extended arm with his. "What is this? I was given to believe that you had already said vows some days ago."

"Yes," came a booming voice from the rear of the throng. "Tell us, milord Grandaise, just what is going on here?"

A score of men on horseback were arrayed behind the speaker, an older, barrel-chested man in elegantly crafted mail and an elaborately tooled helmet. On the sleeveless midnight blue tunic he wore over his armor, there was a coat of arms Griffin had never seen before.

"A wedding," Griffin answered with a questioning glance at Reynard and then a look at the men who accompanied this demanding guest. That was when he noticed that among the dark blue tabards, there were a dozen wearing white and purple with accents of gold. The royal colors. King's men. And near the rear, there was one tabard that bore the dreaded red and white of Verdun.

"Your Grace." Sir Reynard strode back toward the mounted nobleman, and swept a hand toward Griffin. "May I present my lord Griffin, Comte de Grandaise." Then he turned to Griffin. "The duke of Avalon, my lord. Sent by King Philip himself to investigate the recent troubles."

Griffin felt the bottom drop out of his stomach. Everything in his middle seemed to slide toward his knees. Here in the middle of what would surely be a controversial wedding . . . the king's own emissary arrives . . . and it turns out to be the very man to whom he was already answerable for a reluctant but nevertheless punishable breach of his word.

"Welcome, Your Grace," Griffin pulled Julia forward with him, where he bowed and she curtsied. "It has been some time since we met."

"I see we have arrived in the midst of a wedding. How very appropriate." The duke dismounted and stretched his back for a moment before coming to reach for Julia's hand. "Since it is news of *a wedding* that has brought me here in the first place."

"Your Grace, I believe when you hear what we have to say—" Griffin began but was cut off by a motion of the duke's hand.

"Later, Grandaise. I believe I have interrupted this good couple's sacred moment long enough." He smiled benevolently at the bride's pale face and the groom's controlled countenance. "There will be time for our business later."

He placed Julia's hand on his arm and proceeded toward the chapel doors where the bride and groom waited anxiously for the completion of their vows. He flicked a glance at the red-and-white tabard Sir Martin wore, then looked back over his shoulder at the lone red-and-white tabard in his party.

"Sir Thomas—it would seem we have one of your comrades here!"

As the knight dismounted and hurried forward, Sir Martin went to meet him with a look of relief and pleasure. "Thomas? Is that you?"

The knights of Verdun clasped arms and thumped each other on the back.

"What the devil's going on, Martin?" He looked around and spotted Sophie at the chapel door. His face drained as he realized the implication of Martin's and her proximity to that door and to the priest stationed before it. "Don't tell me you're—"

"Yes, I am," Sir Martin said, suddenly sober and communicating the seriousness of the situation to his friend and comrade with looks, not words. "It must be done. And I ask that you stand with me."

Indecision flitted across Sir Thomas's face, but after a moment he stepped back a pace and nodded, supporting his commander's chosen course. He could hardly do otherwise, here in the den of their enemy. As they made their way to the doors of the chapel and Sophie's side, the duke—who had watched intently their cryptic exchange—turned to the couple.

"And who are we to give praise to God for joining in blessed matrimony this day?" he asked.

"Martin de Gies, First Knight of Verdun." Sir Martin bowed stiffly.

"And I am Sophie Marie of Verdun, daughter of Bardot, the Comte de Verdun." Sophie lifted her chin and produced a dazzling smile. "If you don't mind, Your Grace, we were just about to have our vows and future blessed."

Sophie pulled Sir Martin around to face the flustered Father Dominic, who managed to speak a quick but nonetheless heartfelt blessing. In that short interval the identities of the bride and groom and the implications of their wedding—here, at Grandaise—had bloomed in the duke's agile and innately political mind. As soon as Sir Martin and Sophie exchanged the customary "kiss of peace," the duke turned to Griffin with eyes as cold as winter ice.

"What in hell are you up to, Grandaise?" His anger was palpable. "If you would keep your title, your lands, and the head on your shoulders . . . you will explain yourself to me. And your story had better be damned good."

Chapter 30

THE DUKE STRODE INTO THE HALL OF Grandaise ahead of that mixed party, and immediately called for the doors to be closed to those not of knightly standing. Julia hurried along beside Griffin, wishing she could just escape to her kitchen and throw herself into preparing the meal that in the space of one day had already traversed an arc from "pleasant supper" to "wedding banquet" to possibly a "last meal on Grandaise." But she knew her testimony might be critical to making the duke understand what had happened, and began to prepare herself for a spate of hostile and accusing—

The duke stopped in the middle of the hall and turned to look at her.

"You are the 'Julia,' are you not? The demoiselle at the center of this vexation?" Using the excuse of his office, he gave her a thorough looking over as she nodded. "My son still speaks of the hedgehog you made for him."

"I-It was a pleasure to watch him enjoy it, Your Grace," Julia said, with a half curtsy and a helpless glance at Griffin.

The duke saw the way she looked at the man he had come to confront and grew more stern. "It is claimed that the Comte de Verdun abducted you and that in order to get you back unharmed, the count was required to wed you. Did you hear Verdun make such a demand?"

"No, Your Grace," she said with an apologetic look at Griffin. "I was not privy to the negotiations that resulted in my marriage and my freedom."

"Who told you that you had to wed Grandaise?" the duke continued.

"His Lordship."

"Of course he did . . . to shame my lord Verdun . . . by wedding his mistress instead of milord's daughter right there at milord's gate!" Sir Thomas charged, bursting to the front of that group of knights.

"Either you were not there, *boy*," Baron Crossan shouted, lunging through the crowd and caught in the nick of time by his son and Sir Greeve, "or you are a damnable liar! I saw and heard it all. Verdun called out his priest and his swordsman and told Grandaise to choose between the two for the demoiselle. He could marry her or watch her receive the last rites."

"That's a lie! The count would never murder a woman in cold blood!" Sir Thomas raged. "If Lord Bardot were here—"

"He would face a wall of steel for his treatment of Lady Julia," Axel shouted, reaching for the hilt of his blade and igniting a cascade of similar motions. Griffin grabbed Axel's and Crossan's arms to prevent them from drawing their blades just as Sir Martin grabbed his friend's arm and demanded, "Think, man! For God's sake!"

The hall was suddenly a tinderbox of charges, counter-charges, and blades just waiting to be unleashed. The duke stood in the center of that narrowly avoided melee, seeing firsthand the tensions he had come to quell and realizing that to reach the truth here, he would have to employ something considerably more facile and effective than the hammer of royal authority. Luckily he had lived long enough to know there was more than one way to get people to talk.

"Lady Julia," he said with calculated calm. "This kitchen Reynard has rattled on about for days . . . I've a yen to see it. Be so kind as to show it to me."

"O-Of course, Your Grace." She looked up at Griffin

with widened eyes. He frowned at the duke, clearly suspicious of this sudden change in strategy, but then nodded. "The kitchen is this way."

"The rest of you"—the duke gestured irritably to the assembly as he exited—"try not to *impale* each other while I'm gone."

With no little anxiety, Julia opened the upper kitchen door and escorted the duke onto the landing that provided a splendid view of the grandly proportioned chamber. She pointed out the specialized hearths, the ovens, the larder and doors and rope-operated lifts to the scullery. The hearths were glowing, the aisles were full of potboys and hall servers doubling as porters, and the work tables were ringed with women and young girls chopping, grating, and rolling. The intense activity and production were being shepherded by an apple-cheeked nun in full habit . . . who looked up and waved at them.

"This is my chaperone, Sister Regine," Julia introduced her when the duke reached the bottom of the stairs. Regine curtsied and bade the duke welcome without so much as a stumble. Then she clapped her hands and told everyone to stop gawking and return to their work . . . and miracle of miracles, they did.

Julia led him by the hearths, explaining some of the improvements that made Grand Jean's kitchen such a joy to work in, and then shared with him the menu for the evening's meal . . . which now would be augmented by sweetmeats, wafers, and tarts in celebration of Lady Sophie and Sir Martin's wedding.

"This wedding today . . ." the duke mused, snitching a slice of fennel bulb from the table where greens were being prepared for the pot. "Why was the count of Verdun's only daughter being wedded to Verdun's First Knight in Grandaise's chapel?"

"That's a bit of a story, Your Grace," she said, watching the way the duke munched and swallowed and looked about for more.

"I'm all ears," he said, snatching a number of almonds.

Julia led him to the bench just outside the door and

shooed the duty-dodging potboys back inside. He waved her to a seat beside him and she began.

"It started when I was abducted and taken to Verdun."

"Were you hurt in any way?"

"Only my pride. Though being bound hand and foot wasn't particularly pleasant. Anyway, the count had me locked up in a tower room and Lady Sophie sneaked in to my prison to see me. Feeling like fellow prisoners, we quickly became friends. She told me how much she hated the idea of marrying Lord Griffin—whom she believed to be a raging beast of some kind. I told her how wrong she was about him . . . and how handsome and strong and honorable he was. She apparently got the notion that I had fallen under his spell." She looked toward the door. "Milord duke, are you thirsty? We have just brought up some excellent wine from the cellar."

"So, when Lord Griffin brought a force of men to demand my freedom," she continued as the duke sipped his wine, "Sophie suggested to her father that the price of my freedom should be that Lord Griffin would marry me. It served her purposes, since she wanted to escape marrying him, and she believed it served mine. Your Grace, would you mind testing the cheese fritters? The first batch has just come out of the fryer."

The duke alternately blew on and munched on his golden lumps of savory cheese and herb dough.

"Of course I can't say I wasn't pleased in some way. His Lordship is a deeply honorable man . . . fair-minded and generous and very manly." She smiled at that. "And as to violating his arrangement with the convent . . . he tried valiantly to protect me and keep my 'gifts to God' intact. But—flawed and willful creature that I am—I was never meant for religious vows. I didn't want to be a nun and Reverend Mother knew it. She wanted to keep me there as the convent's cook because my food made for harmony among the sisters and maids. Good food will do that . . . make for good feelings and good relations. Sister Boniface used to say that there aren't many problems that can't be solved over a cup of wine and a fine roast joint of meat. How about trying some of my baked buttered wortes and minces in vinegar, Your Grace? This is a new recipe. . . ."

The duke ate and listened and nodded, making encouraging "umhmm" sounds. She told him about Sophie's flight from her father's house and about Sir Martin's daring appearance that morning. She confessed that she and Sophie had put Griffin in something of a corner, making him agree to protect his enemy's daughter against her father. But, the count was behaving monstrously in trying to provoke Griffin and to marry his only remaining child off to a giant dumpling.

"The main course is Chicken Ambrogino with Dried Fruit. Would you like some almond rice with that, too?"

When the serving began in the hall, the duke suggested that she bring Lady Sophie back with her, so that he might have a word with her in private.

Sophie was surprisingly shy, having never set eyes on a nobleman of such rank before. Julia brought her a cup of wine, and she warmed and began to answer the duke's questions.

"I told my father that if Lord Griffin wanted his cook back—I knew by then that she was his cook and not his mistress—that he should have to wed her. Later, when she sent for truffles and that book of recipes, I seized the chance to escape and asked for sanctuary here. I mean, can you imagine a lifetime of sleeping with one eye open, in constant fear that your husband might roll over and suffocate you? And Sir Martin is the perfect knight. My father hardly deserves to have such a strong and capable right arm."

"Your father has no son to inherit, does he?" the duke mused.

"That's why my father keeps trying to marry me off to some wealthy nobleman. So he can protect our lands from"—she looked around her—"from Grandaise. But Julia is my dear friend and the Beast isn't nearly as beastly as my father seemed to think." A new thought caused her genuine distress: "I only hope my father doesn't try to kill Martin when he learns he married me."

The duke asked Sophie to send him Sir Martin when she returned to the hall. It proved to be a difficult interview for Martin de Gies, who struggled with his loyalty to both his lord and the truth. In the end, he confessed to the duke that his lord had indeed coerced Grandaise to wed Julia under threat of violence . . . though the beheading threat was meant just as a coercive ploy.

"Damned dangerous ploy," the duke declared irritably. "Tell me, de Gies . . . why did you come to Grandaise alone to reclaim Lady Sophie?"

That was difficult for Martin to explain without exposing Sophie's scandalous behavior. He was able to say that he knew Sophie was impetuous and that her father was already furious with her intractable attitude. He hoped to convince Grandaise to cooperate and to return her to Verdun before the count realized she was missing. But time dragged on and when confronted with the demand that he wed Sophie, who would not leave otherwise, he felt he had no choice. Matters were growing worse by the day. He believed if he didn't get her home straightaway, there would be bloodshed between the houses.

Looking back, he could see that he hadn't showed the wisest of judgment.

"Well, now you have a chance to redeem your judgment," the duke declared testily. "You must refrain from making Lady Sophie your wife in earnest. If the marriage may be annulled, the situation may yet be saved."

Sir Martin took the suggestion as the command it was, and nodded manfully. But as he walked back to the hall he looked like a man who had just wrestled a badger and lost.

Next Baron Crossan and the duke shared a full cup of wine as the baron related what he had seen and heard before and since his arrival. "Verdun's a treacherous old goat. I was there, I saw it all. He tried to make it look like Lord Griffin was the one who broke the truce, but it was him all along. Thank Heaven our wise king has seen the falseness of his nature and sent someone to search out the truth. Say, are you going to eat that fritter?"

Lastly, the duke called for Griffin to join him on the

bench beside the kitchen door. They shared almond cakes
with cherry sauce, hot spiced nuts, stuffed dates and figs,
and wafers dipped in blackberry confit . . . while the duke
quizzed him on the details of the two weddings and his
abysmal failure as a guardian of young females.

"In wedding the cook you vowed to protect," the duke
declared, "you have broken your word and insulted both
church and state."

Griffin nodded grimly. "The fault is entirely mine, Your
Grace, for trusting that Verdun would deal with me honorably and abide by the truce. For not keeping Julia under lock
and key for the balance of the year. And for not having the
strength of will to keep her at bay once the vows were spoken. I truly intended to seek an annulment and allow her to
return to the convent." He propped his elbows on his knees
and stared off into a memory. "I lasted all of a week. Once
she started cooking . . . Sweet Jesus, what that woman can
do with a truffle. A man doesn't stand a chance."

After a bit more wine, the duke and Lord Griffin saun-
tered around the great hall to the main doors. They heard
raised voices in what sounded like shouting and rushed inside to find the voices were raised in song, not conflict. At
the head table sat Sir Martin and Sophie, bound together
with a garland of flowers, enduring rounds of ill-sung
bridal songs with nervous grace.

All around the hall, faces were wine warmed and merry,
and even the contests and wagers between knights, which
often grew contentious, had a genial tone to them. The
duke strolled through the hall, watching and listening.
Over and over, he heard comments about the fritters, the
chicken ambrogino, the almond cakes, and even the buttered wortes and minces.

A fleeting recall of a comment Lady Julia made left him
scratching his head and trying to call it back again. Something about food and . . . relatives . . . or music . . . or
something. He sighed. He'd remember it in the morning.
He quit the impromptu wedding feast to trudge up the
stairs to the lord's chamber and fall asleep the instant his
head touched the pillows.

*   *   *

THE HARMONY, CAMARADERIE, AND GOOD
relations that dampened the tension in the hall during supper evaporated the next day with the morning dew. The
night's respite had also laid to rest the duke's food-
sweetened approach to gathering testimony. He announced
to the hall over breakfast that he would be questioning
more persons on the accuracy of the accounts given hereto-
fore. And as soon as he downed the last swallow of his
morning ale, he began with Axel and Greeve.

Then midmorning, shouts came from the sentries on the
west walls: a force of men riding hard on Grandaise.
Alarms rang continuously as the folk of the village
streamed through the gates and Grandaise's guardsmen
rushed to take up positions on the walls. It wasn't long before word came down from the lookouts that the force, as
expected, rode under a banner of red and white.

Griffin grimly donned his armor and sword and shouted
orders to his knights and men along the walls. He exited
the hall into the midst of the villagers streaming in to take
refuge within the walls and sent to the armory for weapons
with which to defend themselves.

"Grandaise!" The duke hurried to confront Griffin. "I'll
have no blood shed this day, is that clear? I shall meet
Verdun outside the gates with my men and deliver the
news of his daughter's marriage." The duke's fleshy face
was filled with resolve. "Close the gates behind me. And if
you value your life, you'll see that no 'stray' arrows are
loosed."

Griffin studied the duke's face and realized he had no
choice but to comply. Only through a direct confrontation
of his own would the king's noble emissary begin to understand how treacherous Verdun could be. He nodded and escorted the duke to the gates.

By the time Verdun and his knights arrived at the gentle
slope approaching the front gates of Grandaise, the duke
stood outside the closed iron gates, flanked by Sir Thomas
de Albans and the captain of the king's men. The duke had

prevented Sir Martin from joining them, insisting that it would be best for the bridegroom to remain inside the walls until the count's reaction to the marriage was known. Behind them and stretching out along the wall on either side was a rank of purple and white—a score of the king's men— weapons at the ready. To the duke's left, farther along the wall, stood a collection of tents flying the king's banner. The duke had ordered the royal guardsmen to camp outside the walls, to maintain a royal presence separate from his person, outside the walls of both combative houses.

Now the wisdom of that strategy became clear. As Bardot of Verdun came thundering up he faced the burly duke, and a handful of knights—including one of his own, and a rank of soldiers bearing the purple and white tabards and the insignia of the king of France. As the duke intended, it appeared that the king of France had inserted himself into the conflict.

"Bardot of Verdun!" The duke called as the rider at the head of the force slowed and raised his hand to halt the column. "Come forward to talk!"

Another motion of Verdun's hand sent the men behind him spreading out into battle lines on either side of him. In the prickly silence that followed, Verdun studied the royal banners, the presence of royal guardsmen, and the barrel-chested figure wearing a coat of arms indicating ducal rank. Then his gaze fell on his own vassal, approaching.

"It is the Duke of Avalon, seigneur," Thomas de Albans said, striding forward to greet his lord. "Sent from the king to investigate the troubles. He has news of your daughter and insists you come and talk with him before moving further against Grandaise."

Verdun chose a handful of men to accompany him and dismounted. He ordered his men to stay alert, then approached Avalon.

"The king sends greetings, Verdun," the duke declared loudly enough for all to hear inside and atop the walls of Grandaise. "And a command that you render unto me as his emissary all possible aid in resolving the conflicts between your house and this one."

"Then you should know, Duke, that Grandaise has my daughter within his walls . . . and I intend to retrieve her." The count's hand went to the hilt of his blade and his men reacted instantly, reaching for their weapons.

"Hold there!" the duke roared, taking one threatening step forward. "If you draw that blade, you'd better be prepared to shed my blood with it and make yourself an outlaw to your king!" Behind him, the king's captain and men were matching Verdun's men, hands on hilts and lances ready. After a moment his words had the desired effect; Verdun eased his hand from his sword.

"What makes you think Grandaise has your daughter?" Avalon demanded.

"It's an eye for an eye—" There Verdun halted.

"And what wrong would Grandaise be redressing, Verdun?"

The count refused to incriminate himself by answering, but the duke supplied the answer.

"One abduction for another, eh? Well, I have seen your daughter and spoken with her," Avalon continued. "She is indeed within Grandaise's walls. But I can swear to you, on the king's honor, that Grandaise had nothing to do with her being here. She took it upon herself to ride to Grandaise and seek sanctuary."

"Sanctuary?" That unexpected claim set Verdun back on his heels for a moment. "What the devil could she need 'sanctuary' from?"

"From *you*."

It took a moment for Verdun to react.

"That's absurd. I am her father—her lord—her guardian. She has nothing to fear from me."

"Except a marriage she found repugnant and possibly deadly. She claims you would force her to wed a portly German to cement an alliance. Is that true?"

"It is." Verdun reddened furiously. "It is my right, as her father, to determine who and where and when she will wed." He thumped the tabard-covered mail over his chest. "My right. She is mine, to do with as I think best."

"She feels differently. She has, in fact wedded another . . . one Martin de Gies. I believe you know the man."

"M-Martin? She wedded *my* Martin de Gies?" His anger, stretched and thinned for a moment by those revelations, snapped back. "That cannot be true. He's my First Knight—he would never have—" But the reality that his trusted right arm and daughter had gone missing at the same time struck him and he sputtered, then silenced. After a moment, he clenched his hands and growled, stalking away from the duke and then back. "I don't believe it—I demand to see him—to hear it from his own mouth!"

The duke strode closer and lowered his voice.

"This Martin de Gies did not wed your daughter entirely of his own accord. He was forced to do so in order to get her to return home. I believe he did it to try to avoid bloodshed between your houses. I arrived just after the vows and immediately advised him to go no further with the marriage than spoken words. The situation may yet be saved. . . ."

The count looked up at Grandaise's gate and spotted Sophie and Sir Martin standing with Griffin and his ransomed cook . . . just inside the iron bars. He sensed the satisfaction on his rival's face and swore, shaking a fist at him.

"This is all his fault—I'll have your head for this, Grandaise—"

"No, you won't!" came a feminine voice from the gate. In a heartbeat, Sophie was wrenching open the gate and running out to face her father. She stopped a few yards away, well within the safety of the duke's and king's men. "Lord Griffin had nothing to do with it, except to give me shelter when I was desperate for help. I would never have needed sanctuary if you hadn't insisted on selling me into bondage with that horrid German. And I would never have thought to come here if you hadn't abducted Julia and brought her to Verdun. It was *her* I came to for help . . . and she turned to her husband to help me . . . the very husband *you* forced upon her. So in a way, most of this is *your* fault, Father. Your pride and scheming set into motion events you couldn't control. And now you must live with consequences."

"You'll come home with me right now, Sophie Marie, and submit to my authority and do your duty as my daughter," Verdun commanded, advancing on her. She skittered back to the safety of the king's men and they closed ranks around her. Verdun halted, speechless with frustration, and looked from the duke to the gates of Grandaise. "I'll have this marriage annulled!" he called out. "And you, Martin"—he scoured the iron gates and pointed at his errant First Knight—"I've treated you like a son—trusted you—and you betrayed me!"

"How is that, Verdun?" the duke intervened. "He tried to bring your daughter back to you . . . tried to keep you from having to shed blood. How does that make him a traitor?"

Verdun trembled as he stared between his First Knight and his daughter's faces. Martin de Gies pulled open the great iron gates and strode outside to take his place beside Sophie. Griffin exited the gate and came out to stand with them.

"I had nothing to do with her coming to Grandaise," Griffin called to Verdun. "When I tried to send her home with your Martin de Gies, she declared she would only go if she were duly married to him." He smiled a bit smugly. "It seemed a fitting turnabout, since I was forced to marry at your hands."

"This is an outrage," Verdun sputtered, looking to the duke of Avalon.

"No, Verdun," the duke said, jamming his fists on his waist. "It is justice."

A frantic call came down from one of the sentries in the south tower. The alarm was relayed clearly . . . causing Griffin and everyone present to look to the sky. And there it was. A growing plume of smoke.

"The south village!" Griffin snarled and made for Verdun—but was caught and restrained in time by Sir Martin and the duke. "You bastard! Burning my villages while we stand talking! You see, Your Grace? You see his treachery?"

"That is not *my* doing!" Verdun protested, staring in confusion at the smoke, then turning defiantly back to

Griffin. "Unlike you, I prefer to settle my differences with honor, on a battlefield. I don't go about firing villages and terrifying cottagers!"

"No, you send your *henchmen* to burn out my shepherds!" Griffin charged, thrusting closer to Verdun, his body coiled to strike.

"I've burned no cottages—"

"Then explain that smoke!" Griffin roared.

The duke thrust Griffin back and took the ground midway between the pair of opposing lords.

"Lord Bardot is not responsible for any burnings," Martin stepped forward to declare. "In fact, I was riding out with some men to investigate a fire myself when I spotted Lady Sophie coming here." He looked to Griffin, making a connection in his mind. "Sir Gerard came back from patrol the night before Lady Sophie left with word that two of our outlying cottages had burned."

"*Someone* is burning," the duke declared, turning to Verdun. "On your oath, count . . ."

"It is not my doing, Your Grace. How could it be—when I am here and the rest of my garrison guards my own walls? I swear on my faith, I have nothing to do with it."

The duke turned to Griffin.

"And you, Grandaise . . . on your oath . . ."

"I swear by all that is holy—I have not raided or burned. This is *my* south village." He glared at Verdun. "I'll soon prove who is behind this destruction!" He turned to the gates and called for horses.

"Wait!" The duke grabbed him back by the arm and held him. "We will go and discover the truth together. Take ten of your men, Grandaise. And you—Verdun, the same number. I will bring a dozen. We ride together or not at all."

Griffin stared at Verdun, who glared back at him. Both nodded.

"Reynard, we'll need a score of men," Griffin charged back through the gates issuing orders. "Axel, you and Greeve—bring a half dozen of your best archers. I want some wounded to question."

Chapter 31

TOGETHER, GRIFFIN AND VERDUN LED the main body of men straight into the chaos that once had been a sleepy little hamlet on the southern edge of Grandaise. The smoke was thickening fast, coming from everywhere. Now and again, the wind rolled back enough of the haze, as they approached, to give them a glimpse of the fighting going on all over the village. It also revealed that there was scarcely a cottage, byre, or shed that hadn't been set ablaze. Like the attack on the shepherd's cottage a few days before, this assault was focused more on wanton destruction than thievery.

There were at least a score of brigands, wearing no armor and clad in ragged garments that seemed oddly incongruous on their powerful, muscular frames. Only a few were mounted, but there were a number of horses left in the field between the village and the forest. They wielded their weighty blades and stout shields with what could only be called restraint against the harrows, sickles, and spades of the cottagers who were trying desperately to defend their homes.

Then as Griffin's and Verdun's men charged into the

fray, the villagers were quickly pushed aside in the raiders'
eagerness to engage men of battle. It was almost as if the
brigands had been waiting for their true opponents.

Griffin drew his blade and saw Verdun drawing his. The
men eyed each other as they charged in, wielding swords
from horseback, using the advantage of height to rain down
heavy blows. Then one of the mounted attackers charged
Griffin and soon he was battling eye to eye with a power-
fully built swordsman whose choice of weapon and skill in
using it spoke of military background and experience in
battle. This, he realized, was no ordinary band of brigands
and thieves.

The clash of blades and the panicky rearing of horses
added to the roar of flames devouring the wooden roofs
and starting on the walls of the cottages. The smoke made
gauging the progress of the attack impossible. Each man
was fighting blind, battling for his life and the chance to go
on to the next opponent without knowing whether his side
was winning or losing.

The fighting raged for a time, and the smoke and heat
began to take a toll on both sides. Shouts came through the
smoke and roar, distracting Griffin's opponent enough for
him to find an opening between the cur's blade and shield.
He thrust hard and his blade pierced his opponent's shoulder, though the man twisted at the last moment to deflect
part of the force.

Swaying, the man gripped his saddle and wheeled his
mount, heading for the edge of the village. And as Griffin
turned his mount and searched the smoke, he saw two
more of the marauders racing on foot in the same direction.

They were withdrawing—fleeing!

Giving his mount the spur, he shot toward the western
edge of the village and the field where the attackers had
left their horses. Several of Grandaise's and Verdun's men
were giving chase to retreating raiders and Griffin shouted
and waved, signaling Axel and Greeve to have their archers
take aim on the fleeing men. A hail of arrows caught the
brigands by surprise, taking down several. Those who

hadn't already reached their horses abandoned their
mounts and made a frantic dash for the trees on foot.

Reynard and the duke had broken off from Griffin's
force with a dozen men and ridden south through the edge
of the forest, intending to cut off the attackers' retreat. The
duke suggested that with fields and vineyards to the north
and east and a river to the south, the most logical route of
escape would be west, into the cover of the forest. Now as
the mounted attackers reached the supposed safety of the
trees, the trees came alive with Reynard's and Crossan's
men. Some of the attackers drew blades to defend themselves, while others wheeled and ran for their lives. Soon
even those who had begun to fight broke off and fled
through the trees with the duke's men in close pursuit.

Almost as abruptly as it had begun, the fighting was
over and the clang of blades and shouts of battle gave way
to the hiss and crackle of burning wood and the wails of injured and grieving cottagers.

Griffin sheathed his blade and dismounted. His heart
was still pounding and his blood was still roaring in his
ears as he bent and braced with his hands on his knees,
dragging breath after breath of clean air into his smoke-
clogged lungs. Around him his men and Sir Martin and Sir
Thomas and their lord were emerging from the pall of
smoke to cough out the smoke they had swallowed and
gasp fresh air.

As his men recovered, he sent them back into the village to check what was left of the cottages for survivors,
report on the wounded, and take stock of the damage. As
Griffin's men began to regroup and tend their own injuries,
Verdun, who had inhaled a good bit of smoke, staggered
over to Griffin.

"Those brutes were not my men," he declared in a
smoke-strained voice. His expression was grim and he
fought to suppress a cough at each breath. Griffin coughed
and bent over beside him, breathing, sensing the truth in his
words. He had seen Verdun and his men fighting hard, risk-
ing injury and death, working to beat back the attackers.

"I know every man in the garrison, Your Lordship,"

Martin de Gies said from nearby. "Not one of the men who did this was from Verdun. These men, they fought like—"

"Soldiers," Griffin finished for both of them. "But they weren't."

The brigands were battle hardened and fought with skill and ferocity. But their ragged garments, long, shaggy hair and beards, and grimy, soulless faces . . . spoke of an undisciplined and unprincipled existence. The cities were full of men like them . . . deserters, braggarts, and cruel brutes who enjoyed inflicting suffering . . . men who would do anything for a bit of silver. But they seldom ventured this far into the countryside. Not unless they were *hired*.

"Milord!" Axel and Greeve hurried toward him with their archers, who were pausing along the way to inspect the fallen brigands for survivors. "It looks as if our archers were a bit too deadly with their aim. We've not found any of the curs still alive."

Suddenly there were shouts from the edge of the forest, across the fields. It was Reynard and the duke, hailing Griffin. He left his mount where it was and hurried across the pasture with Axel and Greeve and their archers hard on his heels. As he approached he saw that there were four bodies sprawled on the ground, three with arrows in their backs.

"We've got one alive," Reynard called, kneeling on one knee to roll the man up onto his side. He froze over the body and Griffin watched the knight cross himself and raise a look of horror to him.

"What is it, Reynard? You look like you've seen a ghost."

"It's—it's—"

Griffin looked down and froze himself as an icy finger of recognition dragged through his fire-seared senses. For a moment everything stopped: his breath, his heart, his instinct to reach out, and his impulse to recoil.

There on the ground at his feet was a face he knew better than his own . . . had trained with and fought with . . . and trusted.

"Bertrand." He sank to his knees, staring at those slack

features and feeling fully the horror Reynard had exhibited. "Get this arrow out of him!" he commanded furiously, struggling to contain his rising emotions. "It's Bertrand!"

Two of his archers fell to their knees and tried desperately to remove the arrow one of them had just shot into their old captain. Their hands trembled and Griffin could see when they looked up and reported that they couldn't remove it, that they were devastated by what they had done. He ordered them to break it off and they complied.

"Bertrand." Griffin rolled him gently onto his back, careful to avoid the arrow shaft. "Bertrand, can you hear me? It's Grandaise . . ."

Bertrand's eyes opened.

"Milord? Is it really you?" When he focused on Griffin's face, he raised a hand but didn't have enough strength to reach it. Griffin clasped his groping fingers with one hand and put his other under Bertrand's shoulders to hold him.

"Why?" Griffin had to force each word from his constricted throat. "Why did you do this? You were always one I counted on."

"I didn't want to. My grandfather . . . hates you . . . hates Verdun. Wants you to fight. The land was ours . . . he says . . . the forest is again." He coughed and brought up bubbles of blood. His eyes rolled aimlessly and then closed.

"Bertrand—Bertrand, stay with me. We'll get you back to Grandaise—"

"He said we must take back our birthright. . . ." Bertrand's breath began to rattle in his throat. "Never meant to hurt . . . forgive . . ."

"Your grandfather—Old Thibault—these are his men? Bertrand, tell me—we must know." Griffin was both frantic to know and loathe to hear it.

Bertrand nodded and opened his eyes one last time.

"Forgive me, milord . . . forgive . . . I beg . . ."

Grief surged in Griffin with volcanic force. It felt for a moment like his chest might burst. Then he struggled to produce even a whisper.

"I forgive you, Bertrand."

Bertrand's face grew peaceful. Then his eyes closed and he was gone.

In the hush that fell, all present crossed themselves and said a prayer for the knight who—unknown to them—had dwelt in two worlds . . . one of friendship, respect, and loyalty, and the other of covetousness, vengeance, and betrayal.

Griffin staggered to his feet and floundered for a moment, feeling swamped by grief and anger. He looked around him, groping for direction, and found it in the sympathetic eyes and loyal faces of the men who had pledged themselves to him and had faithfully kept those vows.

"You heard?" He looked from Reynard and Crossan to the duke and then to Verdun. "This—the burning—the strife—Old Thibault de Roland is to blame." He looked to the south and west, the direction the brigands had fled, and realized it was also the direction of Old Thibault's hall. He looked down at Bertrand, seeing recent events in a new light.

"He was responsible for abducting Julia."

"He came to me with word of her arrival," Verdun said, shaking his head. "He often brought me news from Grandaise, late at night. He complained that he was not advanced in your garrison." He looked chagrined to admit, "I believed him. I promised him a place in my service and a purse to help restore his grandfather's keep. But after he brought Lady Julia to us, he disappeared. I assumed he went back to Grandaise and that you must have found him out."

"I did find him out, but only after Julia told us who had abducted her. We looked for him, but he had fled." Griffin looked at Verdun. "I assumed he came to Verdun, since he was obviously your agent. But it appears he went home to his grandfather instead." He turned to look at the smoldering village. "They began to raid and burn, knowing we would accuse each other."

He looked to the duke and back to Verdun, chastened by how nearly Thibault had succeeded.

"How much of this feud between our houses has been the work of Old Thibault and his house?" He didn't expect an answer, but the duke responded.

"We may never know, Grandaise. We cannot change the past. We can only live now to change the future."

The burly duke looked from him to Verdun and back.

"This Thibault de Roland must be dealt with," he said. "It is your chance to truly end the feud and to put the violence to rest between your houses. Do I have your word that you will work together?"

THERE WAS A BRIEF BUT HEARTFELT CELE-bration when the motley force of defenders returned to the hall. None of the men had been killed and few of the injuries sustained were serious. Only one of the cottagers had died in the attack . . . an old man whose heart gave out when he tried to keep the brigands from setting a torch to his house. All in all, their losses were more in replaceable property than irreplaceable lives.

"Thank God you're safe!" Julia met Griffin in the front court and threw her arms around his neck, holding him tightly. He endured her embrace, then set her back with a brief and oddly guarded smile.

"We have much to do, Julia," he said gravely. "And I must ask you to see to some food that will ease the tension in the hall tonight."

"You know I will do my best, milord." She stroked his cheek and felt him stiffen and pull back. "If food can sweeten the air, you will breathe nothing but honey in your hall this evening."

He nodded and turned away to escort the duke and his old enemy Verdun into his hall. His supremely controlled, utterly emotionless mien alarmed her. She wanted desperately to take him aside and get him to talk to her about what happened. But there were more urgent things afoot. The first tentative steps were being made toward settling the feud between Grandaise and Verdun, and plans were being laid to move against old Thibault de Roland. She would have to settle for speaking with him later that night, in the privacy of their bed.

Sophie rushed to hug and kiss Martin, tearfully thanking God that he'd returned safely. Then she turned to her father, who had seen her display toward Martin and strode past her refusing to acknowledge her presence. Martin withdrew his hand from hers with a troubled expression and followed the rest of the knights into the hall, leaving Sophie alone.

Julia hurried to put an arm around her and usher her to the kitchens, telling her that they were all tired and shaken by the day's events. But once in the kitchen, she found her faithful staff also reeling with shock. The news of Bertrand's betrayal had reached them and struck them hard; a number of the young girls had flirted with Sir Bertrand when he came by the kitchens, in the days before Julia came, and he had never failed to compliment the cooks. The thought that he had presented such a charming face while working to undermine their lord and destroy their home was deeply unsettling.

It took all of Julia's considerable powers of persuasion to move the kitchen folk back to their duties. The bruised spirits in Grandaise's hall needed the healing solace of good food more than ever, she told them, and they had a chance to show the Count of Verdun the quality of Grandaise's kitchen. With fresh and selfless resolve, they lifted their chins and set aside their own concerns to render service to their lord.

She threw herself into overseeing the production of an exceptionally fine supper while dealing with a weepy Sophie, who was devastated to find herself caught in the same nuptial netherworld Julia had recently inhabited. She was wedded in name and "volition"—despite an initial bit of coercion—but not in the more critical area of the consummation. And she had learned from Martin on their wedding night that the duke insisted that he make peace with his lord by suing for an annulment and returning her to her father.

During a momentary respite in the preparations, Julia pulled Sophie outside and used a cool, wet cloth to soothe her reddened eyes and puffy nose.

"That wretched duke—it's all his fault." She groaned as Julia tended her tear-scalded skin. "Sticking his nose in other people's affairs. Who asked him?"

"The king, actually," Julia said ruefully.

"I mean, Martin loves me and wants to be married to me! For pity's sake—he braved the 'Beast of Grandaise' to rescue me. No offense."

"None taken."

"He likes my father, and my father likes him. Or at least he did."

"Well, there *are* the little matters of a title and a castle and an heir . . ."

"What can I do?" She looked even more despondent. "The duke's going to make me go back to Verdun, and my father will probably beat me black and blue and stick me in a dungeon somewhere. My marriage will be annulled and I'll be shipped off to Frankfurt and never get to see Martin again."

"You know," Julia said, giving Sophie a comforting pat, "we're assuming the worst of your father. But he's having to change his thinking about Griffin and this feud . . . maybe he will change his thinking about your marriage, too. He has always liked and respected Sir Martin. Maybe when he's had a chance to cool down and when this battle is over . . ." She thought about it for a moment. "Maybe he can be talked out of an annulment." Her eyes narrowed as she scrutinized another possibility that occurred to her. "Or *cooked* out of it."

Chapter 32

SUPPER THAT EVENING WAS POSSIBLY the most nerve-wracking experience of Julia's life . . . as well as the supreme test of her culinary skills. She had surveyed her larder and dragged out every spice and delicacy within it to create dishes that would tantalize palates and promote harmony in the uneasy company that would assemble in the hall for supper. There were too many possibilities, she realized, staring at the spices and meats and the soft dough ready for rolling. And she thought of the convent . . . of the nights she had heard of an argument or bit of contention between sisters and crafted a menu meant to bring the arguing sides together. But men required a more potent, meat-oriented approach to culinary satisfaction. She had to find dishes that combined sweet and sour, soft and hard, hot and cold. Was there time to make it as succulent and sense-charming as it needed to be?

The most unsettling part of the planning was the fact that instead of supervising the serving from the kitchen and putting last touches on dishes the instant before they were served, she was now required, as Grandaise's lady, to be in the hall beside Griffin, entertaining their guests. The thought of trying to warm the heart of the fierce, sardonic

Count of Verdun made her want to scuttle back to her pots
and kettles and renounce all rights to her place in the hall.
When she confided her fears to Regine, the sister declared
that she would see to the finishing and dispatching of the
dishes.

It was a lot to ask of one meal, Julia realized—pacifying
a king-by-proxy, forging a lasting peace between two war-
ring noble houses, and securing two marriages that by all
rights shouldn't exist—so she insisted the kitchen staff say
aloud the "*paternosters*" and rosaries they used to time
their cooking, and she sent one of the potboys for Father
Dominic and asked him to bless each dish before it left the
kitchens.

At the last possible moment, she hurried to her chamber
to wash and change into the silk gown she had worn at her
marriage. Sophie appeared to help her lift her hair and
dress it in a fashion befitting a married lady. Then together
they descended to the hall to do battle for peace and love.

The hall had never looked more impressive. The tables
were all draped with white linen, and the main chairs at the
head table were set with great silver chargers. The cellar
master provided the wine for her to serve to their honored
guests and she carried individual cups to Griffin, the duke,
Sophie's father, the baron Crossan, and the first knights of
each house . . . Sir Reynard and Sir Martin. Then she received a nod from the kitchen stairs, clapped her hands for
the serving to begin, and seated herself beside Griffin.

The duke, as custom dictated, took the chair of the master of the hall, and Griffin and Julia were seated to his
right. To his left sat Verdun and according to custom, the
baron Crossan was seated next to him. That same custom
of precedence required Verdun's daughter and first knight
to be seated next, so Sir Martin was forced to take a place
beside Sophie, who would hardly look at him.

Cinnamon-dusted almonds served as an *aperitif*, to
open the stomach, and were followed closely by an elegant
salade of lettuce and cress topped with a vinaigrette of several kinds of beans and sliced onions and fennel. The men
at the lower tables—an equal contingent of Grandaise's

and Verdun's men—were quiet at first. But as they began to
eat, Grandaise's men began to groan silently, grin, and look
with pride to their lady . . . raising their cups silently to
her. She blushed and looked down, praying that the Count
of Verdun would have a similarly pleasant experience.

The duke tried valiantly to raise safely neutral topics of
conversation, but all failed until he settled on the dish being served. He seemed quite pleased by the food and complimented Julia on her choice to the beginning of the meal.
Verdun said nothing, but Julia noted that he ate quickly and
occasionally closed his eyes as if analyzing the dish's com-
ponents. Fortunately the baron Crossan was not so reticent.
As the second course, a lovely white porée made with
cream and leeks and spiced chicken broth, was served the
baron groaned with pleasure and ignited a wave of audible
sounds of pleasure along the Grandaise side of the hall.

"Milady, you have such a delicate touch with a porée,"
he declared, hoisting a cup to her. "I don't know how you
do it."

"Thank you, Baron," she said. "I must carry your compliments to my kitchen staff. I don't know what I would do
without them."

"A fine cook is a blessing from Heaven," the duke observed sagely, sipping the porée with gusto. "A fine wife is
an even greater blessing. Damme, Grandaise, that must
make you the best-blessed man in all of France!"

Nettled by the duke's words, Verdun glanced at Julia from
the corner of his eye and focused even harder on his food.

Then came the third course . . . a Hungarian Torte made
of thin, flaky layers of dough stuffed with a mixture of
minced chicken and pork, seasoned with saffron and fine
spice. The dough was so golden and so rich and flaky that
it elicited groans from both ends of the head table. Knights
of all colors were nodding and grinning at the unexpected
lightness and savory taste of the dish. They called for more
and before long, the lower tables on both sides of the hall
were making their enjoyment of the dish widely known.

By the time the first meat dish, an almond chicken
cuminade, was being served to the lower tables, the men of

Grandaise were boasting about their habitually fine fare and offering the men of Verdun a place in their garrison . . . for a price. The men of Verdun tossed back good natured answers, until one wine-foolish wag suggested they might just abduct the cook instead.

A deep silence fell over the hall. Verdun's head snapped up, searching his men for the culprit, then steeling himself and looking to Griffin. All eyes turned to the lord of Grandaise, who wiped his mouth and looked out over the hall to the red-faced fellow already counting the stripes that would fall on his back for his thoughtless words.

"That, I believe has already been tried, my good man." He felt Julia's hand on his thigh and reached beneath the table to hold it. Then he grinned. "And when I came to get her back, I brought home not only a fine cook but a fine wife as well!" He turned to Verdun. "I must thank you, Verdun, for that remarkable bit of sorcery . . . turning one woman into two!"

A wave of relieved laughter went through the hall and the count reddened as he began to appreciate the irony of being the author of his adversary's pleasure. Seeing the duke's chuckle and prodding look, he allowed a wry smile to lift one corner of his mouth.

"If only you would do me the same favor," he said tartly, tossing a suffering glance down the table at his way-ward offspring, who reddened.

"I shall see what I can do," Griffin said, looking at Sophie and Martin.

Another round of mirth rolled through the hall. The tightness in Julia's chest began to loosen and by the time the stuffed honey-glazed pork was served, her prayers for the evening were being answered.

"Write my wife," the duke cried, sinking his teeth into the tender pork stuffed with pears, apples, brie cheese and chestnuts and glazed to a golden turn with honey. "I've died and gone to Heaven!"

"Sweet Mother of—" Verdun looked down the table to Julia and then to Griffin beside her, his eyes wide with un-derstanding. "Damme if it's not true. She is the blessing of the age." He scowled. "More than you deserve, Grandaise."

The noise level in the hall lowered considerably as Verdun's comment carried. All paused and looked to Griffin's response.

"On that, Verdun, we do agree," he said, with a pained bit of honesty that drew a husky laughter of understanding from the men in the hall.

Griffin's and Verdun's gazes met and held. And in that moment of honesty and acceptance, a true peace was begun.

As the supper ended, Julia asked the duke to join her in thanking the kitchen staff and tasting a new sweetmeat she was trying to perfect. He gladly complied, but as soon as his thanks were proffered, she ushered him outside to the bench where he had conducted his interviews earlier.

"Have some of this nucato. Your Grace, and give me your opinion. I've used a combination of nuts in the boiled honey instead of just walnuts, hoping that almonds and filberts would round out the nut flavor. Walnuts can be a bit strong. And I used nutmeg instead of ginger. Of course, some people think pepper and nutmeg aren't good in combination. What do you think?"

The duke munched thoughtfully for a moment.

"I think . . . you didn't ask me here to talk about nucato."

His steady regard convinced her that this was a time for plain speaking.

"It's about these marriages, Your Grace." When he groaned she merely grew more determined. "I know you have a lot on your mind—like this campaign against Old Thibault and how to arrange and enforce a lasting peace. So, I want to propose that you allow me to take some of that burden from you."

The duke drew a heavy breath and sighed. "I don't suppose I'll get out of here without hearing this. And just how do you intend to do that?"

She brightened.

"The king believes there must be ties between the houses in order to ensure peace, right? Well, let Sophie and I be that tie. We're dear friends and we're wedded—mostly—to men who respect each other. You're the king's agent, right? You have authority to make the peace. Then insist Sophie's father allow them to stay married and make Sir Martin his heir along with Sophie . . . and recognize milord Griffin's and my marriage as being not only honorable, but necessary to the stability of the peace. Then you can go to the king with a sound and viable peace that he can't help but accept."

The duke looked at her in astonishment.

"Meddling in statecraft now, are we? I don't think you know what you're asking, my lady. Sophie cannot inherit. She is a female."

"Other women have inherited."

"The king's claim to the throne of France is staked on inheriting exclusively through the male line. He will never agree to such an arrangement."

"Well then, don't think of it as Sophie inheriting, think of it as *grafting* Sir Martin into the Verdun line." When the duke still looked skeptical, irritation got the best of her. "Look, does the king want peace here, or not? If he does, then he has to be willing to be a little flexible. . . ."

MAKING PEACE AND SETTING THE WORLD TO rights was an exhausting experience, Julia thought as she trudged up the steps to her bedchamber later. And she still had her own part of the world to set to rights.

Griffin stood in the darkened chamber by an opened window. As she approached she could see the pain in his face and knew he must be thinking of the raid and Bertrand's death.

"I'm sorry, milord." she said, making her way to his side.

"Why?" he said coolly. "You've done nothing wrong."

"I meant about Bertrand. I know it must have been difficult for you."

"He was a traitor. I'll lose no sleep over his fate."

Alarm crept up her spine as she touched his arm and he withdrew it. His night-darkened eyes seemed like bottomless wells of sadness.

"I know you trusted him—"

"He was a traitor," he said, looking away. "I was a fool to trust him."

"You couldn't have known what was in his heart. The fault was in *him,* not in your trust of him. You cannot live in this world without trusting others."

She reached up to remove the band from his nose, and he grabbed her wrist and held it. There was a long silence, in which she quit reaching and he released her hand.

Aching with the need to reach him and make him respond to her, she removed her clothes, hung them on pegs, and then slid naked between the bedcovers. He still stood by the window, staring.

"Come to bed, milord," she said softly, intending to offer him her warmth as comfort, to draw him back from the coldness that was claiming him. "You will have a hard day tomorrow. You need to rest."

"Go to sleep, Julia," he said thickly. "You may have the harder task tomorrow: *waiting.*"

MILES AWAY, IN THE HALL OF THE HOUSE OF Roland, Old Thibault sat in his ancient chair, staring at the treacherous rabble that filled his neglected hall and hating them almost as much as he hated Verdun and Grandaise.

The brutes had failed him that day; they had allowed his grandson to be killed, and in so doing, they had stripped him of all possibility of fulfilling the dream that had kept him alive these many years . . . that his house and line would rise again and take back the land and prominence they had lost when Grandaise and Verdun surpassed them.

Now the boy was gone. And it was all for naught.

When they told him of Bertrand's death, he flew into a rage and struck out at them with bony fists and the staff he used to walk. They backed away, watching, and in desperation he seized a blade and began to hack viciously at his great chair and table, knowing they would never see the good life he had schemed and even murdered to return to them.

When his strength was spent and his fury had cooled,
only icy and dreadful determination remained. He called
his hired captains to his side to reiterate his plan for tomorrow . . . with one slight modification.

As hardened, murderous eyes flicked speculatively over
his wasted frame, he sweetened the bounty he had promised for the heads of the two men he hated more than death.
Taking two bags of coins, he drove an iron spike through
each into the wall behind his chair.

"I will retreat to this place after the assault begins. Whoever brings me the head of Grandaise or Verdun will be allowed to take one of those bags of gold from the wall." There
was murmuring at that and the old man raised his hand and
spoke in a voice that sounded eerily like a death rattle.

"If they reach this far, waste no time protecting me. Aim
all of your efforts on killing Grandaise and Verdun. Two
men. That is all I demand of you. The deaths of two
wretched men." His eyes glittered. "Nothing else matters."

THE NEXT MORNING KNIGHTS OF FIVE COL-
ors exited Grandaise's hall into the cool gray of dawn,
pulling up hauberks and drawing on gauntlets and helms.
Julia's kitchens had made boiled eggs and fresh bread and
morning ale available for those men who would be riding
into battle. Griffin and Verdun met over tankards of ale and
watched each other giving orders to their men and preparing for battle. There was a moment when they exited the
hall and stood on the steps together.

"I thought I would hate you for taking Julia from me,"
Griffin said quietly to his longtime adversary. "But I don't,
at least not now. What I cannot seem to forgive is your taking Bertrand from me."

Verdun glanced at him guardedly, then drew on his
gauntlets.

"I did not take him from you, Grandaise. He came to me
with the offer of news. You may have loved him, but
Bertrand de Roland was never truly yours." He shifted his

gaze from Griffin to Sir Martin who was coming toward them. "Betrayal is always a bitter thing."

"You." Verdun called as he descended the few steps, right into Sir Martin's path. "You ride with your new lord, but under your old colors? What—has Grandaise not seen fit to provide you a simple tabard?"

"I wear the colors of my oath of loyalty, milord count," Martin said with both earnestness and dignity. "I have in all ways tried to further your interests and protect your family as if it were my own."

"And seized the first opportunity to make it your own, didn't you?" the count snapped.

The moment of decision had come. The duke had to act on Julia's peace plan right now, or let a potentially golden opportunity slip through his fingers.

"I would have you know, Verdun," the duke declared, "that Sir Martin has demonstrated nothing but restraint, loyalty, and sound judgment regarding the affairs of your house. You have been better served by him than you know. And if you must take my word on it until you know better, then do so. I would be proud to have a man of such qualities ride at my back *or marry my daughter.*"

Stunned by the duke's forceful defense of Sir Martin and the implication that Sir Martin's marriage with his daughter had found favor with the king's agent, Verdun reddened and looked back at Sir Thomas with a scowl of confusion.

"Very well. You may ride with us, Martin de Gies." Verdun tried to cloak the resentment in his eyes. "But until this matter is settled, I would prefer you ride before me, instead of at my back."

Chapter 33

THE KEEP AND HALL OF THIBAULT OF
Roland sat at the bottom of a forested hill, facing
some rocky, ill-tended pastureland and surrounded on all
sides by the "south" forest that had been at the heart of the
dispute between Grandaise and Verdun for three generations. The castle, a wall-and-bailey structure, was surrounded by an ancient moat that was now just a soggy ditch
littered with rubble from the decaying walls. The keep was
built in the old round style and had been augmented over
the years with brick and stone to give it a squared appearance. But neglect had leached the mortar and cracked the
stone and brick so that weeds sprouted from the dust collected in holes in the walls.

It was a shabby, forlorn heap of stone, presided over by
a man who—they determined by discussion as they rode—
was at least eighty years old.

Thundering down the rutted path, they arrived at midmorning and arrayed themselves in ranks that for now
faced the one part of the structure that hadn't fallen entirely into disrepair, the front gate. When a significant part
of their combined force was in position, the duke selected
Griffin to speak for them.

"Thibault!" He bellowed, feeling strangely liberated by the power used in producing that volume. "Thibault of Roland! We've come in the name of justice. Show yourself!" Nothing happened at first. The gates were closed and the stone pillars on either side stood mute and empty. He tried again.

"Thibault de Roland! Show yourself . . . if you're not too old and infirm to climb your own walls!"

A rustle of impatience wafted through their troops just as a pale, balding figure in a simple linen tunic and robe appeared in the tower above the gates.

"So you've come, have you?" The voice was thin and strained, struggling to project across the field that lay between them. "Figured it out at last, eh? Idiots! Only took you sixty years!" There was a sound like a rusty laugh.

"Open your gates, Roland, and submit to the king's justice!" Griffin demanded. "The king's emissary is here— the duke of Avalon. He will guarantee your safety and escort you to Paris!"

"The king courts me now. Sends *dukes* to my door." Beneath the sarcasm the old man's voice was almost gleeful. "You'll not enter these walls until you pay the toll . . . in blood!"

"We know what you did, Roland," the duke called out.

"You don't know half of what I did, you horse's arse! You don't know how close you came to losing everything! And you deserved every bit of it. You took my land and forests—planted your vineyards where *mine* should have been. You wedded and increased—while robbing me of everything." He gripped the stones at the top of the tower for support, his anger and venom rising.

"Well, I took something from you, too. Made you pay where it would hurt most! I took your fathers! And then I took your sons!"

A stunned silence fell as every eye from Grandaise and Verdun alike fixed on the old man who was coming unhinged before their eyes.

"Your feud began in this very forest—not far from here. Your grandfathers argued and fought over who harvested what on this land—*my* land! I watched as they fought over *my* truffles and *my* oak and *my* game. Then when they were both spent and panting on the ground—I moved in and killed them both—each with the other's sword!"

"He's mad," Verdun said, just loud enough for the duke and Grandaise and Crossan to hear. "They fought to the death. Killed each other."

"And then your son, Verdun. Your brother, Grandaise. The day when they met in the forest to fight . . . I was there, too. And I saw that each was bled with the other's sword. I still have the golden cap you gave him, Verdun." He held up something that glowed golden in the early sun. He tossed it over the edge of the wall, and it sailed down to the edge of the moat.

Verdun looked like he'd been impaled. Sir Thomas rode out to get it and brought it back to his lord. Even before he had it in his hands, Verdun was quaking with fury. He crumpled the cap with its gold-embroidered crest of Verdun's arms, and pressed it to his heart.

"It was my son's. I had it made for him when he was sixteen." Something in Verdun seemed to snap and he faced the duke and Griffin with his eyes blazing. "I don't care if he did it or not. One this cruel deserves to die."

Griffin raised his arm and lowered it in a signal for the archers to begin firing volleys over the walls. Then he raised his blade and kicked his mount forward.

"To the gates!" he roared.

With a thundering shout, three ranks of soldiers closed on the crumbling walls with scaling ladders. Defenders appeared suddenly at the tops of the walls, but none were archers and their only defense was to push the ladders back or wait until Grandaise's and Verdun's men topped the wall and hack at them with blades. But Thibault's men were spread too thinly along the ramparts of the walls and soon knights and men-at-arms were streaming over the walls and opening the gates for their comrades.

Once inside the walls, surrounded by men and horses and frantic clangs of steel on steel, Griffin swung down quickly and looked up to find his erstwhile rival doing the same.

"I want him, Grandaise," Verdun shouted above the din.

"To the hall, first," Griffin replied, already headed across the crowded bailey for the weathered doors of the main hall. There he was met by a pair of burly swordsmen. He felt the burning draw of battle reflex racing along his nerves, preparing him. His entire pace of being quickened . . . breathing shortened, reactions quickened, perceptions became like flashes of lightning.

In three swings of his blade he felt himself sliding into the cool, layered cognition that allowed him to detach from the consequences. In this place there was only fighting and surviving . . . paring away sensations . . . concentrating on the essentials . . . dart of eyes, blade angle, shift of shoulder, arc of swing . . .

Suddenly the last large body blocking his path was falling. From behind him came shouts. He wheeled and found a handful of Thibault's mercenaries bearing down on them. He had time only to cry "Inside!" before shoving Verdun through the heavy doors to the hall and planting himself in the doorway.

Sir Martin appeared out of nowhere and bolted up the steps to his side, deflecting blows and sword thrusts as he came. The odds deteriorated as more mercenaries appeared and rushed them, pushing them back into the hall, where there was some fighting already. Verdun, Griffin saw from the corner of his eye, was battling three swordsmen and being backed steadily toward a corner.

"To your lord!" Griffin called to Sir Martin, jerking his head toward the count. He locked swords at the hilt in order to shove his closest opponent back into several others, buying a moment's reprieve. A moment had to be enough; they were back in a heartbeat . . . all around him . . . climbing on tabletops and ducking under benches, swinging blades at his head and curtains ripped off the doorways at his feet.

Doors slammed, and beyond the circle of men besieging him, he spotted Thibault's mercenaries lowering the bar over the doors, locking them all in. He lurched back, struck a table with his hip, and rolled and slid across it, sending dishes and debris flying. The jackals pursued him as he retreated toward the front of the hall—the dais and the remains of Old Thibault's chair—where splinters and hunks of the damaged seat crunched underfoot.

Suddenly blades were everywhere. He was being swarmed. This wasn't knightly, one-on-one fighting— A pained cry pulled his attention to the sight of Verdun crumpling to the floor and Martin rushing to stand over him, fighting back a number of men bent on reaching the wounded count despite the fact that he could no longer fight.

"Outta the way!" One attacker yanked another back. "His head is mine!"

Martin sent man after man shrieking to the floor, but somehow the numbers never seemed to decrease. Outside, they outnumbered Thibault's men a dozen to one, but in here—

Thibault's men had barred the doors to keep help from getting through. *A trap!* They'd gone for the old man himself and walked right into a trap!

Griffin sprang up onto the head table to buy time to breathe. Below him, he spotted Old Thibault braced against the wall with a crossbow in his hands. Above the withered old cod were leather pouches hanging on nails. In his age-faded eyes was a gleam of pure destruction.

"You'll never leave here!" the old man shouted as his men approached the table where Griffin stood. "You'll die before my eyes!"

Scanning the hall, Griffin realized there must be more than a score of men left—though eight or ten lay on the floor in growing pools of blood.

They rushed him all at once and every muscle in his body contracted . . . crouching, lunging, and dodging. It wouldn't be enough. There were too many of them and no one knew where they were or what trouble—

Something whizzed by, ripping into his arm and he realized belatedly it was the bolt from the old man's crossbow. Pain raked the edge of his consciousness and a gash of red opened across his vision. The hopelessness of the situation bore in on him, sending dying flashes of Julia and home and hall through his awareness. And something inside him snapped.

With a blood-spattered hand, he ripped the band from his nose. A slurry of decay and stench—blood, soured sweat, decaying food, dog filth, and rotting rushes—struck him like a hammer. He fought to breathe and to keep from breathing. Then the scent of the hot red blood making the floor slippery washed through him and purged all else from his head.

With a roar he filled his head and lungs and began to swing his blade with every bit of might he possessed, transferring his pain and desperation to the edge of his blade. He kept moving, always moving—until he saw Sir Martin go down. With a roar, he rushed the men who were poised to sink blades into Martin and Verdun. Time seemed to stand still as he cut and hacked and deflected blows and dealt cuts and wounds . . . pushing the others back, taking them down one by one . . . slashing . . . thrusting . . . hacking . . . until there was one left . . . an aged fury . . . swinging an empty crossbow at him. . . .

Suddenly he was alone, staggering to stay upright. Everywhere there was red. Everywhere he turned there were men on the floor, blocking the way. His lungs were full of blood-tainted air and his eyes burned and his head throbbed. There was a pounding that wouldn't stop, and he heard someone calling his name. When it registered that the pounding was coming from the doors, he stumbled to them and struggled to lift the bar.

The doors swung open, admitting a blast of light into the darkened hall.

With an animal-like cry he shoved blindly through the crowd surging inside. He stumbled and half fell down the steps, sinking onto his hands and knees in the courtyard, spilling his guts on the cracked and sunken paving stones.

Hands lifted him . . . faces appeared in his vision . . . someone called for water . . . and everything went mercifully black.

*   *   *

JULIA AND SOPHIE STOOD IN THE SOUTHERN
watch tower of the house with a few of the guards Griffin
had left to protect them and Grandaise's gates, and
watched the troops trudging back through the vineyards
and across the pastures toward home, bearing a number of
wounded. The women looked at each other in dismay and
hurried downstairs, discarding their plans for a victory
feast in favor of working to heal the injured and comfort
the battle weary.

Little did they realize that among the wounded coming
through the gates would be Sir Martin, Sophie's father,
Bardot, and Griffin . . . each with a different kind and
severity of blade wound. Sophie ran first to Martin. He
convinced her that his sliced ribs weren't a critical injury
and sent her on to see about her father, who had taken a
blade in the chest and was fortunate that he hadn't bled to
death before the fighting was done. Julia spotted Griffin
riding slumped forward on his horse and ran to meet him.
His garments were so bloody that she was frantic, but his
squire assured her that he had only a small wound.

Griffin seemed dazed, but otherwise well as his men
helped him from his horse and ushered him though the hall
and up the stairs to his chamber. There, as Julia stripped his
clothes and sent them for burning, she was chilled to realize that most of the blood that drenched his clothes was the
blood he had drawn from others.

Gently she bathed him and then had his squire stay with
him while she went to the kitchen to make him and the
other wounded a proper Flemish broth. As she carried the
piping hot bowl through the hall, she heard some of the
men talking about Griffin's "amazing feat" and how it had
required such "strength" and "courage." When she returned and tried to feed him some of the broth, he recoiled
from the smell as if expecting something vile. It was then
that she realized he wasn't wearing his band on his nose.

The glazed look in his eyes and his unresponsiveness
alarmed her. She sorted through the chests in the chamber

and searched the parchments and articles on his writing table. Finally, in a small leather pouch near his shaving blade she found a familiar band of curved metal and slipped it on his nose. His tension subsided, and she sat with him as he finally relaxed enough to sleep.

The story of the battle and of Griffin's part in it came out in pieces that, when assembled, made a remarkable story.

Thibault's taunts were repeated to shocked audiences all over Grandaise. Wicked old cod, folk said. The devil would have a fine time with pitchforks and his pruney old bum. The crazed old lord had seventy men in his employ . . . hired killers and mercenaries, every one. Small wonder, folk said, that Sir Bertrand never went home. Knowing he would be out-manned, Old Thibault planned to lure the two counts into his hall, bar the doors, and have his mercenaries murder them before his eyes. At his age, folk snickered, it was surprising that he could see well enough to watch.

Once inside, the three men had faced thirty of Old Thibault's cutthroats. Verdun was wounded and went down first. Sir Martin stood over him, protecting him from the men trying to take his head to collect a special bounty. Folk had to gave Old Thibault credit there, for finding a way to motivate a band of cutthroats using limited resources. Then when Sir Martin went down, Lord Griffin was left facing almost a score of bloodthirsty mercenaries alone. He began to wield his sword with all his might and when it was done, Lord Griffin was still standing. He might be a killing "beast" at times, folk whispered with pride, but he was *their* beast.

A remarkable account, Baron Crossan and the duke seemed to think.

An alarming one, Julia thought, remembering Griffin's revelations about the first time the Beast had made a battle-field appearance. Then after nearly two days of deep, dreamless sleep, Griffin awakened looking so much better that Julia heaved a huge sigh of relief and thought the worst was past.

With Griffin somewhat recovered, Julia left his side to visit the sickroom where Sophie tended her husband and her father together . . . an arrangement dictated by the duke of Avalon, who seemed to think that it might help the lord and the knight get to know each other better. What they learned from that exploration wasn't hard to imagine:

"He snores like a bellowing bull all night long," Martin whispered, pointing to the dark circles under his eyes as proof.

"He slurps his sops like a hog at a trough," the count grumbled, making remarkably accurate imitation of a pig. "And the horny goat thinks I can't see the way he grabs Sophie every time she comes near."

"Bulls, hogs, and goats." Sophie rolled her eyes. "You see what I have to deal with? I have a regular barnyard, here."

On the brighter side, word of the mysterious cause of the feud also spread. Two aging lords had come to blows in the forest, the story went, and a wicked man had seized the opportunity their anger gave him to drive a wedge between two houses. It was a lesson to all on the way evil could enter even small conflicts and make them grow into ugly and destructive battles . . . even wars.

Then on the third night after the battle at Old Thibault's Hall, Julia's uneasiness concerning Griffin's state of mind was confirmed. He came down to the hall for supper and was welcomed roundly by cheers and greetings that made him smile. Attuned as she was becoming to his moods and expressions, she could see that his smile didn't reach his eyes.

Then as they ate, the duke launched into the subject of his visit and the outcome of the battles fought and the odd twist of fate that had landed Griffin's rival in a sickbed in Griffin's hall. Julia's heart climbed into her throat as the duke looked at the two of them.

"I have watched you, Grandaise. And you, Lady Julia. I have seen the good your union has brought to your people and to the possibilities for peace in this region." The duke paused for a moment. "I believe that you not only behaved honorably, Lord Griffin, I believe you exercised admirable restraint in the face of great provocation. I would have you know . . . I will recommend to the king that your marriage—along with Lady Sophie's and Sir Martin's—be allowed to stand."

Sophie, who was sitting farther down the table, listening with eyes as big as goose eggs, cried out "Bless you, Your Grace!" and launched herself at Sir Martin, who had risen as the duke spoke. He seized her around the waist and whirled her around and around, laughing, flushed with desire he hadn't dared show until now.

Julia threw her arms around Griffin's neck and kissed him right there in front of everyone. It was the surprise, she told herself, that kept him from kissing her back. Or the public nature of her impulsive gesture. But in her heart she worried that there was more to it.

When they retired to their chamber that night, her fears were confirmed.

"Come to bed, milord," she said swaying toward him as he sat at his desk, looking over neglected ledgers and tallies. "You still need your rest."

"I doubt it's *rest* you have in mind, milady. And I've neglected these reports," he declared with a lighter tone as if trying to mask his seriousness.

She slid an arm across his shoulder.

"Would it make a difference if I told you I've hidden the essence of an apple, a grape, and a plum for you to find?"

"Not tonight, Julia," he said, stiffening, dropping his pretense of calm.

"I thought . . . we could celebrate the duke's blessing."

"It's not over yet. The convent may still press its claims to you."

Julia retreated a step. "The convent? Why are you worrying about that when the duke has just declared that honor is satisfied?"

"With the king," he said shortly. "Not with the convent."

"But the duke should know if anyone does, since he is the one to whom you're responsible for that vow. If he says our marriage is right and good, who could possibly argue?"

Staring at his tightly controlled frame, she suddenly understood. The one who was arguing with that conclusion was *him*. Why? Why would he doubt the wisdom of their bond now and seek to put distance between them?

"Come to bed, milord. Whatever is bothering you will seem less dire if you share it with me . . . if we face it together."

"Some things," he said with a flash of heat in his otherwise chilled eyes, "cannot be shared. Ever. And you should thank God for it."

He rose and strode furiously from the chamber, leaving her staring after him with hurt washing through her. After all they had been through together, he should know that she would share any burden, help with any problem he faced. What could be so terrible . . . ?

Stifling her perennial impulse to blame herself first in any situation, she forced herself to recall that the chilliness and distance had begun the day of the burning, the day they had fought Old Thibault's mercenaries and learned the truth about Bertrand. Since then, he had hardly touched her. Then this latest battle . . . he had returned home without his nose band. . . . She should have paid more heed to the whispers the kitchen and hall servants thought she couldn't hear.

The Beast was back, at least in Griffin's mind. The battle in Thibault's hall had brought it all back to him, made him relive all of the horrors that caused him to want to cut himself off from all of his emotions and feelings.

He was protecting her, she realized. Or he believed he was.

She had thought that once the duke gave them his blessing, the questions and doubts would be over. She and Griffin would be truly married. Lovers and partners, as Sister Rosemary said.

But there was more to a marriage, she was learning, than just vows or "volition" or sharing bed and board, or even the pleasures of physical joining. The real marriage test was the one that occurred every day, as people lived their lives together. Always facing one more obstacle. One more difficulty to grow beyond. One last test.

Wiping away one traitorous tear, she vowed that this was one last "marriage test" that she did not intend to fail.

Chapter 34

THE NEXT AFTERNOON, JULIA SAT AT dinner watching the pleasure her food brought to everyone dining in the hall. The duke, the baron, Axel and Greeve, Sir Martin and Sophie . . . they all enjoyed her Civet of Hare and the savory cheese and herb rissoles she had made especially for Griffin. She looked at his empty place, beside her, and felt a wave of despair threatening to engulf her.

Griffin had left early that morning with a handful of men and several masons and carpenters to lay plans for rebuilding the south hamlet, even though there was no great urgency to the rebuilding. The displaced folk were housed adequately, if not comfortably, in the village or within Grandaise's walls and a number of them spoke of remaining in the main village instead of returning to the smaller hamlet.

It was dinner time and he was somewhere else. Her hopes for restoring his heart and wooing him back to her arms with food didn't stand a chance if he was never there to eat what she prepared. She would have to take more direct and drastic action, she realized, and pray that Grand Jean and Sister Boniface and the blessed Saint Martha, the busy patron saint of cooks, would lend whatever support they could from Heaven.

After thinking about it for a while, she went straight to Sophie.

"WHERE DID HE GET THE TRUFFLES?" SOPHIE repeated Julia's question as they stood together in the hall. "I have no earthly idea."

"Well, I have to find out," Julia said quietly. "I have to have some more of them. Could you send a message to Francois and ask where he got them?"

"He is probably still furious with me for taking that first batch," Sophie said with a hint of righteous indignation. "I think Francois holds grudges."

"Please, Sophie, send to him. I'm desperate. I must have some truffles."

"What for?"

"Never mind what for. Will you send to him or not?"

A reassuringly canny look appeared on Sophie's face.

"How about if I have *my father* send for them instead?"

When the messenger returned from Verdun empty-handed, Julia was in the kitchen with Jean's great black book, selecting ingredients and making decisions on recipes. The whirlwind of activity she had generated among the folk of the kitchen came to a complete stop at the sight of the messenger's empty hands and rueful expression.

"He said he don't have none, milady," the messenger declared. "Not a truffle to be had in all of Verdun."

"What's a 'truffle'?" she heard one of the friskier pot-boys, Sully, ask a kitchen girl as he hefted a pail of scraps and peelings to carry outside.

"It's like a mushroom."

"Oh. Then why don't she just ask Fleur?" he responded glibly. "She's always findin' mushrooms. She can find anything."

Mushrooms . . . forest . . . truffles . . . Julia wiped her hands and rushed outside to find Demoiselle Fleur digging enthusiastically into her duty.

"Jacques, have you ever heard of truffles?" she asked, clasping her hands anxiously and looking from keeper to beast.

The laconic pig keeper frowned and thought for a moment. "You mean the leetle smelly bits . . . that my Fleur digs up now and again?"

"She digs them up?" She could hardly believe her ears.

"Sometimes. She is quite fond of them. But, it is such a way to go to get them these days. It grieves her . . . they are found no longer in the north forest."

"I have to have some of them," she said anxiously. "Do you think Fleur could find me some?"

"I suppose. Except, it is a long way to the south forest." He scowled. "And ma petite Fleur, she is not much for walking these days. . . ."

That was how Julia came to be rattling along in a cart down the narrow forest path with Jacques, Fleur, and the enterprising potboy, Sully. They stopped here and there along the way to let Fleur trudge down the ramp of boards they'd brought along and sniff around at the base of some trees. But, inevitably, she abandoned the quest and tromped back to the cart, where she waited like long-suffering royalty for her subjects to help her into the cart.

After the fourth such stop, Julia waited until they had stowed the ramp boards and Jacques had climbed up on the driver's seat to look the porcine matriarch in the eye.

"You're enjoying this, aren't you?" she muttered. "Look, you find me some truffles and I'll see you get to ride in the cart every blessed day."

Whether it was the offer Julia made or simply a matter of finding a better scent, at the next stop Fleur took off through the trees with significantly more enthusiasm. They fought their way through the old trees and woody undergrowth after her, watching the great pig pause here and there to sniff at things they couldn't begin to guess. Julia was getting hot and irritable and young Sully had taken to wearing the truffle basket on his head when they came to a small clearing, around which a number of huge oaks stood. Fleur was showing some promising interest in the bare patches around some of the roots, digging daintily at the soil, when out of nowhere a pair of hounds came rushing out of the trees and headed straight for her, barking in alarmed possession. Jacques and Sully tried to intervene, grabbing sticks and bashing at the frantic animals.

Two men appeared on the far side of the clearing, with another dog that raced to join its comrades in harrying Fleur. Jacques was furious—alternately cursing the hounds and shouting at their master to call them off. The first man finally gave a short piercing whistle and the hounds stopped barking and retreated toward him. Julia was furious.

"What do you think you're doing," she yelled, "letting your dogs run wild like that? They were attacking our pig!"

"And what the devil are you doing out here with that monstrous pink beast?" An oddly familiar voice demanded. As he approached, Julia recognized Francois, Verdun's larcenous head cook . . . carrying a basket just like hers.

"We're looking for truffles," she declared, folding her arms and looking at his basket. "So this is where you dig *your* truffles."

"Me? Dig truffles? Hardly," Francois said haughtily. "I always bought my truffles from old Lord Thibault. He had quite a tidy little trade in them. And now that he's gone, I have to get my own . . . like in the old days."

"Old Thibault harvested the truffles?" She was struggling to fit that piece into the puzzle of the past when Francois gave Fleur a dismissive gesture.

"You'll never take home any truffles if you're using one of *those* things."

"She is no 'thing.' " Jacques shook his fist. "She is a *finder* of lost things."

"She's a *pig*," Francois insisted pugnaciously. "If and when she does find a truffle, she'll eat it herself and you won't take a single one home. If you really want to hunt truffles, get some dogs."

"Dogs?" Jacques spat. "They tear up the ground. That is why there are no truffles left in the north. These stupid dogs . . . they have killed them . . . dug them all up and killed them!"

Julia watched with dismay as the hound master weighed in to defend his dogs. Just then, Fleur, who had ambled off, began to snort and dig in earnest at the base of a tree, attracting the attention of the hounds, who came racing over to begin digging wildly and destructively at the earth.

"Make them stop!" Julia demanded of the hound master, who looked to Francois. Francois merely folded his portly arms and gave her a fierce look.

"You stole my book," he snapped.

"It's not your book—you stole it from Grandaise," she snapped back, growing frantic that the truffles would be destroyed. "Call off your dogs. I *need* those truffles!"

He glared spitefully at her, bent on exacting a bit of revenge.

Well, two could play at that game. She folded her arms, mirroring him.

"Call them off or I'll tell your employer you're a thief and a fraud and I'll show him Grandaise's kitchen as proof." She saw her words had an impact and continued, "Even now Lord Bardot lies recovering from his wounds in Grandaise's hall. On the other hand, if you help me dig a basket of truffles, I can almost assure you that the count will never see our curiously 'similar' kitchens."

Francois lost his smug expression and, after assessing her steely look, motioned to the master of the hounds to recall his beasts.

It occurred to Julia as they jostled along toward home in the cart, later, that she and Francois had been arguing . . . in the forest . . . just like the original counts of Grandaise and Verdun. Only this time, they were able to settle the argument peaceably. A little agreement between cooks. A peaceable exchange of benefit.

She lifted the linen on the basket of truffles and selected one of the fragrant dark tubers, turning it over in the dappled sunlight streaming down on the forest path. She closed her eyes and smelled, trying to imagine what more Griffin could smell when he experienced them. Dark, moist earth . . . the very soul of the soil . . . with hints of garlic, shallots, and mushrooms . . . all subtly bound together . . . a culinary—

Treasure.

She began to laugh.

GRIFFIN SPENT A GOOD PART OF THE NEXT morning with the duke and a much improved Comte de Verdun, discussing the fate of the south forest and the holdings of Old Thibault de Roland. The count, having recovered enough to reclaim his usual canny nature, maneuvered for the lands to be granted to Sir Martin, who would have to be ennobled so that his designation as the count's male heir could proceed. Griffin was of the opinion that the lands should be surveyed and divided equally . . . or held in joint trust for succeeding generations. The duke, ever the diplomat, agreed to take both under consideration.

After helping to resettle some of the cottagers in tents near the hamlet that burned, and determining what would be needed to rebuild their homes, Griffin was tired and a bit irritable and found himself longing to return to his chambers and strip off his clothes and sink into a warm, comforting bath. Except that Julia would be there in a heartbeat . . . with her warm eyes and mischievous smile and tantalizing food. . . .

He felt bound and tightly contained inside, unable to reach out past the shell that had formed around him in the bloodbath of his battle at Thibault's hall. He had lost what she most wanted him to give her and he didn't know how to even talk about it, much less get it back. He climbed the winding stairs and paused outside the door, preparing himself to see her.

What he saw when he opened the door was something altogether different. His bed was missing. A bed that measured seven feet by seven feet and had posts six inches thick. He stalked over and stared in disbelief at the blanched square on the darkened wooden floor that marked where the bed had stood.

"What the hell?" He ducked back out the door and stood on the first landing bellowing for his squire. The lad didn't appear. He quieted to listen over the pounding of his heart and heard—nothing. Silence. Damned suspicious silence.

She was up to something. He glanced back at that shocking void where the bed of his ancestors had stood and told himself that it was a bad sign. She was declaring war on the distance he'd put between them and he didn't know whether to try to meet her head on or to run like hell.

Where the devil could she have taken a bed that big?

A noise on the stairs above him made him look up, and there she stood, dressed in the white silk gown she was married in and wearing her burnished hair loose around her shoulders. She seemed to glow in the dim torchlight of the stair passage and he groaned, wishing he could find a way to look at her without *looking* at her.

"What have you done with my bed?" He pointed into the chamber.

"Well, I thought it was time for a bit of a change and so I had it moved."

"Where?"

"Where do you think?" She glanced up the stairs and he recoiled a step.

"Ohhh no. You call your porters and hall servants—whoever helped you move it up there—and tell them to bring it back downstairs where it belongs."

"Yes, milord."

"Yes, milord?" He had to focus more directly on her in order to see if she was mocking him. Damned if she didn't look perfectly sincere. "You went to all of the trouble of hauling my bed up all those steep steps and through that miserably narrow passage, and now you're just going to haul it all back down?"

"Certainly . . ."

She was being entirely too reasonable.

". . . first thing tomorrow."

"Ahhhh." There it was. "And just where am I suppose to sleep tonight?"

"You're welcome to join me in the lookout tower." She

smiled sweetly. "Which, by the way, is where we're having supper."

A bolt of alarm shot up his spine.

"The hell we are. I'm taking my supper in the hall."

He pivoted and stomped back down the stairs to the hall . . . with a nagging sense that something was wrong. It was the silence, he realized as he stepped into the hall. He rubbed his eyes but the view remained the same; there wasn't a soul in the place. And not a single cup, spoon, or crust of bread, either.

He stomped back up the stairs to demand an explanation, but when he reached the landing outside the master chamber, she was gone. He jammed his hands on his waist and turned around . . . and around . . . before he spotted something lying on the step where she had been standing.

It was piece of linen . . . a folded napkin . . . on which sat a lump of coal. Clearly, she had left it there for him to find. Knowing that she had, he would be mad to pick it up. But something wouldn't let him walk away. He bent to pick it up and found that instead of a hard, glossy bit of mineral, he held a velvety black vegetable sphere. An *edible* sphere. His stomach slid.

In the dim passage he ran his fingers over it and fought the urge to take the band from his nose and inhale the dark, earthy fragrance that had always meant freedom as much as food to him. His hand hovered briefly over the band, but the next instant he was taking the steps two at a time with it still in place.

She stood in the evening breeze on the balcony, her burnished golden hair teased and caressed by some invisible sprite. She heard him and turned.

"You changed your mind." She smiled and took a seat at the dining table.

"What the hell is this?" He held up the truffle.

"A treasure."

"It's a *truffle*."

"Exactly. The 'treasure of the south forest.' A truffle."

"How do you know that?" He glanced briefly at the table set on the balcony, seeing his cup and tray, pristine linen, and even a few heliotrope and phlox in a flower bowl. He turned to see his bed and was surprised to find it fit better in the chamber than he expected. It was spread with freshly washed linen and rose petals and piled with multicolored silk pillows.

"In Grand Jean's book, he refers to arguments over how to claim the treasure of the forest," she said, spreading what appeared to be butter with shallots and truffles onto a delicately browned white flour roll. "Well, I think I had one of those arguments yesterday, when I was out collecting truffles. It started me thinking. Truffles grow in the south forest, and the people who harvest them hold vastly different opinions on whether it's better to use pigs or dogs to harvest them. Milord, why don't you pour us both some wine?"

She spread more truffle butter on her roll and groaned as she took a bite.

"It's so obvious that it's astonishing we didn't see it sooner," she continued. "After all, truffles are on your coat of arms."

"They are not." He set a cup of wine down before her.

"Then what are those little dark lumps on the third chevron of your arms?"

"I . . . they're coal."

"Where on your land, milord, has anyone ever dug coal?" When he had no response, she smiled. "Yet, truffles have been dug here for nearly a century. And Grandaise's animal of choice for locating the truffles in the ground is the pig . . . which is also on your coat of arms . . . and on your grounds."

He spotted Grand Jean's large black book on the nearby food table and opened it to stare at the coat of arms in astonishment. It was so obvious; how could he not have seen it until now? Truffles, pigs, and grapes. Grandaise had always been a feast for the senses.

Frowning, he sat down hard on the bench.

"Verdun, by the way, uses dogs. Dogs have an equally keen sense of smell, but are enthusiastic diggers and can tear up the mother plants under the ground. Pigs are more gentle, but they have the same taste for truffles we do . . . so they often eat whatever they harvest." She smiled and shook her head. "The things you learn when you're trying to find a crack in your husband's stubborn heart."

He froze in the midst of reaching for a piece of the roll she had buttered.

"Tell me what happened in Thibault's hall the other day," she said quietly.

"Leave it, Julia." He drew back his hand and gripped the edge of the stone bench on either side of him.

"Are you afraid if you talk about it, it will come back to haunt you?"

"I don't want to remember or to talk about it," he said emphatically.

"Because you killed people?"

He felt his heart beating harder and his breath quickening.

"It was battle. Kill or be killed," he ground out.

"I understand that. Tell me what happened."

"Why would you want to hear such horrors?"

"Because they're lodged in your heart and mind, no matter how hard you try to pretend otherwise," she said. "They're a part of you. And if *I'm* to be a part of you, I need to understand them. Help me to understand."

Her appeal shook him to the core. He'd never imagined talking with someone about what had happened. Especially a woman. Women didn't understand the necessities of battle . . . or the way men had to deal with it after.

"Tell me what happened that made you want to lock your heart away."

"I don't have to listen to this nonsense," he said angrily, rising and starting for the door.

"That's right, you don't." She shoved to her feet and followed him to the middle of the chamber where he stopped with his back to her. "You don't have to listen. You don't have to talk. You don't have to love or to care or to trust me with your problems. You don't have to share anything with me. That is your choice. But if you choose that, you'll be choosing something a lot colder and more lonely than the life you were meant to have. Is that what you want for you? For me?"

He was trembling. Emotions were stirring beneath his becalmed surface.

"This has nothing to do with you, Julia," he said fiercely.

She darted around him and planted herself between him and the door, her shoulders back and her head held high.

"Begging your pardon, milord, but it has *everything* to do with me." Her expression hardened with a hint of anger. "It was me who peeled the blood-soaked clothes from your body and bathed the sweat and blood from you when they brought you home. It was me who found another nose band to help you rest, and then sat with you for two long days while you slept. It was me who watched over you . . . praying for your heart and your mind to heal and for you to return to us."

She edged closer, raising her face to his, making him look at her and deal with her presence, making him acknowledge her place in his life. Then came the words that shot truer than Old Thibault's crossbow . . . piercing his heart . . . striking sparks of light in the depths into which he'd retreated.

"And it is my heart that leaps at the sight of you, and my heart that aches with misery each time you turn away."

The ache in her was visible through the prisms of tears in her eyes.

"I love you, Griffin of Grandaise. Talk to me. Let me be the partner of your heart."

He could feel his emotions roiling, surging nearer the surface than he'd thought. Panic gripped him at the force of that rising. The magnitude and the intensity of it. He could feel his heart drumming faster and his hands beginning to tremble. His skin was suddenly cold, even though he could feel a bead of sweat trickling down the middle of his back. His eyes began to burn from staring at her so fixedly that he forgot to blink.

He could see his silence wounded her, but he had no

words to collect the turmoil and pour it out of him in a way that might make sense to her.

In the middle of that rising panic, he focused desperately on her eyes and felt one strangely calm fragment of memory surfacing in him. During the fight, in that awful moment he realized he was outnumbered by more men than he could count and would likely die, his final thought was of Julia and home. In that moment he had seen her face, felt her presence in his mind, and understood in a way too deep for words what would be lost if he were defeated: all of the possibilities of life . . . of joy and passion and discovery . . . of sharing each moment and living each experience . . . of love . . . with her . . .

Julia watched the hollowness of his eyes transforming, filling, reflecting the light she was trying to bring to him. Seizing that as cause for hope, she ventured one more step.

"Griffin, the band was gone from your nose when you arrived at home. How did it come off? What happened to it?"

She watched him grappling with the question and could see from the turbulence it cause in him that it was close to the heart of the matter.

"Lost," he said thickly. "It was lost."

"How did it come off?"

For a long moment he didn't speak. She could feel the trembling of his hands in hers as shards of shattered memory reassembled in his mind. Her chest ached as his eyes darted over the horrific images returning to him. She squeezed his hands.

"Can you remember losing it?"

He shook his head, his eyes widening, his body stiffening.

"I didn't lose it," he said hoarsely, astounded by what he saw in his mind's eye. "I took it off."

His entire body quaked as for a moment he was there again, reliving that moment of desolation and decision. His eyes began to fill with tears.

"I took it off. I did." His voice strengthened and rose. "I reached up"—he acted out the movements as he recalled them—"and I grabbed it and ripped it off."

In horrified wonder he looked down at his empty hand.

"You took it off?" She had to swallow the lump in her throat. "Why?"

He shook his head, unable to form words to express what he could barely bring himself to recognize.

"Because you knew what would happen," she said for him, reeling from the insight. "You knew it would unleash the Beast."

"I—I couldn't think . . . I saw them coming . . . so many of them. Just like that time in Spain . . ." He grappled with the thought, turning first one way and then another as if looking for an escape, unable to bear the thought that he could do such a thing intentionally.

"You knew what was inside you . . . the power to fight and to survive . . . and you chose it." She squeezed his hands and pulled him back to her, making him look into her eyes and see that there was no judgment, no revulsion in them. "Don't you see, Griffin, you chose it. You knew what was inside you . . . the power to fight and to survive . . . and you used it to defend yourself and others, too." Her voice rose as the warmth of love poured through her heart, displacing the chill of fear. "It's not like Spain at all. You weren't mad with bloodlust or sick in your heart or even overcome by the smells. You did it to survive. You summoned it out of your depths. . . ."

He looked at her through a haze of tears and whispered the truth he now knew.

"So I could come back to you. I did whatever I had to do . . . to come back to you."

The tension in his face as he said it betrayed his hope that she would understand and his fear that she might not. She understood and honored the risk he was taking . . . the gift he was offering . . . full access to his aching heart.

With tears streaming down her face, she threw her arms around him and buried her face in his chest. He clasped her to him, holding her fiercely against him, letting her stubborn love melt away the shell that separated them.

"Oh, Griffin, I love you. With all that I am. With all that I can be."

He kissed her softly, reverently, acknowledging the preciousness of the bond strengthening between them. Then his kiss deepened and grew exuberant, celebrating the freedom that with her help he had just discovered and claimed.

"I love you, Julia of Grandaise . . . more than I can ever say."

Through her tears she smiled up at him.

"Then don't say. Show me. Touch me. Love me."

He picked her up in his arms and swung her around, laughing.

Breathless, they sank onto the bed and began to remove and discard garments with an eagerness that at any other time would have shamed them. But this was no time for decorum and expectation . . . no place for rules . . . except the rule of love. They kissed and nuzzled and loved each other, exploring the sensations of touch and taste. . . .

Then as he braced above her on his arms, looking at her tousled hair and pale, sleek body, he groaned and pulled the band from his nose.

"Wait," she said, pushing him back up when he sank over her, "I have to get a truffle. . . ."

"Oh, no," he said, countering her force until she sank back on the bed. With a husky laugh he lowered his nose to the base of her throat and inhaled deeply. "You smell like Julia . . . the warm scent of 'woman' about your hair . . . the lavender and soap on your skin . . . a tang of salt and a little musk . . . that roe-like scent when you're aroused. . . ." Then he looked up with a liquid glimmer of desire in his eyes. "Why would I need truffles, when I have you?"

She laughed and pulled his head down to demand another kiss.

THEY LAY TOGETHER IN THE LINGERING sweetness of loving, warm and complete, with the night breeze kissing their naked bodies. They had made love and then drank wine and ate Truffled Eggs in Pastry, and goose stuffed with grapes and truffles and covered with a truffle cream sauce, and Baked Truffled Brie en Croute. She fed him blueberries and sugared almonds and his favorite sweetened custard topped with flamed sugar.

"You know"—he looked around at the cozy chamber and relaxed back as the air slid over him, drawing heat from his body—"I like this. Having our bed here. Of course, it will probably be a little drafty in winter."

"Then we'll just take the bed apart again and move it back downstairs." She grinned and rubbed the side of his leg with her toes. "We'll have a summer chamber and a winter chamber."

When his chest rumbled against her cheek but he didn't speak, she raised her head, knowing he had something that needed airing.

"What is it?"

"What if it happens sometime that I haven't chosen it?" he said, sharing one last echo of doubt.

"It won't," she said, running her palm across his chest. "The two times it's happened you've been in battle and fighting for your very life. How likely is that to happen again?"

He took a deep breath and thought of all of the people and events that could conspire to drag him and the folk of Grandaise into the quarrels of the age.

"It's not impossible to imagine."

She took a deep breath, too. And looked up at him with that stubborn smile that never failed to make his heart skip.

"If it happens again . . . at least you'll be better prepared." The love in her heart shone through her eyes. "And whatever happens, we'll face it together. We'll always face it together."

IT WAS LATE THE NEXT MORNING WHEN JULIA and Griffin emerged from their bower and descended to the hall. Everyone from the duke to the lowliest servant could see that tensions between the two had been laid to rest. Julia glowed with health and the happy air of a well-loved woman. Griffin beamed with strength and vitality and the relaxed air of a man sated with loving pleasures.

Sophie and Sir Martin were still casting wistful, longing glances at each other, and Julia laughed sympathetically and gave Sophie a tight hug.

"It will be worth the wait," she whispered. And she knew it must be true love when salty, impatient little Sophie sighed and looked across the hall to Sir Martin.

"I know."

A joint wedding celebration, that was what they needed, the count of Verdun declared when he arrived in the hall that morning. He was still weak, but not so weak that he couldn't contrive to pass off some of the expense of a wedding feast onto his neighbor and longtime rival. Julia embraced the idea straightaway, and Sophie—as soon as she was assured the vows themselves wouldn't have to wait another two months—was delighted to be able to share her celebration with her best friends.

Julia was just giving Griffin a parting kiss, heading for the kitchen to consult on the day's menus when a runner came from the gates, saying that a party of travelers approached . . . two men and a cart full of nuns.

Julia looked at Griffin, who looked at the duke, who—after a moment—took refuge in his ducal authority and sat a bit straighter in the master's chair. A cart full of nuns, his air of confidence said, was not necessarily a bad thing.

He changed his mind, a short time later, when a trio of nuns in black habits sailed into the hall demanding to be shown into the presence of Griffin of Grandaise and looking like a trio of angry crows.

"Welcome, Sisters," Griffin declared, rising. "I am the lord of Grandaise. What can I do for—" He stopped dead as a pair of venomous brown eyes fixed on him. "Reverend Mother. Well . . . this is certainly a surprise."

"Where is my cook, Grandaise?" the abbess snapped, seizing the long silver crucifix that dangled from her belt and looking for all the world as if she was considering stabbing him with it.

"Well, Reverend Mother . . . um . . ." He looked to the duke, who blanched and slid lower in his chair, as if trying to make himself a smaller target.

"I got a message from Avalon saying something about a marriage and an annulment and the king—" A twitch from the head table drew her all-seeing gaze and she recognized and pounced on the duke. "So, there you are." She stalked toward him with her veil flapping. "Where is my cook? What has the wretch done with her?"

"Here I am, Reverend Mother," Julia said, rising from a bench beside the hearth, where she and Sophie had been talking. The abbess squinted at her and paled as the sight of her registered.

"I've come to collect you, girl. Gather your things. We're leaving."

"I'm afraid not, Reverend Mother," Julia said. "I'll be staying here."

"With her husband," Griffin said, coming to put an arm around her.

The abbess turned on the duke. "Why are you just sitting there? Do something about it—you were supposed to protect her."

"I'm afraid, Reverend Mother, that it is out of my hands now," the duke said, clearing his throat and sitting a little taller with each word. "The marriage is part of an intricately balanced peace settlement authorized by the king himself. Julia of Childress was required to wed and is now the Lady of Grandaise. I doubt that even I could influence a change in her status."

"This cannot be!" The abbess stomped a foot. "I won't allow it! I have come all of the way from Rheims—" She turned from the duke to Griffin to Julia, finding only the same solidifying determination. She edged closer to Julia, scrutinizing her changed appearance . . . her unbound hair, her white silk gown, her regal bearing, and the earthy, womanly glow about her that spoke of experiences that put her forever outside the purview of the convent. The resolve in Julia's face caused her shoulders to sag briefly. She turned to the other sisters, her eyes dark with desolation and they hurried toward her. She clasped their hands for a moment, drawing strength, then she turned to Griffin with her fighting spirit rebounding.

"So you're breaking our agreement and keeping my cook. *Fine.*" She glanced at the duke. "Then I demand compensation. And plenty of it."

Thus began a prickly bit of negotiation that ranged from the convent taking over Grandaise's entire estate, to a season's production of wine, to cold, hard, coin to nothing at all . . . at least for the balance of the year that Julia was to have served at Grandaise.

Seeing the abbess's intractable attitude and knowing her susceptibility to good food, Julia hurried to the kitchens and used the last few truffles to produce another batch of the lovely Truffled Eggs in Pastry and a delicious Baked Truffled Brie en Croute like the one she prepared for Griffin the night before. Regine, who was out collecting herbs from the kitchen gardens, returned to find Julia hot and flustered and a bit desperate.

"Here, let me—you'll get your lovely gown dirty," Regine said, taking the grater from her and finishing the grating of the truffles over the finished product. "His Lordship must have really like these dishes for you to be making them again so soon."

"Oh, Regine." Julia looked stunned. "Hasn't anyone told you?"

Shortly Regine was running flat out for the hall, bearing the egg and truffle dish and letting out a cry of joy at the sight of the abbess and her fellow nuns. After a brief reunion, the duke suggested they adjourn for a bit of sustenance and Julia served her truffle dishes, which were paired with some excellent wine.

As Julia suspected, the Reverend Mother was enraptured by the food and mellowed enough to hear what Sister Regine related about her own experiences at Grandaise.

"I'm becoming something of a cook myself," she beamed. "I confess, I find it so much more interesting than stitchery and inspecting the girls' dormitories. There's always something new to learn. Like these truffles. Did you know that they only grow in a few places in the world, and they're harvested by pigs. No, *truly*. And it's good that one of the few places they grow is right here in this province, because they're very dear and usually can't be enjoyed by any but the very rich." She scowled. "I wonder what will happen to all of those truffles on that old baron's land. It would be a shame to have them go to waste. . . ."

Julia looked to Griffin, who looked to the duke, who looked to the abbess.

Thus was born the single solution to the problem of the compensation for the convent, the disposition of Old Thibault's lands, the continued harvesting and care of the truffles, and the potential for Verdun's acquisitive impulses to get the better of him. Grandaise and Verdun would both donate their interest in the southern forest, which they had mostly avoided for years anyway, to the convent . . . which would send a group of sisters to live there and tend and harvest the truffles. Sister Regine volunteered to head the new residence and to study the care and harvest of the truffles . . . which meant she always would be close to Julia and Griffin.

Over the next several days of the abbess's visit, the abbess ate a great deal of wonderful food and had the sisters who accompanied her record on parchment several of Julia's recipes for the kitchen at the convent. When Julia and Griffin stood on the step and waved farewell as the nuns rattled off in their donkey cart, the abbess waved and then turned back to face the front with a sigh.

"Well, I won't miss the chit's stubbornness. That's for certain. And I think we got a pretty good deal out of them."

"You know," the youngest sister said, "I've always like the kitchen. I wouldn't mind learning to cook.

"I think we should have the maids spend much more time in the kitchen . . . I mean, it would probably make them more marriageable if they had more in the way of cooking skills."

The abbess, never one to let a single scrap of information lie idle, inserted her hands up her sleeves and thought about the possibilities that were opening up for the convent.

"Hmmm," she said, narrowing her eyes. "You know, the

Author's Note

PASSIONATE AS I AM ABOUT BOTH FOOD and history . . . as I researched and wrote *The Marriage Test*, I found myself enjoyably lost in the culinary world of the High Middle Ages. It was a time very different from our own in its approach to nutrition and taste and understanding of the chemical and physical properties of food and the needs of the human body. Attitudes toward food ran the gamut from punitive regimens of denial to lavish displays of consumption that make our annual bit of Thanksgiving gluttony seem puny by comparison.

A great deal of research and experimentation went into making Julia's meals both authentic to the times and palatable (if not alluring) to the modern reader. Fourteenth century people had a taste for "sour" the way modern westerners have a taste for "sweet." Their favorite dishes often involved vinegar—even meat marinated in vinegar, which is probably the origin of the old German standby "sauerbratten." And, contrary to our current thinking about food, the more a food was processed (converted into a "made" dish), the more healthful and desirable it was considered to be. Thus, fruits were thoroughly cooked whenever possible and meats might be boiled, pounded, fried, and then spiced and sauced heavily before serving. "Mystery meat" was a highly desirable thing!

Another major challenge in developing scrumptious menus for this book was the difference in foods available then and now. A cook in a wealthy medieval household had a tremendous range of foods and spices available, and readily made use of items we westerners consider delicacies: patés of goose liver, oysters and exotic seafood, almonds, capons, suckling pigs, etc. On the other hand, many of the foods we take very much for granted were totally unknown to them. Imagine trying to concoct savory meals without potatoes, yams, vanilla, sugar, corn of all kinds, chocolate, coffee, tea, citrus fruits, and tomatoes! Cow's milk, cream, and butter were used sparingly, and the fat of medieval times was almost exclusively pork lard . . . preferred by medieval diners one thousand to one over butter!

Also . . . if a heroine going from "cook" to "lady" seems unlikely, be aware that fine cooks were highly prized and often jealously guarded in the medieval world. Cooking for a great house required the skill and organizational ability of a general on campaign, and a lot more tact and diplomacy. Cooks, after all, occupied positions of great trust; they held the health, safety, and all-important reputations of their masters in their hands.

Hospitality, in an era where inns were unknown, was serious business. Nobles who could not or would not spread a proper table for guests were considered miserly. Then, as now, the good opinion of others was often the difference between living in safety and having to take up arms to defend one's self and one's household. As the reputation and fortunes of a lord increased, so did the rewards and honors due his cook. There are numerous stories of cooks being granted lands and incomes of their own and, on occasion, a title.

Rest assured that the details of Julia's kitchen (borrowed from the magnificent kitchen of the abbey of Glastonbury, England) are quite authentic, and the methods and equipment described are accurate. The attitudes toward food and the conflict of the devotees of pigs and dogs in gathering truffles are also well recorded in history.

If you are interested in further research on medieval cuisine, I suggest Bridget Henisch's imminently readable book *Fast and Feast* and the more scholarly *Food and Eating in Medieval Europe*, by Martha Carlin and Joel T. Rosenthal. For actual recipes, I recommend *The Medieval Kitchen* by Odile Redon, Francoise Sabban, and Silvano Serventi; *Pleyn Delit, Medieval Cookery for Modern Cooks* by Constance B. Hieatt, Brenda Hosington, and Sharon Butler; and *Early French Cookery* by D. Eleanor Scully and Terence Scully.

Finally, it has long been my opinion that a great deal of conflict in the world could be resolved if the hostile parties would just sit down together at a kitchen table over a top-notch rissole . . . or a blintze, a baklava, a crepe, a cannoli, a torte, a bit of frybread, a pudding, or a piece of pie . . . and *talk*.